£14·00

Shadow on the Moon

ARCHIE COULTER

Trafford
PUBLISHING

Order this book online at www.trafford.com/07-0584
or email orders@trafford.com

Most Trafford titles are also available at major online book retailers.

© Copyright 2008 Archibald H. Coulter.

Note for Librarians: A cataloguing record for this book is available from Library and Archives Canada at www.collectionscanada.ca/amicus/index-e.html

Printed in Victoria, BC, Canada.

Cover design by Alan Taylor.

ISBN: 978-1-4251-2182-2

We at Trafford believe that it is the responsibility of us all, as both individuals and corporations, to make choices that are environmentally and socially sound. You, in turn, are supporting this responsible conduct each time you purchase a Trafford book, or make use of our publishing services. To find out how you are helping, please visit www.trafford.com/responsiblepublishing.html

Our mission is to efficiently provide the world's finest, most comprehensive book publishing service, enabling every author to experience success. To find out how to publish your book, your way, and have it available worldwide, visit us online at www.trafford.com/10510

 Trafford PUBLISHING™   www.trafford.com

North America & international
toll-free: 1 888 232 4444 (USA & Canada)
phone: 250 383 6864 ♦ fax: 250 383 6804 ♦ email: info@trafford.com

The United Kingdom & Europe
phone: +44 (0)1865 722 113 ♦ local rate: 0845 230 9601
facsimile: +44 (0)1865 722 868 ♦ email: info.uk@trafford.com

10 9 8 7 6 5 4 3 2

This book is dedicated to my parents, Archie and Greta Coulter. Without their love and guidance through my life and especially my formative years, I would never have joined the merchant navy, or written this book.

Chapter One

The Nigerian pirate was getting angry. The Greek master would not co-operate and stubbornly refused to open the ship's safe. The pirate had first tried to intimidate the small fat, balding Greek, forcing the dull black barrel of his pistol into the thick fleshy folds of the man's neck, while screaming dire threats at him. When that failed, he quickly resorted to crude violence, beating him about the head with the pistol. The captain had staggered about in a daze, moaning loudly. Bright red blood flowed freely from the wounds on his head, down his pallid face, before splattering vivid red blotches onto the worn grey carpet on the deck of his cabin.

But still, the Greek obstinately refused to open the safe.

The pirate had obtained reliable information from the ship's agent in Lagos, that the safe contained a considerable amount of cash. He was an incredibly ruthless man and would not allow the stubborn captain, or any one else for that matter, to stand in his way. In fact, he would stop at nothing until the safe was open and he was in possession of its lucrative contents.

So without compunction he pointed the pistol at the left foot of the captain and fired one round at point blank range. The noise from the gunshot, in the confined space of the cabin, was deafening and the air filled with a cloud of cordite fumes. The captain fell screaming to the floor, writhing in agony, gripping his injured foot with both hands.

More violence and more intimidation, but the safe still remained firmly closed.

The frustrated and by now severely enraged pirate then mercilessly put a bullet in the man's other foot, but still, though in horrendous agony, he would not co-operate. The pirate was astounded at the man's fierce resistance. But then he was unaware that this particular captain had a share in the ownership of the vessel, like so many of his counterparts from Greece. The money in the safe, in the region of fifty thousand dollars, partly belonged to him, which was the reason he put up such fierce, though foolish resistance.

The pirate was beginning to realise that perhaps this time he would not get his way. There was nothing more he could do to the captain. It was a pity he thought, that the man did not have his wife with him, as the threat of rape or other harm to a spouse always achieved the desired results. So he sighed resignedly, kicked the screaming captain viciously in frustration and thrust the pistol back, into the army-style webbing belt, round his waist.

Through the brass-rimmed porthole, he could see the first few flecks of grey morning light, drifting over the barely visible horizon. He knew that a police patrol boat would soon be leaving the harbour. So reluctantly, he decided to return to the land, leaving the screaming captain bleeding profusely on the heavily bloodstained floor of his cabin.

He quickly, made his way out of the accommodation and along the main deck to his dugout canoe, bobbing up and down out of sight, under the bow of the ship. Once on board, the powerful one hundred horsepower Evinrude outboard motor thrust the dugout rapidly over the smooth undulating swell and he was soon ashore.

The ageing ship's master died an hour later from shock and loss of blood.

Henry Kaduna was that pirate, a thief and a murderer, who had lost track of the number of people that he had killed. He was also a chameleon who had carved for himself an opulent lifestyle from the proceeds of piracy. But absolutely no one knew, or could have guessed, what the tall well-dressed African, who walked slowly across the car park towards the entrance of the Holiday Inn casino, actually did for a living.

As his powerful body moved he could feel the smart new tan safari suit, sticking ever so slightly to the perspiration on his back. But this troubled him little, as he was used to the suffocating heat that prevailed for most of the year in Nigeria.

He had dined well that night just over an hour ago at Marcel's, a small French restaurant in the centre of Lagos. A huge local crayfish, followed by a prime fillet steak, accompanied by a full bottle of expensive claret had more than satisfied his voracious appetite. Only the over-effusive nature of the proprietor, when he paid the bill, had irked him slightly.

In retrospect, he found it hard to believe, that for the greater part of his life all he had known, was the dull ache of hunger that wracked his body daily as he laboured from sunrise to sunset, with the rest of his family, trying to scratch a living from parched soil. But that existence was in the past and he was fiercely determined that it would never be a part of his life again. In fact after so many years of deprivation, he would do anything and stop at nothing, to preserve his present lavish lifestyle.

Now that he had considerable money, he had decided to enjoy all the pleasures his new found wealth could provide. He visited the most expensive restaurants and feasted heartily on the best food available; seduced as many beautiful women as possible and indulged in the other love of his life, gambling. The bug had really bitten him after a big wins initially on black jack and roulette, though he had not been so lucky lately. He loved the feel of the chips and the excitement of winning. It made him feel like a 'Big Shot' whenever he won a hand or two and amassed a pile of chips in front of him. So, as he often did after enjoying a fine meal, he made for the tense smoky atmosphere of the gaming room.

As he approached the dimly lit hotel entrance, he saw a couple of ragged beggars hiding in the shadows of a large flowering bush near the entrance of the hotel. They were careful to keep out of sight of the doorman, who would not hesitate to lay into them with his nightstick if they were unfortunate enough to catch his gaze. When he got closer to the steps of the hotel, he could see the furtive, crouching shapes more clearly. The tattered dirty clothes they wore, too large for them by many sizes and they were both gaunt and painfully thin. As Kaduna passed by them, the closest beggar spoke in a barely audible whisper.

'Master help us, we is starvin', three days we no chop.'

Kaduna did not feel the slightest grain of compassion towards these two unfortunates. In his mind, because they were beggars, they were weak and he despised them for this. Years ago he had been in an even worse position than them, but had acted ruthlessly to improve his situation in life.

He was born and grew up in the harsh environment of sub-Saharan bush, in the most northern part of Nigeria; a land where for many years hunger and deprivation was his constant companions. However the land that he struggled to exist in with his family had given him a keen sense of survival and honed his instincts to a fine edge. As the eldest, he had little regard for his four brothers and five sisters, who were just extra mouths to feed which ultimately, meant less for him.

The area that he came from, known as the Sahel region, was far from the capital Lagos and consequently saw little of the foreign aid which arrived in the country. Though the government did eventually build twenty miles away, what purported to be a hospital though in actual fact it was little more than a crude doctor's surgery. A school was also started in the next village and it was decreed that all children must attend for two hours each day.

The young Kaduna was not enthusiastic about schoolwork in the beginning, but soon realised it was, at least, the means to escape the backbreaking work in the fields for a few hours each day. Once he learnt the rudiments of reading and writing, he became more interested in schoolwork, seeing that it could have some possible benefits for him later in life. The photographs he saw in the various books depicting life in other lands fascinated him, Europe and America in particular. This fuelled his desire to leave home at the earliest opportunity.

The year of his seventeenth birthday the rains failed to come.

Famine and disease wracked the land. There was little to eat and he was getting thinner and weaker with each successive day. He knew if he stayed, he would probably perish with everyone else in his family. So well before sunrise one morning, he left home taking with him as much of his family's meagre supply of food as he could carry. He felt no remorse in the act and reasoned that he owed them nothing, having toiled in the fields since he was a small child.

It was over a thousand miles from his home to the capital. The terrain to begin with was much as he had known all his life, harsh, arid and unforgiving. He hitched rides in trucks and ox-carts wherever he could and walked the rest of the way barefoot. He had never owned a pair of shoes and the soles of his feet were as tough as tanned buffalo hide.

After many days travel the dry bush gave way gradually to lush verdant scenery. He passed though arable land, with neat farms either side of the rutted road he trod. Eventually he reached the main north south highway, a two lane tar MacAdam road, stretching like a huge black artery from one dusty horizon to the next.

Kaduna soon found out to his dismay that the highway was fraught with danger. Many thieves and brigands preyed mercilessly on the highway's travellers. He was held up many times by these desperadoes, who would slit a throat as easily as cutting the top off an apple. When they found he had nothing of value, they would grudgingly let him go, though sometimes he was not so fortunate and he was sexually abused. The lowest point in his life came when he was gang-raped by four of them. He was scared for life by the experience. It was probably that act, which consumed the final grains of respect remaining in him for the life of other human beings.

Life on the highway was tough and vicious. Only the smartest and meanest could survive. Soon, like the brigands, he resorted to stealing from farms and the small roadside stalls that dotted the highway, rickety structures where long distance truck drivers stopped for crudely cooked food and refreshments.

It was during the journey to the coast, that he killed his first man.

It happened in the twilight just before dawn. Desperately hungry once again, he stole a loaf of bread from one of the hawker's stalls. He then quickly ran off into the shadows with it under his arm. After only twenty meters or so, he tripped over the broken remains of a crate and fell heavily to the ground. Before he could get to his feet, the stall owner came bounding towards him with a knife in his hand.

When the man was virtually on top of him, the panic stricken Kaduna picked up a rock the size of his hand and threw it with all the strength his wasted body could muster. At such a close range he could not miss. The rock struck home on the hawker's head with a dull thud. Then as the unconscious man tumbled to the ground, Kaduna just managed to roll clear. He was on his feet in a flash. He picked up the knife and without hesitation, in a complete frenzy, drove the blade repeatedly into the prostrate man's back. He could feel bone breaking as he plunged the knife into his victim and heard a hissing sound as one of the dead man's lungs deflated.

Kaduna paused for a brief moment, picked up the crude blood splattered knife and the loaf of bread then scurried off into the dim morning light. He was elated by his victory. He felt no sympathy at all for his victim or revulsion at the act of murder. It was no different to killing a chicken, he reasoned.

Almost a month after departing from his home, Kaduna arrived at the seething metropolis which was the capital Lagos. But his troubles were far from over. He soon found out that thousands of people like him from the countryside, all trying to escape the famine, had descended on the capital in search of work. There was no work. Thieving and looting were rife and Kaduna soon joined the mob, stealing whatever he could to sustain himself. The army was eventually called and patrolled the streets day and night, shooting thieves and looters on sight and anyone else who happened to get in the way.

On more than one occasion, he was a trifle lucky to escape extinction, at the hands of the army or the mob. It was apparent to him, that he had to get out of Lagos at all costs, before his luck ran out. He was on the coast, so there were only two choices available to him. Either back inland to the famine, or somehow, out to sea.

He tried a number of times, to sign on ships as an ordinary seaman or an oilier, but was always refused, as he had no passport or any seaman's papers. He then attempted to obtain the necessary papers at the Maritime Board, but the clerk just laughed at him and told him to get the hell back to where he came from. Humiliated, he felt like plunging the hawker's knife into the miserable little clerk. But common sense prevailed. If only just.

With nothing else to do with his time, he spent many hours loitering at the entrance of the port. He often saw crew joining or leaving ships, mainly in the daytime, but sometimes at night. The port of Lagos, did not allow cars or taxis into the docks at night time, due to port security regulations. So these seamen would then have to walk a mile or so though the docks with their luggage, usually a grip or a small case, to their ship. Kaduna watched this scenario many times, over the desperate months he was in Lagos. Eventually, an idea came to him. He knew exactly what he would have to do to achieve his objective of a job on a ship.

So he waited patiently for weeks, till one night a young seaman who vaguely resembled himself, was walking through the port to join a ship. He followed the man and in the quiet dimly lit docks, without pity or compunction, murdered him with couple of swift venomous stabs of the hawker's knife. Amongst the dead mans papers, was a letter of introduction with the name of the ship. He easily found the vessel as there were only three ships in the port at the time.

The next morning he went on board and presented himself to the captain, to sign on the ship's articles. The gaunt cigarette-puffing master looked up at the scrawny youth through hooded bloodshot eyes; shook his head, then without speaking, pointed with a bony nicotine stained forefinger at the form in front of him. He did not even bother to check the photo in the discharge book. Kaduna quickly signed his name. He had done it! He was a seaman.

He settled in quickly to the life on board, and after the deprivations of his life until then, no job was too hard or dirty for him. The food on the ship was wonderful and this diet coupled with the hard work, improved his physique dramatically. During the next eight years he sailed the oceans of the world and learned everything about the ships and the life at sea. In his spare time during ocean crossings, he became an avid reader and his crude English improved beyond recognition. He even managed to loose most of his pigeon English and African accent. In those eight years at sea, life for the scrawny youth from the Sahel region of Nigeria had improved far beyond his wildest dreams.

Redundancy came as a bitter blow.

A world wide recession in shipping caused him to loose his job. He took this very badly and became quite bitter about the downward turn in his fortunes. So when his money ran out, eager to find something to get ahead once more, some nefarious acquaintances of his, introduced him to an extremely lucrative profession. Piracy. It was the proceeds of this, which now fuelled his new opulent lifestyle. So as he walked casually towards the casino, he completely ignored the beggars, staring imperiously ahead as he passed. They would have to make their own luck in life, as he had done many years previously. Or perish. The latter seemed a distinct possibility he thought and chuckled to himself at his macabre sense of humour.

He then climbed the twenty or more wide marble steps that lead up to the dimly lit entrance of the hotel. The fat jovial doorman, in his grubby green uniform and crumpled peaked cap smiled expansively, as he opened the heavy plate glass door.

'Good evening sah,' the doorman said, bowing slightly, as Kaduna passed.

'Jus let me know, if master wants anythin' later this evenin'.'

'I'll see how I feel before I leave,' he replied evenly, the slightest flicker of a smile crossing his lips.

The doorman had in the past procured young girls to satisfy Kaduna's almost insatiable sexual appetite. He could also obtain drugs of any kind if required but Kaduna never indulged in anything more than the local hash, called Ganja, which was smoked by many of the local population as part of the norm anyway.

As he made his way through the hotel lobby to the gaming rooms beyond, he nodded occasionally to the various people that he recognised. He was a regular visitor to this establishment and was well known because of this. None of these casual acquaintances knew how he obtained his affluence and most didn't care. On the few occasions, when someone had become over inquisitive, he would fend off their questions with a stock answer. 'Private business.'

Kaduna was a handsome man, by anyone's standards, with a lighter complexion than the locals. He was from the far North of the country, where the Arab influence over the years, had left the populace with more refined features than their counterparts in the south. His nose though hardly slim, had a good shape that enhanced his face. His eyes were narrow and deep-set and small goatee beard served to give him a sophisticated, though sinister appearance.

He had an excellent physique a legacy of his time in the merchant navy. He maintained his shape by running a few miles daily up and down the sand dunes along the coast and by working out in a local gym, at least three times a week. His strength was awesome and he knew it.

Feeling extremely relaxed, he walked at a leisurely pace as he entered the gaming room. The deep red pile of the carpet felt luxurious beneath his expensive Gucci shoes and the air conditioning was refreshing, after the oppressive heat of the night outside. It was just after ten o'clock, but even at this relatively early hour the casino was quite crowded.

The clientele this evening was as usual mainly Africans, but the occasional white expatriate or businessman could be seen here and there. Some of the Africans, like Kaduna, wore lightweight safari suits but others were clothed in the long brightly coloured national dress, with distinctive plant pot hats on their heads. Despite the air conditioning, the air was thick with smoke. Everyone seemed to be fully occupied with gambling and oblivious to what was happening around them. It was standing room only at both the roulette wheels and three of the blackjack tables were also quite crowded. So he made his way to the far side of the room, to the fourth blackjack table where he could see a couple of spare stools.

He sat down at one of he free stools, took out his money clip and removed a hundred naira note, which he placed on the green beige in front of him. The girl croupier was about to start dealing, when Kaduna caught her eye.

'Ten chips,' he said quietly with a hint of arrogance in his voice, as he gently shoved the note towards the croupier with his forefinger.

The girl took the note and deftly pushed it down the slot at her side of the table, into the locked box below.

'There you are sir,' she said in a pleasant manner, with a soft English accent.

'Ten chips for one hundred naira cash,' stretching slightly as she passed the small pile of chips towards him at the far corner of the table. Her low cut black dress revealed to him as she leaned forward a tantalising view of her ample bosom. She looked up at him through clear blue eyes, for just a moment longer than necessary and he saw the slightest flicker of a smile on her moist pink lips. The dapper African was quick to recognise those small, almost primeval female signs which she had transmitted and found himself paying more attention to the croupier than to how he was playing blackjack. Which as the night progressed, through lack of concentration, was quite badly.

She certainly had class, he mused as he absently fingered one of the black, gold embossed casino chips, head tilted, looking up at the croupier, through appraising eyes. Her pretty face and long smooth honey blonde hair was enough to captivate the attention of any hot-blooded male. When she leaned over, to pass some chips to a punter at the other end of the table, Kaduna's eyes were transfixed by her perfect rear. Which thanks to the tight dress she wore left nothing to the imagination. He felt himself becoming aroused and he was sweating slightly, even though, the air conditioning in the casino, was very efficient. She was fast becoming one lady, which he simply had to seduce, no matter what it cost. With women, as in life, he always got what he wanted.

Lesley Granby continued dealing for another twenty minutes, during which time Kaduna changed two more hundred naira notes. With other things on his mind, he had been losing quite heavily. Then suddenly at the end of the next hand, another girl croupier replaced her. A local, dressed in a long brightly coloured green and red evening gown, of distinctive African styling. She was no beauty. About two stones overweight, Kaduna guessed and the dress bulged in many of the wrong areas because of this. He would have no trouble concentrating on his game now, even though he was disappointed to see the other croupier leave the table.

As she made her way to the croupier's rest area, Lesley was thinking about the tall well-built fellow who had played blackjack like a beginner, losing a fair sum of money in the process. She could easily tell by his demeanour and actions that he was very interested in her and a small note passed by one of the waiters, would assure her of some lucrative after work business.

Although she did not consider herself to be a prostitute, if a punter came into the casino that she liked and of course, if she felt in the mood, then what was the harm of boosting her wages, she often reasoned. After all, why should she let the gamblers seduce her for nothing, when they lost thousands on the tables? Besides, she quite liked black men and had been out with a number in her hometown of Leicester in England. This had shocked her middle class parents and friends. But she had a devilish streak and had always enjoyed the effect on others of her outrageous behaviour.

The man, who had caught her eye tonight, was a particularly fine specimen. With a lighter complexion than most locals he had broad shoulders and muscular arms that made the short sleeves of his shirt bulge. Back home she would have readily gone to bed with him for nothing, but out here it was different. After all, if he could afford to lose three hundred naira in twenty minutes, he could afford a couple of hundred dollars for her.

When she reached the staff rest area, a small dismal room with some worn out easy chairs and a battered coffee machine, she was clear in her mind what to do next. So she sat down, took a pen and some notepaper from her handbag, thought carefully for a moment and neatly wrote out a little note. She put this in an envelope, sealed it and gave it to one of the waiters who was coming out of the toilet, at the back of the rest area. The casino forbade fraternisation with between its employees and clientele, so she found this tactic best to approach suitable punters.

Kaduna's luck had picked up dramatically since the departure of the first croupier, as he was now able to focus on the game, instead of carnal matters. He had quickly clawed back his earlier losses and now had a sizeable pile of chips in front of him. However, his thoughts did drift back from time to time to the white croupier and what he would love to do with her, before the night was finished. Looking round the crowded gaming room, as the present croupier got ready to deal the next hand, he could see her expertly spinning one of the roulette wheels a few tables away. He smiled to himself and resolved to catch up with her later that night.

By this time, his mouth was becoming quite dry, caused by a combination of the tension playing the game and the smoky atmosphere around him, so he called one of smartly dressed, ever-attentive waiters over and ordered a beer.

With each successive hand of cards still his winning streak continued. During this hot run, face cards and aces were being attracted almost magnetically to him. The dealer amazingly kept busting, in fact, he thought jovially, it seemed she was a loser in more ways than one. He was on a roll, adrenalin coursing through his veins, becoming more and more confident, placing larger bets with each successive hand.

Kaduna was by now was so engrossed in the game, that he did not see the waiter, standing patiently next to him, with the beer he had ordered.

'Scuse me sir.'

'Yeah,' Kaduna said without turning round.

'I have brought your beer.'

He turned sideways and saw the glass of beer on the waiter's tray with a small white envelope propped against it. His cold menacing eyes looked at the envelope and then accusingly back at the waiter.

'One of the boys he ask me to give you dis letter. It's from the English girl,' said the waiter quickly.

Kaduna smiled weakly, picked up the tall glass of cold beer, took a deep draught then placed the glass carefully in one of the plastic holders on the side of the table. He could see the croupier was getting impatient to start dealing, so he picked up the envelope and put it in his shirt pocket. Then he placed bets on the two squares that he was playing. After a few more hands, the plastic marker came out of the card shoe and there was a pause in the dealing, while the croupier shuffled the cards and put them back in the shoe.

So he took out the small letter he had received and read the contents. Written in a clear neat style, it told him that her name was Lesley and she was available for some fun later, if he was interested. Two hundred dollars would be all it would cost. A warm feeling of anticipation flowed through him and he suddenly felt relaxed and contented. Two hundred he thought was quite cheap compared to what some of the white women charged. Anyway, price was unimportant. He had to seduce this woman and would have agreed to pay double, if required.

The time went quite slowly until the casino closed at three in the morning. He had been over five thousand naira up at one stage. But like all compulsive gamblers, he could not resist having another couple of hands of cards. By the time the last game of the night was played he was over four hundred naira down. But this did little to dampen his spirits as he made for the residents bar. After all it was only money, he mused. There was plenty more where that came from, these days.

The hotel by this time in the morning was quiet, most of the gamblers having left or gone to bed hours ago. When he reached the bar, this was also virtually empty, with just a couple of people leaning against the counter, looking into their drinks with bleary eyes. She was waiting for him at a table, in one corner of the comfortably appointed bar lounge. Her long blonde hair flowed over the shoulders of her elegant black dress as she gently sipped an exotic cocktail. Impassive, she watched him approach, at a leisurely pace.

'Hi, I'm Henry. Let's go, honey,' he said casually in a level tone.

She took one more sip of her cocktail, stood up slowly, smoothing her dress as she did so and left the bar with him.

During the short car journey to his apartment he said very little, content only to rub his hand up and down the inside of her thigh. When they got inside his apartment, he wrapped his powerful arms round her and lifted her effortlessly across the living room and into the bedroom, where they both tumbled in a writhing mass of arms and legs on his sumptuous king-size bed.

Lesley lost count of the number of times that they made love. Initially she had been a little frightened by the violent nature of his lovemaking. But this had given way to ecstasy as he continued to satisfy her time after time.

He had seduced innumerable women, virtually from the day he reached puberty, though almost all of them were of his race. The few white women that he had experienced had been cold and unfeeling, almost frigid in fact. But this girl was very different to them, participating with much gusto in his extensive sexual repertoire. It felt good to lie next to her on the bed and feel her soft hair on his skin, that in alone was an aphrodisiac to him. So after hours of intense lovemaking, they both succumbed to the deep cavernous sleep only exhausted lovers' experience. When they awoke it was late afternoon.

Lesley lay on the bed, body tingling, refreshed by sleep, listening to the steady whir of the air conditioning unit and the surf crashing on the beach below. The occasional noisy car could be heard rattling slowly past; the driver no doubt being careful to avoid the potholes on the rutted road. The room was almost in complete darkness, save for bright light that spilled over the upper edges of the thick curtains. She looked round at the man lying in the bed beside her, who had satisfied her many times during the night. She thought it was quite comical; she would be paid money for something she had enjoyed immensely. But she had already made up her mind not ask him for this when the time came to leave.

He stirred gradually from the depths of his sleep and felt the warm smooth body next to him. It was a strange feeling to wake up next to a woman. Usually after sex, he would just pay them and unceremoniously show them the door. In fact, he really couldn't remember the last time a woman had stayed all night. He wasn't sure if he liked the idea either. He did not really feel like making love again, but had the problem of getting rid of the woman. He rolled over onto his back and saw her looking intently at him with those big clear blue eyes. She leaned over to kiss him. But he gently pushed her away.

'What's up Henry? Did I wear you out last night?' the girl chided.

He laughed shortly.

'You must be kidding. No woman alive can wear me out.'

'I wouldn't be so sure of that. I'm willing to give it a hell of a try. That was quite a mind-blowing night.'

'It was okay, but you are talking too much, which is annoying me. I think you should go soon. Don't worry, I'll get you your money in a minute,' he replied caustically.

She was a little put out with his offhand tone. She could not understand why suddenly, he was being so horrible to her. But then again, she did not know the volatile nature of the man she was dealing with. She made a serious mistake in deciding to carry on with the conversation, especially as she could sense he was becoming a little vexed.

'I don't know why you are being so nasty. I mean, that was a fantastic time we had last night.' She raised her voice slightly, glaring at Kaduna. Then something snapped in his brain and he got quickly out of bed. He grabbed her roughly by the arm and said.

'Listen, you damn whore. You ask me for money for sex then the next day start to get other ideas. Well it doesn't work like that. Now you get your bloody clothes on and get out of here.' He held her slender pale arm, in the vice grip of one hand and dragged her off the bed.

'Let go of my arm, you blinking ape. You are hurting me!' she screamed at him.

Her acerbic words hit Kaduna like a punch on the nose and his short-fused temper exploded. He raised his arm to backhand her across the face, but incredibly, somehow, at the very last moment, managed to stop himself. Probably because he knew the casino owner, would not appreciate one of his best croupiers, lying in a hospital bed with a broken jaw.

He let go of her arm and went across to the dressing table. He took out a crumpled pile of dollars and naira and threw it at the terrified girl's face. Then he turned round and stormed out of the bedroom onto the balcony, almost ripping the heavy curtain from its runners as he closed it sharply behind him, clearly emphasising in no uncertain terms his intense anger.

Lesley was by now very upset and got dressed quickly, wishing to be out of the flat immediately. Initially she wasn't going to take any money, but then decided if she was going to be treated like a whore, she would act like one. So she hurriedly picked up handfuls of the crumpled dog-eared notes and stuffed them into her handbag.

He was out of sight on the balcony, so she let herself out of the apartment. The elevator door was open. She got inside and pressed the ground floor button. As the elevator creaked its way downward, she suddenly felt very unclean, filthy in fact. Whoring to her had previously just been a laugh, for which you were conveniently paid. But now, the full gravity of what she had become involved with became blatantly clear. Something that was exceedingly sordid.

She cursed loudly, remembering, they had taken no precautions. But the night before, passion had consumed her natural defences, to such an extent, that she couldn't be bothered to insist. She swore once again and said to herself, 'Good God! I could catch something really awful.' West Africa she knew had a high heterosexual incidence of AIDS. She felt sick. On arriving at the Holiday Inn, she raced up to her room and filled the bath with near boiling water. She got into it and stayed there for an hour. She had been stupid and now she felt humiliated and very worried.

After the girl had departed, virtually every muscle in Kaduna's body was tense with rage. 'The stuck up white cow,' he seethed. If any black girl had talked to him like that, he would not have hesitated to teach her the lesson she fully deserved. But she was

British, and he did not want to risk drawing attention to himself. So, after a cold shower and a joint of Ganja, whilst sitting on his balcony, he eventually regained his equanimity. He sat for a while and enjoyed a second joint, staring out at the shimmering expanse of ocean laid out like a huge blue carpet from the beach below, to the distant horizon. The effect of the drug sent soothing waves though his body, erasing the last remnants of tension, till eventually he started thinking about the night's work.

He leaned over the table and picked up a pair of powerful Zeiss binoculars he had stolen from the bridge of a ship a few years previously. The fact that they would have been the personal property of a master or deck officer troubled him not. He scanned the horizon for a few moments and eventually his gaze settled on the anchorage area, about two miles from the jagged moles, which protected the entrance to the port.

There were a few ships at the anchorage, gently rolling back and forward on the long swell. But it was the one closest to the shore, which caught his attention, as this was a large multi-purpose vessel, with three tall yellow rust streaked cranes on deck. This type of ship, he knew from experience, could carry a great variety of dry cargo in the holds. The decks he could see were crammed with containers stacked three high in places. He also observed that this particular vessel was low in the water. This suited his purposes admirably, assuming the captain was foolish enough to remain in that vulnerable position overnight.

He knew from his time at sea that more experienced skippers steamed away from the land during the night, as this coast was well known, for its extensive pirate activity. However some companies were not so well informed and if the vessel had never been to Nigeria before, the normal practice, of anchoring close to the shore, was usually followed. Where the depth of water was shallow enough to drop the anchor safely, an officer had once told him.

If this ship was still near the shore tonight he mused, he would make everyone on board pay for the captain's naivety, just as he had done to many others in the last couple of years. His lips twisted into an evil smile as he sat like a general, surveying the field of battle. Everything was on his side. He had all the essential elements; surprise, numbers, weapons, experience and cunning. By the end of the night, luck permitting, another captain and his ship would be wishing they were back in the middle of the ocean, many miles from Lagos.

Chapter Two

The moon cast a dull glow on the peaks of the smooth oily black swell, as the four large dugout canoes crept slowly from the dark inhospitable Nigerian coastline, towards the anchored ship. The pirates had no difficulty locating the ship as it was brightly lit from stem to stern to comply with the international collision regulations for vessels at anchor.

The master of this vessel was complying with the law. However, a more prudent captain, with knowledge of this particular coast, would have ignored the regulations and kept his vessel blacked out and as difficult to see as possible. As it was, this ship was advertising its presence to all and sundry and like a huge magnet, would attract every pirate on the coast. Henry Kaduna perched on the stern of the leading canoe, licked his dry lips in anticipation. He was going to make sure he would be the first to take advantage of this ignorance.

The engines of the canoes were on minimum throttle and a thick wet Hessian blanket had been thrown over the tops of the outboards to deaden the sound even further. The container ship was still over a mile away and no movement discernable on the vessel from this distance.

Some ships had patrols on deck, where members of the ships crew walked up and down dressed in white overalls and yellow hardhats, flashlights flickering along the deck to deter intruders.

Others had powerful searchlights, sending accusing fingers of light into the inky darkness, ready to illuminate possible trouble. Kaduna would never attempt to board a ship that was alert or had already detected his approach. There was no point taking a risk when perhaps, the next night, a less well-informed ship would arrive. This ship was one of the latter, apparently taking no precautions. Kaduna hoped all the crew and officers would be partaking in the seafarer's favourite pastime, telling lewd stories about rip-roaring nights ashore in port, whilst getting drunk in the ship's bar.

He relaxed a little now as there was still a short while before they would arrive at the vessel. His thoughts drifted back to the bitch he had bedded the night before. A good screw, that was for sure and a hint of a smile crossed his lips. But they tightened as he remembered how enraged she had made him.

As the group of canoes neared the ship, Kaduna leaned over and whispered into the ear of the man who was holding the tiller of the hundred horsepower Yamaha outboard motor and told him to stop the engine. The man, who was called Asamwa, was virtually Kaduna's right hand man. He was much smaller than Kaduna but quite muscular and had all the typical Negroid features of short crinkly black hair, wide nose and thick lips. He did as he was told and pushed the cut out button of the engine, which spluttered softly and stopped. On hearing the engine of his canoe stop, the other three canoes also cut their engines. A dozen or so men in each boat picked up short pointed native paddles and hunched over, began to paddle the boats quietly towards the unsuspecting anchored ship.

Only the most vigilant of ship's crews, would be able to detect the approach of these silent predators of the night. The only noises to be heard, the gentle sloshing sound the bow of each canoe made as they progressed through the water. In the distance behind the advancing canoes, the dull thumping of the surf on the steeply shelving beach could also be heard. This was an ever-present reminder to all of the treacherous nature of the coastline. Finally, intermittently, the sound of laughter somewhere on the ship could be heard and the faint strains of music from a stereo drifted towards the pirates.

Kaduna said under his breath. 'Enjoy the music while you can, you dumb bastards!'

Creeping forward, silently, the canoes made their approach to the ship's bow. Kaduna could now make out the ship's name, 'Cuidad de Valencia'. A strange name, he thought, but gave it no more attention, concentrating all his thoughts on the final approach to the vessel. There was no sign of life on the fore part of the ship and as the canoes got closer, automatically, they split into pairs. Two of them went down the port side and the other two down the starboard side.

As his boat came alongside the black rust encrusted hull of the ship, the swell suddenly pushed the bow of the canoe against he steelwork with a dull thud. Kaduna cursed at the noise, and then hissed at the men in his boat.

'Okay brothers, this is far enough. Let's get on board and see what we can find in all these nice shiny containers.'

'Right on man,' one of the pirates replied excitedly.

Shadowy figures stowed their paddles and stood, legs apart, on the thwarts of the gently rolling canoes. They then started throwing manila lines, with sturdy hooks attached, up towards the ship's rails. The first two lines were unsuccessful in their search for a secure hold and tumbled down into the water. But then, the distinctive ring of metal on metal told the listeners below that a hook had found its target. The man, who had thrown it, gave the rope a good tug to make sure it was secure. Then he started to shin athletically up the line, his feet pattering on the ship's side as he went. He was soon on board. By this time, other lines were fast on the ship's rails and the pirates were scrambling on board in numbers. All were armed, some with knives and others even had pistols, bought cheaply on the back streets of Lagos.

Kaduna had a lightweight Uzi submachine gun, which a contact in the police force had procured for him at a cost of just one hundred dollars. He liked the firepower and ease of use of the weapon. Six hundred rounds per minute would stop anything. It was slung across his back as he climbed the five or so metres to the ship's main deck.

The pirates on deck were now busy breaking the customs seals and padlocks of the containers. Then throwing the various cargoes from within, onto the hatch tops and down onto the deck itself. When Kaduna saw what his men had found, plastic toys, car tyres and clothes, he was not pleased and shouted angrily at the men.

'Leave this bloody garbage, you idiots. Open up some more boxes and get something worthwhile to take back to shore with us.'

Just then one of the men let out a squeal of delight. 'I got cameras over here.'

'That's more like it.' Kaduna said with authority. 'Get them down into the boat.' The deck at number one and two hatches was knee deep in merchandise and opened cardboard cartons, which the pirates had scattered wildly around them in the search for valuables. They were now using the scaling lines to carefully lower cardboard boxes full of cameras and electronics into the canoes below. In the pitching heaving dugouts, eager hands quickly untied the lines and stowed the boxes. The canoes were rapidly becoming full.

The commotion and noise somewhat resembled that of excited children in a toyshop and had now alerted the ship's crew. Searchlights shone down from the bridge, to try and illuminate the canoes. But they had come alongside just past the bow, at number one hatch, cleverly out of sight of the bridge.

Kaduna looking aft towards the accommodation, could see a number of the ship's crew timidly creeping forward, dull beams of their flashlights moving back and forth ahead of them. The crew were furtively dodging in and out of the ship's structure, hoping to take the pirates by surprise. It looked more like a pathetic gesture, to make the captain's paperwork appear better, rather than a concerted effort to actually get rid of the pirates.

Kaduna had expected something like this and stood in the shadows with his gun at the ready. The safety catch was off and a bullet in the chamber set for firing. He smiled to himself as he gently, almost lovingly, caressed the handle of the gun. The seamen would not expect the pirates to be so well armed. After waiting a few more seconds, he squeezed the trigger and sprayed a long burst of fire down the deck, aiming slightly to one side of the advancing seamen.

A tremendous crescendo of noise erupted as bullets ricocheted off the metal deck; clattering and clanging into the base of the containers and hatch coamings, then out to the ship's rails. This created instant mayhem amongst the sailors, who fled screaming and terrified, back to the safety of the accommodation. When all of them were secure inside, they frantically battened down all the steel watertight doors, cursing and swearing loudly as they worked, praying that the pirates would not follow them. Luckily none of the seamen was hit in the hail of bullets.

Meanwhile on the bridge of the ship, the sleep-fuddled mind of the master, Captain Eduardo de la Cruz, was attempting to fully understand what was happening to his vessel and the various implications. It was piracy. No other word for it .He had been woken up half an hour previously, from a very deep sleep, by an extremely excited and agitated second mate, with the unwelcome news, that the vessel had been boarded by a gang of pirates. Now he was trying desperately to raise the shore signal station, to request police help. 'Sécurité, sécurité, sécurité. This is Spanish container ship, 'Cuidad de Valencia'. Come in East Mole Signal Station. Pirates are attacking us. We are in grave danger. Please send assistance quickly. These pirates are armed and we are all in fear of our lives.' He repeated the message several times, in heavily accented English but there was no reply from the shore signal station.

The Spanish captain was wasting his time. No help would come. The radio at East Mole signal station was not even switched on. Kaduna had paid the radio operator a few naira to ensure that the shore receiver would be conveniently broken down at night time.

'Sécurité, sécurité, sécurité.' Again the captain tried to raise the signal station and once again received no reply.

A dark feeling of despondency was creeping over him like a huge black storm cloud poised overhead, ready to unleash its wrath. His ship was only two miles from the shore, with dozens of armed natives on the foredeck helping themselves to the cargo. He was powerless to stop them.

What use was the puny ship's gun, a Beretta .22, against the raking fire of the machine gun, which had shot at his deck patrol a few minutes earlier? Thankfully, mercifully, the patrol had reported to the bridge that no one had been injured. Another very worrying aspect, which ate viciously at the wall of his stomach, like a ravenous beast, was the fact that the pirates would undoubtedly have other firearms and weapons, as well as the deadly machine gun.

God what a mess, he thought. The shore won't help us and we can't even steam out to sea, because the pirates are between us and the anchor up forward. The company, or even the local agent who he had spoken to earlier that day, should have warned him of the situation outside this port at night time. So many thoughts were going through the captain's mind and still the pirates could be heard breaking into the containers up forward. Shouts of jubilation from time to time came drifting back on the humid night air, as they uncovered more valuable booty. By this time he was sick with worry. This intensified even more, when he thought what would happen, if the rabble became confident and decided to attack the accommodation; in an attempt to raid the ship's safe.

'Madre mia!' He cursed softly under his breath. There was almost twenty thousand dollars in that safe, which he had taken a few weeks ago in the USA. This large amount of cash was required to pay off some of the crew, who were due to complete their contracts and be flown home from the next port, Abidjan.

On the foredeck, Kaduna felt pleased with the night's work so far. Three of the four canoes had already returned to the shore crammed full of cameras, cassette players and many other highly saleable consumer goods. His men were now lowering the most valuable cargo of the night carefully into the last canoe. This was video recorders, which would fetch an excellent price ashore.

Kaduna was now thinking of the icing on the cake. The ship's safe. Normally that was one area that he left alone. Although most seamen were not so keen to fight his men on deck to protect the charterer's or owner's cargo, when it came to the accommodation this was a different matter. Crews tended then to feel threatened personally and with this, their behaviour then became unpredictable.

In the past some crews had been overcome very easily and entry gained to the accommodation, then his ultimate goal, and the contents of the master's safe invariably achieved. But when others had been prepared to fight, this had caused bloodshed and even death on both sides. He was not particularly concerned about how many of the crew he would have to kill to obtain the money in the safe. Murder was something he had come to terms with a long time ago.

If some of his own men were killed that would be no loss either, as he trusted none of them. Besides, there were many more ashore who would eagerly take their places. No, it was his own safety he was thinking about. There had been a few close calls in the past. Once in particular he nearly died as a result of an enraged captain and he didn't want to take any unnecessary risks. The life of luxury he planned, away from the stench and squalor of West Africa would never materialise, if he let some desperate seafarer get the better of him.

However, the pathetic effort the ship's crew had made to try and stop him taking the cargo, made him think that perhaps this may be easier than most ships, when it came to gaining entry to the accommodation. He weighed up in his mind the risks involved and possible rewards. The money generated by the cargo they had stolen would have to be split with the rabble now on their way ashore. When all the officials had been paid off and there were many of those, the profit would be eroded even further. This money would be in the local currency, naira that converted poorly to U.S. dollars.

This was a big ship with a large crew, so there would be a sizeable amount of money in the ship's safe. But how to achieve this was the question he kept asking himself. By now all the entrances would be secured shut with steel watertight doors. The only entrance that did not have this kind of door was the wheelhouse on the top deck. But the steel ladder leading up to the wheelhouse would probably have been removed as a precaution against thieves in port.

The only way to get up to the wheelhouse now would be to actually scale up the side of the accommodation, using the lines and hooks from the initial boarding of the vessel. That had worked in the past many times, but surprise was on his side then and that element had long since gone. The crew would probably be waiting on that top deck, ready to hurl any objects at hand down on someone foolish enough to try and climb.

No matter how hard he thought, he could not come up with a good plan where the odds would be sufficiently in his favour. Also it would be daylight in under an hour which concerned him, not wishing to encounter a police patrol on the way back to dry land. It looked increasingly likely he would have to forget about the safe on this vessel and concentrate on getting the last canoe full of cargo safely to the shore. He sighed resignedly and walked along the deck towards his canoe through the piles of cardboard, paper, plastic, clothes and all the other debris of the night's plundering. He kicked the occasional carton or box in frustration as he went.

While Kaduna watched the last of the video recorders being loaded onto the remaining canoe, Captain de la Cruz paced nervously up and down inside the wheelhouse of his ship. This was just about the worst thing that had happened to him in twenty-four years at sea. He used to think that a typhoon was the mariner's biggest enemy. But he had changed his mind this night and the problem was not over yet. He knew some of the boats had left the ship taking their cursed occupants back to the land. But he was not sure if they had all gone. He was tense and starting to become desperate. The stress and pressure of command was weighing heavily on his shoulders. More than at any time he could remember, in all his time in command. This was a desperate situation. A machine gun on his ship in the hands of an uneducated cold-blooded killer had to be the ultimate nightmare. He was puffing furiously on his fourth cigarette in succession since arriving on the bridge. He looked round the wheelhouse almost seeking reassurance from the chief mate, the second mate or even the duty A.B. None was forthcoming. They were all as terrified as he was. Eventually he spoke.

'Third Mate,' he said gruffly. 'How many of those bloody boats are still alongside us?'

'I'd say just the one now sir. I counted four of them when they first came. Then I saw three of them making for shore about ten minutes ago.'

'Are you sure that three of them have gone?' the captain asked tersely.

'Yes sir. I heard three separate engines starting up as the boats left, one by one. I am certain there is only the one left now.'

The captain wondered what the last canoe was waiting for as now it should be full of cargo like the ones that had left earlier. Perhaps they were not satisfied with what they had already and the ship's safe would be their next target. He puffed nervously on his cigarette, shoulders hunched as he paced anxiously up and down.

'Captain,' said the chief mate excitedly. He was standing out on the bridge wing looking forward. 'The last boat has just started its engine.'

De la Cruz went briskly out on to the bridge wing. Sure enough, the high-pitched buzzing of an outboard motor could be clearly heard, punctuating the still night air. Also, the faint outline of a canoe, rolling and pitching over the swell, moving away from the ship, was just discernible.

The little Spanish captain felt a great feeling of relief sweep over him as the tension drained from the muscles in his shoulders. He knew exactly what he was going to do now. Heave up the anchor and get away from this vile coast as quickly as possible, before some more pirates decided to pay him a visit.

'Third Mate, ring down the engine room and tell them that we will be moving off soon,' he said sharply.

'Aye aye sir,' replied the third mate as he strode purposefully towards the engine room phone, located on the control consol in the centre of the wheelhouse.

The captain had told the chief engineer, to get the main engine ready over an hour ago, when the pirates first boarded. It just needed to be briefly tested on air and fuel, and then the ship would be ready to move. He would steam many miles off the coast, far away from his current perilous position. On reflection, it is what he should have done in the first place, he thought bitterly.

The captain turned to the chief mate, who had just come into the wheelhouse from the bridge wing.

'Okay Ramon, you had better get the carpenter and go forward. When you reach the foc'sle, put the anchor in gear and let me know when you are ready to heave away.'

'Right Captain, I'll pick up my radio from my cabin on the way.'

'My radio's already switched on. Give me a call when you get up forward.'

'Will do,' said the chief mate, as he went out of the chartroom door and down the stairs to his cabin two decks below.

Chief Mate Ramon Padilla collected his radio and flashlight from the coat hook just inside the door of his cabin. Then he quickly descended another two flights of stairs to the main deck where the carpenter's cabin was located.

He was a short man, a shade over five feet six inches tall, with typically swarthy Spanish looks. His broad shoulders and heavily muscled arms had been developed over the years, turning valves on the decks and pump rooms of tankers. This was only his second trip on a container ship, but now he longed for the peace and quiet of weeks at sea, far away from land so typical of the tanker trade. If he had known a year ago, the problems and general hassle that was involved in the day to day running of these 'Box boats' as everyone called them, he would never have transferred in the first place. The chilling experience, with the gun toting pirates swarming all over the ship tonight, was just about the final straw for him.

Tankers for him again next trip.

He met chippy, as the ships carpenter was known, at the bottom of the stairs together with three sailors. There was an excited buzz of conversation, with much gesticulation, as the men talked loudly and nervously amongst themselves. They had been fired upon by a machine gun earlier and were still exceedingly shaken by the experience. The talk tapered off and stopped, when they saw the chief mate coming down the stairs towards them.

As he reached the bottom of the stairs where the men were standing one of the sailors called Lopez, was the first to speak.

'What's happening, Chief? Have those bastards gone yet? They could have killed us all with that damn machine gun! A bullet missed me by less than a centimetre! I had a very lucky escape.' He was extremely excited and talking rapidly.

'We were all lucky not to get killed,' a tall slim Basque called Bakero said rather morosely. 'The Old Man shouldn't have sent us along the deck. It was a hell of a risky thing to make us do. He should have known the pirates would have had guns and that he would be putting our lives on the line, making us go along the deck like that. What the hell was he hoping to achieve anyway?'

'Listen, he is in command. We can't question his orders; otherwise nothing would get done on a ship,' said the chief mate firmly.

The carpenter, a stocky Catalan, was determined to say his piece as well. 'Anyway, we were not happy with the situation and the Union will have something to say about this whole affair, when we get back to Spain.'

'Now come on, amigos,' the chief mate chided. 'The worst is over now I am sure. We saw the last of those bloody canoes leaving a few minutes ago, now we are going forward to heave up the anchor and get away from this cursed place.'

'Thank God,' said Lopez. 'This place gives me the jitters.'

The chief mate passed Lopez on his way to the steel watertight door, at the end of the alleyway. Then, standing clear of the door, his back against the bulkhead, he said to the carpenter. 'Come on Chippy; let's get this door opened up.'

The carpenter took a small steel hammer from his canvas tool bag and with a couple of skilfully aimed blows on each of the steel handles of the accommodation door, released them one after the other. Once all the handles were free, he put the hammer down on the deck and with both hands, pushed the heavy steel door outwards. The door swung easily on well oiled hinges and landed with a loud crash against the steel of the accommodation side. Now that the door was fully open, chippy felt an appreciable rush of warm humid African air past his face. Then he turned round and walked a couple of paces back to get his torch which was lying on the deck where he had left it earlier.

The chief mate was about to step over the door sill and go out onto the deck outside when the sailor Lopez shouted to him.

'Hey Chief, I heard on the radio tonight, Athletico got beat tonight in the Copa del Rey.'

The mate paused, smiled, turned his head slightly and called over his shoulder.

'You must have been tuned to the wrong station Lopez. The station I had on, said they won five nil.' A chorus of nervous laughter broke out from behind the mate. He was glad the crew were at last starting to relax a little.

When the chief mate turned his head back, from the crew behind him in the alleyway to look in the direction of the deck outside, his eyes filled with horror. Standing less than a metre away from him was a pirate. He was a tall powerfully built black man, dressed in what looked like some kind of green combat uniform. An ugly snub-nosed machine gun was pointing directly at him. They had been tricked! The last boat had departed. But some of the pirates must have stayed behind. Now with the steel door to the accommodation open, they were at the mercy of the pirates.

The African moved forward in a flash and pushed the gun to within a few centimetres of the chief mate's forehead. There was an evil spine-chilling look on his face. His lips were tightly closed, his nostrils flared and his eyes narrow cold and menacing. The mate's heart beat like a hammer in his chest. His stomach muscles were so taut that he felt they would tear at any moment. He was so intensely frightened he could hardly breathe. He knew death was staring him right in the face and each second seemed like an eternity.

'That's far enough,' said Kaduna, his voice heavily laden with menace. 'Now turn around and go back inside.'

Completely unprepared for this trauma, the short stocky Spanish mate froze where he was standing and felt his legs turning to jelly. He knew enough English to understand what the black man had said, but his body would not respond. The short muzzle of the gun was so terrifyingly close to his forehead. Violent death looked imminent, but he was so terrified he was powerless to do anything about the situation. The carpenter and the rest of the crew, who were only a few metres from the chief mate, stood petrified in silence watching the drama unfold in front of them.

The mate could not have stood transfixed for more than a

couple of seconds, but that was too long for Henry Kaduna, who screamed at the Spaniard, 'Come on you little bastard. I haven't got all night. Now bloody move!'

Then completely without warning, the African lunged forward and viciously stabbed the gun on the mate's forehead. This caused him to stumble and fall backwards into the accommodation, blood spurting from the wound on his head as he fell. He landed heavily on the deck and lay there groaning and writhing in pain, clenching his bloody temple with both hands.

Kaduna was through the door in an instant and stood over the injured mate. More armed pirates swiftly appeared behind him. But they were unable to enter as Kaduna and the chief mate, who was still on the deck, blocked the narrow entranceway.

'Get up you little shit. It's only a scratch.'

The injured Spaniard rose slowly, unsteadily, one hand gripping the alleyway rail while his other hand was pressed on his forehead. His head throbbed terribly and he felt nauseous as the warm blood trickled through his fingers and down his face.

'Bastardo,' he hissed in Spanish, looking dejectedly up at Kaduna.

The pirate let out a short sarcastic laugh and then said, 'Shut up. You are lucky I didn't blow your brains out. But if you don't do as I say, I will shoot you and your friends as well.'

The pirate didn't really want to shoot anyone at this stage, as the noise would alert other people on the ship. He wanted to keep the element of surprise on his side as long as possible. He had a heavy double bladed hunter's knife in a sheath in his right boot. He would soon use this if anyone refused to co-operate, just as he had done on occasions in the past.

'Okay you people,' he intimated with his gun towards the ashen crew, who by this stage were shaking with fear.

Although they did not speak a great deal of English, it was clear what the African wanted. So without taking their eyes off him, the crew cowered back slowly down the alleyway. The mate followed them, still clutching his injured forehead. Blood continued to ooze through his fingers, leaving bright red spots on the floor behind him. Kaduna moved out of the entranceway and the rest of the pirates came in from the deck outside, and stood beside him.

There were another seven pirates, all with pistols in their hands. These were smaller than Kaduna but most were quite well built. They were, for the most part, dressed in scruffy stained trousers and shirts. They all looked half crazed, as if they were drunk or high on drugs. All of them were smiling sardonically, watching the unarmed Spaniards moving slowly, nervously down the alleyway. The atmosphere was extremely tense, the Spaniards to a man believing that it would take nothing for this rabble to start shooting indiscriminately.

Kaduna broke the silence, 'You,' pointing his gun menacingly at the mate. 'Where is the mess room on this ship?'

'It's on the next deck up on the port side,' the mate replied haltingly in heavily accented English. He was so afraid and his reply so quiet that it was barely audible to Kaduna. However he did grasp enough of what the Spaniard had said.

'Okay brothers. Listen carefully. This is what we are going to do,' Kaduna said to the group of pirates. He spoke directly to the smallest pirate, a weasel like man called Mensah who was standing closest to him. 'I want you and Umboko to take these men up to the mess room and keep them quiet. Here take my Uzi, this will be better for keeping them all covered.'

Mensah passed his battered .38 and gleefully took the Uzi machine pistol from Kaduna, beaming like a child, who had just been given a shiny new toy to play with.

'Asamwa, you and me are going to find the captain. The rest of you are to search the cabins and bring anyone you find to the mess room.'

Mensah went towards the seamen and motioned with his gun for them to move up the stairs. One of the younger seamen was trembling quite noticeably and having difficulty climbing the stairs.

Umboko jabbed him between the shoulders with his gun, which brought a squeal from the youngster who then quickened his pace in fear of further punishment.

Kaduna and Asamwa followed behind the group, ever wary, guns at the ready. They left them at the next deck and continued at speed up the stairs towards the bridge, where they expected to find the captain. The remainder of the pirates stayed on the bottom deck and went off in high spirits to the cabins down the alleyways on the port and starboard sides. Kaduna let them keep what they found in cabins, so they were always pleased when given this task by him.

Although the deck crew and officers had been involved for hours with the pirate attack, there were still a number of other crew who had not been called; stewards, engine room ratings and some engineer officers. They had heard the commotion on deck earlier on, but for the most part, they had elected to stay behind locked doors, in the apparent security of their cabins. They were now about to be subjected to the full horror of a pirate attack.

The boarders methodically went from cabin to cabin viciously kicking down the lightweight pine doors and forcing the petrified occupants out into the alleyway, under gunpoint. Then whilst one of the pirates covered the occupants, the other men went through drawers and lockers. The personal belongings of the crew were strewn all over the cabins, as the pirates searched for valuables and money.

Some of the crew pleaded with the pirates not to take belongings, which were irreplaceable, such as wedding rings and personal jewellery. But a blow from a gun or a fist was only response the pirates gave. The pirates were utterly callous, as they wrecked cabins one after the other. Anything that was too large to take ashore was ruthlessly smashed. Televisions, videos and stereos were all systematically destroyed.

While mayhem reigned out of control in the crew's quarters, all they could do was to stand back terrified and sickened by what they saw. They were powerless to do anything about the situation. Some crew were crying openly, as the pirates appropriated their possessions and hard-earned money. The pirates were by now working themselves up into an uncontrollable frenzy, fuelled by hard liquor found in some of the cabins, which they gulped down straight from the bottles.

The mad rampage continued swiftly through the crew's quarters and progressed to the officers' accommodation, located two decks above. Eventually the crazed and drunken gang of pirates reached the cabin of Danilo Eduarte, the ships fourth engineer. Here they encountered difficulty entering the cabin as chairs and other furniture had been piled up against the door in a vain attempt to thwart entry. This pathetic effort at resistance was soon overcome by two of them who kicked the door in unison, till it came right off its hinges.

Young Eduarte confronted the pirates as they burst into his cabin and leapt surprisingly nimbly over the debris of the furniture. He had a small knife in his hand, which he was going to use to defend himself but he was soon dispossessed of this by one of the intruders, who first feinted one way then kicked the knife clean out of his hand.

The pirate then viciously clubbed the fourth engineer on the side of the head with the butt of his gun; knocking him senseless to the floor, blood pouring from the gash left by the gun. The reason for the valiant, though feeble attempt at resistance became apparent to the pirates, as they looked around the small neat cabin. For there in the far corner of the bed, with the sheets pulled right up to her eyes, was Eduarte's beautiful young wife of only two months.

He had been married on his last leave and after a honeymoon in Marbella; he had proudly brought his beautiful young wife with him on the voyage. He had joked about the trip at the time, calling it a pleasure cruise round Africa. This particular cruise was about to turn into a nightmare for the poor innocent girl. A nightmare from which she would never recover.

The sweat-glistening faces of both pirates shone with delight, at the treasure they had just discovered. They walked slowly towards the terrified young girl, licking their lips in eager anticipation of what they were going to do next.

'I wants to be first!' the larger and meaner of the two said, eyes narrow, glowering at his accomplice, saliva trickling from the side of his mouth.

'Take those people in the alley up to the mess room, and then come back later.'

'Okay keep cool man. I ain't in no hurry. You wants me to tell the others?'

'Yeah you better. If they find out there was some pussy on board that we didn't share with them, they would go crazy.'

The smaller pirate turned round and walked back into the alleyway. Then he motioned with the gun in his hand for the officers to move. The Spaniards could see what was going to happen inside the cabin. One of them, the second engineer, a close friend of Eduarte, and best man at his wedding, became agitated, cursing and shouting at the pirate in Spanish.

'Bastardos, hijos de putas!' he screamed. He then tried to lunge forward and grab the pirate, but the other officers restrained him in time, as certain death would have ensued.

The pirate thrust his rusty revolver up close to the left eye of the hysterical man and held it there for a few seconds, saying nothing, staring menacingly at him through cold black eyes. 'Okay you son of a bitch. Let's go.'

The second engineer went reluctantly along the alleyway with the others, cursing under his breath as he went.

In the cabin the beautiful though fragile young girl was sobbing uncontrollably. Her slim body was heaving up and down with fear and revulsion beneath the sheets of the bed. The hideous African came towards her, holding his gun at his side in one hand and undoing the belt of his trousers with the other, eyes glazed with a combination of lust and drugs. He had a sardonic smile on his revolting thick lips. She pleaded desperately with him in Spanish, cowering tightly up against the bulkhead, wishing that somehow the wall would open up and let her escape. He let out a deep sickening laugh and then said mockingly, 'No understan honey. You gotta learn to speak English.'

By now the man was so close she could smell the awful stench of his unwashed body. She vomited down the side of the bed. The pirate kept moving towards her, grinning with perverse pleasure at the vile crime he was about to perpetrate.

A few minutes earlier on the bridge wing, Captain de la Cruz had been trying desperately to contact the chief mate up forward on his radio. He was totally oblivious that the security of the accommodation had been compromised. The captain pressed the call button of his Motorola radio for the umpteenth time.

'Bridge to forward. Come in forward.'

'Hello forward. Come in please. Do you read me?' His speech was laced with anxiety, as a dark feeling of foreboding crept over him once again.

He had checked the battery level on the radio and that he was using the correct channel. But he couldn't understand why the mate had not answered. It usually took about five minutes to get from the accommodation to the ship's bow, and it had been almost ten minutes since the mate departed from the bridge. Perhaps, the captain mused, he had fallen over some debris left by the pirates on deck. But if that had happened, the carpenter would have informed the bridge using the mate's radio. There was something seriously wrong. He was full of dread as to what that might be.

He was just about to send the second mate to find the chief mate, when he heard a loud crash from the direction of the wheelhouse. The noise had been caused by the door to the accommodation being thrown open with considerable force. He spun round suddenly and looked from the bridge wing towards the wheelhouse, just as two Africans rushed into view across the wheelhouse.

It struck him like a sledgehammer. They had been tricked! His shoulders dropped again and he sighed resignedly as the hopelessness of the situation became brutally apparent to him.

The second mate was leaning against the window ledge of the wheelhouse, gazing towards the coast. It was hot on the bridge and he was looking forward to the end of his watch and a few beers in the bar with the third engineer. The sound of the door crashing open shattered his reverie. He turned round with a start and saw a dark figure rushing towards him, with what appeared to be a gun in his hand. Instinctively he put his hands in the air.

Kaduna came up close to the second mate and thrust his gun at the side of the young officer's head. 'Where's the captain?' he asked loudly.

The second mate had been badly frightened, by the sudden appearance of the pirates and was having difficulty replying to the question.

'Come on son. Frigging capitano,' Kaduna screamed, forcing the gun so hard against the youngster's head that he winced.

'There's no need for that, leave him alone. It's me you are looking for. I am capitano,' a small voice said quietly, wearily, from the other side of the wheelhouse as the captain came in from the bridge wing and walked towards the pirate.

The Spanish captain was in a state of shock. His nerves had enough difficulty just coping with the daily problems and tension of a master's job on a large ocean going vessel. Tonight, with the pirates swarming all over his ship, those frayed nerves had been pushed to breaking point. The immense relief at hearing the last pirate boat depart had now given way to awful despondency.

His actions were sluggish and his thoughts slow as a result of the unusually high stress level his body had to cope with. There was no alternative. He would just have to comply with whatever these people required and hope for the best. The most important thing was that none of his crew was harmed.

Kaduna left the trembling second mate and strode purposefully, triumphantly, towards the captain, waving the battered pistol in the face of the smaller man. His hand was shaking with the excitement of the moment.

'There is no need for the gun,' the ship's master said passively. 'I will give you whatever you want.'

Kaduna relaxed slightly, thinking by the captain's attitude the robbery could be easier than he had envisaged. Some captains, mainly Greeks and Indians when confronted with this situation were foolishly stubborn. However this man looked like he might co-operate.

'Okay' Kaduna said, moving back slightly from the captain. 'Now you listen, and you listen real good.' He paused a second, for effect. 'I want all the money in the safe,' he went on, talking slowly and firmly. 'All the money, no tricks, understand?' He was speaking louder now. 'If I think you are trying to conceal anything from me or trying to be clever, some people on here are going to get messed up real bad,' he shouted at the Spaniard who cringed at his words.

'All right, all right. I understand,' replied the captain, a note of irritation creeping into his voice. 'We go to my cabin. All the money is there. Please don't hurt any of my crew.'

Kaduna just grunted at the man's pathetic request. He was in command of this ship now. The grubby gun in the palm of his hand assured him of this. During his time as a sailor, haughty white captains such as this man had made him feel like he was an inferior person, because he was just a sailor and also black. But the tables had turned full circle. He held all the cards now and he would do as he damn well pleased. He turned to Asamwa.

'Take this man to the mess room.' He pointed to the second mate. 'I'll join you as soon as I have the money.'

He wanted to be the only one in the master's cabin when the safe was opened so that most of its contents would go into the various pouches of his army issue combat suit.

When they reached the master's accommodation, on the next

deck down, De la Cruz opened the door and Kaduna followed close behind, pensive, gun at the ready. The captain led the way, through a narrow lobby into the dayroom, where he conducted the ship's business. In the forward part of the cabin, there was a settee and some easy chairs. At the rear of the cabin was a large wooden desk with some papers piled neatly on top.

To the side of the desk, recessed into the bulkhead, was a cabinet with an upper and lower door. The ship's safe was in the upper part. The Spaniard went unhurriedly towards this, extracting a substantial bunch of keys from his trouser pocket. He selected the correct key and opened the top door of the cabinet.

Kaduna was standing in the middle of the cabin. From here he could see clearly what the captain was doing and also if anyone tried to enter the cabin through the lobby. His gun was levelled at the Spaniard, who was partly concealed behind the door of the cabinet. This was moving slowly back and forth due to the easy rolling motion of the vessel, squeaking slightly on dry hinges.

'No funny business now man. Or I will not hesitate to blow you away and your damn crew if I need to.'

'Yes, all right, I am not stupid,' replied the captain, who was starting to be perplexed, at the way this intruder was ordering him round and humiliating him on his own ship.

As he worked the combination back and forth, the captain was becoming increasingly angry and frustrated with the night's events. He was master of this ship and the one who gave the orders. To have this apparition, as he regarded the pirate, bossing him around, was intolerable. By now he had regained most of his composure and was thinking more clearly.

The fact that this dangerous man was pointing a gun straight at him seemed not to worry him any more. He was focusing all his thoughts in an attempt to find a way to teach this pirate a lesson.

He had just got the door of the safe open when he heard it!

A long spine-chilling scream, from somewhere on the deck below.

Then again the same scream, only shorter this time as if cut off by some force. It could only have come from one place. The stark realisation of what was happening totally sickened and incensed him; the animals were assaulting and perpetrating untold evil and misery onto that sweet innocent child, the fourth engineer's wife. The same lovely girl, who only a few weeks earlier, had been so excited at making her first trip to sea on his ship. De la Cruz could stand no more, the short fuse of his temper, was now rapidly burning out. Then he saw it. There, to one side of the money in the safe, the cold black shape of the ship's handgun. He had reached the stage where he was ready to throw caution to the wind. The assault on the fourth engineer's wife was the final straw.

The African would not know there was a gun in the safe, as most ships did not carry firearms. If he could distract the man, this might give him a chance to serve up some retribution. Also he reasoned, the pirate's gun was old and rusty, obviously poorly maintained, perhaps it might not even work.

He carefully reached inside the safe with both hands. One hand gathering up the bundles of money and the other releasing the safety catch on the gun. He was amazed how calm he had suddenly become. Picking up two large wads of crumpled twenty-dollar bills, he turned slowly, walked a couple of paces and put the money carefully down on the desk.

The captain saw out of the corner of his eye, a look of sheer joy cross the African's face as his eyes lit up at the sight of the money. Just like a child being given a birthday present. His heart pounded like a drum in his chest. But his mind was clear as he returned to the safe, reached inside and picked up the gun.

With the adrenalin coursing furiously through his veins, he spun round quickly to try and catch the pirate off guard. Before he had half turned, a .38 bullet smashed though the thin wooden cabinet door, hitting his chest like a pile driver, throwing him against the bulkhead at the aft end of the cabin. His body fell, blood splattered and lifeless to the floor and lay in a pool of deep red blood.

'You dumb stupid bastard,' Kaduna said quietly, as he wedged the smoking gun into his webbing belt, a look of disdain etched on his face. He stepped over the dead captain, as he made his way to the safe.

The pirate was pleasantly surprised at the amount of cash actually in the safe. He gleefully stuffed the piles of ten and twenty dollar bills into the deep pouches in his combat suit. There was a thick bundle of one hundred dollar bills, which he kissed before depositing in one of his pouches. There were also a few bundles of one and five dollar denomination bills, which looked like a lot of money, due to their bulkiness. He kept these till last and crammed them into a thin white canvas bag, which he found in the safe. This would suffice to share out with the morons below. Although he knew more would have to be given to Asamwa, as he was not so easily fooled. The safe was now empty, so he moved towards the desk and picked up the remaining two bundles of money that the ship's master had placed there before his demise. He put these in the canvas bag, as these were also of small denomination.

Before he left the cabin, he looked at the crumpled blood-stained shape of the captain. He felt no remorse or pity for the man. He had been stupid and deserved to die. Finally he reached down and picked up the ship's revolver, lying on the floor next to the body and jammed this into the belt round his waist. Another weapon was always useful.

He found the rest of the pirates in the mess room. All were in high spirits due to the success of their night's work on deck and the subsequent plundering of the cabins. They had bags of various sizes taken from the helpless crewmen and crammed full of their valuables. Most of them, to a man, had taken part in the rape and defilement of the fourth engineer's wife. They looked pleased with themselves and were joking about the vile things they had done to the helpless girl.

Some even had dark bloodstains on the front of their scruffy ragged trousers, indicative of the pain and suffering they had inflicted on the poor girl. Most of them were now very drunk, holding the various bottles of spirits appropriated from the cabins. Spirit trickling down their stubbled chins from overfull mouths as they drank. Kaduna noticed one of the men was missing.

'Where's Mensah?' he said impatiently.

'He is gettin' some action with the girl,' came the slurred, though rather cheerful reply from one of the pirates.

'Someone get him quickly. We are moving out now and I don't want to find a police patrol between us and the shore.' Kaduna spoke tersely.

One of the pirates staggered to the door, then up the stairs and shouted urgently along the alleyway. A few seconds later, the remaining pirate appeared hurriedly from the fourth engineer's cabin, sweating profusely, tying his trouser belt with one hand, while carrying a bulging bag in the other.

The other pirates were now starting to leave the mess room. They swayed and lurched as they went, sacks of booty over their shoulders, talking loudly amongst themselves. The pirates then stumbled down the narrow stairs and out that fatal accommodation door, which still swung freely back and forth. They then weaved their way slowly along the deck to the waiting canoe up forward, chattering amongst themselves as they went.

Kaduna, who had stayed in the mess room, levelled his gun at the motionless seamen and said in an extremely menacing tone of voice. 'Any of you bastards try to leave this room and you will get some of this.' He then fired two shots in rapid succession, just above the heads of the men. The noise from the .38 was deafening. Fire and thick acrid smoke belched from its barrel. The seamen all fell to the deck some screaming, uttering in Spanish all the obscenities they could bring to mind.

The pirate laughed long and loud. Then he fired one more shot into the far bulkhead and left the room rapidly. The seamen lying motionless on the floor could hear the loud boom of his laugh, as he made his way down the stairs. They were completely helpless to do anything to stop him and his gang leaving. That was the way it had been all night and there was absolutely nothing they could do about the situation. In fact this was the way it had been in West Africa for many years. This state of affairs would continue until the maritime nations of the world and the United Nations, began to pool their collective resources to exert pressure on countries to make a concerted effort to bring piracy into check in their territorial waters.

Until this happened, Henry Kaduna and his ilk would remain free to perpetrate with impunity, whatever heinous crimes they so desired on unarmed merchant ships.

Chapter Three

The bullet caught the drug courier squarely at the back of his right knee and pitched him headlong, into the murky oily waters of the harbour in Antwerp. Unfortunately for him, his head struck a concrete pillar as he fell, killing him instantly. The black airline bag that had been slung over his left shoulder, spun through the air and landed on the damp cobblestones of the dock, bursting open and spilling a river of white powder as it slithered along.

Inspector Martin Ellis was an excellent shot and practiced regularly at the Interpol firing range in London. Tonight he had only meant to hit the area of the jetty close to the man's leg as a warning. However, the dock was poorly lit and he was around thirty metres away when he opened fire. Despite this, he still felt angry with himself that he had not hit the area he was aiming for. He wanted to question the man, not kill him. Make a deal, less time in prison perhaps for some useful information. Anyway, as he looked at the body floating face downwards amongst the paper, plastic and oil of Antwerp's Leopold dock, he felt no remorse for the man, only frustration.

He had been assisting the Belgian Drugs Squad to track down a shipment of cocaine. Information given by the United States Drug Enforcement Agency (USDEA), to Interpol indicated that there was a drugs shipment on board a British vessel, due to arrive in the port of Antwerp. Inspector Ellis had worked on similar cases for the last six months, making depressingly limited progress. He had hoped to achieve something positive tonight and was bitterly disappointed to have failed in that objective.

This particular episode started when the USDEA recruited and trained a Filipino living in the USA and then arranged with a manning agency in Manila, for him to join the ship as a sailor. When the vessel arrived at Baranquilla in Colombia, he had contacted a drug supplier who put a trial shipment on the vessel. This had been hidden in an empty paint drum, skilfully concealed out of sight, right at the back of the vessel's paint store. There were ten kilos of pure cocaine in the drum, worth around two hundred thousand pounds at street value.

The Filipino came ashore that night, to meet a pre-arranged contact with a black bag slung over his shoulder. He walked through the huge docks complex for about ten minutes in full view, until he was approached by a scrawny man of similar size to himself. After a brief conversation he passed an envelope to the Filipino and was given the shoulder bag. The seaman turned and hurried back past the concealed police officers in the direction of his ship.

Ellis and the Belgian chief inspector that accompanied him began to follow the courier. All was going very nicely to plan as they meandered through the port, when suddenly; two customs officers appeared and tried to arrest the courier. There was a struggle and the courier shot one customs officer, he then started running along the dock. Ellis immediately gave chase and ran past the injured customs man and his companion. The courier, who must have heard Ellis, turned and shot his pistol erratically at the pursuing Interpol man. It was when a powerful motor launch appeared from behind the bow of a ship that Ellis decided to try and stop the courier.

A match fizzed behind him and he turned to see Chief Inspector Andre Bouliver, of the Belgian Drugs Squad, lighting a cigarette. The acrid smoke of sulphur from the match hung briefly in the air.

The chief inspector flicked the match into the water near the body, and took a deep drag on the cigarette, exhaling the smoke a few seconds later into the chilly, damp January night air, then walked slowly towards Ellis.

The Belgian was a slim figure, no more than five feet seven inches tall, short dark curly hair, thinning noticeably on top. Casually dressed and his black three-quarter length leather coat was open at the front. He nodded his head sympathetically and pursed his lips, in that typically Gallic style of nonchalance then began speaking to Ellis in French.

'Hard luck Martin, it was really unfortunate he hit his head on the pillar.'

'Not half and a real pity that we will have nothing more to show for the weeks of work, than that bag of coke over there.' Ellis sounded disconsolate.

'Well it is something, I suppose and better in our hands than out on the street,' Bouliver said, trying to cheer up the Briton.

'Yes you are right on that count, but it is such an insignificant amount compared to what gets through daily. I really thought we were going to make some progress tonight. Just a small step closer to the ringleaders would have been something. Damn!' He punched his palm in frustration then continued speaking.

'If those frigging customs hadn't blundered onto the scene, I could have stopped him long before that launch appeared.'

The Belgian shrugged his shoulders and opened the palms of his hands, a gesture that intimated what he was about to say.

'Hell man, these things happen. Tomorrow is another day.'

'Any chance of tracking the launch down?' Ellis asked.

'We will try but not much hope really. He disappeared into the fog, so he could be anywhere by now. I've radioed through to the station and requested the information be relayed to the water police. But I think the boat will be too far away for us to find him.'

'Well that most certainly is that.' Ellis sighed resignedly, looking at his watch. It was almost eight-fifteen in the evening. It had been a tense few hours.

'There is no point me hanging round Antwerp now. I don't expect the Filipino sailor who brought the drugs ashore will have any more information for us. The only other person he knew at this end is floating in the dock beneath us at the moment. Ellis sighed and massaged his forehead with the tips of his fingers.

'Yes, I may as well clear off back to London in the morning. I'll send you a copy of my report on this incident in a few days.'

The Belgian took another long drag of his cigarette then flicked it casually into the dock. He nodded his head slowly, resignedly, agreeing with what Ellis had said.

'Yes that would probably be the best thing for you now. We will tidy up any loose ends here. Get statements off all the people on the ship, though that will be in all probability just a waste of everyone's time, of that I am quite sure. But you know that's police procedure and we have to go along with it. The Filipino seaman of course, will have to be secretly flown home tonight. Before 'The Mob' come looking for some compensation, for the drugs they have just lost no doubt in the form of his hide. He was a brave little bugger, I will give him that. I certainly would not like to be standing in his shoes at the moment.'

They both turned and began to walk in silence, ponderously, over the wet cobblestones, the half-mile or so to the dark blue unmarked Citroen police car. Ellis pulled up the collar on his thick wool coat, as protection against the damp chilly night air. He reflected on the week spent in Antwerp with the Belgian Drug Squad, waiting for the ship to arrive. A week used to plan meticulously, a chain of people to follow the drug courier to his final destination. There had been great euphoria, when a telex the Filipino seaman sent to his Mafia contact was intercepted. The trap had been baited and the chance of a positive result against the traffickers had looked promising.

A large squad of Interpol officers were working full time on drugs in London and in other offices throughout the Continent, in an attempt to break down trafficking in Europe. But it was an extremely onerous task. One that Ellis knew in all honesty, was an almost a hopeless undertaking. There were so many huge ports such as Hamburg, Rotterdam and Antwerp to be policed. Places where, every week, vast volumes of cargo arrived. With countless numbers of containers being imported, what chance had anyone of finding a few kilos of drugs amongst all that cargo? In reality to mount a serious challenge, thousands of customs officers with specially trained dogs would have been required. Even then the drug barons would find a way to avoid detection.

Usually Interpol, working with the various local forces, found that any progress made on a particular case, always had the same ending. They could catch couriers and middlemen, but never get close to the hierarchy. Ellis had been given the assignment in Antwerp because he spoke fluent French. He also spoke fluent Spanish and passable German. Interpol preferred their officers to have at least two foreign languages. He had joined 'the firm' as it was often referred to, straight from university with a degree in international law and foreign language. After a training period of one year, he joined the London branch with the rank of sergeant.

He had held a fascination for crime and crime detection from an early age and knew that this would be his niche in life. Being somewhat of a romanticist, he needed something more involved and adventurous than the drudge of regular police work. This is why he chose to join Interpol.

After a few years, his superiors could see his potential and he was invited to join a new elite group within the British part of Interpol, called the Special Investigations Squad. This was a small highly effective group, with just fifty personnel, of which around half were agents in the field. What it lacked in numbers it made up for in quality and had an excellent record since its inception in 1978. It was formed due to the increase of international crime, which affected, or could affect, British interests at home and abroad. The squad was designed with the intention of wherever possible, assisting local police resolve such cases. However it was not beyond the bounds of their mandate to go it alone, particularly as happened sometimes, where local law enforcement may be less than helpful, or even in collusion with the perpetrators.

Ellis had been with the SIS part of Interpol London for three years and had made excellent progress with the various cases assigned to him. Eventually, after a number of high profile successes against counterfeiting rings and organised crime syndicates, he was promoted to the rank of Inspector. He was twenty-eight years old, still single and what women often referred to as ruggedly handsome. Just less than six foot tall with short fair hair. A nose broken at rugby was not quite straight and he had a large square jaw. His eyes were brown, which always struck people as strange because of the colour of his hair. Due to a youth spent rowing his shoulders were broad with well-developed muscles. There was not an ounce of fat on him and his slim hips drove women wild.

The police car soon arrived back in the centre of Antwerp, as there was virtually no traffic at that time of night. Ellis said goodbye to the Belgian policemen at the dimly lit entrance to his hotel and went up the broad staircase to his room on the first floor. He then took a short stubby brown bottle of local beer from the fridge and sat down at the desk. He thought it would be best to start on the report whilst it was still fresh in his mind. So he lifted a thick notepad out of his briefcase and started writing down neatly the events of the last few hours. He would get a secretary to type this up when he got back to London.

After almost two hours and four beers, sipped from the bottle, he became tired of writing, closed the pad and tossed the pen onto the desktop. He was just about to leave his room and sample some of the Antwerp's raucous nightlife, when the phone rang.

'Hello Martin, its Andre,' said an excited voice.

'I've got some good news for you; we could be on to something.'

'Yeah go on, what is it?'

'One of the crew in the engine room, an oiler or a wiper, heard strange knocking sounds on the port side of the engine room, while the ship was in Baranquilla. He thought at the time, that someone was welding or drilling down number three hatch, which is just in front of the engine room, this had happened before apparently with other cargoes.'

'Interesting, sounds like there might be something attached to the hull of the ship,' Ellis said thoughtfully.

'Well, it certainly would not be the first time drugs had been smuggled that way. I've got divers on the way at this moment, to check out the bottom of the ship.'

'Good, let's see what the divers find, give me a call if anything turns up.' Ellis put the phone back in its cradle and lay back on the bed, to consider the latest information. He had thought the case was effectively closed, with the death of the courier earlier that evening, but this information cast new light on the affair.

Nearly two hours elapsed before the Chief of the Belgian Drugs Squad rang back. This time he had some excellent news for Ellis. The divers had found a large canister, attached to the underside of the port side bilge keel. Ellis was unfamiliar with the term, bilge keel. So the Belgian explained briefly its purpose and location.

The bilge keel was in fact a plate, running along the outermost extremities at the bottom of hull, about thirty or forty centimetres wide. It was a part of the ship's structure to help reduce rolling, an appendage on the smooth steel of the ship's hull. A few years ago however, drug smugglers discovered that this would be an ideal place to attach canisters full of drugs known as torpedoes. If the canister attached to the bilge keel of this vessel was full of cocaine, it would represent a multi-million pound shipment, possibly a whole month's supply for a large city.

However, it would be very difficult to find out who was going to receive this shipment. Divers working for the drug traffickers would remove the canister before the ship sailed and take this away underwater. Then the opportunity to seize a large quantity of hard drugs and stop them reaching the market would be lost. Ellis thanked the Belgian for the call and said he would be at his office shortly, to discuss a plan of action.

He arrived at the Police Headquarters twenty minutes later and found quite a crowd in the outer office talking rapidly in French, no doubt discussing the latest find. Almost all of the drugs squad seemed to have been called in, fifteen or sixteen officers in total. Chief Inspector Andre Bouliver was at the centre of the crowd, sat on the edge of a battered metal desk. As soon as he saw Ellis, he got up and welcomed him, shaking his hand.

'Welcome back, Inspector Ellis,' reverting to his title, as using Christian names were 'bad form' in front of the other ranks or on the radio. 'We have been discussing the new situation that has presented itself to us. It looks like we still have a chance, to follow this shipment to the receiver. Then hopefully we will have the next link in the chain. How far we can progress of course, will depend on our old friend, lady luck. One important fact that must be taken care of is the drugs must be removed from the canister and some thing of equal weight put back inside to replace them.'

Ellis took a deep breath before replying, conscious of the many sets of eyes focused on him at that moment.

'Yes sir, I was thinking on those exact lines on my way here. We must stop such a large shipment hitting the streets. Then at least, if we are unsuccessful with the rest of the operation, we will have something positive to show for our effort. Do you think the drugs can be removed in time?'

The Belgian chief inspector pursed his lips and nodded slowly before replying.

'Don't worry; I think we can have that taken care of. Two divers are at present in the process of opening the canister and replacing the contents with plastic bags full of flour. Unless there are any unexpected problems, they should be finished that part of the operation soon.'

'Good that's very reassuring to hear, what's the plan to follow the canister when it's removed?'

'Well, one of my officers suggested attaching a simple radio bug to the canister. That way we will have visual and electronic coverage as a back up, should we lose sight of the smugglers.'

'That's really good to hear sir. It seems like we have covered all angles.'

While Ellis continued the discussion with the officers of the Drugs Squad, two divers toiled seven metres down, in the freezing water of Antwerp's Leopold dock. Both had extensive training of diving in these conditions, having been employed for a number of years working on oilrigs in the North Sea. So the situation that night was nothing new to them. Both wore thick black rubber divers' dry suits, as protection against the effects of cold. After around thirty minute's arduous labour in visibility of only one meter, they were able to remove the cap at the end of the torpedo and replace the contents with plastic bags full of flower. Finally, they attached a small round metal radio bug with a magnetic base, to the under side of a bracket that connected the torpedo to the ships hull.

Satisfied that the bug was adequately concealed in this position, both divers were soon on the surface and ensconced in the back of their specialist truck. The packets of cocaine lay on the floor, safe in the black diver's bag they had taken with them. They swiftly took off their dive suits and dried themselves with towels from a rack in the side of the truck. Then one of the divers, picked up the radio handset at the front of the truck and reported to Chief Inspector Bouliver, that the mission they been given had been accomplished. The luminous hands of the clock on the dashboard showed a time of 2:00 a.m.

Thirty minutes later, Ellis was sitting in an unmarked blue Renault police car, beside Sergeant Marcel Dennis, a slim serious man, with thin fair hair and a moustache. They had positioned themselves at the far side of the dock from the cargo ship, concealed between two warehouses and had a good view of the ship from their position. Other men were carefully positioned in unmarked cars in various parts of the docks and in a launch belonging to the water police. A man was situated in the engine room of the ship and there was a listening device attached to the hull. Any sounds heard, he would immediately pass the information on by radio.

Special tracking devices were located in the chief inspectors car and the launch. As soon as the divers came to the surface with the canister, a signal from the bug would show up on these. The ship was due to sail the next evening, so it was inconceivable that the traffickers would attempt to retrieve the canister in the daytime. It would have to be within the next six hours under the cover of darkness. Ellis was pleased with the preparations. The plan appeared to be watertight, the only thing to do was to sit back and wait for the drug smugglers to make a move.

At first Ellis tried making conversation with Marcel Dennis, but found him to be a man of few words. So after ten of fifteen minutes he laid his head back on the comfortable headrest and closed his eyes. He was not thinking of anything in particular, just relaxing for a few moments. But the drama and tension of the last few days, coupled with serious lack of sleep, finally caught up with him. The four beers consumed in his hotel room, combined with the other effects, provided the catalyst to enable him to doze off. He was soon fast asleep.

'Okay gentleman, mama's come to collect her shopping,' the voice said calmly in French over the police radio on the dash. It was five-fifteen in the morning and Ellis who had been asleep, came instantly awake rubbing his eyes as he looked around the car. His mouth felt like it had a layer of guano, due to the beers consumed the previous evening in his Antwerp hotel. Oh for a bottle of cool clear mineral water, he mused ruefully.

In the dim light, sat next to him, he could see the quiet Belgian sergeant. He was fully awake, alert and listening attentively to the words being spoken by the policeman in the engine room of the ship. In other cars throughout the port bleary-eyed police officers also came alive.

'Hell! These bastards could wake the dead; they are making so much noise. I don't even need the listening device,' the voice on the radio said, sounding faintly amused.

Ellis's attention was fully focused as he listened to the animated voice emanating from the radio. Eventually after about ten minutes, the policeman in the engine room of the ship said the noise had ceased, indicating the torpedo had been removed.

Ellis sat quietly for a few moments, and then turned to the sergeant.

'Well I guess those divers will now be heading towards a rendezvous with someone on the shore, or perhaps, even a boat in the harbour.'

'Yeah, we just need to get an echo on one of the tracking units, and then we can close them down. Well, that's the theory at any rate. But these docks are huge and even if everything goes smoothly, we will still be lucky to catch up with them in my opinion,' the sergeant said quite morosely in an even flat tone.

They sat there in the darkness for another ten minutes then the police radio on the dash suddenly hissed and crackled into life once again. This time it was the voice of the officer in charge of the police on the launch, Luc Melville.

'Come in all units. We have the blip on the tracker and an echo from their boat on our radar screen; we are about one hundred metres behind the suspects. The fog is pretty thick here only about forty meters visibility so they can't see us. Anyway it looks like they are heading for berth 604 at the north end of Albert dock.'

The chief inspector came on the radio next a note of urgency in his voice.

'Okay everybody this is it. Units in the vicinity proceed to the north side of Albert dock. Remember this is a tracking operation not an arrest, so we must not draw attention to ourselves by driving too fast. All other units move closer to the general area.'

Without saying a word to Ellis, Sergeant Dennis started the car, expertly turned it and drove off along the dock road. After a few seconds he started talking in slow measured tones.

'The north side of Albert dock! Humph.' He laughed shortly.

'What's funny?' Ellis enquired.

'Clever bastards, that's the extreme north end of the docks complex, right next to the Auto- route. If we are not careful, they will be half way to Brussels before we can blink.'

'How long will it take to get there?' Ellis asked.

'Not long four or five minutes perhaps, we are one of the nearest I would say.'

As unmarked police cars converged on the area, the police launch had accelerated to find out what was happening and was first on the scene. The cool voice of the boat commander, Luc Melville came over the radio.

'The fog has thinned a bit here; I can just about see the outline of the launch next to the dock wall.'

'Okay Melville, get as close to him as you can and try and find out what is happening.' The chief inspector said.

Meanwhile, Ellis and Sergeant Dennis were proceeding steadily along the waterfront in their police car, berth 604 was rapidly approaching. Dennis slowed the car to 30 kph and their eyes strained in the dim misty light, for any sign of the traffickers or vehicles on the jetty. Just as they arrived at berth 604 the radio burst into life again, but this time Melville was talking in a rather deflated tone.

'Well… We got the boat alright and boarded it unopposed, but the boat is empty. The only thing we found was our tracker bug on the table in the cockpit.'

Ellis grabbed the mike on the police radio.

'This is Ellis speaking. We are at berth 604 there is no sign of the traffickers. We are going to check the fence at the back of the shed near the Auto-route.'

'I hope to hell hope you get something. A number plate, car colour or make, would give us something to continue with, now that we have lost the tracking bug.' The chief inspector added a taught edge to his voice.

'We'll do our best sir.' Ellis replied rather flatly.

Sergeant Dennis changed down a gear, braked and nosed the car slowly round the edge of the warehouse and down the road parallel to the Auto-route. They had only gone a few yards, when they found a large hole in the wire fence, more than big enough for a man to get through.

The red tail lights of a car, a few hundred meters up the Auto-route could be seen for a brief second, before the car was enveloped by the mist.

'Shit! We've just missed them.' Dennis said as he brought the car to a halt, pounding the steering wheel in frustration.

Ellis relayed the bad news to the chief inspector over the radio.

'Damn them to hell and back!' The chief inspector cursed loudly over the radio, then continued more calmly.

'They must have been slippery as snakes to wriggle through our security cordon. Okay all units, there is nothing else we can do, we may as well stand down. It just wasn't our night once again.' The various units called in, acknowledging the chief inspector's instruction to stand down.

Twenty-five minutes later, Ellis walked slowly up the worn sandstone steps and through the stained wooden doors of the police headquarters. He was feeling frustrated and extremely disappointed, that nothing had been achieved once more, in the war against drugs.

He found the chief inspector sitting behind his ancient wooden desk, pounding away on an equally ancient typewriter, cigarette as usual hanging casually from the side of his mouth. He looked up impassively at Ellis through the narrow slits of his bloodshot eyes, indicated with a slight nod of his head the chair on the other side of his desk, which Ellis slumped down wearily upon.

'What a night! I can't believe they got away.' Ellis said.

'Don't worry my friend, these things happen,' said the Belgian not looking up from his typewriter.

'It was that bloody fog that screwed the whole thing up for us,' said Ellis bitterly.

'As I said these things happen, it's winter. We always have a lot of fog at this time of the year in Belgium, as I'm sure you do in England.'

'Anyway the bottom line is the drug traffickers won again,' Ellis said resignedly.

The Belgian stopped typing and looked Ellis directly in the eye.

'Not quite. We managed to hijack their drugs shipment. Forty kilos of pure cocaine is no small amount.'

'You are right! I had forgotten about that, with all the excitement of the last couple of hours. There will be some mighty mad people somewhere in Belgium tonight, that's for sure.' Ellis said brightening slightly.

'Yes it's the one of the biggest seizures for some time. The press will be here soon to take some pictures.'

'Ah well, in that case I shall leave you to get all the glory, Andre. I am a little allergic to photos anyway.'

'You're not going back so soon are you? The boys on the bust are all going out on the town to celebrate tonight. Antwerp is one hell of a party town and there's always plenty spare girls around. Why don't you stay and make a night of it, I'll even pick you up in my car at your hotel.'

Ellis was sorely tempted, but after a week in Antwerp, he wanted to get back to the solace of his house in London.

'Aw, thanks for the offer, Andre. But I have a few people to see over the weekend so I think I'll get the afternoon flight back.'

He shook hands firmly with the Belgian and then left the police station for his hotel.

Chapter Four

The heavily laden dug out canoe, powered towards the foreboding Nigerian shoreline. The throttle of the one hundred-horse power Evinrude was fully open, hard up against the stop. The craft was lurching violently at times, showering the occupants with cool salty spray, as it pitched and rolled in the long undulating swell. Seawater was coming over the sides and accumulating in the roughly hewn bottom of the canoe.

'Take it easy man, or you are going to sink us,' screamed Kaduna over the din of the high-pitched engine.

'I is real worried about the police, sometimes they have patrols around this time of the morning,' replied Asamwa who was at the tiller.

'Just you let me do any worrying about the police,' shouted Kaduna 'Now slow down before I make you.' Kaduna glared at the other man.

Asamwa knew this was not a man to argue with, so he relaxed his grip on the throttle control and the engine revs dropped noticeably. The canoe soon obtained an easier motion, much to the relief of the rest of the pirates on board, who were glad Asamwa had been told to slow down. They had also been quite scared, most being non-swimmers, but were afraid to say anything.

The rest of the trip to the shore did not pass without incident. A high-powered boat was heard in the distance and a dark shape with a conspicuous bow wave came out of Lagos breakwaters. Tension gripped the occupants of the canoe. For a few moments the pirates feared the worst, being caught in the open with a canoe full of contraband. Their weapons were no match for 30 mm cannon, which the police launch carried. After heading straight towards them for a short while, the mystery launch eventually turned away to the south. It was probably an oilrig supply launch heading for the oil fields off River State. The pirates heaved a collective sigh of relief.

It was still quite dark and the entrance to Badagry Creek was barely visible. Only the surf crashing on the beach at each side of the entrance, gave any hint of a break in the coastline. Asamwa pointed the canoe at the gap between the breaking surf. Suddenly a large roller loomed behind them. The huge wave caught the boat as it broke and cast it rapidly past the headlands into the creek. The boat yawed back and forth alarmingly for a few seconds till the wave subsided. Meanwhile the crew clung on nervously. All on board were thankful to be safely through the entrance. It was now only a short journey of a mile or so up the creek, to the secret place where the cargo was to be offloaded.

Asamwa increased the speed now the boat was in calm water and the bow lifted slightly as the powerful outboard thrust the craft forward. The pirate boat quickly made its way up the creek, past the mangrove trees and dense undergrowth that lined its banks. The odd bird squawked and fluttered skywards out of the trees as they passed. The wash from the canoe creamed along the bank after them, disturbing a crocodile, which launched itself into the water, disappearing menacingly from sight.

Finally they came to a small secluded sandy beach, the scene of feverish activity. The other canoes had already been partially dragged up the beach. The pirates were busy transferring the stolen cargo, to a line of ramshackle huts on the edge of the jungle. Some were panting and all were swathed in perspiration, in the heavy dank morning air.

As their boat sped towards the shore Asamwa skilfully cut the engine and lifted the motor clear, just the right distance from the beach. The boat ground quickly to a halt with a judder, as the bow ran onto the soft sand. Men jumped overboard in to the shallow warm water of the creek, to manhandle the craft a few metres further up the beach and make the unloading operation easier.

One of the pirates from another canoe called Abokwe, conspicuously brighter than most of the others, shouted over to the new arrivals.

'Hey Kaduna, where you been man? We all thought the police had got you and screwed you over real bad.'

'No way, I am too quick for those bastards,' replied Kaduna cheerfully.

'Too quick! Lucky that's all you is man.' A few pirates laughed at the exchange.

'You make your own luck in this world Abokwe.' Kaduna replied rather astutely.

Mensah was determined to join in the banter.

'Hey Abokwe, why you leave so soon. We all got us some ass on that ship, and screwed some bastard's wife real good. Man… you shoulda heard that bitch scream when I stuck it in her. She was bleedin' like a pig by the time we finished.'

'Aw shit! Sounds like you had some real good action. Hell! I sure is pissed now.' Abokwe bent over one of the canoes and picked up a large brown carton marked 'Hitachi Japan'. Lifted the valuable box carefully onto his shoulder and made his way ponderously to wards the line of huts.

The stolen cargo would now stay in the huts till that evening, when Kaduna hoped he would return with a buyer. Six heavily armed men were left to guard the plunder. Other thieves had in the past tried to raid the storage place. These had been gunned down mercilessly and their bodies disposed of in he muddy waters of the creek. This had discouraged any more attempts for the moment. Kaduna knew however, that it would not be too long before someone else tried to seize the cargo from them. Being poor as the dirt they stood on, made people desperate. Perhaps next time someone would be better organised, Kaduna thought ruefully.

When all the booty had been offloaded from the canoes, Kaduna ensured that only the most trustworthy of the men was left behind on guard. Then he made his way by boat through the maze of creeks until he arrived at the city of Lagos. The phones had not worked in this country for years, so he had to take one of the broken down taxis from place to place to try and find a suitable buyer.

Kaduna wanted to find a person who would pay a reasonable price and had enough money to buy all the contraband. He was tired of dealing with more than one person at a time, which always made the sale more complicated and less secure. By mid-morning, he eventually found a suitable businessman, called Mohamed Attandah. It was arranged that the man would organise a large truck and bring sufficient money with him for the deal.

The businessman also wanted to bring four of his men with him, to help load the gear into the truck. Kaduna agreed to this, as long as they were unarmed. The man protested vehemently that he would need to protect his investment on the way home. Kaduna reluctantly agreed to this request, as long as they kept all their weapons in the truck. They would meet at dusk and drive down the narrow muddy jungle trail, just wide enough for a truck to pass down, to the place where the contraband was stored.

Kaduna then went home feeling pleased with the night and the morning's work. On arriving at his apartment, he went into the bathroom and removed the small panel on the ceiling at the far side of the shower. Next, he took the wads of dollars from the pouches of his combat suit and placed them into his secret compartment. Finally, he carefully fixed the panel back in place. He must have liberated around eighteen thousand dollars from the safe of the immensely stupid captain, which pleased him greatly. Tomorrow, when he looked more like a businessman, and less like a pirate, he would deposit the money at Banc Suisse in the centre of Lagos and have it wired through to his account in Zurich. They never asked any questions. The only thing that interested them was confirming on their dollar-checking machine that the money was not counterfeit. They often encountered money that was forged, though never from Kaduna.

After a long cool shower he lay down on his bed and smoked a joint of Ganja. As he watched the sinewy smoke rise from the end, he reflected on the last twenty-four hours. Screwing the English girl, that little tart! She had got him mad all right. But she was good, though he hated to admit that fact and he wouldn't actually have minded some more of her at that moment. Perhaps he had been a little hard on her after all, he mused.

He then thought about the raid on the ship. The best thing for him about that was the action and buzz it gave him; culminating in getting his hands on some real money. Yes, he pondered idly, life was working out quite nicely for someone who had started off with absolutely nothing. Suitably relaxed, he stubbed out the remains of the joint and was soon in the depths of sleep. The fact that he had killed a man a few hours ago did not trouble him in the least. He slept with a clear conscience. He always did. As far as he was concerned, the deprivations he suffered in his past were justification for anything he did at present. His past was like a jury that would always acquit him. In his eyes at any rate, this was all that mattered to him.

Later that day as Kaduna sat on the small balcony of his apartment at Echo Beach, Lagos, refreshed from six hours solid sleep, sipping on an ice-cold bottle of beer, condensation dripping from the green bottle onto the top of his muscular thighs, he looked down at the ocean below him, stretching like a huge azure carpet, towards the distant horizon.

He remembered those years when he had sailed on that sea. A lot of good times and a few bad ones, but he had grown to love the life. When he was laid off due to a recession in shipping, it had been a bitter pill to swallow. But what he had learned in eight years at sea, all that knowledge, was now being put to excellent use in his new career. Piracy. An evil trade that he could carry out with impunity. He had ultimate control and held all the aces in this particular game. He was a lucky man, but as he had told one of the pirates, earlier in the day, 'You make you own luck in life'. That had certainly been the case where he was concerned.

His new profession had been particularly good to him. He was fast becoming a rich man. He thought cheerfully about the secret compartment in his bathroom crammed full of dollars. They were changed days since the scrawny youth from Sahel Region battled his way down the highway to Lagos. His only possessions in the world at that time being, the tattered rags he stood up in. But now his future looked as bright as the sun that shone on the shimmering ocean. He now had a status that he would maintain no matter what the price. He had the money. He had the power and nothing or no one could stop him achieving what ever he wanted.

Immersed in his euphoria he had forgotten about one person.

The tall slim, impeccably dressed police sergeant strode purposefully towards the entrance to Kaduna's apartment. He lifted his dull black machine gun up to chest height and crashed it several times against the heavy wooden panels of the door. The sudden and unexpected din shattered Kaduna's reverie. He leapt up from the reclining chair on the balcony and rushed into the living room.

A high-pitched voice, almost like a scream penetrated through the mahogany door.

'Com on Kaduna. Open up the door. The police chief is here.' Bang, bang, bang. He crashed the metal stock of the gun against the door again, caring little for the damage he was doing to the varnished mahogany.

'Open up Kaduna. I already tol you the police chief is waiting out here and he wants to see you.'

His mind started racing, wondering why the police had suddenly decided to pay him a visit. He cared little for the police, as in this country they could be your friend one minute and lock you up the next. He did not like this situation one little bit. But there was nothing he could do. He would have to open up the door. This particular problem was not going to go away on its own.

'Okay, okay, don't break the door down, I'm coming.' He pulled on some shorts from the chair by the bed and slipped a pistol under the corner of the settee for insurance purposes.

Kaduna went to the door, looked through the spyglass and saw two men standing there, one of whom he instantly recognised as the Chief of the Lagos police force, Godwin Azubikas. Damn! He cursed inwardly as he removed the security chain. Next he turned the door handle several times, to release the multi bolt locking system, an essential security measure in that part of the world.

He pulled the door open to find the sergeant standing smartly to attention, as the police chief walked past him into the room. He said nothing as he passed Kaduna, who did not offer any form of greeting either, as he knew the man did not appreciate pleasantries. The sergeant remained outside and Kaduna closed the door.

The police chief was many kilos overweight, due to over indulgence in rich food and a healthy thirst for Star, the local beer. His uniform though immaculate and festooned with service ribbons of dubious origin, was bulging around the midriff. The collar gripped his thick neck tightly and beads of sweat were clearly visible on his forehead. He looked distinctly uncomfortable, as he walked laboriously across the room. Kaduna noticed he was carrying a newspaper, but gave it little thought.

When eventually he reached the nearest comfortable chair, he sat down and slumped back rather ungraciously, glad of the air conditioning in the apartment. Kaduna, who had followed the police chief's ponderous movement across the room, sat down on the chair opposite him, becoming rather nervous with the icy cold attitude of the newcomer, who was now staring at Kaduna and drumming his stubby fingers on the arm of the easy chair.

At last Azubikas broke the silence.

'Congratulations. You made the newspapers!'

'What newspapers, the Nigerian newspapers?' Kaduna said puzzled, as knew the police chief controlled the editor.

'No you asshole,' replied Azubikas caustically, 'the Spanish papers, the British papers and just about every other damn newspaper in the world. Here, see for yourself.' He tossed the paper he had been carrying disdainfully onto Kaduna's knee.

It was the Daily Mail an English newspaper that had arrived on that afternoon's British Caledonian flight from London Gatwick. The front page was devoted to a landslide in North Japan. But at the bottom of page two, he found graphic details of the previous evening's attack. He was visibly shocked.

'Hell! I don't understand how they found out so soon.'

'That ship you attacked yesterday phoned their company boss in Spain, using the ship's radio telephone. He then phoned the Spanish Ambassador here in Lagos. This resulted in me getting a call at five a.m. from the Home Secretary, telling me to get out there and personally see what the hell was happening. I was not pleased with what I found; a dead captain, a half-dead woman, who had been gang raped and a hysterical crew. I sure as hell am mad with you, Kaduna.' When he had finished lambasting Kaduna, he fixed him with a cold hard stare.

The pirate spoke quickly, emphatically in his defence. 'Aw shit, I'm real sorry about the mess last night, but you know, that crazy captain, he tried to kill me. He had a gun he had hidden in the safe. As for the raping of that woman, I did not even know about it until we were leaving the ship.'

'Shut up you miserable crud, you think you are some kind of big shot round here. I know you dress up all fancy and go down to restaurants and then to the casino. Well it does not impress me. All you are is a common thief and murderer. I am extremely annoyed with you and when I get pissed with someone, as I am sure you is aware, they start to wish they was never born.' Azubikas said a heavy menacing edge to his voice.

Kaduna clearly understood what the other man was intimating. Azubikas had a formidable reputation, which was known all over Lagos, as a sadist and a callous torturer of prisoners at Kala Kiri, the infamous local prison. Suddenly he felt incredibly vulnerable, totally at the mercy of this evil bastard. He would have to go along with what this man wanted, or they would be attaching electrodes to his private parts before the day was over.

A chill of fear swept though his body and he shivered involuntarily. This was not how he envisaged his life to be these days. This was something out with his control and that fact displeased him immensely.

The police chief held Kaduna in his ice-cold stare. 'I could resolve this situation very easily Kaduna and get the praise and much esteem from the Home Secretary; by arresting the leader of the pirate gang. I could do this right now as I have a truck full of police waiting outside,' the police chief said, raising his voice threateningly.

Kaduna's pulse was racing and his mouth was becoming dry. Real fear was pervading his body. Nervously, he put his hand under the cushion of the chair and drew reassurance from the serrated handle of a gun. If he were going to be arrested, it would be better to try and make a run for it. Once inside the prison, that would be the end of Henry Kaduna.

After a few tense seconds, during which Kaduna could barely breathe the police chief started talking again. 'However, I am prepared to give you another chance,' Azubikas said firmly, never taking his eyes off Kaduna. 'But first, let us consider the facts. The countries of the world are putting more pressure on our government to stop acts of piracy off this coast. So your operation will take more covering up and more risk will be involved. I am going to have to take some action, to show that we are doing something about this situation.'

Azubikas paused to swat a fly that was buzzing round him. Kaduna relaxed slightly and took his hand out from under the cushion. The fly taken care of, the police chief continued talking.

'But the main thing now will be that I will require four thousand naira each month, instead of the miserable thousand you have been paying me. Also from time to time, I shall expect some bonuses from you, if you have been particularly successful in your work.' A thin smile crossed the policeman's lips and he laughed softly.

So that was it! Kaduna thought, as he smiled inwardly to himself. It was all about money. Of course the police chief wasn't going to arrest him. After all, he would not be able to contribute any money to the police chief's bank account, if he was in prison, or dead. Also he surmised Azubikas was well aware that without his leadership, the amount of money he would receive from the pirate operation would be vastly reduced. The rest of the rabble being so disorganised.

Kaduna felt considerably more reassured and was breathing normally again. The momentary tightness in his chest had disappeared. He was thinking logically now.

'As it happens I was just about to come to see you with a sizeable bonus this very day.' Kaduna said with conviction.

'Yes, I am sure you was Kaduna,' the police chief countered sceptically. 'I always know when you is doing well. As you will be aware, nothing happens round here without me knowing. So a word of warning, never ever try to cheat me. You really don't want to be brought to my prison. This is a place where even the toughest resolve is broken down eventually.'

Kaduna shivered at the mention of the place. He remembered passing a few hundred yards from it one night, on his way to see a trader who lived in that neighbourhood. The agonising screams of a poor soul under torture, could clearly be heard in the still night air. The spine chilling sounds were indelibly etched in his memory. People who were taken there for interrogation, rarely came out alive, unless to join Azubikas's army of informers. There was bound to be someone amongst the pirates, giving their master up to date information. So he would know all about the previous night's success and require substantial and immediate remuneration.

'Well brother I is waiting,' the police chief said, a note of impatience in his voice, his podgy fingers once again drumming on the arm of the chair.

Kaduna went into the bathroom and removed half the dollars from their place of hiding. He placed them in a small white canvas money sack and went into the living room where Azubikas was waiting.

'Here take it. Its nine thousand dollars.'

Azubikas peeked briefly into the sack, nodded his large head slowly and said.

'Good Kaduna. I am pleased to see we understand each other perfectly. Of course, I knew exactly what was taken from that safe. I personally went to see the chief steward on the ship and he showed me the cash account of the master. So I am glad to see you had enough sense to give me half of what you took.' Kaduna did not show it, but he was stunned by the police chief's revelation.

'Yes Chief and you can count on plenty more in the future.'

'I know I can Kaduna and that is the only reason you are not on your way to jail at this very moment.'

The police chief rose slowly from the chair, like some overloaded jumbo jet, struggling to get airborne at the end of the runway. He clenched the small sack of money in one fat fist and slowly made his way to the door. Kaduna followed him and opened the door to let him pass through.

'By the way,' Azubikas said casually and quietly, as he walked past Kaduna.

'Stay on the land for the next few days. I have a plan to relieve the pressure on my superiors. Also, I want you to leave a few cartons full of goods and some empty ones in one of your huts at Badagry Creek.' He paused and looked Kaduna in the eye. 'Oh yes, just one more thing. The gun under the cushion of your seat was rather obvious. As I said before, nothing escapes my attention. That is my job, after all.' For the second time in as many minutes, Kaduna was taken aback by the awareness of the man. His appearance certainly was the perfect cover. No one could ever have imagined some one so grotesque and sluggish could possibly be so astute.

Azubikas laughed heartily on his way to the lift with the sergeant. Kaduna closed the door and went back out onto the balcony once again, hand trembling slightly as he stroked his goatee beard, wondering how Azubikas knew about the gun.

Chapter Five

The ageing Bedford truck, with its garish red and green paintwork, high wooden sides and perpetually smoking exhaust, creaked and lumbered slowly along the rutted jungle track. Occasionally the road appeared to have ended, as the way ahead was completely overgrown with creepers and undergrowth.

Kaduna sat in the front with the driver, a youth of around nineteen years of age, who kept turning to him with a toothy grin every time the truck hit a bump. The youth was in need of a good bath and the air in the cab was distinctly unpleasant, even though both windows were open. Kaduna would be glad when they reached the pick up point for the contraband, if only for the chance to breathe some fresh air.

The third person in the truck was the businessman who had agreed to buy the contraband, Mohamed Attandah. He was wearing a brightly coloured, loose fitting traditional costume, favoured by most of the populace. His face was decidedly chubby and his narrow eyes peered out from under his plant pot hat. Attandah was becoming impatient, as they had been travelling for around half an hour along the dank jungle track. He was starting to fiddle with some brightly coloured beads, which hung loosely round his neck.

'Kaduna, are you sure this the right way? Looks like we has been going round in circles for hours now.'

'Yeah, I'm sure it's the right way. There is only one track and it goes directly to huts where the gear is stowed,' replied Kaduna irritably.

'I would never have agreed to come, if I had known it was as far as this. You will have to find a place nearer to Lagos if you wants to do any more business with me in the future.'

'Okay, okay, but let's just concentrate on this deal for the moment.'

Just then, something glinted dully in the moonlight on the left hand side of the road.

'Ah ha! What did I tell you Attandah? That's the river over there on the left, the huts are another fifty or so metres further on. Okay, stop the truck and switch off the engine.'

'What for?' said Attandah nervously, wishing that his four body-guards in the back of the truck still had their guns, instead of being in the bag currently at Kaduna's feet.

'We have to make the arranged signal, or my men will open fire.'

'What's the signal?' Attandah asked.

'Two short and one long blast on the horn,' replied Kaduna.

'Okay Mofi, stop the truck and switch off the engine. Then make his signal on the horn.' Attandah ordered the driver.

Once the truck had rumbled to a stop, Mofi turned with his toothy grin to Attandah.

'Can't make the signal boss, horn, she no work.'

'Shit! What we gonna to do now, Kaduna?' said Attandah, his voice trembling slightly.

Kaduna had already made provision for this, as transport in Nigeria had a reputation for poor maintenance.

'Don't worry; just flash the lights two long and one short.'

The driver did this and a few seconds later; the sound of a can or empty drum could be heard, being struck slowly four times.

'Great, everything is fine, we can move into the area. Start up the engine, Mofi.'

Attandah immediately became more relaxed and a sly grin

flickered across his lips.

'Very good Kaduna, signals and all. The only thing is, I can come here anytime I wants, now that I know the signal.'

'You must think we are stupid Attandah and you must be very naive.' Kaduna laughed softly then continued talking slowly, precisely, his voice laced with menace.

'We change the signals regularly. The last people who tried to come into the camp using a signal that had been discontinued were all shot dead. Then the crocodiles in the river disposed of the bodies for us very efficiently. There were eight of them and some had guns. So don't even think of playing around with us. We are volatile and highly dangerous. Do you understand clearly what I am saying?'

'Yes I do,' replied Attandah. He suddenly felt cold, as he shrunk back into the battered leather passenger's seat. He wished that the business could be over as quickly as possible.

As the truck lumbered slowly forward, five or six men armed with rifles or machine guns suddenly emerged out of the inky black undergrowth and walked silently unemotionally, on either side of the truck. Fear instantly gripped the businessman and he could feel cold beads of perspiration on his brow, as the full gravity of the situation came home to him. Here he was, effectively unarmed, deep in the jungle with a thick money belt round his waist, surrounded by desperate killers. For all he knew, the demise of the eight men Kaduna had so graphically described to him might actually have been honest people like himself and his associates.

He silently berated himself; 'how could I have been so stupid, to allow this uneducated ruffian to persuade him to come into the jungle?' But the chance to acquire so much expensive Hitachi electrical equipment and Nikon cameras, all at a bargain price, was too good an opportunity to miss. Now, he thought with immense dread, there was nothing to stop this bandit killing him and taking his money. That thought had also occurred to Kaduna.

Kaduna could tell the businessman was very uneasy, probably scared witless at the sight of the other pirates. But to waste him and his five employees would not have been good sense. After all, he had to get rid of the contraband and if he killed off potential purchasers, no matter how tempting, eventually no one would wish to deal with him.

This fellow Attandah could lay his hands on large sums of money, to buy all the cargo in one go. So Kaduna decided to placate him and put his mind at rest, he could prove to be a valuable contact in the future, tonight must also become an exercise in the building of trust.

'Hey! Attandah, relax man, everything's cool. There is going to be no monkey business, you will get your goods. Besides I need you for business in the future. Believe me.'

The businessman felt a little better; however he would only really be completely at ease, when he was out of the jungle and back on the main road heading for Lagos.

When they reached the huts the merchandise was brought out for him to view, Attandah felt more confident now and quickly slipped into business mode, haggling with the pirate for the goods on show. He could tell by the amount and quality, that the trip was going to prove particularly worthwhile. The cardboard cartons for some of the radios and tape recorders were missing but this did not matter, as the goods were apparently undamaged. Kaduna for his part did not haggle very hard. Also as instructed by Azubikas, he had left four cartons full of cheap radios and a few empty cartons out of sight from Attandah, in one of the huts.

When all the haggling was completed, the final price to be paid for the haul was soon agreed. The jungle clearing then became the scene of feverish activity, as the pirates and Attandah's men helped to load the truck, which was well down on its worn out suspension by the time they had finished.

Kaduna then gave the anxious pirates generous shares of

the money that he received for the goods, which they all gladly accepted. Just like children being given pocket money. No doubt, they would spend most of the money on booze and whores in the next few days and soon be back looking for more action. That situation suited Kaduna nicely. He retained the largest portion of the money, the other men in the gang not present still to be paid and of course, his own lion's share. There was plenty of cash this time for everyone, because of the success of the previous evening's attack, even though some was missing. This irked Kaduna greatly.

When the truck was loaded, the pirates excitedly and noisily made their way to the one remaining canoe. Kaduna went with them, leaving one of the other pirates to show Attandah the way out of the jungle. He had no wish to make that unpleasant journey again. Apart from the stench of the driver, there was also a possibility that robbers could attack the truck. He had no wish to become involved defending the cargo, which was now Attandah's concern.

The warm almost perpetually calm waters off West Africa absolutely teem with fish, brought from the Atlantic on the Guinea Current. Tuna, Red Snapper and Mackerel abound.

The fishermen in this part of the world tend to fish wherever they please, with no fisheries protection vessels enforcing national boundaries. The evil brain of Godwin Azubikas was counting on this fact, as he boarded a police gunboat that night in Lagos harbour.

The powerful craft bought from Vosper Thorneycroft of Southampton, together with four sister vessels, was a fine example of this class of boat. Two sleek gleaming sixteen-cylinder high-speed diesels in the small engine room pushed the dramatically flared bow through the water at speeds of up to thirty-five knots, sending a fine spray either side of the craft. The wake from the twin propellers erupted in two frothing trails astern. With such a powerful craft at his disposal, Azubikas was able to cover the thirty or so miles to the Benin border in sixty-five minutes. He then instructed the launch driver to slow down to around five knots.

As the boat cruised up and down the fishing grounds, on the border of both countries its strong searchlight picked out fishing canoes from time to time. But these had all been the smaller brightly painted Nigerian boats, not the larger Benin boats with the distinctive eye painted on the bow.

After a fruitless search of over an hour and a half Azubikas was starting to despair of encountering a craft from Benin. Then fine on the port bow, the searchlight caught the faint shape of a large canoe stopped in the water. His pulse quickened as he gave the order to the launch driver to investigate.

As they got closer he could see the distinctive eye on the bow in the glare of the searchlight. It was a Benin boat and he could see eight or nine figures standing in the canoe busy heaving in the nets by hand. Some were waving at the police launch and others were shouting greetings.

Azubikas turned to the five armed men from his elite Panther unit. 'Right men; you know what to do. These Benin people are stealing the fish of Nigeria. We have to teach them a lesson to discourage others.'

The men pulled the bolts of their machine guns back into the firing position. They crouched out of sight below the low gun wall of the launch awaiting the order to fire.

Ten or twelve metres from the canoe, the fishermen started shouting loudly, protesting that the launch was going to damage their nets. Azubikas's eyes gleamed and a thin smile crossed his lips, at the thought of the pathetic fishermen worried about their nets. Soon, they would have no more worries.

The launch driver cut the engines and let the craft drift the final few meters towards the canoe. Then as the dug out full of shouting fishermen came alongside, he gave the order to fire. The five men leapt up from their places of concealment and unleashed a murderous hail of fire on the unprotected and totally unarmed fishermen.

A few fell, mortally wounded, into the sea but most of them died where they stood in the canoe. There were no survivors. In the space of thirty seconds, nine harmless fishermen had been turned into blood sodden corpses. A policeman got a boat hook and brought the canoe alongside. Two more men got in the canoe; they destroyed any evidence of this being a fishing craft; cutting nets and throwing the accoutrements of the fishermen into the sea. Finally they searched bullet-riddled bodies, for identification and found six battered and dog-eared passports. Four were from Benin and the other two Ghanaian.

The remaining policemen on the launch were bringing cardboard cartons onto deck. Some were full of radios and tape recorders, but most were empty. These were passed down into the canoe and placed around the dugout. A body was lifted here and there and laid on top of the cartons. Next, a few old rifles were placed around the corpses to make it look like they had been armed.

The police chief looked down at the gory scene in the canoe beneath him and felt well satisfied with his handiwork. It looked very realistic, even to his trained and ever critical eye. He focussed the Nikon SLR camera that was slung round his neck on the canoe. Then he quickly fired off a full reel of film from various angles and distances, capturing clearly, the dead pirates, next to the boxes of cargo that had been taken from the Spanish ship.

He had already obtained as a legitimate part of his police work, copies of the bills of lading for the stolen cargo, with the details of the shipping marks. These shipping marks were clearly visible on the boxes in the canoe, next to the dead fishermen. This was concrete proof that it was not only Nigerians who were involved in this piracy.

Within a few days the Home Secretary had all the information and photos collected by the police chief. He was a parochial man, a tribal chief from the hinterland in central Nigeria, he was also the cousin of the President. But he was very naive and uninformed on most matters regarding the pirate situation. The police chief gave him occasional shreds of information. So he was pleased with Azubikas for providing this valuable evidence that could be used to take the pressure off Nigeria. For all he knew, it could actually have been pirates from Benin that attacked the Spanish ship in the first place.

Chapter Six

The hard plastic ball spun rapidly round the mahogany periphery, to the accompaniment of the steady clicking of the roulette wheel. Kaduna's gaze was transfixed on the ball, as it dropped tantalisingly towards, the circle of segmented numbers. Once the ball had slowed down sufficiently, it bounced into one slot then bounced out into the next… red ten.

'That's my number!' he said loudly, arrogantly, punching the air triumphantly.

'Red ten.' The girl croupier said impassively, as she put the plastic marker on top of Kaduna's chips, and then deftly scooped all the other loose chips on the table into a pile in front of her.

Kaduna was smiling profusely as he waited for his payout. He was pleased with himself, having just put his last two hundred naira on the winning number. He had actually been on his way out of the door at the time, having had a bad night at the tables. Then on the spur of the moment, he decided to place the bet, which happened to be the table maximum, and now seven thousand two hundred naira would be his when he cashed in the large pile of chips.

Once the cashier had paid him, he resisted the temptation to have one more bet, as in the past this had always proven to be disastrous. So on this occasion, he left the table and ambled contentedly towards the door and the car park beyond. However, even though he had a noticeable buzz, after winning a substantial amount of money, the night had still been a disappointment. He had actually come to the casino to see the English girl, but she was nowhere to be seen.

It had been almost two weeks since the night he met her. During that time, a number of local women had not given him nearly as much pleasure. He could not get away from the fact, that he was thinking about her a lot more than the majority of his sexual conquests.

The lights were out in the car park once again. He had just put the key in the door of his beat up, though functional car, when he heard footsteps behind him. He spun round quickly his body rigid, senses on full alert. He wasn't about to risk life and death attacking ships, to be taken out by a desperate mugger in a dark car park. However, he was pleased to see it was no mugger, but the English girl croupier. He relaxed immediately and a smile flashed across his pearly white teeth.

'Oh it's you. I wondered who it was creeping up behind me. I was looking for you in the casino.'

'It was my night off, but I saw you in the hotel foyer earlier on, so I thought I would come out and say hello.'

'Well.., I'm real pleased to see you. Hey… don't mind too much about last time, hell, shit happens.' He shrugged and gesticulated with his hands.

'Yeah, I know.' She replied in an understanding tone.

He put his arms round her and their lips met in the frantic crush of a passionate kiss. She clung tightly to him and he could feel her fingernails through his shirt. Her tongue searched deeply into his mouth and her hips thrust into his crotch in a slow grinding motion. He was instantly aroused by the intensity of the embrace and could easily have made love right there in the car park, but he managed to prise her away from her.

'Come on, there's a better place than this,' Kaduna said quietly and then added.

'Same price as last time?'

'It's up to you. I'm not bothered about money tonight.'

The ride back to his apartment, through the dimly lit potholed streets, took a little more than ten minutes and they talked very little during this trip, both looking forward with relish, to the sexual feast they would soon be enjoying.

By the time they reached the apartment, bursting with raw desire for each other, the bedroom was too far away for them so they made love passionately on the mat in the centre of the living room. Later they resumed with new vigour, in the sumptuous comfort of his massive round bed. Dawn was not far away, when finally with all strength consumed, they fell into a deep cavernous sleep.

It was late in the afternoon before they stirred. Lesley was the first to wake. The rhythmic crash of the surf on the beach below, she decided, was responsible for disturbing her sleep. But she didn't mind being woken, as the hours spent asleep had refreshed and invigorated her body. She had no idea of the time, as her watch was on the dressing table at the other side of the room.

After a while, she sat up against the headboard of the bed, rolling her head from side to side to relax her neck muscles, which were a little stiff, probably caused by sleeping in a different position to normal. As she sat there on the bed, the room was still quite dark, except for a shaft of bright sunlight, which shone through a gap in the heavily insulated curtains. She watched the soft rays of light, play across Kaduna's naked torso. The bulging muscles of his back and arms were clearly visible and impressive. So she reached over and caressed them gently with the tip of her fingers.

Her eyes became more accustomed to the light in the room and more of his back became visible. She followed the contours of his body down to his waist. Then something strange caught her eye. She was startled when she saw it, an ugly round scar, just above his right kidney. Looking closer, she could see it was about two or three centimetres in diameter. It was rough at the edges and smooth in the centre. What the hell can that be, some kind of operation, she wondered as she reached down and touched it with the tip of her forefinger. She felt him tense. Then it came to her. Something she had read in a book, or seen in a film perhaps.

That's a bullet hole! Where's this guy been, to get a hole like that in him, she wondered, deeply disturbed at her discovery.

Kaduna lay completely motionless, slowly awaking from the depths of sleep. He could feel the erotic touch of the girl's slim fingers on the muscles of his shoulder. It brought back pleasant memories to him of the night's passion and he was becoming aroused once again. It never took much. He was just about to spin round and grab her, when he felt her finger touch the scar.

He was now completely awake, eyes narrowing, staring intensely at the wall. Body rigid and lips pursed tight as the memories of that awful night came rapidly flooding back to him. The terrible images flashing through his mind were so clear, it was just like watching a movie and he was the central character.

There had only been one ship at the anchorage. Indian or Pakistani, he was not sure exactly where it was from, as people from that part of the world all seemed to look the same to him. There was nothing of value in the cargo, just a few containers full of machinery on deck. While most of the pirates lowered the ships ropes and paint into the canoes, he went into the unlocked accommodation with four or five others.

He went straight to the captain's cabin with one pirate. The three other pirates proceeded to terrorise the officers and crew, ransacking their cabins, and removing their meagre possessions. The captain and his wife had both been sound asleep. The door of the cabin was not even locked. The first thing they knew, that the ship had been boarded, was when Kaduna put on the light in bedroom and dragged the captain from the bed. His wife was hysterical, screaming continuously. The other pirate gleefully slapped her couple of times and eventually she quietened down, a thin trickle of blood, running down her chin from a small cut on her lip.

That particular skipper had been incredibly arrogant and stubborn for a person in such a perilous situation. He would not initially co-operate with Kaduna and open the ship's safe. Though after many dire threats and a vicious beating, the blood stained mariner eventually succumbed to the demands and opened the safe. Kaduna did not normally encounter problems with seamen, who were usually compliant to the extreme after a few seconds staring down the barrel of his gun.

The fact that this master had been so stupid and un-cooperative had irritated him considerably. Then he found the safe was empty, except for a few bundles of virtually worthless Asian money. This made him feel immensely frustrated, as though somehow, the captain had conspired to cheat him.

The short fuse of his temper was rapidly burning out.

Then he saw a thin condescending smile etched on the captain's face. That had been the final straw. In a flash, he decided to vent his frustrations in the most evil manner. While the other pirate held the struggling master in a vice like grip, Kaduna raped his screaming wife.

When he left the cabin, the captain was wailing and sobbing uncontrollably, trying to comfort his beloved and hysterical wife. As a final gesture, Kaduna threw the bundles of worthless money, at the captain's face and thought that was the end of the matter.

He was wrong…

That particular master was normally a very calm and placid person. But the despoiling of his poor wife and the ransacking of his vessel had pushed him over a precipice and plunged him into a mad rage. He sought to exact revenge for terrible acts perpetrated by the Africans on his vessel.

Eyes glazed, palms of his hands sweating, small rivulets of spittle trickling from his mouth, he retrieved a .38 Smith and Wesson automatic pistol from its hiding place in his office. He phoned the second mate on the bridge and told him to fire distress flares to illuminate the pirates. Then he quickly went down the spiral staircase inside the accommodation to the darkness of the main deck.

He could see the hateful canoe near the port side of number two hatch, clearly illuminated in the incandescent light of the flare. The vile pirates were trying to push it away from the ship's side with their short pointed native paddles.

He unhooked the safety catch on the pistol and expertly drew back the slider on top, which sucked a shell from the magazine into the chamber. He took aim and fired two shots in quick succession. He saw spray kicked up as the bullets hit the water around a metre from the canoe. He tried to adjust his aim, but his hands were shaking badly, the trauma of the events racking his painfully slim bony body. So he took a deep breath, to try and steady his nerves, held the gun in both hands and continued firing methodically, shot after shot towards the canoe.

The tables had emphatically turned.

It was Kaduna who was now terrified, as he stumbled and fell in the tossing bow of the canoe, while inches away from him, bullets continued to thud into the woodwork of the boat. To further compound the gravity of the situation, the outboard would not start, despite one of the pirates tugging frantically, on the starter rope at the side of the engine. They would have to use paddles, still more bullets whistled past, too close for comfort. He grabbed his machine pistol and fired a long burst up to where he thought the gunman was located but it was useless. The man had perfect cover under the blanket of the darkness, up on deck while they were fully illuminated, as yet another flare lit up the night sky. He had the lead role in some kind of hideous nightmare.

The heavy southerly swell that was running that fateful night continued to push the dugout up against the ship's side. Seawater was breaking over the crudely hewn sides of the canoe and sloshing about at their feet. The situation was becoming extremely grave. Then by sheer luck, Kaduna managed to get a short brightly painted native paddle hard up against the ship's side. He gave a mighty push with all his strength and the boat inched away from the cold black steelwork that had held the canoe in its grip like a giant magnet.

He started paddling frantically with the other pirates, sweat pouring from his forehead, stinging his eyes as it ran down his face. But the canoe was heavy and deeply laden, full of paint drums stolen by the pirates from the vessels paint store and despite their desperate efforts, it hardly moved. Suddenly, unexpectedly, the outboard coughed and fired into life. A wave of relief washed over Kaduna. They were going to make it. Everything would be fine, he thought. Then the gunman, at last hit his target.

The bullet struck Kaduna in the lower back and the force hurtled him over a thwart onto the paint tins, which were haphazardly stowed in the bottom of the canoe. His back felt as though, it had been had kicked by a mule. He lay stunned and disorientated for a few seconds, as the effects of shock flooded through his wounded body. Anger and disbelief wrestled together in his mind when he realised he had been shot.

He could not believe this had happened to him. Only losers got themselves shot, something he had never considered himself to be.

When he touched the wound, his hand he could feel the warm blood trickling out. It was bad. He was terrified of losing too much blood before he got ashore to a doctor. One of the other pirates casually threw a filthy shirt to him and he had the presence of mind to keep it pressed on the wound.

Thankfully, the dugout was pulling away more rapidly from the ship, the high-pitched scream of the outboard motor clearly audible, as it strained to move the heavily laden canoe through the water. Kaduna's head was swimming and he vomited into the bottom of the canoe. Then he drifted in and out of consciousness for what seemed an eternity.

The journey to the doctor's house took around forty minutes and, although angry at being disturbed late at night, the doctor still agreed to attend to Kaduna. Whether it was his doctor's code, or the sight of the machine gun, Kaduna didn't care. He was only in the cramped surgery for a few minutes when he lapsed into unconsciousness, to awaken twenty-four hours later and be told by the doctor, that he was lucky to be alive. He had lost a considerable amount of blood and the wound had been badly infected by the dirt in the bottom of the canoe and the filthy shirt he had used to staunch the flow of blood.

That night had been a stark reminder of the dangers of his profession, that he was every bit as mortal as the next man. After six months of being virtually unopposed, he found out the hard way that he was not invincible and that ships sometimes could hit back. Lying there motionless on the bed, thoughts of that terrible night were still crystal clear in his mind. He could feel the English girl close to him. There was still a faint hint of her perfume from the night before which was pleasant. Her smooth white arm was draped over his shoulder and her red sculptured fingernails stood out against the black skin of his chest, fingernails that probably had some of his skin underneath. But his mood had changed and he lifted the slim, almost weightless arm off his shoulder and let it fall down on the bed beside her.

'What's up?' The girl said, she was already wide-awake. 'You've been laying there all tense for ages now.' There was a note of concern in her voice.

'Aw nothing, I just had a bad dream that's all. These things happen.'

'It can help sometimes to talk about these things.'

'I don't think a woman needs to know my problems,' he said rather mordantly, a note of arrogance evident in his voice.

She was more than a little perplexed with his rough and arrogant manner, especially after such a night of intense lovemaking. What a Jekyll and Hyde character he was she mused, but wisely resisted the temptation to give him a piece of her mind for his abruptness. She still had vivid memories of the scene he created last time and wished to avoid a repeat of that at all costs. She sighed resignedly then chose her words carefully.

'Well, I suppose it's time for me to be making a move. I'm working at six o'clock tonight.'

'Yeah, that would be best,' replied the almost motionless African lying on the bed.

She could feel an atmosphere of tension developing between them, which worried her but she was not about to rush out of the house. She needed to freshen up first.

'Do you mind if I take a shower before I leave?' she asked politely.

'No, just help yourself;' he replied and then added, 'I'm going out for a run. Don't know when I'll be back, just let yourself out when you are ready to leave.' He needed the exertion a hard run would give to release the tension locked up within his body.

She got up from the bed and went into the bathroom which adjoined the bedroom. It looked like it hadn't been cleaned for years. Being a particularly fastidious person, she cringed at the sight of the grubby unclean floor and tiptoed towards the shower. The shower cubicle wasn't much better, almost all the tile grouting had turned black and the soap was mashed up in the holder.

The shower water felt good, even though it was lukewarm and far from clear. She heard the door to the flat close loudly as Kaduna went for his run. She was glad he had left her alone. His mood once again had turned ugly, a repetition of her previous visit when he had almost thrown her out of the flat. She pulled back the shower curtain and stood there dripping. She surveyed the bathroom looking for a towel, but none was visible. She cursed quietly under her breath. Then she stepped out of the shower and made her way towards a locker on the other side of the bathroom, water running off her, forming little pools on the grimy tiled floor as she walked.

Inside the locker, all she found to her dismay was a pile of rather odorous dirty washing, no sign of any towels. Becoming a little frustrated, she went into the bedroom and opened the wardrobe; thinking that if she did not find something suitable, she would have to use the bed sheet to dry off with.

The air conditioning in the flat was now making her soaked body feel cold, she didn't want to catch a chill. So standing on tiptoes, she reached into a fitted wardrobe beside the bed, hoping to find a towel. She was relieved, when at last she located some right at the back of the shelf. Shivering she dragged the top towel towards her quickly. Strangely though, the towel felt much heavier than it should have. The reason for this soon became apparent. She looked in horror, as a gun fell off the end of the towel and plummeted down onto the edge of the bed, before clattering noisily onto the floor.

She jumped back involuntarily at the sight of the firearm. Then after recovering from the initial shock, she began to dry herself slowly, methodically, without taking her eyes off the ugly, dull black steel object lying inertly on the floor. It was no ordinary gun; this was a small machine gun, with a short snout for a barrel and a small handgrip. The magazine seemed too large for the gun and a considerable amount of the matt black paint had been scratched off this. There was second magazine attached to the first with brown plastic tape.

She was astounded! What could anyone possibly want with such a lethal weapon? This type of gun went well beyond the requirements of self-protection. It occurred to her that her lover must be involved in something so bad, beyond the bounds of comprehension, to need such a powerful weapon.

The idea, that the man she had just spent a passionate night with, could be a cold blooded murderer, sent an icy chill of apprehension through her body. The fine golden hairs on her arms were now standing up, as she shivered once again.

Her mind was racing, rapidly coming to the conclusion that she could be in mortal danger if Kaduna discovered she had knowledge of the machine gun. Everything would have to be left, exactly as it had been found. But the towel she had used was by now quite wet. She soon discovered there were more towels in the locker to the left of where the gun had originally been located. One of these, she found, was almost the same colour and size as the one she had used. She gingerly picked up the gun, which was surprisingly heavy in view of its size. She put it on a dry towel and slid it to the back of the shelf. Now that everything was back in place she heaved a sigh of relief.

She hurriedly searched the bedroom for her clothes, all of which she soon found. Then dressed quickly, wishing to distance herself from the apartment, the machine gun and Henry Kaduna as fast as possible. She put on her shoes, grabbed her slim handbag and was just about to leave, then decided to check through the apartment to see if anything had been overlooked. Everything seemed to be in order, as her eyes methodically scanned each room.

She was pleased however, that she had taken the time to check, when she found her gold Rolex on the dresser in the bedroom. To have lost that treasured possession would have been heart breaking. It was a genuine Rolex watch, a present from an Arab businessman that she met whilst working at a London casino.

Heart racing, she made her way quickly to the door, frantically wondering what would happen if he suddenly came back. She could never face him, after making such a horrifying discovery. But her luck held out, as she made her way from of the flat along the landing. Not wishing to spend a second longer than necessary in the vicinity of the apartment, she did not wait for the creaking elevator but instead scampered down the bare concrete steps of the staircase and out onto the sun-baked street. A battered green taxi, with a door that would not close properly, stopped and took her back to the Holiday Inn.

Later as she lay on the bed in her air-conditioned room in the hotel, sipping a large whisky on the rocks to calm her down, eyes closed and the vapours of the spirit drifting through her mind, she punched the bed with her free hand and said softly to herself,

'Oh bugger. What the hell have you got yourself involved in this time, Lesley? Boy, you sure can pick them.'

Chapter Seven

The United Nations general assembly in New York was around three quarters full for this particular morning session. The debate, which was scheduled to start at ten-thirty, had to be delayed a few minutes, as delegates were still finding their places. Most of them had just enjoyed a leisurely breakfast and were in no hurry to begin yet another monotonous debate. This in all probability would have little to do with them, or their country for that matter.

Ulf Litmannen, the incumbent speaker, was from Finland. At fifty-two years of age he still retained the archetypal Scandinavian look, tall with a thick head of wavy blonde hair. He was still considered to be a handsome man, even though the ravages of heavy spirit drinking over the years had taken its toll on his facial features, which had now started to sag noticeably. He sat arms folded, in his comfortable high backed chair and viewed the scene in front of him.

The semi-circular hall, with its rows of linked desks, reached backwards and upwards, to the main entrance door at the rear of the hall. The vast auditorium spread in front of him with scores of delegates, their aides and advisors, was a living ocean of colour. Most of the delegates were smartly dressed, in the most expensive suits their huge salaries could afford. Interspaced with the delegates in Western dress, were numerous brightly coloured national costumes, mainly from the African nations. It was indeed a cosmopolitan scene.

Mr Litmannen looked at his watch as the minute hand reached ten forty. It was time to start the debate. Regardless of the few stragglers, who were still making their way ponderously to their respective places, he tapped the microphone in front of him to get the attention of the assembly. Then he cleared his throat quietly and started to speak.

'Good morning. The first item on the agenda for discussion to-day, ladies and gentlemen, has been tabled jointly by three nations, namely Spain, the United Kingdom and Greece.' The assembly was settling down and starting to pay more attention to what was being said as the speaker continued.

'This is the grave situation of the increasing number of acts of piracy, on unarmed merchant ships that are taking place all over the world. This year alone, there has been a thirty per cent increase in attacks, in three main areas. The South China Sea, the Straits of Malacca and West Africa.' He paused and looked at the assembly over the rim of his glasses. 'By far the worst area is West Africa.'

There was a perceptible rumble of dissension and uncomfortable shifting of feet from a number of the African delegates.

'In fact, the statistics I have here in front of me show the worst area this year to be Nigeria, off the port of Lagos, where it would appear, a highly organised gang of pirates are operating.' The Nigerian delegate, remained tight lipped and impassive, but still had to use his arm, to stop one of his assistants from standing up and protesting.

'In the past two months alone, there have been five such attacks on vessels at anchor off the port of Lagos. There have also been a further two on vessels waiting for a pilot up to Port Harcourt at the bottom of the Bonny River.' The speaker paused briefly, consulted his notes then continued.

'On each occasion, cargo was stolen from these vessels by armed raiders and the ship's personnel held at gunpoint while their possessions were stolen. The masters on three of these vessels were also forced at gunpoint, to hand over the contents of the ship's safe, a very disturbing and harrowing experience for the poor people who had to undergo this treatment.'

He stopped speaking and looked up gravely from his notes .He noticed that, for a change, he had the attention of virtually the whole assembly. This was surprising, he thought, being a subject that most of the delegates knew little or nothing about. He could see, by the looks on some of the faces in the rows closest to his podium, that they were actually quite astounded by the revelations he was making.

'The worst attack so far documented this year happened on the night of January 22nd, just over three weeks ago, when the Spanish vessel 'Cuidad de Valencia' was attacked. Numerous containers of cargo were pilfered. Most of the crew's personal effects were stolen. An officer's wife was raped and left for dead by the pirates.' A low groan permeated through the auditorium at the mention of the word rape. Most of the men present thought of their own wives. The women in the assembly had their own private feelings on the subject.

'But finally, most tragically, the captain of the vessel was murdered by one of the pirates.' He paused and looked directly at the Nigerian delegate.

'I wonder if Mr Enegbe the delegate for Nigeria would be good enough to explain to the assembly, what progress his government have made in tracking down the perpetrators. Also what measures they will be taking, to address this problem in the future?' The speaker then sat down and waited patiently for a response from the delegate in question.

The slim bespectacled figure of Mr George Enegbe sat in his seat for a few moments, scanning over a pile of papers in front of him and then slowly rose to his feet. He was attired in national dress, long green and white patterned shirt, worn outside matching baggy trousers with a plant pot hat perched on his head. He was quite nervous, having only spoken briefly to the assembly on one occasion previously. This was the reason he was slow to stand up, taking the extra minute or so to compose his thoughts. He looked at his notes one more time, adjusted his glasses and looked directly at the speaker and began talking in a dry even tone.

'Mr Speaker, ladies and gentlemen of the United Nations. Let me first start off by offering the sincere apologies of the people of Nigeria to the people of Spain, for the simply terrible tragedy that happened off our port of Lagos three weeks ago.' He looked down at his notes and once again and re-adjusted his glasses.

'It is true, there has been and increase in piracy in Nigerian waters. After all, the facts and figures are indisputable.'

There was a nod of assent from the speaker and a number of the delegates who were listening intently to what the Nigerian was saying.

'But I must stress in the strongest terms, the good people of Nigeria are not responsible for all of this crime. My Home Secretary has had his police chief conduct a thorough investigation into this particularly tragic case and appraised me fully of the facts.'

He stopped talking for a few moments to let the substance of what he was saying be absorbed by the listeners. He was a quite a skilled orator, having studied English at Oxford, which had helped secure his position at the UN. But he was also the brother in-law of the Nigerian President, which had helped him even more. He had the full attention of every member in the auditorium, as they waited expectantly for the conclusion of his explanation.

'The hard facts of this particular case are that it was not the good citizens of Nigeria who committed this crime, but actually criminals and pirates from the republic of Benin.'

The delegate from Benin became noticeably agitated, as if a red hot poker had touched him on a nerve end. He tried to stand up to protest the accusation, but one of his assistants intervened and quickly calmed him down. The Nigerian delegate continued speaking in a calm even tone.

'Just after the attack on the Spanish ship, one of our police patrol boats intercepted the pirates on their way back to Benin. The pirates were given the opportunity to surrender, but they chose to fire on our boat. During the exchange of fire, two of our policemen were injured. One is still in Lagos hospital at this very minute, recovering from his wounds. During this exchange of fire all the pirates were shot dead. I have some photos here, which show clearly the cargo stolen from the vessel in question lying in their canoe. I have also in my possession six identity books which were taken from the dead pirates. Four of these were citizens of Benin and the other two were Ghanaian.'

He held up the stained and battered passports for the assembly to see.

'The shipping marks on the cartons of the stolen cargo correspond exactly with that documented in the bills of lading from the Spanish ship. This proves conclusively that these people were the pirates. I will pass the photos and the books for inspection by the Assembly.'

The Finnish speaker looked at the evidence and had to admit to himself, it certainly seemed on the surface to prove that in this instance anyway, Nigeria was not to blame. The delegate from Benin was indicating that he wanted to speak.

'Perhaps the delegate from the Republic of Benin would like to answer the allegations recently made?' said the speaker. The delegate from Benin who was grim faced, got quickly to his feet.

'The people of the republic of Benin do not accept these allegations.' The man was obviously very angry, which the shrill tone of his voice conveyed emphatically to the audience.

'The day after the attack off Lagos took place, one of our fishing boats with nine men on board, failed to return to Cotonou. It just disappeared into thin air, even though the weather was fine, which we find highly suspicious. We feel the 'so called evidence' presented is a fabrication by Nigeria, to divert attention away from themselves and we utterly refute these allegations.' He sat down as quickly as had had risen.

There next followed a heated exchange across the auditorium between the delegates of Nigeria and Benin and their assistants. The speaker had to talk firmly to both parties to get order restored to the assembly.

Most of the delegates seemed to be of the opinion, in this instance, that the Nigerians were most probably not to blame. But Sir Hugh Spencer, the tall, slim, impeccably dressed British delegate, stroked his chin thoughtfully and was far from convinced.

He had extensive experience in the diplomatic service in West Africa and knew the lengths that some Africans would go to cover themselves. He was familiar with the area in question and found it hard to believe that pirates would travel fifty miles to attack a ship at Lagos, when there were ships at anchor off their own port, Cotonou that could be more easily attacked.

He leaned over to communicate his feelings to the Spanish delegate directly in front of him. He was also deeply suspicious of the Nigerian story. Looking around the auditorium, Sir Hugh could tell by the various heads nodding and the tone of the rumble of voices, that most of those present, accepted the word of the Nigerian delegate. After all, the story he had concocted, he mused, would be quite plausible to anyone not familiar with West Africa.

The speaker brought the meeting under control once again.

'It would seem there is ground for doubt, that all of the piracy off the port of Lagos is being perpetrated by the citizens of Nigeria. However as far as I can see, the vast majority is still being caused by Nigerian citizens, so, to reiterate my original question to Mr Enegbe, what is your country going to do to improve this situation?'

The Nigerian got slowly to his feet and those close by, could see the smallest hint of a wry smile on his lips.

'We are taking as many measures as the resources of our impoverished nation can permit, with the limited funds we have available. We have increased the number of police to track down these people. But it is not and easy task, as there are many small rivers and creeks in our country, where they can hide. A pirate's canoe after all, just looks the same as a normal fishing boat.' Mr Enegbe stopped and looked around, pleased to see the mood of the assembly seemed to be on his side.

'We would like to increase the number of patrols in the anchorage, but unfortunately we only have one suitable patrol boat and even this is broken down at the moment. If the United Nations could provide us with even a small amount of aid, we could buy new patrol boats, to enable us to tackle the problem with proper equipment. Perhaps even Interpol could be of some assistance to us in solving this problem.' The President himself had specifically asked him to request this assistance.

'I am led to believe Interpol has the expertise and training in so many matters such as this, which we Nigerians are lacking. With this, Mr Speaker, I wish to conclude.'

Sir Hugh Spencer was amazed and thought Mr Enegbe, despite his benign appearance, to be a rather an astute person, skilfully turning the situation round to his country's favour. From initially being comprehensively lambasted, to what looked like obtaining a substantial aid package. Sir Hugh, ever the sceptic where Africa and aid was concerned, doubted this would have any effect on the piracy situation off Lagos. As in the past, the lion's share of the money given in the form of aid to these poor countries, just filtered into the pockets of various officials and little or none reached its intended destination.

There was however, one point the speaker mentioned, that he was certain had to be completely true, that one highly organised gang was responsible for most of this piracy. Undoubtedly there would be more acts in the future, which was bound to affect the UK sooner or later, due to the size of its merchant fleet and traditional trade links with West Africa. He resolved to contact Commander Roberts, the head of the Interpol branch in London and inform him of this development at the UN.

Chapter Eight

It was Monday morning, two days after returning from Antwerp. Ellis was relaxed, having had a weekend of exercise rowing on the river and exercise of a different nature after meeting one of his sister's friends in the pub on Sunday afternoon. The girl, a medical student called Helen, was fast asleep in the bed. Nothing could disturb her. Not even a bomb going off next to the bed, he mused. Well it had been a very good night all round, he thought. She was entitled to her sleep.

After a leisurely shower he dressed in a dark blue suit and had a light breakfast of cereal and tea, before making his way out of the house into the crisp January morning air. He then climbed into his yellow Triumph Stag sports car, which was parked in the dusty cobweb-laden garage. The car started at the third attempt, not having been used for a few weeks. Then, after negotiating several quiet side streets, he made his way along the Bayswater Road into the heart of London. This great artery of traffic was in its normal state for a Monday morning, bumper to bumper.

He could have used the Tube, but being cramped like a sardine in a smoky carriage with a heaving mass of humanity was not his idea of how to travel. At least in the car, he had some control over the journey and could be alone with his thoughts. He was partly thinking about the report he would make regarding the events in Belgium last week, but mostly about the carnal events of the last twelve hours. A warm sensation passed through him at the memory.

Just before nine o'clock, he arrived at the garage under the Interpol building and quickly parked his car. That was one advantage of working for 'the firm,' there was always ample parking under the office block, which made the decision to drive in to work that much easier.

On arrival at the fifth floor, where his unit the Special Investigations Squad was located, he went directly through the open plan area to Chief Inspector Peter Morison's small and Spartan office on the far side. He shook hands with his boss and, on his invitation, sat down on the lumpy chair opposite his desk. Peter Morrison was a short slim man of around fifty years of age with a bald pate and a noticeably pale face, as if he had spent his whole life indoors and was averse to fresh air or sunlight.

'Well Martin, I must offer you congratulations for assisting to capture the drugs shipment over in Antwerp.'

'Thanks sir. I was just disappointed that we never made any progress following the traffickers. It was the bloody fog that screwed us up in the end.'

'Anyway, not to worry, I am sure we will make progress in that direction soon. Damn pity about Chief Inspector Bouliver.'

'Oh I don't know. He seemed to be in fine spirits when I left him on Friday morning.'

'You haven't heard then?' his boss replied in a somewhat surprised tone, regarding Ellis over the top of his glasses.

'No. What's happened? Is he all right?'

'Fraid not Martin; Chief Inspector Bouliver was murdered on Friday evening when his car was blown up. It happened while he was driving home apparently. Remote control job they reckon.'

'Good God! It must have been the traffickers exacting retribution!' Ellis was visibly shaken.

'Yes, even worse news I am afraid. Another two officers on the bust have also been murdered,' his boss said gravely.

'Hell, they are probably looking for me right now,' Ellis stated rather flatly.

'Well, there's every possibility of this, but they will have great difficulty in finding you as they do not know you. But there's another reason they will find it very difficult to trace you, as you will be going off on another case soon. Something quite important has come up. The details of which the commander will divulge when he calls us to his office. Meanwhile make yourself at home, get yourself a coffee it's freshly brewed. Excuse me; I have a few things to trawl through.'

As his boss sorted the piles of paper on his desk, Ellis was deep in thoughts dominated by the fate of the poor Belgian. The chilling factor was, had he taken up the offer of hospitality extended to him by the genial Andre, he would have bought it as well. Another narrow escape! Well, he knew about the danger when he joined the force all those years ago. He could have lived a cosseted life in a bank or an accountant's office, but the boredom would have killed him. He felt it was much better to live to the full doing something you enjoy, rather than work with the sole purpose of earning money.

Around twenty minutes later, Chief Inspector Morrison received a phone call from the commander and they both proceeded without delay, up the short flight of stairs to the next floor. The office of Commander Roberts, the head of Interpol's London branch, was a grand sumptuous affair on which no expense had been spared. A burgundy coloured deep pile carpet covered the floor and elegant red leather settees and armchairs were carefully positioned throughout the room. Huge glass windows looked out over the city, the silvery Thames in the distance threading its way between the buildings of the capital. As always, Ellis thought the view to be simply stunning.

Commander Roberts was stood behind an elegant but substantial rosewood desk, topped with red leather, looking down at a folder on the desk. He glanced up momentarily as his two subordinates approached the desk.

'Good morning chaps. Come, please be seated.' He indicated with one hand the two seats positioned in front of the desk. The tall slim boss of Interpol reached over and gave firm handshakes to each of his subordinates in turn. He was a man in his mid fifties and had silver grey hair, parted precisely at one side and swept across to the other. His complexion was extremely healthy, probably due to many hours outdoors in all weathers walking his Alsatian dogs, or rounds of golf at his club in Berkshire.

'Now let me see what we have here,' he said in a precise clipped tone, as he looked down at a crisp green file located almost exactly in the centre of his desk. The man was a perfectionist. From the way he dressed, always immaculate, to the way he ran the agency with precision and efficiency.

Since he had taken over three years previously the number of arrests and crimes solved had more than doubled. It was a known fact that his predecessor, Jack Edmunds, near to retiring age, had been treading water for years, not really wanting to ruffle any feathers or achieve anything remarkable. The agency had been stagnating and morale had been virtually extinguished. The arrival of Commander Roberts had been like a breath of spring air and Ellis had the utmost respect for the man.

He looked up from the file he was studying towards Ellis. 'Good show over in Antwerp, Ellis. That will put a dent in the drugs trade for a while. I believe the street value of that stuff was in the region of twenty million pounds. Damn pity about the three Belgians though. Mind you, it seems there is a price to pay for everything in life.'

'Thank you, sir. I just heard the bad news a few minutes ago.'

'You will need to step carefully for a while, Ellis.' The commander pointed his right index finger at the younger man, a note of seriousness in his voice. He looked down once again at the folder in front of him.

'Now let me see what we have concocted for your next case. I see from your file you were actually born in Africa.'

'Yes that's right sir. Nigeria, Lagos in fact.'

'Where you lived until you were eighteen I believe. Would you care to enlighten us about your time there?'

'Certainly sir, I lived in Lagos till I was eleven, then much of the time after that was spent at boarding school in the UK, though I did return to Lagos at holiday times. My father was with the oil industry and he was transferred back to the UK when our oil boom was starting in the North Sea in the early seventies. He has lived in London ever since.'

'I see, so you must be familiar with the topography of the area in and around Lagos. I should imagine you will also be familiar with African customs and attitudes, in essence how the place works?'

'Oh yes, I would say I am well qualified in all those respects. The layout of the town will have changed somewhat since I was there, as apparently they have used a lot of the money from their oil industry to build a new modern Lagos. But I will soon get my bearings I am sure.'

'All right Ellis, I'll tell you what's come up and this might surprise you, it certainly took me aback. Our delegate at the UN, Sir Hugh Spencer, contacted me last week. Apparently, the Nigerians over there have made an official request for the assistance of Interpol, the purpose being to help in tracking down a highly organised gang of pirates, operating off the port of Lagos at the moment.' The commander spoke in an authoritative tone, regarding the two men in front of him impassively, with his cool clear blue eyes.

Ellis was immediately intrigued. Like most people, he knew virtually nothing about piracy and listened intently to the words of his boss. The commander had a way of speaking, his choice of words and the inflections in his voice that generated maximum attention from his audience. After a brief pause he continued speaking.

'Since last week however, headquarters in Lyon has decided that we shall handle this investigation. Probably because Nigeria is one of our former colonies, though I suppose the reputation of our Special Investigation Squad must have had some bearing on this also. That's where you come in, Ellis. We are going to send you out there to get to the bottom of this affair.'

Ellis waited for a moment before answering, to absorb what his superior had said.

'Well sir, I do know a lot about Lagos and the people, but I know nothing about piracy or where to even start looking.'

'That's no problem, Ellis. We're all more or less in the same boat. I have here a comprehensive dossier supplied by the MNAOA, which is essentially the Merchant Navy Officers' Union. They have one person in their office, almost permanently assigned to this research. You can spend the next week studying this, I am sure you will find it highly interesting reading, even if it is somewhat distressing in places.'

Ellis was excited at the prospect of tackling another form of crime. In fact, ever since he had cleared up an international counterfeiting network almost three years ago, he had been exclusively assigned to the drug smuggling problem. As with the affair in Belgium recently, little progress had been in any direction and he had become somewhat disheartened because of this. So he welcomed this new and different kind of challenge, at this point in his career.

Peter Morrison now took up the briefing.

'Well Martin, it's a serious business and we have given the job by the UN and headquarters in Lyon of putting a stop to it. I have here a letter from the Nigerian Internal Affairs Minister. He is particularly keen to have our assistance. He says that he and the rest of the government are genuinely embarrassed and distressed with the piracy that is happening off Lagos. He mentions how the recent attack on a Spanish ship, shocked him and his colleagues. He also says that he has suspicions of his police chief; whom he thinks could do considerably more to catch these people. So there you have it Martin, a hot potato then.'

The commander remained silent, hands clasped calmly in front of him, regarding each person intently as they spoke. Ellis smiled briefly before continuing, which Commander Roberts took as a sign of the man's confidence.

'It certainly sounds like there will be plenty of work, getting to grips with this problem. But I must say I am looking forward to the challenge and working on this case,' Ellis said with enthusiasm. The commander spoke now, a serious tone once again apparent in his deep voice

'That's good to hear Ellis, but a word of warning old chap, you had better be damn careful when you get out there. This gang will kill you as quick as look at you. There have been seven people murdered on ships in the last year. Anyway you take the file, sit down and absorb its contents for the next week. We'll have another meeting next Monday, to discuss the best way to tackle this problem.'

Commander Roberts stood up from behind the solid rosewood desk. The other two realised this signified the end of the meeting. As they left the room he went towards the window, deep in thought and gently stroking his chin as he walked.

Ellis spent the rest of the morning at his desk in the open plan area composing and writing up his report on the previous week's events in Antwerp. He had been shocked at the news of the demise of the genial Belgian and his two associates. He certainly would heed the commanders' warning and be careful for the next week, starting by checking under his car each time before starting it up.

By nature he was a cautious person, but this had been instilled in him further during his one year of training, at the Interpol College in Brigham Hill, Wiltshire. He had enjoyed his time there, studying international crime and learning the most effective methods to tackle it. He absorbed the details of the mandate given to Interpol by the various signatories to the agreement, which was most of the world.

The firearms part of the course he had particularly enjoyed and had become a crack shot with a handgun, entering and winning a number of minor police competitions. He enjoyed learning about the various types of weapons and how they operated, details such as the rate of fire, how many rounds in the magazine and practising instant recognition. There was a weekly test where a gun was pulled out and a number of rounds fired off. The trainee was then asked how many shots were left in the magazine. Ellis only ever got it wrong once, but his instructor managed to impress on him in no uncertain terms that once, was one time too many. He never got the count wrong after that and had successfully called on this skill during numerous operations.

Ellis found the whole aspect of his job fascinating and highly rewarding. During his time with 'the firm,' he had been involved with the police forces of most European countries and also with the police in the USA, Brazil and Japan. The majority, were always wary of his involvement initially and some downright un-cooperative.

Of all the places he had visited, he found Japan the strangest. In fact, it was a wonder he had achieved anything at all in Japan. During his time there, the Osaka police virtually ignored him and tried to obstruct him at every turn. He started to doubt they had any interest in catching any criminals involved in organised crime. He mused that while the Japanese police tried to reach a decision through one of their committees, the Yakusa went about their business virtually un-opposed. It was not hard to see who the real criminals were in Japan, as they arrogantly strode round in their black suits and dark sunglasses or drove round in huge black cars, with tinted windscreens, which were usually Mercedes. Japan was indeed a strange place.

It was in general frustrating to find that no matter where he went, there always seemed to be, a superintendent or chief inspector determined to put him in his place, almost as he got off the plane. But Ellis knew his international law inside out and the mandate Interpol possessed. A few choice words and phrases usually had the desired result.

Sadly, Chief Inspector Andre Bouliver had been quite the opposite, actually genuinely pleased to be working with Interpol. He had made Ellis feel instantly at home in his station and instructed all his officers to give maximum cooperation.

'We are all on the same side after all,' he had emphasised at the briefing with all his officers on the first day.

Ellis sighed. Then he carefully read through the neatly typed seven page report, ensuring he had missed nothing. Then he signed this at the bottom with his large dramatic signature and tossed it into the out tray on his desk. He then sat back in his chair, hands behind his head, deep in thought. The person at the next desk soon disturbed his reverie.

'Well Martin, you certainly seem to have the world on your shoulders today. What you need is a good screw.' It was Sergeant Bob Wallace, he had been on the same course as Ellis and they were good friends. Ellis laughed.

'I had a good screw last night, thank you very much Bob.'

'Really, details please,' his bemused associate said, leaning across the desk in anticipation of a lurid story.

'Absolutely no chance, bad show old chap. After all, I may want to marry her some day and it wouldn't do if someone was spreading malicious gossip, now would it?'

'You won't be getting married for a while I shouldn't think. Life's too much of a good thing for you at the moment. Anyway, how did last week go? I heard you helped in getting a large shipment seized.'

Ellis told him about the week's events. Bob Wallace was also assigned to the drugs section and had been involved in the build up to the bust in Antwerp. He was quite different to Ellis, smaller slightly built with dark greasy hair. He sported a bushy moustache on his upper lip. Ellis always though he looked more like a crook than a policeman. He did, and had a lot of success undercover because of his appearance.

He gave his friend a detailed description of how the operation had gone in Antwerp, which he thoughtfully absorbed and asked pertinent questions from time to time. Then, with the business out of the way, after some friendlier cajoling by Wallace, he did reveal some of the details of his previous night's liaison, though he played that down somewhat. When Wallace realised he had milked the maximum detail from Ellis regarding his latest conquest, he returned to his own desk and continued with the work he had been doing previously.

Ellis rubbed his eyes, checked his watch for the time, it was two-thirty. So he went over to the coffee machine, and came back with the statutory Styrofoam cup full, and sat down at his desk. As he carefully sipped the scalding black liquid, he began to think of his forthcoming mission. Nigeria. He found it truly amazing that he was going back there after almost twelve years.

His mind flashed back rather fondly to the life he had known in Nigeria, until he was eleven years of age and had to leave for boarding school in England. British Petroleum employed his father, and he was in charge of operations in Nigeria. His office was in Lagos, even though the oil wells were located to the south and east, offshore, at the mouths of the River Niger. If his father ever needed to visit a drilling location, the company plane would fly him down to the River State.

He had lived with his mother, elder brother and sister in a huge rambling colonial mansion set in its own grounds with a tennis court and swimming pool. Manpower was cheap in Nigeria in those days, so a virtual army of servants catered for his every whim. In fact, there were more servants than family members. A cook and two others worked in the large homely kitchen, while the butler and two maids looked after the other side of the house. In addition there was gardener and a chauffer.

Life in those days, prior to independence in 1960, had been

very comfortable for all expatriates living there, a constant round of parties in various people's homes and on the various beaches in the area. Ellis never lacked for someone to play with when he was younger, as his brother Tom was just fourteen months his elder. Besides, there were lots of other children in the area, from wealthy British families who drifted in and out of his home at will. Security was never an issue in those days. What little crime there was would be committed by Nigerians, against other Nigerians. No one would dare commit a crime against the rulers of the country. They truly were halcyon days.

Initially an English tutor called Mr. Clifton had been employed to convey the joys of learning to Ellis, his brother and his sister. Lessons were daily in the vast drawing room, where the three of them would sit for four hours every day, from nine till one o'clock. The afternoons were always too hot to offer any hope of concentration. The strict, unsmiling, middle-aged teacher, managed to convey the basic rudiments of the subjects to them. But eventually it was decided by his parents, a private school in Lagos that catered for children from expatriate families, would best serve their educational needs. They would then be better prepared for mixing with other children, when eventually their time came to return to England to boarding school.

As he was quite young at the time, Ellis did not recall a great deal about his education as a child in Nigeria. What he remembered most was simply growing up and having a wonderful childhood, as a member of a highly privileged British family. Even now, slumped in a swivel chair at his desk in Interpol's London office, Ellis was amazed how idyllic those times still seemed. But he was astute enough to realise that over the past twenty years Nigeria had changed.

How much it had changed he was soon about to find out.

Chapter Nine

Kaduna's heart thumped steadily and he was sweating profusely as he climbed the dimly lit stairs to his apartment. He had just completed, almost an hour's hard run along the beach over the numerous sand dunes on that section of coast. The awful memories the English girl had rekindled by touching the scar on his back had made him extremely tense. So he had pushed his body to the limit along the beach in an attempt to dissipate this tension. Now, although his muscles ached, he felt considerably better, invigorated by the blood that had coursed furiously round his body for the last hour.

When he entered the apartment he was pleased to find the girl had gone, as he wanted to be alone. He stretched out on the balcony, sat on one chair with his feet on another and let the cool sea breeze coming off the ocean cool him down. He closed his eyes briefly but his mind was racing as well as his heart and he couldn't help starting to plan his next move.

He hadn't observed any ships close to port since the last raid. The reason he swiftly concluded probably being the adverse publicity, surrounding the attack on the Spanish ship. He thought ship's masters were being more cautious now, probably staying far out at sea during the night and only coming in at daybreak, to take the pilot on board. Nevertheless, the time had come to spring back into action. In order to discuss the next raid, he had arranged to meet his right hand man Asamwa, around eight p.m. that night at a club in Apapa. After a long cool shower, he dressed casually in slick Levi jeans and a white Nike Tee shirt and then began searching, for a pair of tan slip on shoes. He found these eventually under some old clothes in the bottom of the wardrobe. Without thinking he reached to the back of the top shelf, ensuring his insurance policy, the gun, was still there. He always liked to check this from time to time, as its presence gave him re-assurance that in the event of an emergency he could rapidly bring to bear some impressive firepower.

He quickly located the gun, safe in its place of stowage at the back of the top shelf. But one thing momentarily puzzled him. Why did the butt of the gun feel wet and how did some small pools of water get onto the top shelf? He soon realised the girl must be the culprit. He was reasonably certain she would not have been prying, probably only looking for a towel. But now she had knowledge of the gun, and that worried him.

His clapped out Toyota was where he had left it earlier that day, when he returned from the casino with the English croupier. Just a few parking spaces away from the entrance of the apartment block. Night had now fallen and the air was heavy, hot and humid. There were few sounds to be heard, just the surf crashing onto the beach and the sound of the occasional car rattling its way along the bumpy coast road.

At last he was feeling relaxed and in a good mood as he contemplated meeting his compatriots and having a few beers, whilst deciding when to make the next raid. As he strolled casually towards the car, he was absently humming a tune he had heard earlier that evening and was playing with the keys in his hand. Then suddenly he sensed something was amiss and turned round to find a police sergeant a few feet behind him. It was the same man that had accompanied the police chief a few weeks ago. When Kaduna realised this, his pulse quickened and his stomach muscles tensed as if they were being squeezed through a mangle. The presence of this man was a harbinger that his evil boss was in the vicinity.

Kaduna stopped and confronted the immaculate sergeant, who had a swagger stick under his left arm. He noticed the man's lips twist, then part to form a malicious little smile, revealing stained teeth. The sergeant then spoke to him in a commanding tone.

'Okay asshole. The chief he wants to talk to you.'

'Where is he?' replied Kaduna nervously.

'He is waiting in the car at the other end of the building.' The policeman pointed in the general direction. Kaduna sighed resignedly and walked slowly, with a heavy heart, towards the parked car. As he approached the large black Mercedes, he was amazed to find it highly polished and in excellent condition. A rare sight in Nigeria, as most of the cars on the roads were essentially wrecks. He could see the corpulent shape of Azubikas sitting in the front passenger's seat next to the driver, staring impassively forward. He got in and sat in the back seat next to the sergeant and another police officer. The air in the car was heavy with the stench of unwashed bodies.

After a few minutes, which seemed like an eternity, the police chief started talking slowly, in even tones.

'Hello Kaduna. We have not seen you for some time. In fact we even thought you have leave the country.'

Kaduna took a deep breath appraising the situation and his options before replying.

'Well? I am waiting.' The police chief prompted a harsher edge to his voice.

Kaduna could feel the sergeant getting agitated and managed to blurt out a few words before he could do anything.

'You said to lie low for a while Chief and let the situation calm down,' he said quickly.

'That is true. Yes that certainly is true.' The police chief replied in a slow measured tone.

'But I didn't mean for you to give up altogether, as you seem to have done.' His tone was becoming more aggressive and he was speaking louder.

'I was just on my way to meet some friends to discuss what we are going to do next.'

'Hah!' The police chief laughed shortly. 'So that is what you call the rabble that assists you in your work. Friends! You have no friends. Each one of them would slit your throat for the price of packet of cigarettes and you know it.'

'Yes, I know what they are like, but I can handle them. They know I am not a person to be crossed. A few have found out the hard way, which has gained me the respect of the others.'

'Well I am sure you are right. But how are you going to continue to justify your existence? You will have seen that ships have stopped anchoring off the port, since your last escapade was so well publicised.'

Kaduna though for a moment then replied. 'There are two ways. Either I have to go further out to sea to find the ships, or perhaps I will have to attack while the ships are in port.'

'In port!' the police chief exclaimed, turned round and looked Kaduna directly in the eye.

'You better be real careful if you are going to try anything in the port. It will have to be fast and no rough stuff either. So be warned, no more foul-ups. I don't need any more trouble from the Home Secretary. Anyway I need some money before the week is out.'

'You will have money before the week is out. As I said before, I was on my way to discuss this matter with the others.' Kaduna replied, a reassuring note in his voice. After a few seconds of tense silence, the police chief sighed then spoke tersely to the sergeant.

'Okay Kwado, let him out of the car.'

'Yes sah.' A crisp reply, as the sergeant opened the door and jumped out. As Kaduna got out the sergeant pushed him to one side. He stumbled and spun round, incensed, fists balled at the ready, he didn't like being pushed policeman or not. The sergeant stood back slightly, holding the car door with one hand. Both men eyed each other coldly for a second in silence. Then the sergeant got in the car which sped off along the coast road.

Once the car disappeared from view, Kaduna dropped his fists to his side and breathed deeply in an attempt to clear the tension from his body. He walked slowly, dejectedly, with his head down, towards the Toyota. Then he kicked an old rusty tin that was lying on the rutted sidewalk viciously into the road. It clattered loudly as it tumbled across the road.

'Bastards!' he said loudly, vehemently.

When he reached the car, he got inside and slumped back in the driver's seat, head against the headrest, closed his eyes and tried to relax. Then he remembered there was some Ganja in the glove compartment. He sat up opened the flap and quickly found the joint. Once he had lit this, he lay back once again and inhaled deeply, eyes closed, thinking dark thoughts. This latest altercation with the police chief and his henchmen, only served to confirm a nagging fear that had been eating away inside him for a while. That it was only a matter of time, before his demise came knocking on his door. They were just playing with him at the moment, the way you play with a helpless fly, before crushing it into dust.

He could see no reason why the police chief didn't just dispose of him and put one of his brighter policemen in charge of the pirate operation. The idea was not so far fetched, the police as the perpetrators of the piracy. They did similar things ashore all the time in this part of the world, as corruption was rife at all levels.

It was a hopeless predicament. He could not give up his lucrative business quite yet, as he did not have enough capital to maintain his opulent lifestyle indefinitely. Also his travel documents were not in order. Furthermore, Azubikas would almost certainly have the airport under surveillance. So there was nothing else he could do. He would have to continue and hope that lady luck continued to smile benevolently on him.

He had been put under pressure to make more attacks and take even more risks than before. This was not the ideal way to conduct his perilous business. But first he must contact Asamwa and see if anything had materialised in his absence. He finished the joint, exhaling slowly the acrid smoke, and then flicked the tiny stub out of the open window.

He started the car and eased out of the parking area, onto the dark coast road. He passed a number of people waiting at the roadside looking for lifts. A few waved their arms frantically, indicating for him to stop. Normally he would have given someone a lift, but tonight he was not in a particularly kind mood.

The lights of Lagos glowed brightly in the distance. The skyscrapers gave the city a modern appearance he always thought. Though in reality, most of the facilities within had broken down many years ago, never to be repaired.

As he drove towards the centre of Lagos he was in a sombre mood, but he desperately hoped that by the end of the night, he would have a better idea of how his immediate future would take shape. To eventually enable him to fulfil his ambition, to escape the clutches of Africa and find a life of luxury in safe in another country.

Chapter Ten

Exactly eight time zones away from Lagos is Hong Kong, often referred to as the centre of the Orient. A giant crossroads where East dramatically meets West. A multitude of modern office and apartment blocks reach skywards in front of a backcloth of verdant hills. While below these huge buildings, on the pavements of the packed streets, vendors dispense bowls of steaming noodles from battered kitchen carts to eager customers. In the same street, the driver of a Mercedes may be honking his horn in frustration, as a rickshaw, pulled by a gaunt jaundiced figure of a man, blocks his way.

There is no place more fascinating in Hong Kong than the bay itself. This is absolutely crammed with ships of every description. From the most modern container ship, decks piled high with shining metal boxes, to rusted old freighters, perhaps on their last voyage before going to scrap. A plethora of ships swinging on anchor chains, or moored to buoys. Ships loading cargo from barges or from smaller coastal ships tied up alongside. Inter-mingled with this vast fleet are numerous junks and sampans, buzzing back and forward like busy bees between the ships. One family concerns, just earning enough money to keep operating.

Every five minutes, the double decker Star Ferry goes from Victoria to Kowloon, passing another going in the opposite direction. The whole panorama is punctuated every so often, by the scream of jet engines as huge hydrofoils on their way to Macao cut dramatic swathes through the bay at speeds of up to forty knots. While owners of junks and sampans curse loudly, as the wake from these modern craft cause their ancient boats to pitch and roll violently.

With so much happening at any one time, the onlooker can easily be mesmerised by the scene. Second Mate Thomas Kolskis certainly was, as he leaned on the rail of his ship soaking up the view for the umpteenth time during his watch. He was of average height and build, twenty-eight years old, with lank blonde hair and a straggly beard and moustache. There was pale skin on his face and dark rings under his eyes from lack of sleep on the twelve to four watch.

His ship was the Russian general cargo vessel, M.V. 'Kapitan Penkov,' which was at anchor loading crates of machinery for West Africa. The ship was quite modern compared to some of the old clankers he had sailed on earlier in his career, built just 8 years previously. It had four hatches, all forward of the accommodation. The ship was designed in such a way, to enable general cargo or containers to be carried in the holds, with containers on deck. The cargo handling equipment consisted of four 25-ton SWL – safe working load- Russian designed Velle cranes. There was also a set of derricks at the aft end of number four hatch, which were useful for loading and discharging break bulk cargo. It also enabled this hatch to work two gangs if required. The crew of thirty-five persons were all Russian and included three women who worked as stewardesses.

The second mate was taking a breather from checking the cargo and securing down the hatches. The air on deck was still, hot and humid, with hardly a breath of cool air. But after being down number three hatch, which was like an oven, the deck at least for a few minutes felt like heaven. Intrigued by the scene in the bay, he did not notice the figure beside him.

'Skiving again are we, Sec? Leaning on the ships rail won't get those cargo lashings checked,' the bosun said, with a note of mock severity in his voice.

'Hey you old bastard, you should know how to speak to your officers,' the second mate replied jauntily.

The bosun would tolerate few people talking to him in that manner. But the second mate knew what he could get away with, having sailed with the bosun for a year while he was an ordinary seaman. He had found him, an extremely tough and uncompromising taskmaster, who punched first and rarely asked for explanations later. A crewman under his control had but one thing to remember, to do exactly as the bosun told him.

His background clearly explained the man's inherent violence. When he was fourteen years old, in nineteen forty-one, he witnessed the execution of his family and the burning of his village by the Germans. He fought in the resistance for the remainder of the Second World War, avenging their deaths many times.

He still hated Germans vehemently and would often pick a fight with one, whilst drunk in one of the many seamen's bars that dotted the globe. He would take great pleasure in beating any German to a pulp. This bosun was certainly not a man to be tangled with and the weight of his huge meaty fists was clearly etched on the second mate's memory. He respected him, even though he did not wholly approve of his methods. Kolskis had studied and was an officer now, but in a way the bosun was still the boss. That was the aura the man possessed.

'Yeah, I actually had to restrain myself when I saw you leaning on the rail just now. Otherwise I might have been charged with assaulting an officer. But you know old habits die hard,' the bosun said quite matter of factly.

'Yes Ivan, you don't have to remind me of the years you spent imparting to me gently the finer skills of seamanship.'

They watched in silence, as the ancient skeletal Chinese stevedores, rigged wire slings around a large wooden crate in the barge beneath them. A quick hand signal from the surly hatch foreman on the ships rail and the electric winches on the winch table above their heads, clattered noisily into life. Surprisingly enough, the crate was heaved smoothly, from the tossing barge and lowered into the ship's hold. As it passed over the deck, the markings on the side of the crate could be clearly seen. Nguba Brothers, Apapa, Nigeria.

'Damn cursed place,' the bosun said with venom.

'I'd rather be going to Brazil, or some other decent run ashore, than that stinking hole.'

'Now don't be like that, Ivan. At least the women are cheap there.'

'Cheap! They want to be. They are all full of clap and AIDS anyway! I don't like the bloody country or their women one little bit. The place is full of thieves, pirates and it stinks. The last time I was there, all the fenders in Apapa were covered in shit. The smell got into your clothes, even your hair after a while.'

The second mate cringed at the bosun's accurate description, of the place where the ship was soon bound.

'Don't remind me. Anyway I have work to do down the hatch. Don't forget, we have the commissar's meeting at four this afternoon in the mess room.'

'Da, da! Don't remind me, I can't wait.'

The second mate went across the deck and was about enter the mast house, when the roar of jet engines close overhead caused him to stop and look up in awe. It was yet another Jumbo, making its final approach to Kai Tak airport. He followed the path of the giant plane, as it skipped low over the ships in the bay. Then watched it steadily lose height, before banking hard right and dropping like a stone onto the short runway. An impressive sight, he thought and wished he had become an airline pilot. But he wasn't and he descended once again into the boiling hold.

'Capitalism, comrades, as we all know, is the main problem with the Western World today.'

The large but austere mess room was packed with the entire crew of the M.V. 'Kapitan Penkov.' It was the once monthly lecture, given by the ship's commissar Gregor Kaminsky. A mandatory requirement on all Soviet ships, designed to refocus the minds of ship's crews, of the value of having such a fair system of government in place in their country. The lectures usually failed to achieve their objective, only serving to remind most listeners of the stark reality of communism, that essentially they had no life of their own and were basically just the property of the state.

The crew fidgeted restlessly and tried to focus their attention on the orator, who was standing at the forward end of the room. The small weasel like man, with a pockmarked face and dark close-cropped hair, was dressed in the commissar's dark blue uniform and peaked cap. He was speaking with so much enthusiasm, that he could have been addressing a crowd in Red Square.

'It is totally immoral, this fact I am sure you all appreciate. Free enterprise can only lead to greed and all its inherent problems. Look at the USA, a total cesspool of depravity and corruption. We have Comrade Lenin to thank we do not have its equal in the USSR.'

Second Mate Thomas Kolskis, had heard the argument countless times over the years, even if it was put differently by the various commissars. Like the rest of the people attending, he had to try hard to stop yawning or even worse, falling asleep. Every one on board had to attend these meetings, including the captain. No one dared risk being absent. The commissar was more powerful than the captain, as he was the party man on board. He was always quick to spot any dissension on the ship and send a report to Moscow. He could even have a man sent back to Russia at the earliest opportunity.

As the lecture dragged on, the second mate looked round the room at some of the people present. Litbarski, the tall gangling, gaunt faced, chief engineer from Tallinn, was sitting directly in front of him. He was sitting next to the only other Estonian on the vessel, a grossly overweight third engineer called Korklov, whose huge stomach always protruded from his overalls. He would often pat this proudly, saying, 'Its all been paid for.' A reference to the vast amount of beer he had consumed to produce such a large stomach.

Over towards the bulkhead on the starboard side he could see Lila, one of the three stewardesses on board. She was blonde with a full figure and the most attractive of the women. Her feminine charms were a delight to savour, or so he had been reliably informed, by two other crewmembers more fortunate than himself. Sitting at a desk next to where the commissar was standing, he could see the imposing figure of the captain and he wondered how he was finding the meeting.

Captain Victor Borisenko gave the impression he was listening attentively to what the commissar was saying. Though he knew it was raw propaganda to try and obscure the shortcomings of Russia. He was fifty-eight years old, a tall barrel-chested man with broad Slavic features on his face. His dark hair was neatly parted and slicked across the top of his head. He looked out at the assembled crew with impassive eyes. He had seen too much, in his thirty-one years at sea, to believe anything the commissar was saying. He, like most captains in the Russian Merchant Navy, resented having a party man on board telling him what to do. Especially as Kaminsky, like most of his ilk, had little idea of what running a ship was all about.

As the party man continued his oratory with gusto, the captain's thoughts were with the coming voyage, general cargo and containers to West Africa. Not the most popular destination with ship's crews. He had not been there for almost six years, but had learned from other Soviet masters that the situation there was deteriorating rapidly. Pilferage of cargo and thieving in general of anything that was not securely locked, seemed to be the norm these days.

It was the same the world over, he reflected morosely. As countries became poorer, the people grew more desperate. He sympathised greatly with their predicament and felt genuinely sorry for the poor wretches, just as long as they did not try to take anything from his ship. That would have been a great personal insult to him, his security on board and his efficient running of a ship. Retribution to any perpetrators, no matter how poor, if caught would be harsh.

He had heard that a more sinister menace had manifested itself in West Africa, which caused him great concern, highly organised armed attacks on merchant ships, which amounted to nothing more than piracy. 'Just let them try on this ship,' the captain said to himself and a thin smile crossed his lips, as he thought of the racks of rifles and machine-guns the vessel carried. Russian and Israeli ships are almost the only nations to carry firearms on board in any quantity. All personnel train regularly in their use and are subsequently very proficient with firearms. On this point, Captain Borisenko was extremely enthusiastic, and firearms practice was held monthly. Even the cook had to take part in this exercise.

He had in his possession a directive from the head of the Russian Merchant Service, to use all means at his disposal, to prevent any unlawful boarding of his ship. In a time of war a Russian merchant vessel, would immediately form a part of that war machine. Because of this, secret codebooks and other important documents were placed on board and these must never be allowed to fall into the wrong hands. So like most Soviet masters, he was extremely resolute in complying with this particular directive. In other words, he would use any means possible to stop, or deter unauthorised persons boarding his vessel.

Captain Borisenko had a very tough upbringing, witnessing the callous destruction of his country at the hands of the Third Reich and the horrific atrocities the jackbooted army left behind. He had been a lieutenant in the Red Army and was a veteran of bitter, often hand to hand fighting, to rid his country of a hated foe. Images which, he would take with him to his grave and it had left him as a man with little compassion.

'...and I am sure the captain will echo my sentiments to the full,' the commissar said which brought the captain's attention back to the meeting.

'Yes, Comrade Kaminsky, I agree fully and all that you say should be noted by everyone present.'

Kaminsky could tell the captain hadn't been paying full attention to his lecture, but nevertheless he was satisfied with the captain's adequate reply.

'The captain mentioned to me before that he would like to bring some items to your attention before the meeting closes.'

The great bear like figure of Captain Borisenko began to stand up, carefully putting on his glasses as he rose. Looking across the mess room over the rims, he could see he had the immediate attention of the assembled officers and crew.

'I would like to start off by saying thank you to Commissar Kaminsky, for reminding us of the values of Communism.' A polite ripple of applause came from the crew.

The commissar nodded his head approvingly. The captain's stomach turned at having to pay lip-service to a cretin like Kaminsky.

'I will get straight to the point.' He held up a telex in his right hand, shaking it a little for emphasis. 'I received this telex from our Marine Department in Leningrad this morning. It's to do with piracy. It's not good news.'

He cleared his throat quietly, and then began to slowly read the contents of the telex, a serious note evident in his deep voice.

'All ships must exercise extreme caution in the South China Sea, between the Paracell Islands and Singapore, as there have been numerous attacks on merchant vessels in the last two months by heavily armed pirates. This, as you will all be aware, is precisely the area we will be passing through after we leave Hong Kong,' he said in an even tone.

He abruptly stopped talking and looked gravely round the room, to ensure the full attention of all present. Then took a deep breath though his nose and continued. 'In separate incidents, three crew members have been shot and wounded and in another a Greek captain was murdered. Comrades, this is a grave and dangerous situation that has arisen.' He stopped reading for a moment looking very worried.

The chief officer started to speak. 'But sir, these people should pose no threat to us, with all the automatic weapons that we have on board.' A hint of arrogance in his speech, a few of the crew nodded in agreement. The captain banged his fist angrily on the desktop and shouted at the chief officer.

'Don't be so bloody naive. We don't know anything about these people, do we?'

'No sir, I was merely mentioning the fact that we are well armed,' the chief officer blurted out quickly. He felt intense humiliation at the captain's vitriolic outburst in front of the crew and junior officers. But the captain was only just beginning.

'Well armed, you think I don't know that! When do you suppose these people will come anyway? Ten o'clock in the morning, when we are all on the bridge drinking coffee? No my friend, in the dead of night in pouring rain, when they cannot be seen, out from behind an island in small wooden boats that the radar will not detect. There may be ten or fifty of them, swarming on board in the pitch dark. You start firing automatic weapons then, and there will be as many of our comrades at the bottom of the sea as pirates.' The captain's voice lowered slightly. He had succeeded in imparting to all present the gravity of the situation. The chief officer, whose cheeks burned bright red with shame, quietly seethed and now hated the captain more than ever.

'So this is what we will do,' he continued in an even tone. 'All ladders round the accommodation will be taken down. All doors will be bolted shut at night time and only one open during the day. The searchlights will be rigged on the bridge wings, so that they can point forward or aft. The crew will be on security watch, half of them before midnight and the rest until 0600 in the morning.' A dull groan emanated from the depths of the assembled crew. Seamen never welcomed extra work and loss of sleep anytime, which applied more to Soviet seamen, as they would receive no extra pay for the work done.

The chief engineer muttered under his breath in Estonian to Korklov the 3rd engineer sitting next to him, 'The Old Man's gone crazy. This is like preparing for war. It can't be as bad as he is making out,' Korklov said nothing, merely nodded.

'Did you see the way he talked to the mate? I tell you, the old bastard's cracking up.'

'Yeah yeah, keep your voice down,' Korklov eventually replied.

The captain heard the dissenting groan, but chose to ignore it and continued speaking.

'The engineers will keep watches. The stores on deck are all to be welded up. When we leave Hong Kong, we will test the firearms. All personnel will attend firing practice. That is all the measures for the moment. I may instigate more later should they be required. Does any one have anything to add to the list of precautions?'

A silence followed, his list already being quite comprehensive.

'All right,' the captain said sighing. 'Just one more thing I would like to add. We will not be finished with this accursed problem, once we leave the Straights of Malacca either,' he said resignedly. 'It also mentions at the end of the message, that the utmost caution should be exercised in West Africa, as there have been attacks on vessels there as well. If anything even more organised than here in the Far East. Over the last year it would appear an organised gang has been at work off the port of Lagos. The telex ends with clear instructions, to take all precautions necessary to protect the vessel, the crew and the cargo.'

The captain finally put the piece of paper on the desk in front of him. He took off his glasses and put them into a small leather case, which he slipped it into the pocket of his white starched uniform shirt.

'Okay, that's enough said on this subject for the moment. The meeting is now concluded.'

The officers and crew rose almost in unison and began to make their way to the door.

The bosun towards the rear of the crowd was rubbing his huge gnarled hands gleefully together. He spoke confidently to a pencil thin able seaman, with a thick moustache and greasy hair, who was walking in the throng next to him.

'Well that's good news Serkov, looks like we could get some action this trip. Any pirate, who puts a foot on my ship, will find himself full of holes. I haven't had a chance to take someone out since the war. Well, not legally anyway, should be good sport.'

'You might think its funny now, Bosun. But you may change your tune before the trip's over. Sounds like a bloody nightmare to me,' the A.B. said rather miserably, as he shuffled along head bowed.

'What!' the bosun exclaimed angrily. 'People like you, are all we need when the shit hits the fan. I tell you now Serkov, you better pull your bloody weight if things do get tricky.' He raised his voice and glaring at the man menacingly from heavily hooded and bagged eyes.

'Don't you worry about me Bosun, I killed enough people in Afghanistan to know how to handle myself,' retorted the man flatly.

'Oh!' The bosun was a little taken aback; unaware the man had actually seen action. This fact in the bosun's eyes automatically accorded him a measure of respect.

'Well... You'll probably be all right then, Serkov.' His tone brightened and he smiled expansively, as he clapped the man roughly round the shoulder.

The mess room soon emptied as the officers and crew returned to their various duties. It was another hour until dinner, which was from 1730 till 1800. As he walked past the galley door, located just behind the mess room, second mate Thomas Kolskis was by now feeling a little hungry. He almost stuck his head inside the galley, to ask the cook what was for dinner. However, the pungent odour that hung in the air answered that question for him; boiled salt fish and cabbage again. How disgusting, he thought, no longer feeling hungry.

Chapter Eleven

The week in London had gone surprisingly fast for Ellis, too quickly in fact. He had read the file Commander Roberts gave him several times and fully absorbed its contents. He was quite astounded to find the extent that piracy had manifested itself, with over two hundred reported attacks the previous year. Not being involved with piracy previously he had only heard the occasional vague account, so his perception and knowledge of the problem like most people, was minimal.

Piracy as it transpired was a worldwide problem and the Far East if anything, seemed to be even worse than West Africa, the waters of Indonesia and the South China Sea being areas rampant with piracy. He read reports of what looked like navy gunboats, with heavy machine guns mounted on the bow attacking ships. Some ships were even hijacked and their crews put in lifeboats, while the pirates sailed the vessel and its cargo to a pre-determined secret location to be sold.

Anti-piracy patrols had been set up by various countries. But as far as he could see, some of those were no more than a façade, to placate the nations whose ships were regularly attacked. Virtually no pirates had actually been caught and the incidence level continued to rise yearly. He wondered briefly, if some of these governments were getting 'kick backs' from pirate gangs. But he soon dismissed this thought, scolding his imagination for running momentarily wild. Ellis felt extremely sorry for the seamen who had to face this threat untrained and unarmed.

He had also spent considerable time in the library, reading extensively about the state of affairs in Nigeria. 'The Firm' had even obtained back issues of Nigerian daily newspapers for him to study. However he did not glean much information from them, as they tended to print only the good things that were happening in the country. The only news he could say with certainty was reported accurately, was the football and sport on the back page.

A few issues of an underground paper called 'The People' probably gave him more of an insight as to what was actually happening. Basically as he feared, the infrastructure of the country was crumbling, with rampant corruption at all levels. The oil revenue from Nigeria's high grade crude, in the region of twelve billion dollars a year, should have made it a rich country, with a high standard of living for its citizens. However it was rumoured that as much as two billion was unaccounted for, this cash being filtered off into the already bulging pockets of lofty officials. The people were consequently very poor, with high unemployment and most surviving on one meal a day. Crime was rife, robbery and murder almost endemic. The government retained the death penalty, to combat the crime problem and many criminals were executed annually, usually after the briefest of trials. It made depressing reading, especially when he thought back to how the country was when he was a child.

He could find little information regarding the pirate gang. Only that they were highly organised, heavily armed and totally ruthless. As far as he could tell, they were responsible for fifteen acts of piracy in the last year. Hi-tech goods, to the value of two hundred thousand dollars, had been stolen. Then most probably sold for a fraction of that price he mused.

On six of the vessels, the accommodation had been attacked and cash, in the region of ninety thousand dollars, taken from the various ship's safes. A captain and a chief officer had been murdered in separate incidents. Furthermore, three women had been subjected to the horrors of gang rape during that period. All had since contracted HIV. On receiving the results of the test, one of the women had committed suicide.

What concerned him most once again was that none of the gang had ever been caught. Though he strongly suspected, no one had tried particularly hard to apprehend them. They just seemed to melt into the night after their raids. None of the stolen cargo had ever been traced. The whole scene smelled rather badly of an inside job, which would make his operation very difficult, if not impossible.

But his first problem was where and how to start. This would not be an easy task. A white man in a black country was hardly the ideal scenario for a covert operation. He had some ideas on this subject, which he would discuss later in the morning with his superiors. For the moment though he was tired of reading about Nigeria and pirates, he sat back in his chair and reflected on the events of the last week.

On Monday he had been distressed, though he took care not to show emotion, at the grisly demise of his friend, the Belgian police chief inspector. He now feared for his own safety. It was one thing gaining victories against 'The Mob,' but it had to be remembered they would always try to exact revenge. He felt they would be drawing on their considerable resources, looking for him at that very moment, an extremely worrying fact. In a way he was glad his next assignment was to an obscure location; never mind how difficult a task that might prove.

He glanced at his watch, ten twenty-five. Then he got up from his desk and made his way ponderously up the stairs to the commander's office, wondering what would transpire at the meeting. Morrison was already seated in front of the boss's desk, a small green folder on his lap. Commander Roberts was seated behind the desk, reading some papers, delicately sipping coffee, from a gold-rimmed bone china cup. Ellis shook hands with both men and then sat down on a chair next to Morrison.

The commander started by re-iterating what had been discussed at the previous meeting. He also stated in clear terms the purpose of Ellis's mission which was to attempt to uncover the identity of the pirate gang leader and the location where the gang came ashore after attacking ships. Once he had finished speaking, Commander Roberts spoke directly to Ellis.

'So what do you think of the proposed operation, now that you have familiarised yourself fully with all the information available?' hands together, fingers interlaced on the top of his huge rosewood desk, eyeing Ellis intently.

'Well sir,' Ellis started speaking slowly, aware of his boss's powerful gaze. 'From what I have read, it will be a difficult task. The situation in general in Nigeria seems to be pretty desperate. Corruption of course, is at the core of the whole problem. It seems that every official has his hand in the honey pot, which is Nigeria's oil wealth.' Ellis paused briefly.

'So how do you see this situation affecting your operation?' his boss interjected.

'Well it is like this sir. I don't think it is feasible for me to work with the local police. They could even be in league with the pirate gang for all we know. Also from what I have read about the Chief of police, a certain Godwin Azubikas, he is the last person I would trust.' Ellis took a deep breath and continued speaking. 'Apparently, Amnesty International would like to talk with him, over numerous substantiated allegations of torture at the local prison. Of course the Nigerian government refused the request outright. He must have some friends in high places. So it seems the only way, I will be able to obtain the information required, is if I go in completely under cover.'

Commander Roberts fiddled absently with a gold pen on his desk, nodded briefly then spoke. 'Yes I would tend to agree with you there Ellis, but that in itself will be a difficult proposition. Your appearance alone would tend to make you rather conspicuous, for this kind of covert operation, being a white person in a country full of black people that is.'

Ellis digested what his boss had said, but he had something else on his mind. 'I agree fully with what you are saying sir, but another thing concerns me. If I am successful, in identifying the leader of this pirate gang and the location of his operation how will I be able to bring him to justice without the assistance of the local police?' A puzzled look etched across his face.

'Ah! Both I and Chief Inspector Morrison were thinking this could be a major problem at the beginning of the week, but this problem seems to have resolved itself.' Commander Roberts said enthusiastically. He shook the gold pen a couple of times for emphasis, before continuing. 'The Nigerian Interior Minister who wrote to me last week, wants this matter resolved and has promised that when you pass on to him the required information, he will dispatch military police personnel, or even a special army unit to take care of the problem, thus circumventing the need to involve the local police. So like you, it seems he does not trust the police chief either.'

A special army unit! That sounded a little heavy handed to Ellis. But it certainly demonstrated that means were available to apprehend the pirates, when he had procured the required information.

'I actually had a private phone call with Chief Endofu, the minister in question two days ago. Apparently he and some other members of the government have been highly embarrassed, by the bad international press that Nigeria received over this piracy issue. He will give you every assistance that you require. I have here a list of his various telephone numbers. As an added security precaution, he will not know of your whereabouts.'

Ellis was relieved to find that was going to be the case. As at that moment in time, he did not trust anyone in Nigeria. Not even a government minister.

'Good, that's a starting point anyway and reassuring to know that I should have someone on my side when I go there. He may also be very useful, if I get myself in too deep or fall foul of Azubikas and his cronies. But that still leaves the problem of being able to move round freely asking questions, without inviting the interest of the local police chief.'

'Don't worry old chap, we have sorted out something quite good for you on that score. Cover that will enable you to move freely, in shipping circles at any rate. I'll leave Chief Inspector Morrison to fill you in on the rest of the details. You'll be flying out to Nigeria on Wednesday.'

Chapter Twelve

The small battered Toyota crept slowly along the narrow street in first gear, leaving a trail of thick black exhaust smoke, weaving occasionally as it crept forward to avoid large potholes in the road. Its driver, Henry Kaduna was in possession of slightly less patience than normal, as he cautiously navigated the car through the teeming thoroughfare. The side of the road was full of hawkers and their stalls, tiny businesses at the foot of the entrepreneurial ladder. Some of these sold only one item such as bread from a little table, illuminated by a small flickering candle, giving off a thin wisp of black smoke. The hawkers would sit at these tables twenty-four hours a day, barely making profit for their endeavours.

It was early evening and the street was packed with the local populace, on their way home from work or milling round to see what they could buy from the hawkers. Occasionally Kaduna would blow his horn and gesticulate to someone who was being particularly obstructive. A great torrent of abuse would usually follow from the pedestrian and the car would once again inch forward along the street.

By the time he arrived at 'Club 21' a little after eight p.m., he was sweaty, thirsty and very irritated, he hoped the effort of coming to the place would prove be worthwhile. He passed under the dim neon sign above the entrance, opened the heavy wooden doors and entered Apapa's biggest nightclub. Everyone in the area, including visiting seamen, resident expatriates and anyone else who could afford the price of a beer or a girl, visited the place.

As he strode inside, the chill of the air conditioning hit him like a brick wall. The acrid smell of Ganja and cheap perfume, hung in the air like a toxic cloud from a chemical works. The place was dimly lit and it took a few seconds, for his eyes to become accustomed to the light. The walls and ceiling were painted black with white stars and moons, possibly to give the impression of being under a clear African sky.

A 70's Tamla tune was being played by the D.J. who sat behind a counter at the side of the small dance floor on the left hand side of the long room. Down the other side were a number of alcoves, where a degree of privacy could be obtained to get to know the hookers who frequented the place. As Kaduna passed one of these alcoves, a girl sitting there stood up and tried to get him to sit down with her.

'Want some fon, honey?' the girl said in a low sultry voice in a poor attempt to be seductive.

'Clear off,' Kaduna replied, his voice laden with vehemence as he pushed the girl firmly to one side.

During his time as a seaman, he was more than happy to visit this establishment every time he was in port. But now that he had aspired to greater things, his expectations in life had risen also. The place sickened him now and made his skin crawl. In fact he could not wait to conclude his business and leave.

As he approached the end of the room he could see his associate, Asamwa, sitting at a table with some other men.

'What's up Kaduna? Not like you to turn down such a fine woman.' Asamwa said cheerfully.

'Aint nothing up, I just had enough action last night to last for a few days.' He smiled weakly.

'How you been man?' Asamwa said as he clapped Kaduna round the shoulders with one arm and shook his hand vigorously with the other.

'I've been okay, keeping pretty quiet for the last few weeks.'

'Too quiet man, too quiet. Com sit down, I has some interesting people I wants you to meet.'

As they sat down, Asamwa called over to a waitress and ordered five Star beers. This was fine by Kaduna, being so thirsty he resolved to do his beer justice when it arrived.

While they waited for the drinks, Asamwa introduced the three men seated round the table. The first was a rangy youth called Richard, who was around twenty years old. Kaduna thought there was something familiar about this young man. As it transpired, he was Asamwa's younger brother and had taken part in the last attack, looking after one of the canoes. Kaduna had not taken much notice of him at the time and wondered why this wide-eyed youth had been brought along to meet him.

The other two men sitting on the far side of the table were completely unknown to him. He couldn't help but notice that they looked a little nervous, as the light on the middle of the table cast a dim glow over their faces. One of the men, who was just a little older than Asamwa's brother, called himself Milton Pobee. He looked brighter than most as listened attentively to the conversation.

The final person in the group, who sat directly opposite Kaduna, was called John Ekpe. He appeared to be in his forties and even in the dim light, Kaduna could see he had many grey hairs. A thin moustache was visible on his upper lip and he sat hunched up with rounded shoulders. He fidgeted under the table with something on his lap and cast occasional furtive glances back and forth to Pobee and Richard as if for reassurance. This made Kaduna feel uncomfortable and impatient to find out why they sat here with Asamwa.

The beer was brought by a fat shambling waitress and plonked down unceremoniously in front of them. Then she picked up five grimy glasses, off the battered tray with her thick fingers and placed them on the table.

'Twenty-five naira,' she said in a flat monotone. Kaduna tossed some crumpled naira notes on the tray and the woman departed as slowly as she had arrived.

Kaduna declined the use of the glass, preferring instead to drink direct from one of the ice-cold bottles. He took a long draught, savoured the feel of the cold beer going down his throat, belched and thumped the bottle down on the edge of the table. Beer foamed from the top of his bottle.

'Okay Asamwa, what's going down?' he said, looking directly into his eyes.

'Well, we ain't had no action for a long time now. Me and the rest of the boys, well we is getting hungry. All the money we made the last time jost seemed to run out real quick.' Kaduna knew where the money would probably have gone, booze and whores. Fools, he thought and let the other man continue.

'So we has to do something soon or people is gonna start doing their own thing.'

'For sure, we need to find some action very soon,' Kaduna said in a level tone.

Asamwa nodded gravely then started to speak. 'Well wantin' action is one thing, but findin' it is gonna be something else,' He said, somewhat sagely for him.

'Yeah I know what you mean. The ships have been avoiding the anchor place for a few weeks now, staying way out at sea at night time. I guess they got wise at last.' Kaduna said in a flat tone. Asamwa nodded, his eyes opening larger and a small smile flickered across his thick lips, as if he were about to impart some precious gem of wisdom to those sat around the table.

'That is so, but there is another reason. Mr Ekpe who works for a shippin' agency, say the country have a depression jost now and not much cargo comin' in. That's why less ships is visitin' Lagos than before.'

'Yeah, that's not good news. I knew there was a depression, but hadn't realised it was that bad,' added Kaduna glumly.

'Anyway we got to looks at other places to find the action.'

'Yeah I was also thinking this. What is your idea?' Kaduna prompted.

'There's only one place left till things picks up, where we can find ships and cargo.'

Asamwa paused for a second.

'Inside the port.'

'Jeez.' Kaduna whistled softly, not letting the others know it was an option he had also been contemplating. 'You must be crazy. Inside the port, sounds like a bunch of trouble to me. What do you think the police are going to be doing, as we casually help ourselves to ships' cargo?'

'Well, it will be easier with the help of these three guys.' He motioned to Ekpe and Richard who nodded enthusiastically.

'You see my brother Richard?' He motioned with his index finger, to the young man on the other side of the table. 'He work in the cargo department of Bowman's agency, he's Mr Ekpe's assistant, who is the person in charge of the documents. Ekpe can find plenty of information about the cargo comin' into this port.' Asamwa was starting to talk faster now as he reached the conclusion to his story. 'He has information tellin' what's inside the containers and where they is stowed on the ship. Ekpe, show him what you have.'

The older man brought out a crumpled brown envelope from underneath the table and carefully placed it in front of himself; then pulled out a few sheets of paper and passed these across the table to Kaduna. The light in the club was poor, so Kaduna held the sheets of paper close to the dim lamp, in the centre of the table. Ekpe began to speak in slow measured tones. Kaduna could tell immediately, he had a much superior education to the others seated round the table; so he listened attentively as the clerk spoke in almost flawless English.

'These are Bills of Lading. There are three copies of each printed: one for the ship, one for the cargo receiver and one for the agents, so that they can arrange customs clearance for the inbound cargo.' He paused for a moment to let Kaduna absorb what he was reading. Kaduna nodded his head slowly as he read the information in front of him. There were container numbers and who the shipper and receivers were, but more importantly for him, the type and weight of cargo within. He nodded appreciatively. 'Very good Ekpe, but it would take hours roaming round in the dark, trying to find this particular container.'

'Not really, each ship has a cargo plan on a container vessel, or the semi-container vessels that visit Lagos regularly. The cargo plan consists of hundreds of little squares that represent a container.' He pulled more sheets of paper from the envelope which were stapled together and passed this across to Kaduna, who looked at it with a puzzled expression on his face. He told Ekpe he didn't understand what he was looking at. Ekpe smiled and said.

'That's not surprising; it takes a little practice to know these plans properly. But when someone understands the plan and has the number of a container in which he is interested, it can be located in a few moments.' Ekpe paused again.

'Okay go on, I am listening,' Kaduna prompted.

'Take for instance this container, CTIU 8731112-9. According to the Bill of Lading this is full of VCRs. Ekpe leafed expertly through the plan then half a minute later pointed out to Kaduna the location of the container on the ship. This was at number two hatch, on the port side, just close to the ship's rail.

Now Kaduna understood and the slightest hint of a smile flickered across his lips. This was indeed valuable information to have at his disposal. Now he could go right to containers full of the most valuable cargo, instead of wasting precious time breaking open dozens of boxes full of machinery and other non-transportable or low value cargo. It was in fact evident that, if the operation were planned properly, they would only have to spend a few minutes actually on board a ship. Just enough time, to unload as much of the contents of one container, as they could safely carry in four canoes.

'Very good Asamwa I like it, you have done well. I am sure we will make good use of this information. Just one thing though. Don't ask me to figure out where the bloody containers are on each ship.'

Asamwa grinned. 'No problem man that will be the job of Richard and Mr Ekpe. Pobee here will tell the stevedores on the ship, to put the box we needs at the ship's side.'

'He can do that?' Kaduna looked incredulously, at the fresh-faced youngster.

'Yeah no trouble for him, he is a clever one, so clever that they has given him the job of night foreman. Ekpe have a friend in the stevedore's office; he can have Pobee put on any ship we wants to make a hit on.'

'All sounds a bit too easy to me. There must be something that's been overlooked,' said Kaduna with a frown across his brow.

'Don't worry man. They always recons the simplest plans is the best,' Asamwa said, then let out a nervous laugh.

Kaduna continued to leaf through the Bills of Lading, as he was very interested to see what cargo this particular ship had on board. He was pleased to see Ekpe had only brought bills pertaining to valuable cargo. This ship had some exceptional cargo on board, but without this information he would never have been able to find such quality merchandise amongst five or six hundred other containers.

This was the chance he had been waiting for, the chance to make a big killing before the bubble burst, before Azubikas and his henchmen started getting too close. But he would have to ensure a tight lid was kept on this little plan. He felt the need to assert himself to those present, to ensure no one would get over confident and start talking. He put the papers down and leaned on the table looking directly into Ekpe's eyes.

'So Ekpe, why the sudden change from clerical work to thieving?' Kaduna said sternly.

The clerk had been nervous to begin with but had calmed down when describing the documents. He almost fell off his chair under the intense, blood-chilling gaze of Kaduna.

'Bbbb... because I am sick of struggling,' he blurted out. 'I have been struggling all my life to earn a decent wage, to buy some things for my family. Every year my wage stays the same, but the costs go up. I am getting poorer as the years go by. The company are bringing in younger men to do my job. I don't know how much longer I will be kept on. If I lose this job I am finished. I don't even have fifty naira savings. That is why I will do anything to try and get ahead.' The clerk looked miserable.

Kaduna believed him. He knew the state of affairs in Africa only too well. For the vast majority of people every day was a struggle, most considered themselves lucky to just have enough food to eat. He despised the little clerk as he was a hundred times better off than most and a damn sight better off than Kaduna had been just a few years ago.

But what concerned Kaduna, was Ekpe struck him as the kind of man who would soon betray him, if the wind started to blow from the other direction. Azubikas would not even have to lay a finger on this little shit to get all the information he required. Kaduna would use the man all right. Put his information to good use. Pay him well to keep him quiet, though he was unhappy at having to take on a person with an obvious moral fibre deficiency.

So he leaned over and put his face quite close to the shipping clerk and started speaking slowly in menacing measured tones.

'Now you just listen here Ekpe, as I am only going to say this one time.' He spoke just loud enough above the music, so that all those round the table could hear what he was saying.

'Yes yes, I am listening,' came the barely audible reply.

'Perhaps, you do not quite understand the situation. Well this is the way it is. By coming here tonight, you are now one of us. You are in as deep as you can get. Should you or anyone else, mention a word of this to an outsider, I will personally take a bush knife and slit that person right up the middle. Tell them, Asamwa,' he barked.

'It is true; I have seen him do much worse things.'

Kaduna relaxed and moved his face away from the clerk, grabbed his beer and took a quick draught before placing it back on the table. He leaned back in his chair and regarded the clerk. Ekpe was visibly shaken with what Kaduna had said. In fact he now wished he had not come to this place and had never met this ruffian. Kaduna could see his little demonstration of power had achieved the right result. Ekpe certainly was terrified of him now, as were the other two newcomers at the table.

He continued talking in the calm moderated tones of someone in control of a situation, with the full attention of his audience.

'So you see Ekpe, you and your friends must always make sure to do as you are told. You must always remember where your loyalty lies, as you are now one of us.'

A hint of a smile crossed Kaduna's lips as he spoke. He could see by the expressions on the faces of those sat round the table, that a crude level of respect had been instilled. The show of aggression had effectively demonstrated that Henry Kaduna was not a man to be crossed. Which he was sure would be in the forefront on their minds, should they ever be tempted to talk to the wrong people.

'Yes Ekpe, you are a now a part of our gang. Which most of the time will be a good thing. In fact, I am now going to demonstrate to you what loyalty will achieve for everyone.'

He took out a roll of naira from his jeans and passed two notes to each of the people at the table. Ekpe looked down at the two notes, afraid to take his eyes off Kaduna.

'Go on, pick them up, they are for you.' Kaduna said in a friendly, almost benevolent manner.

The clerk looked down at the two bills in front of him and eventually picked them up with a trembling hand, then held them under the dim light in the middle of the table. He could not believe how much it was. Two hundred naira, almost a months pay! He started to feel a little better, thinking perhaps this fellow Kaduna may be all right to work with after all.

Asamwa's younger brother and Milton Pobee had sat transfixed; as they watched the amiable man, who had entered the club, suddenly turn into an ogre who terrorised poor Mr Ekpe. But Kaduna's actions had made a definite impression on those two young men and their lips were effectively sealed.

Five more beers arrived. Kaduna picked one up and motioned for the others to do likewise. 'Okay brothers. Here's to our little secret and us.' the pirate said expansively.

They all murmured their approval and clinked the bottles together. Kaduna sat back and surveyed the people round the table, taking small sips of their beer as if it was almost too precious to drink. It was only to be expected he thought, as most of them could not afford the price of a beer.

'Okay Asamwa, what's the next move?'

'Well, I was lookin' at the papers Ekpe have before you com in. Looks like there is a ship coming here in a couple of days, with some good gear. Show him the document, Ekpe.'

The clerk thumbed through the Bills of Lading, till he came to the one that was required. 'Here you are this is the one I think you want, M.V. 'Southern Star.' It's due to berth here at Tin Can Port in two day's time,' he said in a remarkably calm voice, considering the trauma he had been subjected to only a few minutes earlier. He placed the paper in front of the others.

The money had worked wonders, Kaduna mused, smiling thinly as he picked up the piece of paper and read the information. It was container full of portable radio cassettes. He thought this was an excellent target. He would get a good price for that type of cargo, being the kind of merchandise always in demand by receivers. So he told the group to be ready for action the first night the vessel was in port.

With the business concluded to his satisfaction, Kaduna slowly stood up, stretched his muscular arms, and nodded his head slightly as a good-bye gesture to those sat in awe round the table. Then turned and made his way at a moderate pace out of the club. Pleased to be leaving the place, but also pleased with his night's work.

Chapter Thirteen

The empty forty-gallon drum seemed to dance in the wake of the vessel, as the withering fire from the Kalashnikov turned it into a giant colander. Though it was riddled full of holes still it would not sink, as it was being towed by a wire from the stern of the vessel. Another automatic weapon opened up and the bullets kicked up a dramatic trail of spray near the bouncing drum. A few seconds later they also found their mark, causing a great crescendo of sound as the lead struck home, rounds rattling round inside the drum adding to the din.

'That was shit shooting Korklov!' the great barrel-chested Russian master barked. 'Put another magazine in the damn gun and hit the drum next time, not the water.'

'Sorry sir, I wasn't concentrating,' the Estonian third engineer said, then deftly ejected the empty magazine and clipped a fresh one in place. He took aim, fired and hit the drum at the first attempt.

'That's more like it,' said the captain. 'Now give the gun to the second mate, let's see how he does.'

The Russian cargo vessel M.V. 'Kapitan Penkov' was on a voyage from Hong Kong to West Africa calling at Singapore and Durban, it had deviated twenty miles to the east of the trade route to enable the live firing practice to be conducted. Almost half of the ships crew were congregated on the poop deck, firing various weapons from the vessel's arsenal at the drum towed behind. Other smaller paint drums and tins, saved specially for this occasion, were thrown into the water, for practice at moving targets. The crew for the greater part were excellent marksmen, having learned that skill during their conscription into the Russian Army.

After half an hour, the captain was satisfied and the crew returned the weapons a special locker in the main deck alleyway. When they were all stowed back in their racks, Commissar Kaminsky locked the heavy steel door. Only he and the captain had a key for this. The seamen then returned to their various duties, leaving one of the oilers from the engine room to sweep the spent cartridges over the ship's rail into the sea.

Later that night as he leaned on the end of the bridge wing, looking out across a glassy calm sea, Tomas Kolskis, the second mate, wondered if the practice they had taken part in that afternoon was really necessary. In the ten years he had been at sea, they had never had to fire weapons in anger. Though in some ports the watchman on the gangway had a rifle, to remind the locals that it was a Russian vessel they were boarding. That was a remarkably effective procedure, as thieving was only really encountered in ports, where there was no armed watchman. An interesting fact, he thought.

He had just spent the last half hour inside the wheelhouse, peering into the screen of the antiquated radar. A combination of the heat from the equipment and the heavy tropical night air had made the atmosphere in the wheelhouse almost unbearable.

So while everything was quiet, he decided to have a short break from the radar and was now enjoying the steady flow of cool air, as he leaned on the ships rail. It was the most tranquil of nights, with a flat calm sea and although the sky was not clear, the moon peeped through occasionally and cast a dull silvery glow over the water. The ship had no rolling or pitching motion movement, as it powered forward at a shade over sixteen knots. It was hard to believe the ship was actually at sea. The storms of the North Pacific he'd encountered on previous ships, when they had almost pounded themselves to bits, a distant memory to him now.

It was a little over three days, since the vessel had completed loading in Hong Kong and headed down the buoyed channel, between the rocky steep sided islands of Victoria and Lamma, then turned southwards towards Singapore. A very quiet trip so far, the captain's fear of a pirate behind every island so far proved unfounded.

However, he had stressed to them all earlier that day in his own unique emphatic style, that no relaxing of vigilance would be tolerated, as now they were entering the area of highest pirate attack incidence. The second mate had a sailor and a cadet to assist in look out duties on the bridge. He was also in radio contact with the carpenter and three sailors, who were patrolling the deck armed with pistols. Personally, he thought the Old Man was being too cautious, almost paranoid in fact.

As he stood on the bridge wing, making the most of his short break from the discomfort and monotony of the radar screen, his thoughts drifted back to the previous trip, when the ship had visited New Zealand. 28 days in Wellington to discharge 850 tons of general cargo. The stevedores were on strike for most of the time and everyone on board had a great time. There were many parties on the ship and ashore and a plethora of lovely willing girls.

His reverie was suddenly shattered, by an excited call from the cadet on the radar.

'Small targets, dead ahead range five miles.'

His pulse quickened as he walked swiftly from the bridge wing to the radar. A few long strides and he was peering over the cadet's shoulder onto the circular radar screen. He watched the rhythmic sweep of the scan for a few moments, to confirm what the cadet had reported. Sure enough, there ahead of the vessel, were the barely perceptible blips of small targets fading in and out. One sweep the targets would be there and the next they would be gone.

It was one of two things, his years of training and watch keeping experience made him think. Either debris floating of the surface of the sea, or small wooden boats…

He picked up the heavy cast iron telephone on the end of the control console next to the radar, and dialled the master's number. It rang only once, before he heard his gruff voice.

'Yes what is it?' the captain enquired somewhat testily.

'Problems sir,' the second mate paused for a moment. 'Small echoes dead ahead, I don't like the look of it.'

'Right, I am coming up,' the crisp reply came from below. The captain was now fully awake and alert.

Within a minute Captain Borisenko was on the bridge. Even in the dim light of the wheelhouse, the second mate could see he had dressed hurriedly. Shirt hanging out from the back of his trousers and his hair which he had no time to comb, sticking out at various angles.

'So what have we got, Second Mate?'

'Look there sir, dead ahead. We have three faint echoes painting in and out.' The second mate pointed to the targets on the radar screen. The ship's master reached an instant decision.

'Alter course twenty degrees to starboard away from the buggers.'

The alteration meant the ship would pass roughly half a mile, from the unidentified craft.

'Tell the deck patrol to be alert.' The captain spoke quickly, tersely.

'Yes sir, do you want me to sound the emergency stations alarm?'

'No don't do that, you bloody idiot, it will just send everyone into a blind panic.' The captain berated the second mate, who cringed slightly at the rebuke. The cadet, glad to see someone else at the mercy of the Old Man's wrath, stifled a gleeful snigger. As they closed rapidly with the craft all eyes on the bridge strained through powerful binoculars for the first sight of the targets.

The second mate standing at the radar screen clicked the large black bakelite switch on the right hand panel and altered the range to three miles. The sinister targets became larger and consequently clearer. They were four points on the port bow range one mile and would pass the beam at a distance of just over six cables, 0.6 of a mile.

Pulses quickened and breathing became shallower, nerves became stretched taut. Everyone had heard many stories about the atrocities pirates had committed. In this part of the world rumour had it, the callous pirates cut off the noses of their victims as souvenirs.

'Switch on the bridge wing searchlights.' The master shouted to the cadet on the bridge wing.

Almost in unison, two powerful fingers of light stabbed through the darkness and illuminated the three passing craft.

The second mate standing on the bridge wing with the cadet, expected to witness an attempted boarding by a pirate gang, but was stunned by the spectacle dramatically illuminated just over half a mile away. It was not boats full of armed pirates, but boats packed so full of people, they were almost sinking under the weight of humanity. He realised immediately what he was witnessing and said quietly, 'My God! Refugees, Vietnamese boat people…'

It was a pitiful sight. The boats were old and decrepit, wallowing slowly as they passed the vessel. These people must indeed be desperate. For so many to cram onto these hulks and risk their lives on a hazardous journey, across the South China Sea from Vietnam to these Indonesian Islands. But they lived with the hope of being picked up by a merciful ship during the journey. The craft were seriously un-seaworthy and would undoubtedly sink in any kind of moderate wind. Typhoons were not uncommon at this time of year, which served to further illustrate how desperate they were to escape.

The three boats were now clearly visible. The people on board were waving wildly at the passing ship, jabbering away to each other in their own language and shouting at the ship. The occasional shout of help could be heard above the din. The Russians on the bridge, stood transfixed by the scene.

The second mate couldn't help but notice that the packed craft were all deep in the water and that it would take virtually nothing to swamp and sink them. His seaman's eye was quick to recognize the perilous motion of these ancient craft, as they came into contact with the wake of the M.V. 'Kapitan Penkov'. They were rolling slowly, laboriously, their spindly masts describing large arcs, on the shiny surface of the water. The sea eating hungrily at the pitifully small freeboard and spilling eagerly onto the decks, soaking the wretched people who sat there, further compounding their misery.

The ponderous motion was a positive indication to him that, due to the overcrowding of the craft, they were dangerously short of stability. In imminent danger of capsize and sinking, with virtually all of the refugees perishing. It was clear in his mind what had to happen next. They would have to slow down, turn the vessel round and rescue these people. Most of his compatriots on the bridge were of the same persuasion. He turned to the captain, who was standing deep in thought behind him and spoke urgently.

'Shall I phone the engine room, sir and tell them we will be slowing down?'

'You will do no such thing,' the master replied sternly.

'But sir, these people are desperate, they need our help. For pity's sake sir, their boats are about to sink. They are in distress. We have to pick them up, it's the law.'

'Law, how dare you tell me what law is? I'm the law round here. Their cursed boats got them all the way from Vietnam to here; they can take them a bit further. Besides, there's an island close by and a patrol craft from the Indonesian Navy could come out at any time and help them.'

The second mate realised that it was pointless to try and argue with him. Obviously there remained not a grain of compassion in the man's body. He felt frustrated and angry, but there was nothing he could do. Control of the situation was completely out of his hands. As it happened, the captain did have compassion for the refugees.

The master had in fact just spent agonising minutes wrestling with his conscience. But he refused to let it cloud his mind, in deciding the best course of action. He left the small silent morose crowd on the bridge wing and went towards the wheelhouse. He passed Kaminsky the commissar who was standing just out side the door, a smug look on his loathsome face. He was not happy with what he had done, but knowing the implications and problems involved, was satisfied his decision was the only sensible course of action he could take.

A number of masters held the opinion, that the concept of distress and the boat people was ambiguous. Open to discussion. Not cut and dried. There to be interpreted, as you saw fit. Some masters at the slightest sign of refugee boats, would alter course many miles away from the craft to avoid physically seeing them in distress. Others would stop and give them food, water and fuel for their boats, without actually picking them up. But the ships which took refugees on board would then invariably be faced, with a delay of many days off-hire in Singapore, while a wrangle ensued as to what would happen to the hapless people.

These factors had influenced Captain Borisenko's decision not to pick up the boat people. Besides he thought ruefully, if they had known his nationality, they may well have preferred to stay on their rotting hulks. Anyway they would probably be all right. They were after all close to the island. The matter was closed as far as he was concerned. He had enough to think about in the next two days.

As he stood on the bridge wing, watching the pathetic craft disappear into the night astern of the vessel, Thomas Kolskis was sickened by the captain's decision, though not surprised. He was a heartless bastard, everyone on board knew that. He wondered what would happen to the people on the craft, perhaps some would not last until rescued. The whole scenario was too depressing to continue contemplating. Anyway, he had to alter course soon so he turned and made his way into the wheelhouse.

After the second mate had brought the vessel onto the new course, he checked the position again and plotted it on the chart. Then he returned to the radar, to check for approaching traffic. The small echoes of the three refugee boats could still be seen, faintly astern on the radar screen. Then suddenly, dramatically, another echo appeared from close to the island. Larger and travelling quite fast, as it left a distinctive white trail on the screen of the radar. Good he thought, perhaps the captain was right after all. It could be a patrol boat from the island. He felt better now, knowing the poor souls were going to be rescued.

He was wrong about the other boat. It was not a rescue craft, but a boat crammed full of Indonesian pirates, who in the next half hour, would bring unimaginable hell to the unfortunate refugees.

Chapter Fourteen

'You has to wake op,' said the Air Afrique stewardess gruffly in a heavy African accent.

Ellis blearily opened his eyes, which slowly focused on the apparition standing in the aisle a few feet away. The overweight Ivorian stewardess in an ill-fitting green uniform was just about the last thing he would have wished to see on awakening.

'We will be landing in Ouagadougou in five minutes,' she announced matter of factly.

He sat up in his seat which was by the window, pulled up the blind and looked out. 'God what a place,' he thought. Nothing but brown scrub and parched grass as far as the eye could see. He wondered how people could exist in such a harsh environment. The plane by this time was quite low in the sky and he saw what looked like wildebeest stampeding, throwing up a cloud of dust as they ran, and proof at least that the land could sustain some life.

Ellis was unable to recall exactly where Ouagadougou was located. But after a few moments the mist cleared from his sleep-impaired mind and he remembered. It was in fact the capital of Burkina Faso, which used to be called Upper Volta. He decided he liked the original name better. He would have preferred the direct British Caledonian flight from Gatwick to Lagos, but unfortunately that had been fully booked. The last remaining available flight was Air Afrique from Paris to Abidjan, capital of the Ivory

Coast, via Ouagadougou. He would then take a connecting flight from Abidjan to Lagos.

It had been a lousy flight. The service was non-existent, the seats were very uncomfortable and the cabin crew sullen. The plane itself was an ancient twenty-year-old DC 10 in serious need of refurbishment. In fact he mused, if he was not mistaken, an aircraft this type had crashed in the desert the previous year. Whether it was one of this carrier's planes or not did not perturb him in the least, as he had a totally fatalistic attitude to flying.

As the plane skimmed low over the city on its approach to the airport, he started to get his first impression of the extent of the squalor of modern day Africa. Something his cosseted life as a child in Lagos had not seen. The buildings of the city were all one-storey flat roofed mud dwellings, which were traversed with rutted litter strewn mud tracks. As the aircraft descended steadily, he could see rangy goats and cows wandering aimlessly in the streets, oblivious to the din of the plane overhead. Ragged children could also be seen playing games amongst the garbage and wrecked cars. It was obviously a very poor place, even by African standards, he concluded and he felt genuinely sorry for the inhabitants.

Once the plane had landed, a trickle of people disembarked. Strangely many more joined and the flight was almost full for the final leg to Abidjan. He assumed the reason for this must be, the lack of daily flights linking Ouagadougou to the outside world. When the plane was safely airborne and heading south to the capital of the Ivory Coast, he took out his briefcase and continued to read the voluminous notes he had been given in relation to his new undercover job. He was going to be a surveyor for the Britannic Protection and Indemnity Club, or P & I Club, as it is referred to in shipping circles.

P & I Clubs handled the insurance of vessels, other than the hull and machinery. Hull insurers, such as Lloyds of London and the Swedish Club, covered those two main items. The type of insurance covered by a typical P & I Club would be: liabilities for damage to a third party, damage caused by ship to shore installations, (such as jetties or cranes), oil pollution damage, accidents to personnel and all the related costs of the accident, cargo damage caused by weather or other means and theft of cargo or personal effects.

Shipping companies joined a P & I Club and paid a certain premium each year to have their vessels covered. If claims were low then the P & I Club made a substantial profit and might give a rebate to the companies in the Club. However if there was a major claim, such as a huge oil spill, settlement could run into hundreds of millions of pounds. The Club that had insured the vessel in question would take a financial pounding and have to dig deep into their reserves of capital, accumulated from profitable years. Premiums of course would then go up the next year to compensate the Club for the loss.

It was a good system, which all parties concerned were satisfied with. The ship owner had the knowledge, that he was fully covered for all losses his vessel might incur. The persons claiming against vessels were always paid, and more years than not, the Clubs always came out ahead of the game.

Piracy however, was a continual thorn in the side of the P & I Clubs. Though compared to a major catastrophe like an oil tanker going aground, the money payable for an incident of piracy was not so substantial. But gradually over the years, it was starting to amount to a considerable sum. So when Commander Roberts at the London branch of Interpol, phoned the Britannic P & I Club and mentioned he needed cover for an agent to operate in Lagos, they were only too pleased to accommodate that request. The Britannic had at that time, actually been considering hiring a special investigator, to try to get to the bottom of the piracy problem in Nigeria. But Interpol's request had now obviated that need.

As far as the correspondent in Lagos was aware, the new surveyor was just a replacement for the one who had resigned two months previously. That particular surveyor had only stayed for six months of his twelve-month contract. Finding replacements was never easy, as Nigeria was a country where surveyors were loath to be posted. Places like Singapore, Tokyo or Miami were much more appealing locations to spend a year and those offices never had a problem with replacements. In fact, surveyors often asked to extend their contracts in those locations.

The plane droned on southwards and Ellis put down the file he was reading, rubbed his forehead gently and leaned back in the Spartan comfort of his seat. He hoped his mind had soaked up enough knowledge, about P & I Clubs and the shipping industry in the last three days, to sound convincing to his new employer. Fortunately for him, he had a virtual photographic memory and had only to read most things once. When his boss told him what his cover would be in Lagos, Ellis protested vehemently that he would never be able to learn enough to convincingly do that job. His boss dismissed his protests with a casual wave of the hand, saying, 'A doddle of a job, Martin. You go on a ship, look around and then fill in a form about what you have seen. Child of four could do it.'

Now that he had read extensively on the subject, he realized a child probably could do a P & I surveyor's job. Providing the child knew all the rules and regulations regarding safety of life at sea, statutory instruments, merchant shipping M-Notices and the pertinent IMO regulations and resolutions.

In addition to learning as much as possible about a surveyor's work, Ellis also had to have comprehensive knowledge of his previous service in the merchant navy. What companies he was supposed to have been with, the composition of and nationalities of the crews on board and where the ships had traded. What college he attended to do his exams, even some of the names of the lecturers and examiners. Luckily there had been a sergeant in the London office, who had served at sea for six years rising to the rank of third mate, before tiring of the life. He had given Ellis an extensive cover story, which he had now just about memorized.

For the rest of the flight to Abidjan, Ellis read a book called 'The Ship Surveyor'. It covered a tedious subject well and was interesting in places and easy to follow. Occasionally he would glance out of the window, at the scenery below and was amazed how quickly it had turned from arid scrub to verdant jungle. Almost as if painted by a landscape artist, who enjoyed dramatic clashes of colour? This lush greenery lasted till the plane arrived at Abidjan on the coast.

He spent an uncomfortable hour in the sweltering heat of the transit lounge, waiting for his connecting flight. When eventually he boarded the plane, he was pleased to be moving once again. Air Ivoire was the carrier for the fifty-five minute flight to Lagos, on a Mark 1 Boeing 727, a more modern plane than the previous flight, if only slightly.

As they approached Lagos just before sunset, Ellis found the view quite depressing. A shanty town of corrugated iron huts seemed to stretch from one horizon to the next. He cringed at the abject squalor and in a way was glad it would be dark soon. The 727 touched down in Lagos at four minutes past seven, just as in the distance the sun dipped beneath the silvery horizon on the Gulf of Guinea.

He was back in Nigeria with mixed feelings, a heady cocktail of apprehension and excitement. Ellis was concerned to be working alone on this case in a hostile environment. Also about the role to be acted out, whilst trying to surreptitiously gain information to achieve his objective. He resolved to take each day as it came, be patient and not become a victim of rashness. As he walked across the tarmac towards the arrivals hall, the early evening air was like an invisible barricade of heat and humidity. The heavy smell of vegetation, mixed with the smell of wood fires hung in the air.

There was a long queue at the immigration desk and it seemed to take forever until his turn eventually came. The acerbic immigration officer, wearing a light green uniform, took Ellis's passport and scanned through the pages with snail like slowness, almost as if he was searching for some information of national importance.

'You cannot enter Nigeria,' the man said eventually, looking up at Ellis with rheumy but impassive eyes.

'What!' He was flabbergasted. 'Why not?' he demanded, his voice rising slightly.

'There is no use getting angry with me. It is not my fault that you do not have a visa.'

'I don't need a visa. That is a British passport and Nigeria is a commonwealth country!'

'I am aware of that fact. But you still need a visa. It looks like you will have to get back on the plane and go back to where you came from.'

'This is ridiculous. I want to see your superior officer.' Ellis demanded.

'That won't be possible, it is now night time and he will not be here till morning. You only have one possibility.' The officer looked directly into his eyes and lifted his eyebrows slightly.

'Oh I see,' Ellis said quietly, now realising what the man was about. 'Could twenty dollars help the situation?'

The man nodded. Ellis took his passport back and deftly slipped a note from his pocket into this. He passed it back to the official, who took the money then stamped the book. Ellis found the situation faintly amusing. The tentacles of corruption had spread to such an extent in this country, as to be waiting to greet un-suspecting new arrivals.

By the time he had retrieved his two grips from the creaking battered aluminium carousel, another large bustling queue had built up at the customs checkpoint. Most cases were being opened by over zealous customs officers. When his turn arrived, another twenty dollars ensured his uninterrupted passage. Almost an hour after landing, he eventually walked exhausted out into the main hall of the airport.

There was the usual crowd that expectantly awaits a newly arrived plane. Necks craning in search of loved ones. He noticed a few people standing round with name boards and was pleased to see his name neatly written in thick black letters on one of these. A slim white man of medium height, around forty years old, held the board. His hair was slicked back over his head and he was dressed in loose fitting tan coloured trousers and a striped short-sleeved shirt. Ellis brightened and walked confidently up to the man and introduced himself. 'Hello, I think I am the person you are looking for. I'm Martin Ellis.'

'Glad to meet you, Martin. I'm Captain Ronald H. Wilson. Just call me Ronnie, everyone else does round here.'

They shook hands and the man took one of his grips.

'Have a good flight?'

'Not really. Air Afrique.'

'Ah! Well they're crap.' The man sighed knowingly and then added, 'A pity you couldn't have got the BCal flight.'

'That was full up unfortunately,' Ellis replied evenly, and then continued, 'bit of a performance getting through immigration as well. The chap said I needed a visa. I had to pay twenty dollars in the end.'

'Welcome to Nigeria, Martin. They always pull that trick.'

The man led him out of the airport building, past a number of beggars who touted to carry the bags and received polite, though firm rebuffs for their efforts. Ronnie had a newish looking Peugeot 604 and they were soon on their way along the freeway towards Apapa. The patter of the tyres evident as they passed over poorly tarred gaps in the concrete road.

After a while Ronnie spoke. 'So I believe this is your first job as a surveyor.'

Ellis had been dreading this moment. The inquisition was about to begin… 'Err… Yes.'

'You sound worried, don't be, there is nothing to the job. A kid could do it, if the truth were known.' Ellis almost burst out laughing and barely managed to control himself.

'Anyway, I've been at this game a long time, so any questions you have, don't be afraid to ask. We will be going round ships together initially, till you get the hang of things.'

'Oh. That's good to hear, thanks.'

'Believe me; your biggest problem will be putting up with living in Nigeria. Most new surveyors don't stay the full year.'

'I should be all right on that score. I was actually born here, so I have a good idea of what the place is like.'

Ronnie unexpectedly changed tack in the conversation. 'So where did you do your time?' The question caught Ellis completely off guard. 'What the hell did he mean by time?'

'Pentonville,' he said quickly. Ronnie laughed.

'Very good, I did my time with Bank Line. Same as Pentonville, only the food was worse.'

Damn! He now realised what time meant. What company had he served his apprenticeship with? 'I did mine with Ellerman's,' he replied, a little hesitantly.

'City, Wilson's or Pap's?' Ronnie said matter of factly. He was enumerating the three companies making up Ellerman's shipping group. Luckily Ellis had been briefed.

'Err… Ellerman City Liners actually.'

'Fine company, how many ships have they got left now?'

'Around twenty-six, they sold another five general cargo ships recently.'

It was fortunate for Ellis that he got that right, Ronnie, being an avid reader on anything regarding shipping, already knew that fact.

Ellis managed to answer most of the man's questions adequately and was glad when they arrived at the small apartment block in Harbour Road Apapa twenty minutes after leaving the airport. A brick wall topped with broken glass surrounded the building like the rest in that road. Ronnie tooted the horn and after a few seconds, the metal gate creaked open. An elderly African appeared from behind the gate.

'That's Eric, our security guard.' Ronnie said a hint of sarcasm in his voice.

Ellis could see the man was quite old and had a limp. The ancient mottled uniform and a crumpled peaked hat he wore, served only to make him look even more bizarre. Ellis wondered wryly, how much security he actually provided.

He nodded and smiled at Ronnie as he opened up the other gate.

'Everything quiet Eric?'

'Yes sah. Everythin's fine. Everythin's real fine.'

Martin Ellis however, felt far from fine.

Chapter Fifteen

The three large dug out canoes, were completely hidden in the dense marsh rushes, on the west side of Badagry Creek. Powerful Evinrude engines stowed, the pirates had used paddles to silently reach this position, directly opposite the wharves of Tin Can Port in Apapa. The marsh toads that croaked incessantly, reminded the pirates they were not alone in the swamp. The shriek of a marsh hen calling its mate pierced the still night air from time to time. Insects crawled over them and mosquitoes bit constantly. A white man would have found the conditions unbearable. But all of these men had known much worse in their lives than simple discomfort. To a man, they all had a history of deprivation and virtual starvation. Days where a handful of roots, picked out of the desert scrub, or rotting scraps from a garbage bin, had to suffice as sustenance.

As they waited, watched and listened, a louder mechanical sound could be heard every few minutes. The low buzz of the electric cranes on the container ship, M.V. 'Southern Star' punctuated the almost still night air. The ship was moored opposite the pirates on berth 23 alone in Tin Can Port. The three twenty-five ton Lieber cranes worked methodically along the deck, discharging the cargo of containers, which had been loaded a few weeks previously in Asia. Crane jibs tracing shallow arcs, across the star-studded black velvet curtain, which was the African night sky, as they went efficiently about their work.

The pirates watched the scene, transfixed, licking dry lips, hearts beating steadily as the minutes dragged into hours.

'Jesus this waitin' is killin' me,' Omboko said, rather impatiently.

'Shut up you idiot,' Kaduna hissed.

'Wait and watch, we will be moving soon enough.'

'I thought Pobee was gonna fix everythin' for us.'

'He is but it takes time to set up,' Kaduna said irritably.

'We should have done a ship at the anchorage .We pick our own time to attack there, instead of waiting for some other bastard.'

'Yeah and what did you get? Garbage most nights. This way we move fast, hit one box and we are history in a few minutes. Now shut up or else!'

Omboko could tell by the inflection in Kaduna's voice that he was not joking and settled back against the gunwale of the canoe, closed his eyes and tried to relax. Soon his thoughts turned to the young fourteen-year-old schoolgirl he had ravished that afternoon. But she wasn't so young really. He could tell she had lost her virginity many years previously. Still, she was nice.

On the fore deck of the container ship, Bob Holden the tall genial second mate from Hull was almost two and a half hours into his watch. The graveyard shift as it was known, from midnight to six in the morning. He looked at the battered scratched Timex on his wrist, rubbed his eyes and yawned. The luminous dial read two twenty-five. He sighed, thinking it was later than that. It was always the same on this watch, minutes seemed like hours, no one to talk with and pass away some of the time. The ship's officers and crew by now would be tucked up nicely in bed inside the cool accommodation.

It had been a very unpleasant watch; the heat had been quite oppressive. The stench from the human excrement on the jetty fenders nauseating and the stevedore foreman, a new guy called Pobee, extremely arrogant and quite uncooperative. In fact, he could see him walking haughtily along the deck towards him at that moment, as if he owned the ship. He was glad he didn't have to go searching for him, as he had a question to ask the scrawny, poorly dressed Nigerian.

'Foreman!' he called.

'Yeah?' came the sullen reply.

'What the hell is happening up at number two hatch? I see one of the containers that was on the middle tier has not been discharged but is sitting on the hatch top.'

'There is a problem with the customs papers for that one. It has to stay there till the mornin'.' The foreman brightened slightly, and then added. 'I hope that's okay, Second.'

'Yes that's okay. But in future tell me if any containers have to stay on board. Oh, and I don't like it so close to the ship's side. Get the crane driver to shift it back into the centre of the hatch.'

'Sure thing Second, as soon as he comes back from his break I will tell him.'

'You better not forget.'

'Don't worry my friend, don't worry. I will fix it.' Pobee then patted the second mate reassuringly on the back and sauntered off along the deck.

Bob Holden did not like people touching him, especially ones he despised and when the foreman patted him condescendingly on the back, he almost rebuked the man. But it was late, he was very tired and he did not wish to become embroiled in an argument with him, though something did trouble him. When Pobee patted his back, he thought he felt a slight prick. It must have been the rough seam of his overall against his skin he concluded and proceeded aft towards the accommodation to obtain a cold drink.

On his way to the accommodation, Bob Holden had to pick his way gingerly along the deck, taking care not to stand on any sleeping bodies. The pay was so poor for the stevedores, that most of them worked both the day and the night shift and consequently spent most of the night shift, asleep on cocoa mats scattered around the deck of the vessel.

Like the majority of the officers and the crew, he really hated coming to Nigeria. Everything was a hassle. The accommodation and the stores had to be kept locked. Nothing could be left lying round the deck. Not even a simple ring spanner or a small rope tail for a mooring rope. It would all be stolen, quicker than you could blink an eye. Even the containers were fitted with special locks, which made it difficult for thieves to open them. The manufacturer was continually improving these securing devices. But as the latest version of these locks was brought into service, thieves would find a new way to break them. This created a never-ending self-perpetuating circle.

The only compensation on this vessel, as far as Bob Holden was concerned, being that nearly all the officers were British. The only non Brit. on board was the third mate from India. A strange moody and unpredictable character called Sunil, who no-one on the vessel particularly liked. So him apart there was a decent social life on board. Even so, everyone looked forward immensely to finishing the coast in West Africa and heading back to Asia, via Durban in South Africa.

After a few minutes he reached the accommodation, let himself in and savoured for a delicious moment the almost icy air-conditioned air inside. He took his shoes off and went to the bar to get a soft drink from the well-stocked fridge.

Around five minutes later, he returned from the almost polar air of the accommodation onto the sweltering deck, slowly sipping a can of coke. But something did not feel right. He thought it was just the transition, from the cold accommodation to the heat of the deck. Then he noticed there was a tingling sensation in his shoulder. He rubbed his shoulder, to try and dissipate the irritation. He was starting to feel light headed and a little nauseous. This strange feeling became steadily worse, until a few minutes later; his head was spinning with dizziness. He sat down on a crate bewildered and felt like vomiting. Just before passing out, the stark realism of what had happened struck him. My God! He thought, 'the little bastard's drugged me!'

Pobee smiled as he saw the officer slump over on the crate. The juice of the Lipia tree was a potent drug. They had used it in his local village on the tips of arrows to kill game. Lesser amounts had worked well to drug people in the past, who usually woke up in one or two hours, feeling like a water buffalo had kicked them in the head. The second mate however, was not the only one sleeping soundly, on the deck of the M.V. 'Southern Star.' The four Filipino seamen, who had been on security watch, were also out for the count. Pobee had drugged them a few minutes before his encounter with the officer.

The two armed navy sailors on board would not be a problem. In fact, they might even help to unload the container. He went quickly onto the foredeck, told one of the stevedores, to open the doors of the red container on number two hatch. Then he let out a shrill piercing whistle across the creek. One hundred metres away at the edge of the marsh three Evinrudes' coughed then sprung into life. The canoes burst dramatically into view, bows high in the water as they sped across the short stretch of creek towards the ship. Meanwhile at number two hatch, the stevedores had virtually emptied the container and had positioned most of the contents close to the ship's rail, waiting for the arrival of the canoes.

When the craft came alongside, the stevedores haphazardly threw into the large dugout canoes below buff coloured cardboard cartons marked 'Sony Japan' full of radio cassettes. Some of these narrowly missed the pirates, who screamed back obscenities to those above. There was much excitement and shouting. Very soon the canoes were piled high with cartons, some of which were dented, damaged by the exuberance of the stevedores participating in the heist. The armed navy sailors, contrary to what Pobee thought, did not participate in the theft, but stood bemused close by, watching the spectacle below them.

Bill Jackson was the master of the 'Southern Star'. He was a dour Yorkshire man in his early fifties, of medium height with a powerful physique. That particular night he retired early but had slept very little, spending most of the time tossing and turning on his bed. By the nature of the job, he worried a lot. After all he was responsible for everything that happened on the ship. Lagos was a bad place to be on a ship, with the constant worry of pirates and thieves who could strike at any time.

Lying on his bed, looking up at the ceiling, he could feel the ship roll from side to side, as the twenty-ton containers were discharged from the deck. This was a normal motion for a ship of this type and did not trouble him. He could hear the buzz of the cranes intensify, as the heavy containers were picked up. The huge electric crane motors, straining to heave in the thirty-millimetre diameter crane wire. Every so often a bang or thud could be heard, but these were not unusual sounds. As careless crane drivers, occasionally allowed the container they were discharging to collide with another container, or part of the ship's structure.

All of those sounds that night were familiar to him. It was only when he heard the sound of a great commotion on deck, that he sat up in bed with a start and realised immediately something was seriously wrong. He picked up the Motorola walkie-talkie lying on the table close to his bed and spoke anxiously into the microphone.

'Come in Second Mate. What the hell is happening on deck?'

He waited a couple of tense seconds, expecting to hear the second mate's response. This never came.

'Come in Second Mate.' He was speaking more impatiently this time, but still no response came. 'Perhaps his batteries are dead or he is next to a crane,' thought the captain.

'Come in duty A.B. or Bosun.' He tried to contact other members of the deck watch a number of times.

After a few seconds with no reply, he became seriously concerned. Why was no one on deck responding to his call? He jumped off the bed and quickly put on a pair of shorts, rushed out of his cabin and up one flight of stairs to the bridge to get a clearer view. When he arrived on the bridge, he peered anxiously out of the window at the front and saw an open container near the rail at number 2 hatch. Men were throwing boxes from this over the ship's rail; he assumed there must be canoes waiting below. To get a better view, he proceeded across the wheelhouse in the direction of the bridge wing and was surprised to find the door open. The reason for this became abundantly clear when he went outside. Someone was stood at the outboard end of the bridge wing. It was the Indian third mate Sunil, resplendent in his baggy Asian pyjamas, leaning over the Taff rail at the end. It took the captains steely eyes a split second to realise what was happening. The full horror of the situation he had stumbled upon, hit him like a sledgehammer blow. The third mate had the ship's distress flare pistol clasped in both hands, pointing forward in the direction of the canoes.

Less than a mile away, like the captain of the Southern Star, Ellis also had slept fitfully since going to bed at eleven-thirty. The drinks with Wilson, out on the balcony of the large airy apartment, had calmed his nerves slightly and helped him to get to sleep initially. But the bed was uncomfortable and the pillow smelt of stale sweat. Also his mind was still buzzing, with the barrage of questions Wilson had subjected him to. He felt his answers, were becoming less and less convincing. This man certainly was astute and an experienced seaman and would probably by now have seen through his story.

Ellis drifted in and out of sleep, but was suddenly awakened by a dull thud. Still lying on the bed he instinctively turned and looked towards the window. The curtain was only partially closed and saw a bright lingering, incandescent flash that pierced the darkness outside. It was the kind of flash that he would normally associate with some kind of flare.

'Stroll on…!' he said aloud. He got of the bed and went quickly to the window. He opened the glass door and went out onto the balcony. Wilson was already there. A dull glow lit up the inky black night about a mile or so away, just out of sight on the other side of the harbour. Then he saw another flare, come from the top of the shadowy outline of a ship, before it disappeared downwards and out of sight.

'What the hell is happening?'

'Looks like our pirate friends are becoming really daring nowadays.'

'How do you mean?'

'Well this is the first time to my knowledge; they have had the balls to try anything in the port.'

Ellis thought for a moment before speaking. 'Looks like they are getting some of their own medicine from the ship.'

Wilson sighed. 'I sincerely hope they haven't hit any of the pirates with that flare gun. Or there will be all hell to pay.'

'But surely the ship is only defending itself?'

The balcony was dimly lit, so Ellis could not see the expression of astonishment on Wilson's face. He was amazed at the naivety of his associate's remark and it further served to confirm his suspicions about this person. Wilson waited a few seconds, and then replied in an even tone.

'Fraid the Nigerian police will not see it like that. It will just be another lever to be used to get money out of the ship owner. You and I will be up to our necks in the proverbial, trying to sort the mess out.'

Ellis realised he had said the wrong thing and tried to make amends.

'You'll have to excuse me. This stuff's all a bit…'

Wilson cut him off before he could finish the statement.

'I accept it may be new to you Martin, but I would have expected you to be a little more genned up than that. Anyone who knows anything about our business, could tell you that the best way to get yourself killed in a pirate attack is to resist. Also, the quickest way to wind up in jail in a port is to shoot someone, pirate, thief or whatever.'

Ellis felt slightly embarrassed at the rebuke, even if it was justified. What happened next rocked him back on his heels.

Wilson turned slowly round and looked straight towards him. 'I think it's time you levelled with me Martin. I could tell in the car on the way back from the airport, that you have never been on a ship in your life. So would you be so kind as to tell me exactly who the hell you are and what you are doing in Lagos?'

Ellis stood in silence for few moments, looking out towards the port, weighing up his alternatives. He quickly came to the conclusion, that any more lies would not enhance his position here. He turned his head slightly towards Wilson, before speaking quietly and deliberately.

'My name is Martin Ellis, Inspector Martin Ellis actually, from Interpol in London.' He paused briefly, to assess the effect of his words.

'Yes… Very interesting. Please carry on.' Wilson prompted in a clipped tone.

Ellis told Wilson the whole story, how he had been sent here to try and find out the identity of the pirate leader. Also that he was given the job because of his previous connections with Nigeria. It took almost ten minutes to tell the whole tale. During this time the other man leaning on the rail of the balcony barely moved, except to swat the occasional bug or mosquito that came too close. Wilson said very little, just the occasional 'yes,' 'I see,' or 'please carry on.' Ellis could tell he was methodically absorbing and analysing everything he said.

'…So there you have it, the whole unabridged truth, nothing left out.'

Wilson stood upright and faced Ellis, who also turned round and back from the rail. 'Excellent! We have needed someone like you here for years, Ronnie Wilson at your service.' He held out his hand. Ellis took it and shook it for the second time that day.

The raid had gone like clockwork, the signal, alongside in under a minute, the cartons full of cassette radios rapidly thrown into the canoes. Even if some had hit his men, the most they suffered was a few bruises. Three large boats piled high with extremely valuable and saleable cargo, ready to make a timely escape into cover of the stygian blackness of the African night and all achieved in less than five minutes. It was beyond Kaduna's imagination, that it could have all gone so smoothly.

That was until he heard a bang and huge ball of fire hit one of his men, exploding red hot phosphorous and sodium, over his chest, arms and face. The man fell writhing and screaming amongst the cartons, which quickly ignited around him. Smoke from the cartons and the burning man, made Kaduna's eyes smart. The awful stench of burning flesh choked him. In a few seconds, the adventure had turned from resounding success, to potential disaster.

Another flare fizzed overhead, landing in the water a few metres from his canoe. They were under attack. Kaduna had to think fast or the fire would spread quickly, aft to the engine and the petrol tank.

'What can we do? Abokwe is fired!' screamed one of the pirates.

Kaduna's reply had been firm and instantaneous. 'Dump him in the bloody river.'

'No! He's my brother. We has to save him,' came the anguished reply.

Kaduna took out a silver pistol from the holster at his side and pointed it at the pirate nearest the screaming burning man.

'Dump him, or both of you will be rotting in the river tomorrow.'

The man could see Kaduna was deadly serious, so dared not argue and complied rapidly with the order. Another two pirates, who were close at hand, assisted him. Soon the burning man was manhandled, writhing, screaming and pleading desperately, over the side of the canoe into the dark waters of the creek. Burning cardboard boxes were thrown after him, as the huge canoe listing to one side, pulled sluggishly away from the ship. The powerful outboard motor screaming loudly, as the overloaded craft took agonising seconds to build up movement. The other canoes had already departed; leaving the scene almost immediately after the first flare had been fired.

Eventually Kaduna's canoe built up speed and headed quite rapidly away from the ship. The spine-chilling screams of the man in the water could be heard clearly, even above the din of the outboard. This sent a wave of fear through the remaining pirates, crouched low in the canoe. They all knew it could easily have been one of them that had been struck by the flare, to be left to die in agony by the heartless Kaduna, like their ex-comrade drifting down the river.

As the canoe progressed up the creek, the screams finally diminished, though the glow of the phosphorous and sodium that was devouring the unfortunate's flesh could be seen until they rounded the turn in the river.

It had been a close call. No one appreciated that fact more than Kaduna. Had it not been for his quick thinking, they might all be dead now. He felt no pity what so ever for the pirate who was killed. In fact he smiled wryly to himself, as he recalled the unfortunate was actually Abokwe, who had been helping himself to cargo and secretly plotting against him.

The flares rankled though, just who the hell had fired them?

Powerless to do anything from where he was, the captain saw Sunil the third mate fire the first flare. He was horrified at the actions of his subordinate. The consequences could be dire. Then he saw the Indian take a second flare cartridge, from a small cardboard box placed on the bridge Taff rail. Quickly, expertly he reloaded the gun and took aim one more time. In the space of a few seconds, like a trained soldier, he was crouched with both hands on the pistol, ready to fire again. The captain rushed towards the third mate.

Fortunately he managed to cover the few paces between them and push his arm to one side, just as he fired the second flare.

'You bloody idiot!' he screamed. Then added still shouting loudly.

'You must flipping mad Third Mate to do a crazy thing like that.'

Sunil turned round and even in the dim light; the captain could see the glazed, half-crazed look in his eyes.

'I hit one of the bastards!' he proclaimed triumphantly. 'I took one of those suckers out!' He punched his chest with his free hand.

The huge meaty paw of the captain, effortlessly grabbed the smoking flare pistol out of the slim bony, child-like hand of the third mate. He then looked forward over the Taff rail and his worst fears were confirmed. There in one of the canoes, was the awful apparition of a blazing screaming man. 'Damn!' He thought, 'the shit will really hit the fan now.' A few seconds later, the powerfully built Yorkshire man was horrified to see; some of the pirates actually dump their stricken comrade over the side of the canoe and into the river. The man continued to scream, though louder at a higher pitch. It was an awful sound.

'I am fired I am fired!' He shouted desperately, as the water in the creek made the phosphorus and sodium of the flare burn even more intensely. The ebb- tide, which was running at around three knots, soon carried the burning man towards the middle of the river and slowly out to sea.

After a few moments absorbing the terrible spectacle, the captain left the bridge and rapidly descended the three flights of stairs inside the accommodation to main deck level. He found the second mate just outside the accommodation, bewildered and rubbing his head. The second mate looked up, and recognised the distinct form of the ship's master coming towards him.

'Jesus sir, my head is spinning and I feel like spewing up.'

'Take it easy lad. Take it easy.' He put an arm, reassuringly round the second mate's shoulders.

'What happened to you?' He asked after a few moments.

The officer spoke slowly, his speech slurred. 'I think that little shit of a foreman, pricked me with something and drugged me.'

'What about the crew you had on watch with you?'

'Dunno about them. Must be down on the main deck, I guess.'

'Okay you take it easy for a while. I'll go and see if I can find what happened to them.'

He found the four crewmembers on the main deck, leaning vacantly on the rail. Even in this light, he could see their faces were ashen, as they looked in a detached way across the creek. The bosun was still alert enough to hear the sound behind him, of someone walking across the dunnage and paper that was littering the decks. He turned slowly round and saw the skipper approaching.

'Damn it sir, we all feel rough as hell. That stevedore foreman must have drugged us. We have been unconscious for ages.'

'He did the same to the second mate. Just take your time men; you will probably be okay in an hour or so.' The master tried to re-assure the dazed crew men.

Further up the deck, the captain could see an open container lying at an angle, next to the ship's side, with the remains of several ripped and torn cartons strewn across the deck. Although the deck was quite dark, a dim shaft of light from one of the cargo clusters on the hatch top penetrated the red steel container. It appeared now to be virtually empty.

The deck was quite eerie, all the stevedores having vanished. Probably with some of the cargo from the container, he thought darkly. The only sound to be heard, was the steady pleading whine, of the electric motors from the now motionless cranes, almost as if the cranes despised inactivity and wanted someone to come and use them, or at least switch them off.

As the captain surveyed the scene along the deck, trying to absorb the cunning and audacity of the attack on his vessel, he heard a commotion and much loud shouting behind him. He turned slowly, resignedly round, broad shoulders hunched, to find his worst fears confirmed. For there, striding confidently along the deck, were several Nigerian policemen. As they approached, he could see they were dressed in ill-fitting green uniforms, with black berets, placed haphazardly on their heads. Highly polished brown leather chest and waist belts, stood out dramatically from the mottled green background of their uniforms. As they got closer, he could see they were armed with an assortment of ancient pistols and rifles.

The officer at the front of the group, a pencil slim weasel-like individual with a thin moustache which was barely discernable on his upper lip, confidently walked up to the captain and spoke loudly, in a clipped authoritative manner.

'Is you the master of this vessel?'

'Yes that is right,' he replied wearily.

'I am placing you under arrest, for the murder of a Nigerian citizen on this ship tonight.'

Chapter Sixteen

The sun rose rapidly, dramatically, like a huge ball of fire in the east; from darkness to daylight in a few minutes, unlike northern latitudes, where the sun takes its time getting out of bed. Ellis was up early and actually enjoying his first dawn in Africa for many years, leaning on the rusted balcony rail of Ronnie Wilson's apartment. The high level of refraction on the horizon, served to enlarge the sun to three or four time its normal size. He couldn't remember it being that dramatic when he last lived in this country. Then again, he was not normally up as early as this and probably didn't appreciate the event, at such a tender young age. But it certainly was impressive now.

The city was quiet at this early hour with little movement discernable in any direction, as he looked across a sea of flat-roofed buildings. An open door or window could be heard in the distance, clanging against a wall. Africans were early risers, probably due to the hot night climate. Besides, most of them would have long journeys, on foot or on rickety buses to work. So they had to start off early in the morning. But at five fifty that morning the city seemed slow to rise from its slumber.

The other occupant of the apartment was by nature an early riser, and came out onto the balcony, with two battered glass tumblers full of what looked like orange juice.

'Here, this should absorb some of the bad taste from the previous night, that may be lingering, possibly even dominating your taste buds, on a hot and clammy morning in good old Lagos.'

'Thanks Ronnie,' Ellis said, as he sat down on one of the iron chairs, next to the large stone-topped table in the middle of the balcony.

He took a sip of the drink and was pleased to find it was ice-cold pure orange juice. His furry mouth, a casualty of the previous evening's gin and tonics, felt instantly refreshed. He sat in silence for a few minutes and watched the last of the sunrise tumble across the horizon, then spoke to his companion.

'So what's the plan for the day Ronnie? Will we be visiting the ship that was attacked last night?'

'Perhaps, perhaps not,' replied the Englishman quite matter of factly.

'Oh, how's that? I thought P & I business dealt extensively with this kind of issue,' Ellis said, shuffling and trying to make himself more comfortable on the iron chair. Had no one heard of cushions in this part of the world, he wondered.

'That's true old boy, but not all the ships are with the same P & I Club. As I am sure you must be aware, there is more than one.'

'No I wasn't aware actually, but then again as we both now know, I am a newcomer to this industry.'

'Yes quite,' Wilson said in a monotone. Then he continued more brightly, as if being asked to give a lecture on his favourite subject. 'Actually our Club is not one of the major players in this league. Other P & I Clubs, like the North of England P & I, or the Swedish Club are much bigger than us. So there is every possibility that the ship attacked is insured by one of those two. Anyway, we shall soon find out when we go to the office after breakfast. There will probably be something on the telex machine, from Head Office in London, regarding the incident.'

'Oh, that's a bit disappointing, I was hoping we would be able to go down and start snooping round a little. I've got to start some-where to get to the bottom of this,' said Ellis rather wearily.

'Don't be so impatient young man, you are just off the plane,' Wilson chided, and then added in a rather sympathetic tone. 'There will be plenty of opportunity in the next few months to achieve your objectives. But let me warn you now, you'd better be careful at all times; this is not longer Nigeria in the sixties. Most people are starving here, which tends to make them rather desperate. Nigeria is a very, very, dangerous place.'

Ellis could tell by the expression on Ronnie's face that he was deadly serious and he was grateful for the older man's advice. There had been a few tell-tale signs he had noticed since arriving in the apartment, to substantiate what his companion had mentioned. The first thing he had observed was all the windows were fitted with heavy metal bars. It was just like looking out of a maximum-security prison. But the metal doors fitted everywhere were more disturbing. Not only was there a steel door as the main entrance to the apartment with multiple bolts and locks, but there was a similar door on each of the bedrooms. He had been to some strange places since joining the service, but this was the first where this type of door was fitted to the bedrooms. It must indeed be a very dangerous place to live these days, he thought.

After a light breakfast of coffee and toast, Ronnie drove them both to his office in Creek Road Apapa, which was situated close to the entrance of the container port. The office was small, very hot and oppressive as the air conditioning had been switched off overnight. But it cooled down soon after the ancient rattling machine was switched on.

When they checked the messages on the telex machine, it transpired that the Swedish Club insured the 'Southern Star'. Ellis was slightly disappointed but took care not to show his feelings this time. However, further down the long white sheet of telex messages, there was another telex from The Britannia in London. They were asking the Lagos office if they could act on behalf of the Swedish Club, with regard to the incident on the 'Southern Star'. Apparently their representative in Lagos was in

Port Harcourt, involved in an oil spill on the Bonny River and would be unable to attend the vessel in Lagos. Ronnie said it was quite normal for the various Clubs to ask assistance of each other. Anyway, his Club would be paid quite handsomely for their efforts. The arrangement suited everyone.

They boarded the 'Southern Star' just after ten o'clock and immediately encountered an air of despondency. This was quite apparent, even as they stepped off the gangway, onto the green painted steel deck of the vessel. The Filipino watchman, sitting on a chair near the top of the gangway, gave them no more than a cursory sullen glance. Even Ellis a newcomer to the trade, could sense something was amiss on the ship.

When they reached the ships office on the third deck next to the captain's cabin, they found a harassed looking officer, in the middle of a discussion with some local officials and a high-ranking smartly dressed policeman, of medium build about thirty years of age.

They introduced themselves to the chief officer, who was acting as temporary in command during the master's absence. They proffered name cards to him and he accepted them with no more than a perfunctory glance at their names. He was under pressure and they were just another two people to be attended to. Wilson and Ellis had arrived in the middle of an animated discussion, in which the chief officer was partaking with utmost vigour.

'So I hope the captain is being well treated in this prison you have taken him to. There was absolutely no need to arrest him. I think confiscation of a passport would have sufficed in the circumstances.' He spoke rapidly with a nervous edge to his voice.

The policeman replied, in a more confident tone. 'Now you listen to me, a major crime have occurred on this ship while in Nigeria. So we shall be the ones to decide how to deal with this case.'

The ship's officer looked fatigued, with pinched cheeks and dark rims under his eyes. His thick brown hair was unkempt, as if he had been running his fingers through it many times in frustration.

'I'm sorry, but I can't help thinking you have over-reacted in this case. After all, the man who bought it was a damn pirate robbing our ship.'

'That may be true, but the penalty for theft is not death, is it?' The policeman fixed the officer with a piercing gaze, from his wide alert eyes.

'But….'

The policeman cut him off before he could continue. 'But nothing, the case is closed. Now I has to inform you, that I am placing your vessel under arrest, until a substantial financial bond can be obtained.'

The other people in the room sat quietly almost impassively, listening to the exchange between the police inspector and the acting master. Sat close to Wilson, Ellis could tell his partner was getting agitated and was keen to participate in the exchange. He waited till the end of the dialogue, coughed slightly which got the attention of the protagonists, then spoke slowly.

'The police inspector is absolutely right of course. This is the normal procedure in such cases.' He had the full attention now of the people assembled, most of whom who nodded assent at his comment. 'I and my associate have had considerable dealings in the past with this kind of case, and hope that we can all work together to achieve a satisfactory conclusion.'

Ellis admired his partner's bedside manner. Involving all present and making everyone feel important. Ronnie continued talking.

'Have you had time yet to prepare a statement of facts regarding, the events of last night, Chief Off?'

The ship's officer laughed, and then rounded on the surveyor. 'You must be bloody kidding. I haven't been to bed since the incident, or much in the days preceding it. You'll all get a statement of facts when I'm good and ready to give it to you.'

Ronnie sighed inwardly; this young man's belligerence could

not possibly help the situation. He would have a quite word with him, at a more opportune moment.

'Well, can you give me a quick run down on what happened?'

The officer talked in a monotone, whilst looking nonchalantly around the cabin, relating briefly an account of the incident.

'Thanks Chief, well that at least puts us in the picture. Can we have a look round the deck for a bit then talk to some of the crew?'

'Yeah that's fine, help yourself.' The officer replied matter of factly.

Wilson and Ellis spent the next hour walking round the ship, watching the discharging operation and talking to any crewmembers, they encountered on deck. Ellis couldn't help noticing as he walked round, the all-pervading stench that surrounded the ship. He asked Ronnie what was making the smell. He just smiled and pointed to the ship's rail. Ellis was shocked when he looked over, to see a stevedore defecating on one of the huge rubber fenders between the ship and the jetty. The fender, like all the others, was covered in the filth. Apparently the toilets provided in the docks were few and had ceased to function many years ago.

After a short walk up the port side of the main deck, they soon discovered the pilfered container had long since been discharged empty. However, there were a number of large empty cardboard cartons lying crumpled on deck. Together with dozens of smaller boxes. Ellis picked up one of these, looked at it and quietly digested what was written on the box, grunted and spoke nonchalantly to his companion.

'Sony radio cassette, nice piece of gear, I used to have one just like this. It's somewhere at home at the moment, under a pile of junk I shouldn't wonder.'

'Yes this is just the kind of thing the locals would buy, small and of high value. There must have been close to a hundred thousand dollars worth of these in that container,' Ronnie said thoughtfully as he rubbed his chin and then added. 'Of course, the pirates will only get a fraction of that money. But still a tidy sum I shouldn't wonder.'

They tried talking to some of the crewmembers during their tour of the deck, but unfortunately they met no one who could assist them with their enquiries. Most of the crew knew nothing, as they were either asleep or had been had been drugged by the head stevedore.

One of the engine room crew however, provided a clearer picture of what had happened in the early hours of that day. He had just returned from a rather unsavoury excursion ashore and was taking a final beer on the boat deck, before retiring for the night, when the pirates struck. Too drunk to be bothered with the hassle of raising the alarm, he had watched rather bemused as the scene unfolded before him. The small slim Filipino seaman, with greasy jet-black shoulder length hair, spoke excitedly in accented English, as he recounted to Ellis and Wilson what he had seen.

'You know the best thing about it, was when the flare hit the pirate.' His face lit up at the memory.

'Yes I imagine it was the best bit,' said Wilson rather acidly.

'But why would the captain fire the flare?' He prompted.

The man looked amazed at the statement, which had been carefully loaded and was above his head. 'Naw.., that won't no captain. That was du crazy third mate, what fired the flare.'

'Really, how can you be so sure?' Ellis enquired before his partner could speak.

'Well I was on the boat deck, just below the bridge and hear the Old Man screaming at him after the second flare got fired.'

They talked to the Indian third mate later in the morning, but he steadfastly refused to admit that he fired the flares. He insisted instead that it was he who actually tried to stop the captain. Ellis mused on the fact, that you didn't have to have a shred of investigative ability, to realise the third mate was in 'save your hide' mode, so any further conversation with him would prove pointless.

It was rapidly approaching noon, as they both stood silently, leaning on the ship's bulwark by the gangway, pondering the situation on board the ship. By this time in the day, the sun had reached its zenith and beat down ferociously from an almost clear sky. Just the odd wisp of high stratus cloud, coloured the canopy of light –blue, that stretched from one horizon to the next.

The air was stifling and Ellis's clothes stuck to every part of his body. Sweat ran freely down his face and dripped onto the deck, while the evil odour of the fenders clogged his nose. He felt awful. He longed for a cool drink and even more so, a cold shower and a change of clothes. Ellis wondered how long he would have to stay in Nigeria to achieve his objective. On the evidence he had seen so far, it would probably be months before he could even get a lead. That in itself made him a little depressed.

As for the pirate, what a mess he had left behind him, disappearing into the night and escaping scot-free. At the meeting with the authorities when they first arrived, there had been no mention of any attempt to find the pirates. The only concern was for the one who had been killed. The poor captain was languishing in a stinking prison cell and he had not even fired the flare pistol. But, as Wilson pointed out to Ellis, it would not have mattered who fired the gun. The master was still responsible and that was why he was being held in prison.

It was their job now acting for the vessel's insurance company, to try and come to an agreement with the Nigerian authorities. Firstly, to have the master released on bail and secondly, to get them to accept a bond so that the ship could sail. A replacement master would be on his way from the UK, to take over the command of the vessel from his imprisoned predecessor.

Wilson perceptive as ever, sensed Ellis' dark mood and prodded him in the side playfully.

'Hey come on Martin, cheer up. Working here is not so bad really. It just takes a little more time than back home. But it will all pan out eventually, you'll see.'

'Yeah, I suppose you are right. So what's the next move?'

'The next move? Best part of the day now old son, a few beers and a leisurely lunch at the Apapa Club.'

Ellis was taken aback slightly. 'Sounds great, but I thought you were going to arrange finances, to have the ship and the captain released?'

'I'll phone from the Club, the line is as good from there as any other location.'

Ellis brightened noticeably.

'Any chance of nipping back to your place for a shower first?'

'Oh I think we can manage that okay. Come on Martin we're wasting time.' Ronnie then turned away from the bulwark and made his way quickly down the rickety gangway, with Ellis close behind.

Lunch turned out to be decidedly inauspicious. The Apapa Club had a very limited menu and Ellis had plumbed for omelette and what turned out to be very soggy, greasy chips. The Star beer was excellent however, ice cold from large green bottles, with heavy condensation on the side and small rivulets trickling down towards the base of the bottle. Also partaking of what purported to be lunch that day was a smattering of expats and a few locals. They either sat at the bar on the bar stools, or at tables on the veranda. No one sat by the pool, as there were no sun umbrellas for protection from the fierce midday sun.

The Apapa Club was the Nigerian equivalent of those exclusive Clubs found in India at the time of the Raja, though not quite as ostentatious. It had been built in the 1940s for the expatriate community living in Lagos, a place where they could meet those of their own ilk without native intrusion. But now in 1982, it was showing distinct signs of dilapidation, due to the lack of maintenance over the last twenty years. The chairs were rickety and the wicker tables somewhat threadbare, in need of extensive repair to return them to their former glory. Even the cushions on the bar stools were stained, lumpy and no longer comfortable. Ellis thought bemusedly, that the Apapa Club needed a manager from Trust House Forte, or some other reputable company, to give the place a complete overhaul. But this was Nigeria and fine detail was obviously lost on the present owners.

Most of the clientele either said hello or nodded to Ronnie, which was not surprising, as he had lived continuously in Lagos for almost ten years. Ellis felt refreshed, having had a shower and a few cool beers, to help wash away the taste of the greasy lunch. Sitting in one of the bamboo chairs in the shade of the veranda, looking out on the inviting dark blue waters of the Club swimming pool, he had a chance to reflect slowly on the events of the last twenty-four hours.

One thing was certain. The previous night's raid had been planned with almost military precision. He was undoubtedly dealing with a professional in this instance, something he had not expected. Another interesting fact was that only one container had been pilfered. One full of high value cargo, which seemed to indicate the pirate, had inside information.

Ronnie was sat on the other side of the table wearing his glasses, concentrating on a file he was reading. Ellis looked towards his companion and spoke.

'I've been thinking about that raid last night Ronnie.'

'Really,' the other replied flatly, as he put down the file and then added, 'I suppose that thought has crossed a few people's minds in Lagos today. It was a big story in the local press incidentally.'

'Oh! I didn't know that. Anyway, getting back to the reason I am here, to try and catch this fellow. I have to make a start somewhere. I think it is fairly obvious the raid was an inside job. You've been in shipping a good while, who would have access to the kind of information needed to thieve the contents of such a valuable container?'

'Quite a few people really. The captain and chief mate on the ship would have access to the numbers of the containers and the contents. It's happened before where ship's staff has been in collusion with thieves.'

Ellis digested what he had been told, waited a few seconds then continued.

'In this instance Ronnie, my gut feeling tells me the crew are not involved.'

'Oh no? What about the dodgy third mate then?' Said Ronnie, raising his eyebrows.

'Oh! I forgot about him. Hmmm.' He pondered a moment. 'No I don't think even he could have been implicated. If he had he wouldn't have fired the flare. He's just a crazy, the kind of imponderable that life throws up from time to time.'

'Yes I suppose you are probably right in this case. So that leaves the people ashore I guess. The agents at the loading and discharging ports would have access to all the bills of lading and cargo manifests, also any amount of clerks in their offices.'

Ellis nodded his head slowly as he absorbed the information then spoke.

'I think we can discount the agents at the loading ports, so that just leaves the local agents in my mind, as the most likely source of the information for the pirate. Do you know who the 'Southern Star's' agents in Lagos are?'

'Yes that's Bowman and Co. The local Nigerian manager is Michael Kafu; he is actually in the Club at the moment, having his lunch on one of the tables next to the bar.'

'I wonder if he would let us talk to some of his employees?' prompted Ellis.

'He has to let us talk to his employees. After all, we are acting for the insurance company who is going to have to cover the loss. We have to conduct an investigation of all the facts, starting at Bowman's office later this afternoon.'

'Well that's good news indeed, Ronnie.' Ellis took another sip from his cold glass of beer, stretched his arms and sat back in the chair, closed his eyes and was asleep a few minutes later.

Located just over two miles from the faded elegance of the Apapa Club, inside the living hell that was Kala Kiri prison, the exhausted captain would have loved to close his eyes and wake up refreshed, to find it had all been a bad dream. But sleep was something he was unable to achieve, while he was locked in a cage, with around thirty tattered stinking inmates. He had stood with his back to the wall, ever since his arrival in the foul cage almost eight hours previously. Because he was the only white man incarcerated, there were thirty pairs of crazed eyes permanently fixed on him. He feared that if he went to sleep, they would probably jump him and steal his clothes and shoes. The distinct possibility of gang rape sent a chill up and down his spine.

The captain was ravenous and his mouth was dry as a bone. The local agent had brought him some chicken and vegetables around lunchtime. But when the food was passed through the bars this caused a riot, the other prisoners fighting on the filthy floor of the cage, for scraps of the now soiled food. The cell was like an oven, with barely any room to move around, so numerous were the other prisoners. The stench was appalling from the sweat of the unwashed bodies and the excrement and urine, which spilled over from a single bucket in the corner.

A dark feeling of despondency and depression had crept over him. He even wondered if he would ever see his lovely wife and two young sons again, back home in Harrogate Yorkshire. As at that moment death at the hands of the crazed mob or the guards seemed a distinct possibility. Earlier in the day, the vicious guards who beat the inmates back with short thick rawhide whips had already dragged one body out unceremoniously. If he ever managed to get out of this awful mess alive, he would probably be deranged like the rest of the inmates. Death in that case would be preferable, he conceded reluctantly to himself.

Meanwhile, in a different part of the prison, a whole world apart from where the captain was held, Police Chief Godwin Azubikas, nibbled on a biscuit while sipping tea from a fine China cup. His office on the top floor of the prison was bright and air-conditioned. Fine antique style furniture and thick carpets filled the room. The large windows looked out over the prison roof, to the palm tree fringed white sandy beach and the sapphire blue sea beyond. From his armchair in the middle of the room, he could appreciate the fine vista stretching away to the horizon. No one could imagine this room was a part of the most notorious prison south of the Sahara. It was more like an exclusive penthouse in a plush hotel.

Azubikas was feeling very pleased with life this day. A large amount of money had come his way that morning, from that arrogant upstart of a pirate. Someone who he already had plans for at a later date, he mused smiling to himself, looking forward to that day with relish. But another stoke of luck fuelled his good mood. That was the arrest and imprisonment of the British captain. He saw the look of abject terror on the man's face, as he was bundled into the large holding cell on arrival early in the morning. He looked like he was almost ready to crack and he had only just arrived. It felt good to know, he had the power to reduce the high and mighty white man, to a blubbering mess if he so desired. Teach these people a lesson, who was really the Master Race in the world. Yes, that was another interesting prospect in store, perhaps.

Chapter Seventeen

While Ellis was dozing, Wilson continued a lively banter with some Europeans and locals at the bar of the Apapa club. Then after about half an hour gin glass in hand, he sauntered casually over to his sleeping companion. He sat down in one of the wicker chairs opposite, sipped his drink before setting it down on the table. Then after a few seconds, he spoke normally, just as if he had never been away and his associate was still wide-awake.

'Bad luck I'm afraid.'

'Wha wha what do you mean?' Ellis said, as he stirred from what had been a short, but very deep sleep on the veranda of the Apapa Club. He sat up and rubbed his eyes, as the reflected glare of the West African afternoon sun, bounced off the white tiles surrounding the swimming pool. Wilson regarded his companion briefly then continued.

'I've just phoned the Britannic in London to arrange the bond for the ship and the captain. The ship is quite straightforward and a million or so U.S. will enable her to proceed from Nigeria to Douala in Cameroon, the ship's next port.'

'A million!' Ellis exclaimed, by now almost fully awake. 'Isn't that a bit steep?'

'No, not at all old chap, I would say quite reasonable in the circumstances really. A Nigerian national has been killed, which was directly attributable to the ship, so I have no qualms with that. The real problem is the authorities are adamant that the poor captain must remain in prison and stand trial.'

Ellis was silent for a few seconds, as the full gravity of what Wilson had said struck home. This would mean the unfortunate English captain, would be exposed to the full degradation and deprivation of the African prison system. This for him would be as close to hell as it was possible to get, without actually being there.

'But surely, there must be something we can do to help the poor fellow?' He said eventually. Then after a few moments thought he added, 'a large bribe to the prison governor or something like that?'

'Well you are learning quickly Martin aren't you?' Ronnie said quite bemusedly, and then continued in an even businesslike tone. 'That will be the solution eventually I am sure, but remember what I told you, about the timescale here in West Africa.' Ronnie mopped his brow, with a rumpled handkerchief, looking directly at Ellis.

'That everything takes time here right?'

'Correct. So for the moment the poor man will have to make the best of the situation, till the U.S. cavalry arrive. But it's impossible at this stage, to tell when that will be.'

'If we can't help him, then what's our next move?'

'We'll go down to Bowman's office and see if we can glean any info there. I talked to Kafu while you were dozing and told him we would be at his office, around three this afternoon to talk to his people. Meanwhile, the Britannic will be transferring funds to the Bank of Central Nigeria, to put up as bond for the ship.' He paused for a few moments, took a short quick breath, nodded his head slightly and said to Ellis, 'Okay Martin, if you are ready we may as well head to the agent's office.'

Ellis yawned and stretched before getting slowly to his feet, feeling the detuning effect that three lunchtime beers tend to have.

They strode out of the Apapa Club and climbed into the Peugeot 604, which was like entering an oven on wheels. Ellis started to sweat profusely, the effect of the shower he had enjoyed two hours previously now emphatically cancelled out. The car must have been one of the few in the country at that time fitted with air conditioning, which took a few minutes to have any effect on the air inside the car. Ellis was grateful when at last the air did cool down to a bearable level.

As they proceeded along the pot-holed road towards Bowman's office, just outside the docks in downtown Apapa, Ronnie said very little and Ellis could see he was obviously quite deep in thought. So he just stared absently out of the car window, into the baking hot Nigerian afternoon.

At this time of day, there were not many people on the streets. Just the occasional plant pot hatted pedestrian, in baggy shirt and trousers, walking slowly along the pavement. As the car carefully made its way down the dusty poorly maintained road, they passed numerous small stalls at the side of the road, selling every type of consumer goods imaginable. Ellis found it faintly amusing, that each stall was piled high with just one specific item; such as long loaves of crusty French bread, cartons of Marlboro cigarettes, small round tins of fish and even a decent variety of electrical goods.

The people that operated these stalls apparently stayed open twenty-four hours a day, ever hopeful of making a sale. He knew this, having seen these stalls on his way from the airport the previous evening; the various goods barely illuminated with small flickering candles or gas Tilley lamps. But this afternoon, the heat was too much even for these indomitable entrepreneurs, who seemed to have given up on the day, most being fast asleep, slumped across their wares. At least they have got that part right. Ellis thought, as the hint of a wry smile momentarily appeared on his lips.

They arrived at Bowman's agency a little after three in the afternoon, to find most of the clerks and other office staff, ponderously going about their various duties. The place was oppressively hot and the hum of an air conditioner could only be heard from the direction of the MD's office. The rest of the building had to make do with ancient rattling fans, turning slowly on the ceilings of the various rooms. Some of the senior clerks however, were fortunate enough to have small modern electric desk fans to help keep them cool. Ellis noticed that most of the furniture was old and well worn; also that the reek of stale sweat pervaded the atmosphere of the building.

At one of the larger desks towards the back of the room, senior clerk John Ekpe looked up briefly and impassively, as the two white men entered the main administration room of Bowman's office. He knew exactly who they were, as Mr Kafu had warned the whole office staff not half an hour ago, what to expect later in the afternoon. Ekpe was quite astounded that so soon after the raid; people had already come straight to the office where he worked to ask questions. The muscles of his scrawny stomach felt tight and it was hard to concentrate on his work, though outwardly an onlooker would see the senior clerk working quite diligently.

Mr Kafu the agency manager, showed Ellis and Wilson into his office. The friendly Nigerian was around forty years old, above average height for Nigeria and although he could not as yet be classed as obese, he was certainly overweight. His light grey safari suit was filled out with his substantial frame and the short sleeves of his shirt pinched his thick arms. He invited the two newcomers to sit down at the side of his modern, polished, luxuriously deep brown mahogany desk. A short discussion followed, with regard to what the visit hoped to achieve. Kafu gave a list of all his employees who could have had access to the information, that somehow found its way into the hands of the pirates. Then it was agreed that a few of his employees, randomly selected, would be interviewed. One by one, these employees were called to the office, where they were asked a series of questions to test their reaction. The last person to be interviewed was the senior clerk.

Ekpe had been very worried, since the white men came into the office over an hour ago. In fact, in a moment of panic, when his mind was not functioning rationally, he wondered if he should just admit how the pirates knew which container to open. But the memory of Kaduna and the raw terror he had quite firmly instilled made that option a non-starter. Besides he knew if collusion was admitted, then he would wind up in jail anyway.

His mind was still trying to think of what to say, if he was one of the staff that would be questioned, when a voice called firmly from the direction of the MD's office,

'Mr Ekpe.'

'Yes sir.'

'Come into my office for a few moments.'

'Yes sir, I am coming.'

Hands shaking, he nervously tidied a few papers on his desk and then walked slowly towards the MD's office. Once inside, the spectre that greeted him was not encouraging. The two white men sat expressionless next to Mr Kafu. There was a lone chair facing them. He was introduced to the two men, then invited to sit down. The elder of the two investigators sat back in his chair, with his arm resting on one of the armrests. He regarded Ekpe for a few seconds, and then began to speak in a calm almost soothing manner.

'Well Mr Ekpe, as you will probably know, there was a raid last night by pirates up at Tin Can Port, on one of the vessels dealt with by this company.'

'Yes, I believe so,' he replied. 'That is what everyone is talking about today.'

'Were you aware that the thieves were very selective?'

'How do you mean?'

'Well they only opened one container and that just happened to be the one with the most valuable cargo,' Wilson said, his voice hardening ever so slightly.

Ekpe swallowed before answering.

'No, I was not aware of that. But I don't know why you are telling me this information.'

'Well it's quite simple,' the other younger man said, speaking for the first time. 'As you are in charge of the freight department here, you would have access to this information.'

'Ha!' Ekpe laughed softly. 'Yes, me and another twenty people in this office. Any one of them could have told the pirates.'

'That's true and we know the people in this office who had access to that information, as Mr Kafu has been kind enough to furnish us with a list. Most of whom we have concluded would not have this information close to hand. But as head of the freight department, you could access these documents unnoticed at any time.'

Ekpe sat in silence, listening to the white man. What he said was ludicrously simple to deduce and seemed to make him the prime suspect. He felt very vulnerable and wished he had never become involved. But that was done now and self-preservation was his priority. 'It look like, you is virtually accusing me of this terrible crime!' His voice was rising, sounding indignant. 'But as I have said, there are many people in this office who could have done this. However there is one thing you has forgotten.'

'Please be kind enough to enlighten us,' Ellis said almost casually

'Virtually the whole of the customs department, many dozens of people, could have gained access to the information any time they wants. All the containers and their contents has to be declared to the customs, ten days before any ship arrives. It is too easy for you to say that the information came from this office and so the head clerk must be to blame. When in fact as I have explained, there are many other people, who could be responsible for this.'

The answer rocked Ellis back on his heels. For his first question as a P and I inspector, he certainly had come off second best. Wilson quickly interjected in a distinctly patronising tone.

'Now now Mr Ekpe, no one is accusing you, of involvement in this affair. It is just that we have to start our enquiries somewhere and of course the agent's office for the cargo involved is always going to be the logical starting place.'

Ekpe nodded briefly, his integrity more or less intact. Mr Kafu was smiling thinly; pleased with his head clerk's answer, as obviously he did not want any blame attached to his operation.

'Okay I think you can go back to your work now Mr Ekpe. I'm sure these gentlemen have no further questions.' Mr Kafu said in a level tone.

Wilson said nothing, though he shook his head, as an indication that as far as he was concerned, the meeting was over.

A very relieved Ekpe got up and made his way back to his desk. His answers had comprehensively shifted any blame away from himself. In fact he now felt so confident; he was tempted to check some more bills of lading that had just come in that morning from Hong Kong. But no, he had better be sensible for a while, till the heat of this particular fiasco died down a little.

On the way back to Ronnie's house, Ellis felt a little disappointed that the time spent at the agent's office, had not yielded any thing more concrete with which to proceed. It had in fact, thrown up a brick wall with regard to pursuing that line of inquiry, as it was inconceivable that the customs could be investigated. However, he had a feeling deep down, that this Ekpe fellow at Bowman's office was hiding something. He had been very nervous when he entered the MD's office, visibly more so than the others. Also his answers were a little too well thought out, to be wholly genuine.

For the moment anyway, he would have to approach the challenge from a different angle. Finding information to track down the pirate leader was never going to be easy, especially as he had to remain incognito from the local police. In the past he had always had a measure of assistance from that area. So not having this facility here in Nigeria, made the job infinitely more difficult. On the plus side though, he reminded himself, he did have the Interior Minister and of course, the very able Ronnie Wilson.

The car turned off the main highway and made its way down River Road towards Ronnie's house. The road here was quite narrow and a rickety truck lumbered along in front of them, slowing their progress. There was just the occasional stall owner in this street, this area not being as populous as the centre of Apapa. As the car crawled along the potholed street, Ellis's mind was drifting back and forth between the events of the last twenty-four hours. Such a lot had happened. He really did feel like a fish out of water and felt it would take a considerable time to get to the bottom of the problem. The idea of working without the assistance of the local police force troubled him greatly. This coupled with the heat and general squalor of Apapa, made him slightly depressed as he looked out the car window at the litter strewn streets.

The truck up ahead suddenly lurched to a standstill. Ronnie braked and had no trouble avoiding the rear of the vehicle, as they were travelling very slowly. He couldn't pass the truck as there was a steady stream of taxis, buses and other various types of ramshackle transport coming from the other direction.

During the time that they were stopped, something caught Ellis's eye and pulled him quite sharply out of his reverie. He would not have noticed had the car not been stationary for those few moments. As it happened, the car had stopped beside one of the roadside stalls. Not three feet from his window, Ellis could see a neat stack of small tan coloured cardboard boxes. On the end of each one it said: 'Sony cassette radio'. He let out a short burst of air from his pursed lips, sat bolt upright and said to himself. 'Well, that's very interesting. Could something as simple as this be the start of the long trail that would eventually lead to the pirate?' Anyway, the boxes on the hawker's stall certainly set his mind racing.

Chapter Eighteen

The Russian general cargo ship lay quietly to her port anchor in the eastern working anchorage of Singapore. It was almost three a.m. and the duty officer on the bridge was thinking of making his second cup of coffee, since coming on duty at midnight. The sea was calm and had an inky back appearance. A weak flood tide made the M.V. 'Kapitan Penkov' tug gently on her anchor cable. In the distance, he could see huge black clouds over the brightly lit skyscrapers of Singapore. A sure sign of torrential rain, which he thought would probably reach the ship within the next half hour. There was little activity in the anchorage at that time of night; just the occasional 'Bum Boat', or a tug towing a barge full of cargo out to a ship, ready for the stevedores to start loading at six-thirty.

Four decks below the bridge, Sergie Dimitri the first trip junior seaman, lay wide-awake on his sweat soaked bunk. The gangly youth from Odessa on the Black Sea, was eighteen years old with a bushy head of brown hair. His pallid complexion had little sign of any beard growth, just the occasional tuft of bum fluff. Almost six feet tall, he was painfully slim and had been nicknamed 'Spider' by the crew.

His cabin was a whole world away from the almost palatial accommodation, allocated to the senior ranks on the ship, the captain and chief engineer. He lived in a tiny box like affair on the main deck at the forward end of the accommodation, next to the main entrance door. This banged constantly against the bulkhead where his bunk was located, as people entered and left the accommodation. On the deck, above his head, lived a cargo winch for number four hatch and when this was in operation his whole cabin would vibrate, making sleep impossible. The cabin was freezing in winter and red-hot in the tropics. In heavy weather his porthole leaked and his deck would be awash with salt water.

To further compound his misery, he had to share his already cramped quarters, with the galley boy. A bespectacled corpulent youth, a few months older than himself, called Malkinov. The crew had even less regard for him than and had nicknamed him 'Blubber'. He was a genial enough type of person, though Sergie hated having to share a cabin with him, as he had an aversion to soap and suffered from body odour. He had to keep the porthole open and the alleyway door ajar on the hook, in an effort to make the air in the cabin breathable.

That night he was even more uncomfortable than normal in the hot and smelly cabin. He decided to get up from his bunk and go onto the winch deck, above his cabin for some fresh air. Standing at the rail looking towards the shore, savouring the sweet air, he could see many ships in the anchorage.

It amazed him that so many ocean-going vessels could be packed into such a small area. He had overheard the third mate saying, that the Old Man was not happy to be anchored so close to some of the ships, with only three cables clearance. He was unsure what that term meant, (it was actually a third of a mile) but he knew if the captain was concerned, there must be a good reason.

The night air was completely still except for the occasional light zephyr and the ship deathly quiet, the steady hum of the generators in the engine room being the only sound of consequence. After around twenty minutes or so on deck feeling much better, he yawned and decided to try and get some sleep, before the four to eight watch keeper would noisily awake him at six-thirty.

He was just about to leave his position on the winch deck and start walking aft towards the stairs, when he heard the faint, almost inaudible sound of hushed voices below him. He became immediately alert, pulse racing slightly. His first thought, perhaps this was the pirates the captain had warned them all to be on their guard against. He cautiously peered over the ships rail, looking forward then aft, to see if any craft were in the vicinity. To his horror, a mere thirty metres away, he could see quite clearly the dark outline of a small boat of some sort, bobbing up and down, close to the stern of the ship.

'Hell's teeth,' he thought. 'I will have to raise the alarm, this could be really serious.'

He was about to rush up to the bridge and inform the duty officer, when an object caught his eye. Something was being taken quickly from the boat, on a line onto his ship. As far as he could make out in the dim light, it was a package of some description. Then a few seconds later, another package came rapidly onto the main deck. He relaxed a little. Something odd was being perpetuated. But it could not be pirates as he was led to believe they took from ships, not the reverse.

Sergie desperately wanted to find out what was happening. But as this was his first trip to sea, he was extremely apprehensive about prying into something he did not understand. He stood for a few minutes longer in his place of concealment pondering. But as more packages came on board, curiosity got the better of caution and he crept furtively along the deck to get a better view.

The deck below was in semi-darkness, the only illumination present being cast from the lights inside the accommodation. But even in the dim light, he could see quite clearly a pair of skeletal Chinese men. Close cropped hair, pinched cheeks and clothes that seemed a couple of sizes too big for them. They were bringing the packages up from the boat, with much gesticulation and the occasional burst of guttural Chinese. Sergie recognized two of the engine room crew assisting the Chinese by lowering the packages down a stores hatch into the engine room.

From his place of concealment in the shadows on the deck above he was entranced by the scene. He wrinkled his brow slightly, trying to imagine what was in the packages. Drugs, perhaps? He had heard one of the A.B.'s talking in the mess room about a Cypriot ship, caught recently trying to smuggle drugs into the USA. But surely he thought in his naiveté, no one in the merchant navy of the Soviet Union would cast aside their conscience and be involved in such a heinous crime. Eventually he concluded it couldn't be drugs, as there were just too many boxes involved.

After a while, he observed the spindly Chinese were starting to tire with the exertion of heaving so many packages up from the boat. It was now taking much longer for successive boxes to be brought on board. Then suddenly, as one of them was passing a package to an engine crewmember, it slipped dramatically from his thin bony hands, landing on the damp deck with a dull thump. The fall caused the cardboard wrapper to open at the seams, spilling the contents onto the green-painted metal poop deck. Sergie gasped. Hundreds of shiny new silver watches were scattered over the deck. He heard one of the engine room crew shout at the culprit.

'You stupid bleeding fool!' He was about to slap the much smaller man, when the oriental in a flash, sprang into the classic 'Kung Fu' pose. This stunned the motorman who immediately put all thoughts of violence aside, quickly trying to placate the angered Chinese.

'Okay, okay, I sorry get angry. You right, me wrong. Better pick watches up, get job finished. Get money, okay?'

But the Chinese still maintained his martial arts posture, looking as if he would still strike, like an uncoiling Mamba, towards the now apologetic Russian seaman. The situation was only defused; when to Sergie's complete surprise and bewilderment, the ship's commissar appeared on deck. He walked slowly towards the Chinese man, with palms upturned, speaking in a soothing tone.

'Come on Li Fung Wa. Relax, man. We are all nervous. My

man is truly sorry he get angry.'

The Chinese dropped his guard slowly. 'All right Kaminsky.' His voice was trembling. 'This time I no kill. But nobody try to strike Li Fung Wa. Now you give money. I go.'

Kaminsky handed him an envelope with fifty dog-eared one hundred dollar bills inside. The Chinese man opened the envelope and quickly counted the bills. Then he stuffed the envelope inside his scruffy stained shirt, turned and disappeared down a rope ladder over the stern. The other Chinese scowled at Kaminsky then quickly followed his associate down to the boat .The motorman then cast off the frayed manila rope that was securing the boat. The boat's large diesel engine, which had just been ticking over gently, suddenly rumbled into life as the throttle was pushed to full power.

A thick blue cloud of smoke emanated from the small exhaust pipe, just above the waterline, as the propeller churned the dark bay water and sent it boiling to the surface. Kaminsky leaned on the ship's rail and watched the boat's departure.

While the mini drama was being enacted on deck, far below in the depths of the engine room, it was a scene of feverish activity. The engine fitter and another motorman toiled to hide the contraband away. Litbarski, the tall lean chief engineer, was supervising the operation. It was him in fact, several voyages previously who had dreamt up the whole idea. Quite by accident, he had stumbled on the perfect hiding place. A small tank originally used for generator lube oil which was no longer in use.

This was where the boxes of watches were stowed. Anyone checking to see what was in the tank would first look at the sight glass at the side. Litbarski had cleverly blanked the bottom of this and filled the glass half full of oil, before fixing it back in place. This gave the impression the tank was half-full of lube oil and would satisfy any curious port official who cared to check. As an extra precaution, in case anyone more knowledgeable than the average official should come prying round, he had blanked off and filled the sounding pipe of the tank, to the same level as the sight glass. The idea was foolproof.

The boxes of watches, carefully being lowered by the engine room fitter through the access manhole, were small enough to pass comfortably through the oval shaped hole. A motorman was inside the tank, packing the boxes tightly into position. After the last box was in place, he climbed out of the tank, every inch of his overalls sodden with perspiration. The two men then sealed the tank shut, by means of a heavy steel plate with thirty-six studded bolts. With this cover bolted back in place, no one would know there was anything in the tank but oil. After all, the sight glass indicated the tank was full of oil, which was enough evidence for anyone.

As he watched the men tighten down the last of the nuts with a ring spanner, Litbarski smiled at his ingenuity, which had worked perfectly numerous times. Of course, when he first thought of the idea, he had to sound out the commissar. He knew everything that happened on board, with informers dotted round the vessel. Just like back in Russia. He had a feeling Kaminsky might accept the idea. The chief engineer's cabin was next to the commissar's and he had noticed many an insalubrious character entering or leaving the party man's cabin. Usually in the middle of the night, at a number of ports the vessel had visited. When he first mentioned the idea to Kaminsky he was very enthusiastic, congratulating the Estonian on such a brilliant idea. In fact it was his contacts in West Africa who actually bought the watches.

Only a limited number of people on the ship were involved in the smuggling operation and these were all sworn to secrecy. Smuggling in any form is a serious business and consequences too dire to even think about would ensue, if ever they were caught. Litbarski shuddered at the thought. But he could make more money in one watch operation than two years at sea, which for him was more than enough incentive to pursue the lucrative business further.

Four decks above where the chief engineer was standing, from his vantage point at the aft end of the boat deck, Sergie found it hard to comprehend the events of the previous ten minutes, thinking that perhaps that he must have imagined everything. How could the ships commissar possibly be involved in anything as underhand as he had just witnessed? After all, was he not the man on board who held himself up to be the most righteous, the most vociferous opponent on board to any form of personal gain? It was all very hard for the youth from Odessa to comprehend, but he had witnessed the parcels coming on board and the party man handing over the thick envelope full of money.

It made him feel bitter and even more disenchanted with life, that such a paragon of the ship's company should be involved with something so dishonest. From where he stood, he could clearly see the commissar standing at the end of the poop deck, watching the departure of the boat. He was nodding slightly and talking in hushed tones to the big motorman next to him.

Sergie wondered vaguely where the other motorman had gone, the one who had been lowering the boxes down the hatch. Perhaps he was assisting with hiding the contraband, he thought briefly. Then suddenly, without any warning, a thickly muscled arm, slimy with sweat and oil, curled round his scrawny neck, almost tearing it from his shoulders. Simultaneously, a massive calloused hand enveloped his face, nearly suffocating him. He was immediately consumed with terror, eyes bulging in his head. The motorman pushed his lips close to Sergie's ear and spoke in heavy menacing tones.

'What the hell do you think you are doing Spider, you little Odessa crud.' The words vibrated through the youth's body and he almost vomited, with the stench of garlic and stale beer from the man's breath.

'You better not speak a single word to anyone, of what you have just seen. Or I swear to you one dark night in a storm, when the seas are smashing across the decks you will become just another statistic for seamen lost overboard. Understand?'

He tightened his grip round Sergie's throat, so that he could no longer breathe. Tears were streaming from his eyes down his cheeks. After a few moments that seemed like an eternity to the suffocating youth, the motorman released his grip and turned him round, gripping Sergie's hair and pulling his face to within a centimetre of his own.

'I said do you understand sonny?'

Sergie was whimpering and gasping for breath and only managed to blurt out an almost inaudible reply. 'Yes. Yes... I won't say a word. Not a word I promise.'

The man released his grip and turned round, pushing him roughly towards the stairs leading down to the poop deck. He was in such a state of shock, that his knees almost buckled, pitching him headlong down the metal rung stairway. But he managed to grab the handrail and steady himself briefly, before proceeding.

'Get to your cabin, boy and don't breathe a damn word, or else you will be history,' the motorman called after him.

'Yes sir' replied Sergie, weeping miserably as he stumbled down the ladder to the poop deck. When he reached the bottom of the stairs, he could see the commissar, arms folded, staring seriously at him. This served to further compound his misery, now that the party man also knew he had been spying on their operation. What a mess he thought, as he made his way along the deck to the entrance of the accommodation and the relative sanctuary of his cabin. All I wanted was some fresh air, he reflected morosely.

The large heavily built motorman followed Sergie to the bottom of the ladder, and then lumbered across the deck to where Kaminsky was standing imperiously.

'How much did he see?' asked the commissar curtly?

'Too much, I'm afraid comrade. But I scared him real good, he won't talk.' replied the motorman confidently.

'I hope you are correct for all our sakes comrade,' said Kaminsky acidly.

'Yes yes, don't worry it will be okay. I will rough him up from time to time, to make sure his mouth stays firmly closed.'

The commissar nodded silently, then turned abruptly and walked towards the accommodation entrance.

Chapter Nineteen

A fine plume of spray arced out gracefully from either side of the bow, as the twenty-foot fibreglass boat sped over the glassy calm waters of Badagry Creek. The boat was tilted aft a few degrees, a direct effect of the Evinrude forty-five horsepower outboard that thrust the craft spectacularly along, at somewhere in the region of twenty-five knots.

Martin Ellis, dressed in a purple beach vest and cut away jeans, baseball cap firmly on his head, sat in the bow of the boat, enjoying the cool air which rushed past. He always found these kind of craft quite exhilarating, as being so close to the water gave a true sensation of the speed. Ronnie Wilson sat in the stern one hand on the outboard tiller, which had the throttle turned to max power. He had an ice-cold can of Heineken lager in his other hand, which he sipped on from time to time. He was dressed somewhat more conservatively that his companion, with a check shirt and tan lightweight trousers.

In the centre of the boat was a large blue cool box, stocked with beer and an assortment of food for their lunch. Two fishing rods lay next to the cool box. When Wilson had suggested a few weeks previously, that the landing place might not be that difficult to find, Ellis had been quite dubious of his assumption. Until Wilson explained, that the authorities either knew where the pirates came ashore, or were not bothered. Either way, it could not be very far along the coast from Lagos. After all, he had reasoned, Lagos was where the contraband was undoubtedly sold. So because they couldn't risk looking like someone snooping round, they decided to look like expats, out for a Sunday 'burn up' along the creek, like so many often did.

The two previous Sundays they hadn't noticed anything suspicious. In fact, they were now starting to go over ground already covered. Though this was the first time they had travelled this part of the creek in an easterly direction. Ellis, who was sitting in the bow of the boat, casually scanned the bank and felt frustrated by the lack of progress on this case. He was used to more action and quicker results. He thought that Wilson's idea, of simply going out to see if they could find where the pirates landed, was slightly ludicrous and would probably prove to be a yet another dead end.

As the mangrove trees, creepers and the occasional small beach or clearing flashed past, he reflected on the case so far. A recent phone call to the Interior Minister, enquiring if he had any information, proved to be fruitless. In fact the man had been somewhat haughty and off-hand. He pointed out to Ellis that he was expecting information from him about the pirates, and not the other way round, though he did emphatically promise prompt and decisive action when the time came to eradicate the pirates. This heartened Ellis, knowing at least one person in authority in Nigeria, was committed to the cause.

After the meeting with Ekpe, Ellis asked Wilson to obtain some local assistance. Two reliable youths had been employed. One, called Johnson, had been hired to follow Ekpe and report on his movements. But so far this had revealed nothing, as all he ever did was go home to his wife. Another dead end. Ellis thought the radio cassettes displayed on the street stalls of Lagos, might provide a clue as to who was fencing the operation. A friend of Johnson, called Ndofu, had been assigned the task of following the delivery trucks, to find out from where the goods were distributed from. This he dutifully did on a Honda 90 moped that

Wilson had acquired for him. He had been instructed to take down details of all delivery trucks and also registration marks if any.

This was another extremely long shot, but in the six weeks Ndofu had been involved, it had at least turned up one shred of evidence. A name, Mohamed Attandah.

Two days previously, Ndofu had managed to follow an old jalopy of a truck back to a yard. The faded sign on the wall outside proudly announced, 'Attandah Trading Nigeria Ltd.' Ellis knew this was the barest of clues, as the truck's owner could be a few dealers down the chain, from whoever actually dealt with the pirate. However, Ellis thought, it might be worth following his truck after the next raid, to see where it goes.

Soon the boat reached the end of the creek and powered out into a windless South Atlantic Ocean. Even so with no wind, the craft rose and fell quite dramatically over the long rolling swell, which probably started off life as a storm many thousands of miles away, somewhere off the Cape of Good Hope. Ellis in the bow of the boat, like some kind of ancient sentinel, stared blankly out into the expanse of ocean, which unfolded like a vast blue carpet before him. The clear sky and the warmth of the sun on his skin did little to dispel his sombre mood. In fact he felt quite depressed, which was not an emotion his personality allowed to surface very often.

The case was weighing heavily on his mind and seemed to have thrown up an impenetrable wall for him to try and overcome, almost single-handed. His career thus far, had been quite spectacular. He was the blue-eyed boy of Interpol, fast tracked by his superiors for rapid promotion. But now he felt his career had ground to a complete stop. He was so engrossed in his dark thoughts, that it was only the violent motion of the craft, pitching up and down on the short steep swell that brought him back to his senses. Wilson, ever alert in the stern, saw the danger and reduced to half speed, to avoid the risk of flipping the lightweight boat over.

'Where are we going?' Ellis shouted to Wilson, above the roar of the outboard.

'Find some place to have lunch and enjoy the rest of the day.'

'Sounds fine to me.' Ellis scrambled towards the middle of the boat, dipped his hand into the cool box and retrieved an ice-cold can of beer.

'To hell with it all,' he said resignedly to himself, as he took a long cool draught of the refreshing beer, which made him feel slightly better.

After half an hour of pitching and rolling over the ocean swell, they approached the two long breakwaters which lead into Lagos harbour. These breakwaters point in a south-easterly direction, like two huge concrete fingers, beckoning vessels to enter the port. They were constructed by the British between 1908 and 1912 to protect the dredged entrance channel from strong wave action and consequent silting up.

They soon rounded the west mole and entered the channel leading to the port. The motion of the boat became a great deal more pleasant as they left the ocean swell behind them. Ten minutes later, Wilson altered course to port and headed for an inviting stretch of palm fringed, sandy beach. He ran the boat up the beach, expertly cutting the engine just before the boat ground softly ashore on the white sand. There were a quite a few other boats, high and dry along the beach. A number of barbeques were crackling away, and the smell of food cooking and burning, as it is so apt to do when barbequed, hung distinctively in the air. There were many groups of expats and locals drinking and generally having a good time, a typical Sunday afternoon booze-up in Lagos.

Ellis helped Wilson get the cool box out of the boat and they sauntered off towards one of the larger groups. Wilson greeted a considerable number of people as they made their way along the beach and they all seemed very pleased to see him. Evidently, a popular member of the expat community thought Ellis, who was impressed that his companion knew so many people. But then again he reasoned, if he had been living in a similar environment for many years, he would also be well known.

Eventually, they ended up talking to a group of people that Wilson had a particularly lively repartee with. Most of these were younger than him, a similar age to Ellis in fact. He couldn't help noticing, that there were some very attractive women amongst the group. Most of whom were European, interspersed with a few stunning Nigerian women, contributing enthusiastically to the general banter.

Almost immediately he could tell that some of these women, by their feminine actions, were particularly impressed with him. He thought cheerfully that it might turn out to be quite a good day, after the earlier disappointments. He soon erased all thoughts of the case from his mind and began to enjoy the atmosphere of the beach party, becoming slowly though quite pleasantly inebriated, laughing and joking with his new group of admirers. Then Wilson turned round to greet the latest arrival at the beach.

'Well it's nice to see you again. Where have you been hiding these last few weeks?'

'Oh you know how it is round here, always something happening.'

Ellis turned round to see a particularly attractive girl in a bi-kini, with blonde hair and long sun-tanned legs, walking casually towards them.

Ronnie beamed at Ellis then said.

'Martin, I'd like you to meet an old friend of mine. Lesley, let me introduce an associate of mine called Martin.'

'God isn't Ronnie so stuffy!' she said mockingly, then added, 'Pleased to meet you, Martin. Just arrived out from England, have you?' A beautiful pearly-white smile on a lightly sun-tanned skin made her look even more stunning; Ellis was immediately attracted to her.

'Er... Yes. I've been here six weeks now.'

'I suppose you are crossing the days off the calendar, like every-one else round here, till your next leave in the UK?'

'Well I was till about 60 seconds ago, but I'm not in such a hurry now.'

'Really, I wonder why?' she teased.

Ellis was so engrossed in conversation with her, that he failed to notice the presence of one more person, who had just finished unloading some items from the boat in which she had arrived. She turned round and smiled warmly at the tall African man next to her, then said.

'Well Martin, if you have just arrived in Lagos you probably haven't met this person either.'

'Hello,' the genial newcomer said, stretching out a rather large hand. 'My name's Henry. Henry Kaduna.'

Chapter Twenty

Just a little over four miles from the gaiety of the beach party that particular Sunday in Lagos, another scene was unfolding in the grim hell of Kala Kiri prison, where Captain Bill Jackson languished. A total shell of the man he had been previously, bloodshot eyes staring out crazily over six week's growth of beard. His hair long and matted and his body racked with dysentery, at least two stones lighter than when he was thrown into the zoo that purported to be a prison.

His filthy hands clinging onto the bars of the cage, he stared out hopelessly to even greater hell beyond. He was the only white man in that cell of thirty black prisoners and they took it in turns to vent their frustration on him. Colonialism, they had always been led to believe, was the real reason why their country was so poor, not the rampant corruption at all levels. The British had 'lorded it' over them for hundreds of years, the supposed superior race. But not in Kala Kiri prison. Everybody was equal here. Except for white people unfortunate enough to end up there.

Bill Jackson had contemplated suicide on many occasions. Only his belief in God and the thought of his family back home in England, had kept him from that final senseless act over the last six weeks. He had been raped by the inmates a number of times and knew that he probably had Aids by now.

Suddenly the cell went quiet, as the clip clop sound of onrushing boots was heard rapidly approaching. The other thirty prisoners looked madly towards the tunnel which led to their cage. A few started whining. The terrifying sound of the boots, that awful harbinger. The guards were coming. When they came and took someone, they never returned to the cell. Screams were usually heard late into the night. Eventually to be followed by silence, deathly silence.

The boots stopped, a frantic rattling of keys, and then the door at the end of the tunnel was thrust dramatically open. The metal door banged against the wall, as four immaculately dressed guards in khaki uniforms strode though. The sergeant in front of the group, took a clipboard from under his arm, scanned it briefly then shouted.

'Attention prisoners.'

Everyone in the cell froze. Bowels twitched.

'Bring prisoner Jackson to the gate now.'

A multitude of hands in unison grabbed hold of virtually every part of his body and propelled Bill Jackson roughly towards the entrance of the cell, thrusting his face hard against the dark rust streaked bars of gate. One of the other guards inserted a large metal key in the lock of the gate and in one swift movement of his wrist, unlocked the cell. The captain sprawled out onto the filthy floor and lay there; panting for a second, till the steel toecap of the sergeant's boot caught him in the ribs, lifting his body a few inches off the ground with the force of the blow.

'Get up or I give you some more, white bastard!' the sergeant shouted, voice laden with vehemence. Wincing, gripping his side with one hand he staggered slowly to his feet. It felt so painful he was sure a rib must be broken. Eyes half-shut with the agony of the blow, he was looking in the direction of the sergeant, who wore a sardonic smile beneath his moustache on the thick lips.

'Now up the stairs before you make me very angry, 'Mr Big Shot' white captain.'

Captain Jackson staggered as quickly as he could towards the door and up the stairs, his mind in turmoil. Half in mortal trepidation of what was in store for him next; the other half strangely relieved that soon it would all be over, as he could not stand to be locked up with thirty wild animals for a moment longer.

After the captain and the four guards reached the top of the stairs, they passed along a low dimly lit alley, through three more locked gates, up another smaller flight of stairs and then turned right into a square, windowless room. It was slightly better lit than the alleyway. He was pushed roughly by two of the guards onto the chair in front of a metal desk. Behind this sat a huge Nigerian, so corpulent that the folds of skin on his neck hung over his shirt. A huge round black face stared impassively at him, through beady little eyes. The man looked hideous and evil emanated from him and filled the room. Three of the guards quickly left and the steel door slammed emphatically behind them, the lock rattling shut. Only the sergeant remained and the man behind the desk. After about thirty seconds, which seemed like an eternity, the man behind the desk eventually spoke, in a deep, voice.

'Do you know who I am?'

'No sir I don't.'

'My name is Chief Superintendent Azubikas, head of Lagos police. I am also the man who hold the power of life and death in my hands for every person in this place.'

Jackson's mouth was dry and he swallowed to try and find some saliva, as he digested what the man had told him.

'Now listen to me very carefully,' the police chief said, voice hardening, a heavy note of menace becoming more evident as he spoke.

'I want you to tell me what you know about the two white men that has brought food to your cell.'

'Well I can't tell you very much, because I never met them before I was put in this prison. But as far as I know, they both work for the Britannic P & I Club.'

'Really,' Azubikas said, huge fat arms folded across his chest, nodding in a sage-like fashion. 'That's interesting what you has just told me, because one of them, the young one, have been doing all kinds of snooping round, asking a lot of questions and getting people to gather information for him.'

'Well I can't tell you anything about this, as I have been in here for the last six weeks.'

Azubikas suddenly exploded, slamming his huge paw on the desk. 'Don't get clever with me you insolent white dog!'

The sergeant strode quickly forward and with great power, backhanded Jackson across the right ear, knocking him to the floor. Then he roughly grabbed his collar and dumped him back on the metal seat.

'Now listen here. I want some answers and if I don't get them my sergeant will. Now tell me what you know, about those two men.'

Jackson looked up slowly, tears running out of his eyes, with the pain from his ribs and now his swollen right ear. He looked directly, almost arrogantly, into the eyes of the police chief then spoke slowly, in a deliberate manner.

'You can beat me up all day and night. But it will be a complete waste of your time. I don't know a thing about those two guys, other than what I told you.' His head slumped down resignedly, staring at the heavily bloodstained floor. Shoulders sagging, he looked a forlorn figure hunched on the chair. After a long time, perhaps a minute, with the room in complete silence, Azubikas spoke, his deep voice reverberating off the dank stone walls.

'You is free to go.'

Jackson was already in a state of extreme shock. His body shook and perspiration ran from virtually every pore. He had expected the true horror of hours of torture, ending in a slow excruciating death at the hands of his sadistic captors. So when the police chief told him he was free to leave, he immediately thought it was a trick. Some kind of sick joke, and certainly not true. He sat in stunned silence for a few moments. Then the Nigerian spoke again, in a slow deliberate tone. He sounded like he was losing patience with the prisoner.

'I said you is free to go. If you don't get up soon, I may change my mind and throw you back in the cell.'

'But I don't understand,' Jackson quickly blurted out. 'What about the poor Nigerian fellow who was killed?'

'Ha! That was your lucky day. The man who was killed turned out to be nothing more than a Ghanaian. If he had been a citizen of the Republic of Nigeria, you would have been tried and executed. Now get out of here, before I lose my patience completely.'

Without saying another word, the British captain got as quickly as he could to his feet and made for the door. The sergeant, who was close behind him, quickly unlocked the door and pushed him roughly through. He still thought it was some kind of trick and would only really believe he was free if he were actually sat on a plane, bound for England.

Azubikas slouched back in his chair and watched the captain depart. He smiled contentedly to himself. He had known for almost a month now that he would have to release the Englishman eventually. But he did not want him to get off lightly. He wanted him to truly suffer before being released, as he was certain his prison system would now have ensured. He had known about the nationality of the dead pirate since just after the incident. Then three weeks ago, the Home Secretary had phoned to tell him that the British government was bringing serious pressure to bear on Nigeria. They were threatening to cut off agricultural aid worth many millions, if the captain was not promptly released. Apparently the man's local MP was a frontbencher (whatever that meant) and quite high up in the ruling party. The MP had been able to use his considerable influence to bring the case to the attention of the British Government.

Then, as a final inducement to get the man released, the P & I Club had produced a considerable sum of money to make sure the right palms were suitably greased. A thin smile momentarily crossed Azubikas' lips, at the thought of the ten thousand dollars, his share of the inducement. However, right at the end before releasing the prisoner, he couldn't resist just one opportunity of terrorising him and he just had that satisfaction. All in all, it had been quite a pleasant day so far for Godwin Azubikas, Police Chief of Lagos. Just a pity he thought, that the captain genuinely did not have any information about this Ellis, the man he had been hearing so much about, from a number of his informants. Not to worry, Azubikas thought. His time will come, soon enough.

Barely three hours after leaving the presence of the police chief, Bill Jackson still could not believe he was on board a British Caledonian jet, thirty- five thousand feet above Nigeria, bound for London Gatwick at five hundred and fifty miles per hour. The speed with which he been turned from a stinking convict, into his present cleansed and presentable condition, was quite astounding. Minutes after leaving Azubikas he was led to a shower room and ordered to remove all his clothes. He stayed in the shower as long as the guard would permit. He scrubbed every inch of his skin viciously, with the remainder of his strength, in attempt to wash away the stench of life in that awful cell.

Emerging from the shower after about ten minutes, he found his shaving equipment and a small bag, with a suit and some of his clothes from the ship, on a chair nearby. He quickly shaved and dressed. Then he was virtually frog-marched to the prison gate by the sergeant and another guard. He watched the sergeant sign some papers, with a great flourish and then he was bundled into a police car and whisked rapidly to the airport. He was taken to the BCal check in, located in the middle of the departures hall. People in the queue for the flight, stared in horror at his crumpled suit and dishevelled appearance. The sergeant thrust his passport and a ticket to London into his hand. Then he turned abruptly, without a word, leaving him to check in alone.

Safe at last on his way home, he sighed and closed his bloodshot eyes, gritty with lack of sleep. He found it amazing that even though exhausted mentally and physically, sleep eluded him as the horrendous images of the last six weeks flashed before his eyes. Psychiatric counselling would be required for many months when he got home to help him come to terms, with the horror of incarceration in a West African prison. Even with the best help available, he would never be the same man again. His confidence permanently shattered, his life effectively ruined. Bill Jackson had become yet another victim of piracy. While the perpetrators, men like Henry Kaduna, acted with impunity, then lived a life of opulence from the proceeds of their hideous trade.

Chapter Twenty-One

Martin Ellis had been told right from day one in the training academy, that if you wanted to be a success at any form of police work, plenty of patience would be required to achieve this. The words of his instructor drifted faintly through his mind. This job is not about shoot-outs, hijacks, hostages etc. etc. Real police work was about grinding the facts available, till eventually something was squeezed out with which to work. Ellis was young and arrogant in those days and he had his own pre- conceived ideas, of how policing should be done.

He now sat as he did every night at this time, on the balcony of Ronnie Wilson's house in Apapa, watching yet another sunset over Lagos harbour. More than six weeks into this case, and still only the barest thread to work with. He was beginning after eight years in the force in one form or another, to see the wisdom of his instructor's words. Perhaps, he thought, his other cases had been resolved too quickly. Perhaps it needed something like this, to slow him down and make him develop other qualities of police work. Deep in thought, he did not notice Wilson padding out onto the balcony, with a gin and tonic in each hand.

'Come on chap, cheer up. You could be stuck in worse places than Lagos, you know.'

'I'd have to think really hard to come up with one,' replied Ellis testily.

'Try one of those countries in the Persian Gulf. At least you can drink as much as you want here and no one gives a toss.'

'That's true, the only complaint I've had in six weeks is from my liver.'

'Oh quit moaning, it's time for sundowners.'

So far, the only piece of information he had to work with was the truck of this trader Attandah. This had been seen on numerous occasions by one of his youths, off-loading Sony radio cassettes to stalls in the area. He was sure this man was heavily involved in fencing the operation. If he could just manage to follow one of the trucks after a raid, he might be able to pinpoint where the pirates were coming ashore. Perhaps even photograph them off-loading the booty. That at least would be a start. However there had been no pirate activity since the night of his arrival. Probably because of the huge furore that followed, due to one of the locals being killed. This state of affairs would not last forever. Eventually the pirates would be tempted back into action. When they did strike he would be ready, having formulated a plan he hoped would resolve the case. He had a distinct gut feeling that he would not have very long to wait.

His instincts as usual, were absolutely right. Barely three miles away from Wilson's house, in a small ramshackle beachfront bar, Henry Kaduna stared across the table at a very nervous Mr Ekpe. He had been inactive for a while and needed more action soon. The enforced absence had made him realise, how much he actually enjoyed what he did for a living. He missed the excitement of the hunter stalking his prey, the feel of the Uzi machine pistol in his hand and the power that this gave him. Also the knowledge that he could never lose, against the unarmed seamen he loved to terrorise. He missed the money as well of course. After all, he was not in the business just for the fun.

But circumstances had dictated that after the last raid, just like the one before, the situation be allowed to calm down. Now though, he was very restless. Wining dining and screwing Lesley was great, but he needed more in life than that alone. He found the arrogant Brits she introduced to him infuriating, though he played his part well, smiling, joking and laughing, though inwardly seething. One such Brit he had spoken to recently, on the beach, albeit very briefly, called Ellis, was typical of the race. Fair hair, well built, self-assured and all the women at the beach virtually throwing themselves at him. He wished he could kick down a captain's door one dark night off the port and find him on the other side, staring down the short stub-nosed barrel of his Uzi.

Another thing that concerned him about the recent inactivity was his band of pirates. No matter how rag tag they were, they would eventually drift away one by one and join other smaller, less successful operators than him. So he was inwardly pleased when Ekpe sent a messenger earlier in the day, to inform him some interesting information had come to light and that they should meet that evening.

It was dark already and looking out towards the sea, only blackness could be seen. Where the ocean joined with the cloudy sky was indiscernible. A light cool breeze blew off the ocean and wafted though the shack, offering pleasant relief from the oppressive night air. Kaduna sipped his ice cold beer, watching the condensation trickle down the side of remarkably new looking glass, silently regarding Ekpe over the rim.

Across the table from him sat Ekpe who was looking towards the floor. He was fidgeting with something out of sight below the level of the table, making no attempt at conversation. He found the little clerk quite reprehensible. The way in fact, he regarded any person he perceived to be weak.

The presence of Kaduna alone made Ekpe nervous. He knew this was not a man to play games with, a cold-blooded killer for sure. Since becoming involved, he had heard enough spine-chilling stories of how he went about his business, to drive even the calmest person to distraction. Apparently, during the last raid, he had ordered a gravely injured pirate to be dumped in the river, threatening to kill anyone who disobeyed him. How someone could be so insensitive to an African brother was beyond the mild mannered Ekpe. His drink lay untouched and he licked his dry lips constantly.

After the nerve-jangling visit of the P and I investigators, he felt like telling Kaduna he wanted no more to do with him. But when they never returned, his morale and confidence improved. The five thousand naira he had received after the heist had helped to pay off most of his debts. It was the easiest money he had ever earned in his life, the equivalent of six months of the measly salary that Kafu paid him at Bowman's office. So he was now driven by both fear and greed to continue the relationship. Eventually Kaduna spoke.

'So, what have you brought me this time?'

Ekpe coughed to clear his dry throat then spoke.

'Well there is a couple of things. I gets a feeling something different is gonna be happening. The boss been getting some long distance phone calls which he always take in his office with the door closed. Very strange. I just gets the feeling something big gonna be happening.'

'Don't sound so exciting to me.'

'Last couple of times it was to do with special high value cargo.'

'Alright, let me know as soon as you hear anything. What else have you got for me?'

'There is a ship anchored at the roads tonight, waiting for a pilot at first light. The captain, well, he wants to drift off the coast, to avoid pirates. But port control say there had been no attacks for months and the problem had now ceased. Also, if he don't anchor close to the port, where the pilot can get him easily, he would miss his turn for berthing first thing in the morning.'

'How do you know all this?'

'I heard them talking on Channel 14 of the VHF this afternoon.'

Kaduna knew from his years on ships that agencies usually had a marine VHF radio set in their offices, listening to Channel 16, in case a ship in the harbour or just off the port wished to contact them. He also knew that conversations were always carried out on another channel, as 16 was for calling and emergency use only. During his time at sea he had silently observed everything. His officers might have thought him to be just another dumb A.B. swabbing out the bridge, or doing some other equally menial chore. But he was actually storing in his memory whatever information came his way, for future use. So far, he had made exceedingly good use of this.

'Okay. So ships are still foolish enough to anchor close to the land. What is so special about this one?'

'Well, I has been watching this one for a while now. I was checking the manifest two weeks ago, when I finds there is one container with five tons of Citizen Watches,' he replied enthusiastically, nodding his head.

'Well that's certainly interesting,' Kaduna replied, sitting up in his chair and leaning closer to the to the senior freight clerk, stroking the goatee beard on his chin, never letting his gaze drop from the other.

'What else can you tell me about this ship?' he said quietly.

'The really good news is' the clerk continued, becoming excited and talking much quicker, 'the container is beside number one hatch, on the deck portside. It'jost like they have put it there as an invitation for someone to com' and help themselves.' He laughed for a few seconds at his joke, till he saw the other man was still looking seriously at him. Kaduna's razor-sharp brain quickly analysed the information he has just been given. Containers stowed at the forward end of vessels were the easiest targets, being so far away from the bridge. More often than not, a ship could sometimes be boarded and a container emptied without detection.

'Gimme the ship's name and the container number,' Kaduna demanded.

'Here, I have write both on a piece of paper for you.' Ekpe pushed a grubby slip towards the other side of the table. Kaduna read the scrawl and sat quietly for a few moments, weighing up his options. This certainly did seem too good an opportunity to pass up. He just wondered if the clerk had told him everything about the ship. He sensed this was not the case.

'Anything more to tell me? Like the nationality for instance?'

'Oh sorry, I forgot. Got too excited you see. She is registered in Le Havre. The captain sounded French on the radio as well.' He paused for a brief moment then continued. 'There is one more thing.'

'What's that?'

'The ship she just com from the USA.'

Kaduna's eyebrows rose noticeably, with the subtlety of a portcullis, quick to pick up the significance of that piece of information. He knew ships calling there, invariably stocked up with U.S. dollars, for the purpose of paying the crew's wages for the next few months. He drained the remnants of his beer, banged the glass on the table and leaned back on the chair, nodding thoughtfully. Yes, he said to himself, it was time to go back to work.

'Wake up Martin, there was an attack last night.' Wilson shouted excitedly, as he banged on the steel door to Ellis's bedroom. The heavy metal door was an integral part of the security in the house, protecting Ellis, or any other guest for that matter, from the attention of unwanted intruders during the night. Ellis had been awake for a good half hour, lying quite still on the bed, trying to dredge up some enthusiasm, for another day's drudgery as a pretend inspector for the Britannic P & I Club. He was watching a brightly coloured lizard called a Gecko, crawl slowly up the vertical face of the wall next to the window, in search of its next meal. It took a few seconds, before he realised what Wilson was saying, as his voice was muffled penetrating the thick steel door. Without speaking, he got up quickly from the bed, covering the few strides over the bare tiled floor to the door, in the blink of an eye. He slid back the two heavy retaining bars and opened the door to find Wilson standing there, fully dressed and eyes wide with excitement. 'What's happening?' Ellis said.

'As I've said a few times now, there was another attack last night.'

'How do you know?'

'I have just received a phone call a few minutes ago from the master of the vessel. We are the P & I Club for that vessel and he can't raise anyone else ashore so he tried us as the last option. The poor chap sounds awfully shook up, had a terrible night of it with one thing and another. Anyway the top and bottom of it, he has two men with gunshot wounds and has had a container cleared of its contents. Also his safe has been emptied, of almost thirty thousand dollars and the crew's cabins ransacked and most of their valuables stolen.'

'Hell! Sounds like a real bad one. Did he say how severely injured the men were?'

'One's pretty mashed up I'm afraid. Shot in the stomach, lost a lot of blood. The other took a couple of slugs in the leg but isn't critical. His main problem would appear to be he is getting zero assistance from the authorities, to get his two injured men ashore.'

'God how awful, people lying all over the place bleeding and no chance of seeing a doctor,' Ellis said with a considerable amount of feeling. He sympathised strongly with the two injured men, who were laying waiting for help that was slow to come, because he had been in that situation himself before. It was not a nice feeling.

'What time is he due to berth?'

'He is supposed to get a pilot within the next hour or so, which in normal circumstances would seem to be the solution to his problem.'

'Why do you emphasize normal circumstances?'

'Simply because the pilot boat has broken down again, the only other craft available is the port's sole remaining tug, but it has been out of service for many months. So it would appear if someone doesn't do something quickly, a poor seaman will die in the next few hours.'

Ellis thought for a few seconds, of some way to help the stricken seaman. But he was pessimistic about coming up with any easy solution. The idea of using Wilson's powerful speedboat sprang quickly to mind. But getting such a critically injured man, from the ship to a small boat, bobbing crazily up and down on the swell, was highly dangerous and would drastically worsen his chances of survival. So he disregarded that idea.

Even if the injured men made it quickly to the shore, the quality of medical care available in Lagos was quite appalling. This was apparent to him during a short visit to the local hospital, to interview a slightly injured seaman. The hospital was both under staffed and under equipped. In fact, the place reminded him of a photo, depicting a clearing station at the battle of the Somme. There were injured people lying round in virtually every location. Some on stretchers, others on trolleys, most were moaning or crying and some screaming in agony, as they waited hours for attention. What hope was there for someone with a bullet wound in the stomach receiving the proper medical help ashore in Lagos?

He moved slowly across the room and sat down on a settee opposite Wilson. His associate's fore head looked like a neatly ploughed field, as he was deep in thought like himself. Eventually Ellis started talking. Not because he felt he had anything specifically of use to say, but mainly to break the deathly hush in the room.

'Well Ronnie. You know this coast and shipping a hundred times better than me. There must be something that can be done.'

Wilson sighed and looked up with a vacant look in his eyes

towards Ellis, the palms of his hands upturned in a gesture of dismay.

'Yes I know this area better than most, which probably explains why I feel more despondent than most at this juncture. Blowed if I can think of anything to help them.'

After a few seconds Ellis started talking again, nodding his head up and down, as if to try and shake out some ideas.

'There has got to be some way to help these poor people. There is always a way. How about the army, they must have helicopters. Yeah, but getting the men ashore is only part of the problem. It's just a shame there isn't some kind of ship nearby that could help; a warship perhaps, with a helicopter and decent medical equipment on board. No chance of that though, I wouldn't think. I don't know. The whole thing has got me stumped.'

Wilson regarded his companion with a look of amazement.

'Now hold on a minute, young fellow. We can't say for sure that kind of help is definitely not available, can we?'

'Highly unlikely, I'd have thought. Not much need for any Navy presence round here,' said Ellis.

'True, it's unlikely, but not impossible,' Ronnie replied. He paused for a moment then added, 'But there are all kinds of other ships that have the same facilities. Survey ships, even passenger ships, have a fully trained team of doctors and nurses on board.'

'How the hell are we going to find out?'

'We're not, but the captain of the ship can put out a Sécurité alert on his MF radio. If there is anything like that in the area, they are duty bound by international regulations to respond and send help. It's an extremely long shot, but anything is worth trying in a situation like this. I'll call the captain on my VHF set immediately.'

Within a few minutes Wilson managed to contact the master of the 'Ville de Lyon,' who thanked him profusely for his idea. The ships radio officer, a short grossly overweight youth of twenty-four years old, from Lille in northern France, who squinted out from behind a pair of heavy greasy glasses, was on the bridge at that time. He quickly went into his radio room next to the chartroom. Soon his thick stubby fingers started transmitting a Sécurité alert, with the Morse key on the five-hundred megahertz frequency. This is the distress frequency used by shipping and International law required that all ships listen to this frequency. So any ship within two hundred miles should pick up the message.

Captain La Conte, a slim man of medium height, with thinning dark hair slicked back over his head, was silently cursing himself for not having thought of the same idea as the P & I inspector. After all, he had been at sea twenty-five years, it should have occurred to him. But he reasoned, after the night he had just endured, the lack of sleep, the debilitating effect of raw terror, plus the fact that he had to act as a doctor to a severely injured seaman, it was a wonder he was able to function at all. So having set the process in motion on the bridge, he headed down the stairs to the hospital three decks below, where the injured seamen were being looked after by the second mate.

When he entered the one bed hospital, he immediately saw the bosun sat on the floor on a cushion, back against the wall. He had been shot twice in the thigh of his right leg during the pandemonium that ensued soon after the pirates broke into the accommodation. He stared blankly at the deck in an obvious state of shock, but did look up when the captain entered, showing at least he was alert to changes in his surroundings. The captain had given him five millilitres of morphine soon after the incident. A tourniquet had been applied to his leg, released by the second mate every twenty minutes to keep the leg alive. He was unable to walk and the captain was sure one of the bullets must have broken his femur, though; at least he was a stable condition.

Lying on the blood-soaked bed, with a trance-like stare into space, was the fair-haired, twenty-six year old second engineer, from Arles in the south of France. He had been shot in the stomach, as he tried to stop the pirates ransacking his cabin and stealing a large sum of cash he had foolishly tried to keep hidden there. His face was becoming so white through loss of blood, it was almost anaemic. The pale face, fair hair and the white pillow on which his head rested limply, almost merged into one. A sickening sight, but worse, much worse, he also kept complaining of feeling cold.

The captain knew from his limited knowledge of medicine, that this was a very bad sign. The man may only have a few hours to live, unless he received expert medical attention soon. He also had been given an injection of morphine and another of penicillin, in an attempt to counter the infection which was undoubtedly spreading from his bowels to the rest of his body. A large thick wad of cotton wool had been applied to the ugly black wound just above his navel. Bandages were tightly wrapped round his body, in an unsuccessful attempt to stop the blood oozing out of the wound.

As the frail figure of the second engineer lay motionless on the bed, Captain Henri La Conte had an all-pervading feeling of helplessness. There was absolutely nothing more he could do for this poor young man. Only the previous evening, before dinner, he had regaled all in the officer's bar with some of his lewd exploits in the various ports he had visited. Most of which would have been regarded as unprintable. He was the veritable life and soul of the party, but if help did not arrive soon, would be making a one-way trip to the ships provision fridge, in a body bag. What a terrible waste of a young man's life. All caused, by an evil bunch of cut-throat pirates, who would in all likelihood never be caught. He had heard stories, that in some parts of the world they were in league with the police and various other authorities. As he watched the life drain slowly out of the second engineer, the memories of the last six hours flooded back.

The first knowledge he had that the pirates were on the ship was when the phone by his bed rang just before five to one in the morning. He dressed quickly and rushed up the one flight of stairs to the bridge, which was on the deck above his cabin. Heart pounding, stomach a tight knot of dread, he walked quickly out on the port bridge wing. Then, he peered cautiously along the ship's side and saw the faint outline, of a very large canoe at the forward end of number two hatch. Banging sounds could be heard from forward, as the boarders tried to open a container, or break the tempered steel padlock into the foc'sle.

The sinister muffled sound of numerous hushed voices could be heard on the Amplidan talkback system, which had been left hidden, out of sight on the foc'sle head. Indelibly printed on his memory, was the expression on the young second mate's face. It was etched with worry, looking perhaps for a few words of reassurance from his captain.

When none came, he spoke haltingly, his nervousness evident in his speech.

'Wha, wha, what are we going to do sir?'

'Absolutely nothing,' he had replied emphatically.

'But, they are stealing the cargo and the stores,' the second mate had pleaded.

'Let them have it. It's all covered by insurance anyway.'

'But what if they decide to attack the accommodation?'

'They will fail,' he had stressed confidently. 'All of the doors are bolted shut on the inside. The outside ladders are down. They could never climb the vertical face of the accommodation. I made it my business, before we reached this hellhole of a coast, to tighten up on our personal security. Believe me. They will leave soon when they have filled their canoe.'

One hour later, the stark realism of how seriously he had underestimated the pirates was being driven home to him. He was locked behind the reinforced steel door to his cabin, with three heavy metal locking bars in place as a sledgehammer pounded away on the other side, probably from the ships bosun's store, a bitter irony. An awful spectre grew before his eyes as the door, slowly but surely, came off its hinges. Panic-stricken, certain his life would end soon, he was tempted, severely tempted to get the ship's pistol out of the safe. But he quickly reasoned, after killing one or two, he would eventually succumb to their superior numbers.

So before the door finally collapsed, he went to the safe and took out all the cash. Thirty thousand U.S. dollars, twenty thousand French francs and some British sterling then left the safe door open. He made no attempt to conceal the bulk of the cash, to try and dupe the pirates. At that instant he was interested in one thing only and it was not saving the company's money.

Next, he quite methodically stacked the cash neatly on his desk. He placed the gun where it could be seen in front of the money, with the clip visibly out, then sat down calmly behind his desk, to await his fate. If he were to die, which he was sure would most probably be the case he was fiercely determined not to give them the pleasure of seeing his terror. After all, he was French and his dignity even in such dire circumstances had to be upheld.

Barely seconds after sitting down, the door collapsed inwards with a sickening crash. Three pirates rushed in brandishing an assortment of weapons. One had what appeared to be a rusted World War Two Sten gun. Another had an equally poorly maintained pistol of some description. Whether these weapons would actually work, he very much doubted, but was never the less, not about to find out.

The obvious leader and by far the tallest and beefiest, had a modern machine pistol. This looked totally efficient and deadly. He was dressed in a green combat suit, heavy army boots and had a soldier's forage cap pulled down tight on his head. This served to accentuate the cold steely eyes, which stared out from under the peak of the cap, directly at him. The other two looked like a pair of vagrants, dressed in ragged stained shirts and torn jeans. On their heads they had grubby woollen hats. The type worn by skiers in winter time, probably sent out to West Africa by Oxfam, or some other charitable organisation. They were both wide-eyed.

High on drugs and they looked extremely volatile and dangerous. However, all three were visibly taken aback when they saw him sitting calmly behind the desk. They had no doubt expected some form of resistance, or to see a quivering wreck of a man pleading pathetically for mercy. Amazingly the leader laughed. He looked at his two accomplices and said vehemently, 'Get out.' The two virtual tramps obeyed instantly without protest and quickly left the cabin. Headed to the decks below no doubt, to see what mayhem they could wreak, unchecked in that location.

After the two had departed, the pirate leader leaned on the captain's desk and looked him straight in the eyes. Captain La Conte expected to be scythed down at any second, in a withering burst from his machine pistol. But he steadfastly refused to avert his eyes from the other. After a few seconds, the pirate stood back and spoke in a surprisingly eloquent voice.

'I like your style, Frenchie. It's the only thing, between you living and me pulling the trigger of this gun. I'm not even going to check the safe or search the rest of the cabin. If you had tried to trick me, like so many before, I would have finished you.'

The pirate quickly grabbed all the cash. He stuffed it into the various pockets of his combat suit. Finally he pushed the clip back into the ships pistol. He waved it briefly, terrifyingly, in front of the captain's face, before thrusting it efficiently into the belt round his waist. Then he turned without another word and disappeared rapidly out of the cabin door. Captain Henri La Conte slumped onto his desk, head in hands, unable to believe that he was still alive. After a few moments, when the tension drained from his body he looked up and tried to gather his thoughts. What a horror story of a night! The first thing his mind could focus on was the sounds of total bedlam on the decks below. Then he heard it, the awful sound of gunfire and someone screaming. Then a few seconds later, the chaos receded like a fast flowing ebb-tide, the noise stopped and the pirates were gone.

As the French captain stood there in the hospital, barely five hours after the whole horrific incident, he looked down sadly at the rapidly fading second engineer. He realised the captain was staring at him and turned his head, looking despairingly into his eyes.

'I've had it sir. I'm going to die.'

'Hang on Second. Don't give up. Listen, we could be in port in an hour or so and you in the hospital soon after.' This he knew was highly improbable, but he had to say something to give the sick man hope. Unable to look at the dying seaman any longer, he looked way. It was daylight now and through the porthole at the aft end of the hospital, he could see the glimmering, endless expanse of ocean beyond. The captain was in an almost trancelike state, his mind overcome with a sense of hopelessness. The only sounds discernable to him were the hum of the generators and creaking of the accommodation, as the ship rolled easily in the low swell. Then suddenly, he heard another sound much closer, the rhythmic pounding of feet along the alleyway.

He looked round at the hospital door in a daze, trying desperately to focus his exhausted mind, when suddenly the radio officer burst though the door, face wild with excitement, triumphantly clutching a piece of paper.

'Sir, sir, it's a miracle. We've had a response to the Sécurité message I sent out.'

It took a few moments for the words of the sparks to register then the captain came rapidly back to reality.

'Yes, yes, Sparks. What have you got? Come on man, what have you got?' he said, suddenly alert, and sounding impatient.

'A real bit of good luck sir.' Sparks was punching the air with delight, he was so excited.

'Calm down man. What do you have to tell me?' The captain said quietly.

Sparks took a deep breath and continued.

'I've made contact with a U.S. Aircraft carrier called the 'Forrestal'. She's on her way from the Cape to Gibraltar, about one hundred and twenty miles to the south of us. I gave them our position and they can have a chopper on our deck in just over an hour. But they need to know the blood group of both the casualties, so they can send the right blood and plasma with the medical team.'

The captain maintained his composure, but inside he was jubilant at the news. He rushed out of the hospital with the sparks close behind, along the alleyway and up the two flights of stairs to his cabin. From the locker behind his desk, he quickly retrieved the personal files of the two injured seamen. He found their pre-joining medical examination reports, and jotted down the all-important blood groups on a piece of paper. He thrust the paper into the eager hand of the sparks, who bounded up the stairs to the bridge, picked up the handset of the radio telephone and quickly contacted the aircraft carrier. He quickly relayed the information regarding the blood groups of the injured seamen. The carrier said they would clear everything with the Nigerian authorities. Telling them it was a training exercise and that a chopper would be at their position in just over an hour.

Meanwhile down in the ship's hospital the second engineer lay incredibly still, almost comatose. He felt increasingly cold and was having difficulty keeping awake. The second mate had to keep talking to him and shaking him gently every so often. But as time dragged on he became more despondent of help arriving in time. He knew the signs. His limited knowledge of medicine told him the man needed blood and plasma soon, or he would be dead within the hour.

The minutes ticked slowly by, as the crew on deck and on the bridge waited for the arrival of the helicopter. The sea was flat calm, with the low sun glinting on the water like vast silver lances. The ship rolled easily on the long swell, as if being rocked by a giant pair of hands. Low cloud just above the horizon to the south spoiled what was a perfect azure sky. Visibility was excellent and a dozen pairs of eyes, from the crew standing by on deck, to the officers on the bridge, scanning the distant horizon with powerful marine binoculars, searched expectantly for the first sign of the American helicopter.

Suddenly it happened. Almost due south, just above the low clouds, a small round shape could be seen approaching at a rapid pace. As the outline quickly materialised into a helicopter, the first sounds could be heard. Faintly at first, barely audible, came the flop, flop, flop of the distant helicopter's rotor blades. Soon this became a deafening crescendo of noise, as the helicopter rapidly loomed large on the starboard quarter. Then it banked steeply, as it made a complete circuit round the ship, so the pilot could ascertain the condition of his landing zone. The ship's VHF radio burst into life, as the pilot's speech, shrouded in the deafening noise inside his cockpit, filled the bridge.

'Okay Ville da Lyon. This is Mike Charlie 5 coming in to make a landing on your deck.'

The helicopter came in slowly from the starboard side, just above the level of the hatch top, skipping over the ships bulwark, inching carefully closer, towards the landing spot. Eventually it set down gently in the middle of the hatch. The pilot quickly cut the engine. A low pitched whining sound could be heard, mixed in with the general din of the rotor, as the turbo in the engine slowed down. The door on the port side of the helicopter sprang open and four heavily built men, dressed in white tight fitting coveralls leapt out. They split into pairs and each pair carried a stretcher. Ducking down instinctively below the slow spinning rotor, they raced towards the aft end of the hatch. Close behind them was a doctor and three medical orderlies, carrying shoulder bags full of equipment.

The chief mate was waiting at the aft end of the hatch and led the medical team into the accommodation through the main deck door, then proceeded up one flight of stairs and along the starboard side of 'A' deck alley, to the tiny hospital at the end. The captain, who had left the bridge after the helicopter had safely landed, was waiting for them at the entrance to the hospital. The stretcher bearers stopped in the alley and were overtaken by the medical team, training having taught them that the doctor would call when they were needed.

The doctor eased his slim frame past the burley stretcher-bearers and recognising the captain of the ship standing at the entrance to the ship's tiny hospital, quickly introduced himself. The captain then swiftly gave him the case histories of the two patients, including what medicine had been administered.

Next the American medical orderlies rapidly connected an intravenous drip to each arm of the second engineer. The doctor checked the patient's temperature and pulse, and then gave him a shot of blood clotting agent and another of morphine. He then had a quick look at the bosun's wounds. He dressed these and fixed a splint to immobilise the broken leg, then called the stretcher-bearers to carry him to the waiting helicopter.

The two remaining stretcher-bearers clattered noisily into the hospital and held the stretcher level with the bed, as the doctor and the orderlies carefully lifted the ashen, shaking second engineer onto it. Then they hurriedly covered him with a blanket, before departing down the alleyway to the waiting helicopter, one orderly each side holding the fluid bottles.

As the helicopter eventually disappeared from view, heading at one hundred and fifty knots in the direction of the carrier, Captain La Conte stared in silence for many minutes towards the distant horizon. The Americans had been on the ship less than ten minutes. Which all seemed to blur into one long ill defined instant of time. He felt light-headed, almost dizzy and was glad to be holding on to the Taff rail, on the bridge wing. Whether this feeling was due to the lightning sequence of recent events; lack of sleep, or worry over the survival of the second engineer, he was not sure and certainly did not care. He hoped desperately that his officer would survive. No one deserved to die as a result of the actions of a savage bunch of pirates, who in all probability would never be caught. Eventually he turned and walked slowly, wearily, towards the open door of the wheelhouse. He felt so drained that he would sleep for a week, given the opportunity.

Just as he entered the wheelhouse the VHF burst into life. But it was not the laid-back American accents this time, but a heavily accented African voice that filled the bridge.

'Dis the pilot boat. You has to com to the breakwater right away. Pilot is waiting to board you.'

The captain took a deep breath, sighed resignedly and said quietly.

'Magnifique…'

Chapter Twenty-Two

Echo Beach is about three miles east of Lagos, a broad expanse of dark sand that shelves dangerously into the sea. Swimming is not recommended due to the undertow from the huge Atlantic rollers, which crash constantly onto the beach. Such is the strength of this powerful off-shore current that it will effortlessly suck an unsuspecting swimmer out to sea, never to be seen again. Most of the West African coast suffers from this phenomenon. Unlike beaches in more civilised countries, there are no lifeguards or any other emergency facilities at Echo Beach. A person foolish enough to go swimming, encountering difficulties would find scant comfort in the fact that the nearest help was Clifton beach at Cape Town, three thousand miles away.

Swimming though, was the last thing on the mind of Henry Kaduna, who was slouched back in the shade, on the worn sun lounger, placed conveniently close to the beach bar. He was sipping a cocktail of some description, which Lesley had obtained for him. Relaxing, reliving the action and the adrenalin surge from the night before. This always gave him a much greater high than any drug. The raw power of a machine pistol in the palm of his hand and the terror it could so easily inflict on an adversary, was a thought worth savouring.

As he sat there quite contentedly, the cool afternoon breeze caressed his toned body. He watched with a degree of amusement that comes only with knowledge, as some drunken expats played an incredibly dangerous and stupid game, dodging the waves as they pounded onto the foreshore. They laughed childishly, as they ran from the waters edge and back to safety, just in front of around forty tons of foaming, angry water. He smiled thinly and thought quite jovially, if one were sucked out to sea, which was not unknown, he would be the last person going to their rescue.

Much earlier that day, from the balcony of his apartment, through powerful Zeiss binoculars, he had watched impassively as a totally different kind of drama unfolded. There in plain sight a few miles from the coast, a U.S. helicopter had dramatically appeared, landed on a ship and airlifted two wounded men. He cared not a jot, that all this commotion was a direct result of him organizing an attack on the merchant ship the night before. In fact it made him feel quite proud of his work. The degree of chaos he was able to create, so infinite that eventually the ship had to call in assistance, from the U.S. Navy to sort the problem out. That was quite an achievement on his part. He would have gone straight out again that that night and attacked another ship, except there were no ships off the coast. Also without doubt, his band of pirates would all be staggering round in a drunken stupor. Or passed out, covered in vomit down a filthy garbage strewn alley somewhere in Apapa.

He felt only derision towards those weaker than himself and the majority of the pirate gang fell into that category. But he now had that wonderful feeling of immortality, which came to him after a particularly successful raid. Only an hour previously he had screwed Lesley's brains out, his desire for her heightened by the previous night's action. She lay exhausted, fast asleep on a sun lounger next to him. He had even been able to smooth-talk her into quitting her job at the casino in Lagos and leave Nigeria with him when the time was right. Women were so gullible, he mused to himself. Furthermore, the police chief had been less threatening than usual, when he phoned him before noon. He had arranged

243

to meet him later in the day, once the goods had been disposed, to give his share of the cash and the loot.

There were still a couple of hours before the meeting with Attandah at the beach in Badagry Creek. So he lay back on the sun lounger and closed his eyes, listening to the rhythmic sound of the waves crashing on the beach. He was suddenly feeling very tired after the exertions of the previous night and the recent passion with Lesley. Very soon he dozed, though still aware of every sound around him, his inbuilt self-preservation mechanism never fully switching off at any time. He felt very contented as he drifted in and out of sleep. Congratulating himself on the mayhem he had yet again been able to create, also committing such exquisitely gross crimes and once again, getting away with it.

That afternoon in Lagos, Martin Ellis was also mildly, congratulating himself, because at last, after seven weeks in Nigeria he had achieved something positive. It was a few minutes after four p.m. and Ronnie had given him the heartening news. The carrier had contacted the ship, to inform them that the second engineer had undergone a successful operation. Although not out of danger, his vital signs were improving and his condition was stable. Ellis was exhilarated by the thought that an idea of his, might eventually have helped to save someone's life.

So even though he sifted laboriously through yet another pile of insurance forms, his spirits were noticeably lifted. He knew that soon, very soon, the pirate would have to dispose of the merchandise. When this happened he would be ready to move quickly. His two assistants, Johnson and Ndofu, were stationed round the clock, watching the merchants' yard for any sign of a truck movement.

He was in contact with them at all times, by means of the matt grey Motorola radio that lay at the end of his desk. This specialised piece of equipment, had radio crystals installed, with exclusive frequencies, ensuring all conversations would be private. He had recently obtained four of these with great difficulty and expense, one thousand U.S. dollars each. Nigeria did not as yet have a ready supply of the technology found in Europe and the USA. However, Ronnie's local knowledge once again proved invaluable in tracking a down a dealer with this specialised Hi -Tec equipment in stock. Ellis and Wilson each had one of the radios, so did Johnson and Ndofu. Johnson had reported in at four o'clock that there was no sign of movement. Now all that could be heard on the radio was the occasional crackle and hiss over the airwaves.

He stretched back on his chair, yawned, and looked round about him. His eyes once again assaulted by the untidy piles of folders, that seemed to endlessly clutter this small office, making working more claustrophobic and oppressive than needed. He couldn't fathom why such a precise person as Wilson, hadn't got a proper filing system in place, to make the office more manageable. When he had casually broached the subject one day, soon after arriving, he was idly swept aside by his companion. He had the infuriating reasoning that the office had been in operation for ten years and was functioning just fine, so why change the system? Ellis pursued his argument no further.

Ellis was just about to stand up and get yet another Styrofoam cup of chilled water, from the bulbous glass cooler in the corner of the office, which looked like some kind of alien, when the Motorola buzzed quietly into life.

'Boss, boss, dis Johnson. Com in boss, dis Johnson,' a distinctive African lilt to his voice. Though his voice was soft, slightly over the level of a whisper, it had a noticeable inflection of anxiousness.

Martin Ellis casually reached over and picked up the radio, pressing down on the transmit button and holding the radio close to his mouth. There had been many false alarms in the last few days, both Johnson and Ndofu finding a child-like glee in using the radios, so he was expecting nothing special from this call.

'Yes Johnson. This is Ellis, any movement?'

'Yes boss. Two trucks jost left the yard. I saw Attandah in the passenger's seat of the first one,' came the breathless excited reply.

Ellis came rapidly alert, his pulse quickening in anticipation of some action at last. 'Which direction were they going, Johnson?' Ellis prompted.

'I thinks they is heading for the motorway and the airport. I'm jost gonna to start the motor cycle and follow the trucks.'

'Good work Johnson, remember what I told you. Don't get too close to the truck, stay about one hundred metres back. Do you copy?'

'Yes boss loud and clear.'

At the far end of the office, Ronnie Wilson had been listening to the exchange between Ellis and Johnson. As Ellis made his way past his desk towards the door, he looked up over his glasses, at the rapidly departing younger man and said.

'A bit of strop chap?'

'Yes you could say so! Perhaps mega strop, by the time the day is out.'

Ellis stopped momentarily, turned round, and looked earnestly at Wilson.

'Listen Ronnie, I'm going to try and track this trader to the hide out. You've got a Motorola, just watch my back in case the plan turns to… well you know.'

'Yes don't worry I'll do what I can if there is a problem. Good luck.'

'Thanks.' Ellis turned and bounded down the stairs two at a time, unbuttoning his shirt and loosening his tie as he went.

Underneath the Britannia P & I office was a garage, with an aluminium up and under type door. At the inner end of the garage, covered in a light film of dust, was what gave the appearance of being a beat up motorcycle. The front forks were rusted and scratched, the tank had a dent and the seat was ripped. The machine beneath the façade however was a 250cc single cylinder Yamaha trail bike in tip-top mechanical condition. When Ellis bought it shortly after arrival in Lagos, he put it into a small workshop recommended by Wilson. He told them to give the machine a thorough overhaul and renew all the worn parts of the engine, gearbox, suspension, and brakes. He even had fitted brand new tubes and tyres, so that the machine was mechanically very sound. When it came back from the workshop, he rather grudgingly set the carburettor to run a tad rich, so that the exhaust smoked slightly. The exhaust of every vehicle, whether two or four wheels in Lagos smoked, due to lack of maintenance and worn piston rings etc. So he did not want to draw undue attention to himself, by having the only machine without a trail of smoke.

Hanging next to the machine, were some scruffy clothes and a well-worn, black three-quarter face helmet. Ellis quickly threw off his crisp white shirt and tan trousers and put on a stained shirt, scruffy worn out jeans and a pair of extremely worn trainers. He secured the helmet on his head and reached over to a shelf above the motorcycle. He then deftly opened a tin and smeared oily black makeup on his face neck and hands. He clipped the Motorola to his belt and a special extension mike to the inside of his shirt. He pressed the button of the mike and spoke.

'Where are you Johnson?' No reply. 'Come in Johnson, where are you?'

Then the mike spluttered to life and Johnson's voice could be heard over the din of a Honda 90 moped.

'Hello boss I'm jost at the start of the motorway now. But the second of the trucks has stopped. I think it have a problem with the engine. I am behind the first truck. We are abouts to cross the Apapa Bridge.'

'Okay, I'll be waiting at the first turning after the bridge. When I come alongside you take the next turn off the motorway and go home.'

'Okay boss loud and clear.'

A few minutes later Ellis was on his way along Creek Road towards the motorway. The road was virtually free of traffic; most of the people still at work in the small factories and offices in that part of town. So he made good time, taking care not to go too fast and attract unwanted attention. Belying its external appearance, the two fifty Yamaha felt exceedingly smooth as Ellis changed effortlessly up and down the gears, delighting in the surge of acceleration between cogs. If required he mused, this would be an extremely difficult machine to catch. A reassuring fact at any rate, as he overtook a slow moving bus and roared up the access road to the motorway, lifting the front wheel of the machine as he did so.

A few hundred few yards along the road, he pulled over onto the hard shoulder, engaged neutral, left the engine running and sat confidently astride the machine, like a rider about to start the Isle of Man TT, or a Grand Prix race at some exotic continental circuit like Assen or Monza. After a few moments the bus passed him and he craned his head to his left looking back along the empty motorway for a sign of Attandah's truck.

The road was almost devoid of traffic and a heat haze rose steadily from the virtually smooth Tarmac. Odd puffs of dust caused by heat thermals drifted across the road, obscuring visibility slightly. After one or two minutes, he saw the wavy form of a high sided vehicle about half a mile distant. Thick black smoke pouring from the exhaust, as it approached from the direction of the city. That must be it, he thought. He pretended to be looking at the engine of the motorbike as the truck passed, but could still see clearly on the wooden planked side of the vehicle, in garish blue and white writing, Attandah Trading. His spirits soared. At last he had something real to work with.

He waited till Johnson and his Honda 90 passed him then fell in fifty metres behind, gradually catching him. When he momentarily pulled alongside, despite the black make up he was recognised immediately, by a nonchalant nod of the head. Johnson knew the drill and slowly fell back, leaving the motorway at the next junction two miles further down the road.

Not wishing to be spotted by the two men in the truck, though it was unlikely as they would be concentrating on the road ahead, he fell back to a distance of just over one hundred metres. There was no traffic on the motorway, so the truck was always in full view. Eventually after another fifteen minutes, the truck turned off the motorway, and down a number of roads in the suburbs of Apapa.

Ellis couldn't help noticing that the houses in this area spoke volumes for the affluence of their inhabitants. Poor, very poor. Single storey buildings, rust-streaked corrugated tin roofs with mud floors. A virtual plethora of ragged, barefooted children playing the street, with squawking chickens, small black pigs and scrawny dogs as their playmates. A heavy odour of the open sewer at the side of the street hung distinctively in the air.

On more than one occasion, he had to take evasive action as a child or animal ran in front of him. He knew from years of experience, that motorcycles were not as forgiving as cars in crash situations. Cars were dented, motorcyclists were injured or killed.

The thought had occurred to him more than once, since starting to follow the truck that perhaps Attandah's truck may have been on some other kind of business. After all until now, the basis of this particular line of enquiry was fairly flimsy at best. However his doubts were soon erased as the houses petered out, and the truck suddenly turned off the main road. It lumbered carefully along a narrow rutted track, just wide enough for the passage of one vehicle. Initially, the track passed through tall marsh grass and bamboo trees, which after a mile or so, became fringed on either side by dense verdant jungle.

It was approaching sunset and light, as it does in the tropics, was fading fast. Ellis gingerly followed the truck along the jungle trail, carefully avoiding the ruts. Knowing that at such a slow speed, if his front wheel caught a rut the wrong way, he would be thrown to the ground, like novice by a black belt at Judo. He was pleased he had the workshop take care to all aspects of the Yamaha's overhaul, including the electrics and the lights. As when darkness set in, the jungle would have as much visibility, as could be had from the centre of a barrel of Nigerian crude oil.

Now he would have to be really careful. A narrow track, the truck up ahead. Suddenly, with the euphoria of the chase fading, he felt incredibly vulnerable. He had assumed the pirates would travel to the rendezvous by water. He hadn't considered what he would do if some decided to come by road. He decided to stop and take stock of the situation before proceeding. Deftly changed down through the gears he pulled up quickly. Hitting the cut out button for the engine, this died immediately.

He removed his helmet and listened for sounds of approaching traffic. At first he could hear quite clearly, the low gear engine noise and the creaking of the suspension of the truck up ahead. But this mechanical sound soon became swamped by a cacophony of other sounds. Jungle sounds. Some discernable like bats, parakeets, and toads croaking in the distance. Other sounds a native would have been able to identify, but not a European city dweller such as Martin Ellis. He was relieved to find that no sound could be heard from the road behind.

He reached down and spoke quietly into the Motorola mike, ears and senses strained for any change in the sounds round about him.

'Ronnie. You there? Come in Ronnie.'

A rustling sound came over the mike, indicating that radio at the other end, had just been hurriedly picked up.

'Yes come in Martin. You're a bit faint mate but I can just hear you.'

Ellis felt relieved, on hearing a friendly voice on the radio.

'Just to let you know where I am, if case things turn nasty. I came through community nine, then about half a mile outside that area, turned left onto a narrow trail. I followed the truck since the Lagos Apapa Bridge. I'm certain now that the truck is heading to meet up with the pirates.'

'Okay Martin, I've got a rough idea where you are. I'll come over in the car and wait just outside community nine. That way you will have someone close at hand, if the wheels fall off.'

Ellis was relieved to hear he was not going to be entirely alone. 'Thanks Ronnie I appreciate that, over and out.'

Before restarting the motorcycle, he listened carefully once more, to make sure he was not being followed. Then he re-buckled his helmet, started the engine and proceeded cautiously down the trail. The truck was no longer visible. It was dark now and he kept his lights dipped to avoid being spotted by the truck, or anyone else who might be in the vicinity. After approximately five minutes, he could see the tail lights of the truck up ahead. He could also make out the truck's surprisingly powerful headlights, rocking back and forth off the side of the jungle, as the truck lumbered along. Watching the floor of the trail for holes and ruts and his rear-view mirror to make sure he was not being followed, he stayed behind the truck for another ten minutes.

The jungle was becoming clearly less dense and he caught oc-casional glimpses of the silvery ribbon of water, he knew to be Badagry Creek. The track turned to the left and came to what looked like an open space, one hundred metres up ahead. He stopped and watched the movements of the truck, as it came into the clearing and eventually ground to a halt. He quickly pushed the machine into the undergrowth. When he stepped back, the green bushes sprang back to their original shape, effectively cam-ouflaging the Yamaha. He smiled to himself and said under his breath, 'Nice job Ellis.'

Then an alarm bell rang in his head.

That it may just be too good a concealment job and if he wasn't careful, he might not find the bike later. He broke some of the branches off the bush. Then as an extra precaution, he placed a rotten piece of wood he found on the floor of the jungle a few centimetres from the edge of the track.

He could now hear the muffled sounds of the voices up ahead. Though he could not discern clearly what was being said, it sounded just like general banter, punctuated with occasional laughter. Keeping as close to the bushes and trees as possible, without touching them, he crept furtively along the trail, towards the position where the truck had stopped. Ever conscious of the exposed situation in which he had placed himself, he was starting to become really nervous. All the training had gone right out of the window on this operation. His instructors at Interpol would surely have though him certifiable for operating in this manner, with no real back up. It was in fact, the frustration of the weeks of inactivity that led him to act in this irresponsible manner. Now deeply committed, he was determined to see this exercise through and glean some information that night.

Almost noiselessly, he closed in on the occupants of the truck and those with whom they conversed. He was starting to pick out odd words that were being said, all of little significance so far. Through the gaps in the trees, illuminated in the trucks headlights fifty metres away, Ellis could see four or five men sat on the ground, in front of what appeared to be a large pile boxes. Creeping ever closer along the jungle track, he could feel his heart beating against the side of his ribcage, his mouth was dry and his hands shaking noticeably. Sweat poured from every pore in his body, as the humidity and heat in the jungle coupled with his own nervous tension, took its toll.

Inching forward, concentrating hard on maintaining cover while trying to eavesdrop on the muffled conversation up ahead almost proved fatal. Such was his desire to actually find out what was being said, he almost failed to hear a new sound. A spear of dread hit him in the heart, as he realised exactly what that new sound was. A car was approaching at speed. He dived into the undergrowth, and looked back nervously along the trail. A dull glow had started to illuminate the track and jungle on either side, rising and falling noticeably on the side of the trees, as the vehicle travelled over the bumps of the trail. Within the space of a few seconds the light, together with the noise of the engine, had increased dramatically in intensity. Till eventually a car burst into sight, headlights blazing, scything a bright swathe of light through the inky blackness of the night.

Ellis caught a brief view of the car, a battered yellow Toyota, as it rocketed past his hiding place, travelling at speed, bounding over the ruts and bumps before powering out into the clearing, skidding to a stop. He was immensely relieved to have remained undetected but couldn't help thinking that the driver must either be completely ignorant of the damage such a bumpy road can do to suspension, tyres and shock absorbers, or he was rich enough to not care. He though the former was the more likely.

Once the car had come to a stop, its driver Henry Kaduna, killed the lights, switched off the ignition and climbed out. He quickly assessed the scene in front of him. Oti, Asamwa and three others had brought the merchandise from its place of hiding into the clearing, ready to be loaded onto the truck when the deal had been made. He strode purposefully towards the small group a few metres away. Asamwa stood up and ambled casually towards him. Hand loosely raised, ready for the classic black brother high five. Kaduna could easily see his compatriot was very much the wrong side of several joints of Ganja. He for one was not amused.

'Yo brother where's ya been man?' Asamwa slurred.

Kaduna roughly swept away the proffered hand and shouted loudly at his fellow pirate, his voice thick with vehemence.

'Listen you little shit. Who told you to move any gear out of the hiding place?'

'Hell boss, I was only tryin' to help by gettin' the boys to have the stuff ready for the man,' Asamwa replied in a rather crestfallen tone.

'Next time, you damn well wait for me, no matter how long it takes. You clear on that?' He pushed Asamwa roughly on the chest, who stumbled backwards slightly with the force.

'Yh… yeah okay boss. No sweat,' Asamwa stammered.

Out of the corner of his eye, Kaduna could see the sickening sight of the ingratiating, plant pot-hatted grossly overweight Mohamed Attandah, standing just out of view in the loom of the truck lights. He hated having to do business with such a veritable snake in the grass. But it was all a means to an end. Which he had decided, was rapidly approaching. Very soon he would be on his way, winging across the skies on a jumbo jet to some tropical paradise, to enjoy the fruits of his hard earned endeavours.

But first he had to deal with Mohamed Attandah.

The trader stepped forward palms upturned. A gesture Kaduna hated.

'Now everybody, we gots to cool it and get this business over as quickly as possible for the benefit of us all.'

Kaduna's insides crawled as the man spoke. There was but one person Mohamed Attandah had any interest in benefiting, himself. The man's demeanour incensed Kaduna more than ever that evening. He would have liked nothing more than to shoot him and his driver with the Smith and Wesson .38 calibre pistol he had in the glove compartment of his car. Then steal the buy cash, dump both of them in the creek and drive the clapped out truck in after them. Now all he wanted was to get rid of the gear and be away from this place, Attandah and his own pathetic compatriots, as soon as possible.

The fractious pirate bent down and took one of the small almost square boxes off the pile. He deftly cut it open with a stiletto he always carried, grabbed some of the contents, which were heavy chunky silver Citizen Watches and tossed them idly towards the trader. Who, taken by surprise at the arrogance of Kaduna, only managed to catch two or three, while the others landed on the damp mossy floor of the jungle. Attandah held the watches close to his beady eyes and leaned over towards the headlights of the truck. He rolled his plant-potted head back and forth a few times, and then turned round; head bowed slightly and faced Kaduna.

'I really think these watches is junk. I can't give you any more than a dollar a watch. Even then I is probably losin' money.'

'Come on, these are Citizen Watches man. I saw the exact model in a shop down town and it cost twenty U.S.'

'Well that may be true. But my clientele can't afford such prices. Also, you gots to remember, that there is a whole world of people to feed, before these particular watches can even be sold.'

Kaduna knew what he said was true. But also knew, from previous dealings with the man, that the watch would most probably sell on stalls for four or five dollars. Even so, approximately one hundred cases each crammed full, with two hundred watches at a dollar each still amounted to a sizable sum of money. But he wasn't going to let this miserable specimen of a human being get off lightly.

'No I don't agree. I also have a lot of people to pay and one dollar is out of the question. Another thing you should consider is that while you were tucked up in bed with your fat wife, I took a lot of risks to get this cargo. So I do not accept one dollar per watch.'

'Well that is my final offer I can't afford to pay no more.'

Kaduna knew that it wasn't even close to his final offer and it was all now a game of bluff, mind games. But he was tired and couldn't be bothered with the hassle. He was just about to acquiesce, when he caught the faintest glimmer of triumph in the creep's eyes.

'Okay Asamwa, we cannot do business with this man tonight. Start loading the cargo back into the canoes and take it to where we can obtain somewhere near its true value.'

Before Kaduna's henchman could pick up the boxes of watches, the dealer quickly interjected.

'Well I may be prepared to come up a little.'

'Yes?' Kaduna replied impatiently.

'Say one fifty per watch.'

'Not good enough. Asamwa, load the boxes.'

'Okay, okay, stop. That's it. Final offer or I is leaving. Two dollars a watch, not a cent more.'

'Done,' Kaduna said emphatically. He quickly shook the cold clammy outstretched hand of the trader, sealing the deal. Without showing it, he was extremely pleased to have earned twenty thousand U.S. by virtue of a few seconds of bull.

From his place of concealment, Martin Ellis watched with fascination as the protagonists, acted out the drama. As the unusually tall and well-built pirate argued with the much smaller and rotund trader, he clicked away every few seconds with his Nikon FE camera, recording the whole scene, from the first meeting, to the conclusion of the deal. He was glad to have loaded a super fast film in the camera. In this darkness the results would be grainy as hell, but after all, they weren't for a photo competition. The images he was sure, would be clear enough, to provide damning evidence against the pirate and his fence.

When the leader of the pirates turned to walk back to his car, Ellis zoomed in to get a close up of his face, which so far had eluded him. As he walked slowly towards him in virtual darkness, Ellis peered into the eyepiece of the camera, finger poised on the shutter button, hoping, that his face would be illuminated for a few seconds by the loom of a headlight. But the man was walking well clear of the truck, looking towards the ground as he went. Ellis cursed silently. 'Damn! I'm not going to get the shot.' Then one of the accomplices, carrying a box under one arm and a torch in his other hand staggered. Perhaps tripping on a broken branch, or rut on the jungle floor. Without warning he shone his torch into the pirates face. Click. Ellis had the shot.

Though something else now troubled him. There was a certain familiarity, with the face he had briefly seen. He followed the pirate through the zoom lens of the camera, till eventually he opened the car door and sat down inside. The car's inside light came on and shone on the pirate. Ellis took more shots, as the light was now slightly better. He was still puzzled by the dimly lit face which he saw in the viewfinder. But now there was something else. The man he was watching had a small goatee beard.

He had seen him somewhere recently, but couldn't quite dredge the details from his brain.

Then it struck him like a bolt of lightening.

'Unbelievable,' he muttered quietly. 'It's the croupier's boyfriend, Henry. Henry Kaduna.' Then he said to himself, 'No never. There must be a mistake!'

For a few more seconds he continued looking down the zoom lens of the camera, confirming what he had suspected. This person, who appeared to be the leader of the pirate gang, was actually the same person who he had met on the beach in Lagos less than a week ago. There were very few Nigerians over six feet tall built like an ox. He had only met one in all his time in the country. It was the same man he was now sure. It was an incredible coincidence and he felt tremendously elated, with this stroke of good fortune. He had at last identified the leader of the pirate gang and could see real progress being made to conclude this case.

Having obtained the information he sought, Ellis knew it was time to carefully extricate himself from his immensely precarious situation. He started walking slowly, as quietly as possible, back along the trail. His feet landing softly on the muddy track, like the paws of a lion creeping through the jungle. Every so often he stopped, turned round and listened to make sure he was not being followed. After ten nerve jangling minutes, he found the piece of wood left as a marker for his hidden motorcycle. Ellis quickly retrieved the machine from the undergrowth. He reached down to the gear lever and pulled it up one click. He tried the machine, and was pleased he had managed to find neutral at the first attempt, as it ran freely along the track.

Ellis didn't want to start the machine, as he was still too close to the pirates and the one with the car would soon catch him if he wasn't careful. So he began pushing the motorcycle slowly along the trail, in the direction of the main road. He had decided to try and push it a mile or so before attempting to start the bike.

At around one hundred kilos, the machine was not heavy by motorcycle standards, but the suffocating heat and the ruts and bumps in the track, made the job of pushing it that much harder.

Ellis was very fit, but after half a mile or so started to feel quite tired. So he stopped for a few minutes to get his breath back. Standing there in almost total darkness perspiring furiously, the air was heavy, dank, and completely still. Not even the slightest zephyr of wind could be felt. He could hear some monkeys chattering nearby, perhaps even laughing at him, and in the distance the shrill of a parakeet pierced the night. He was about to start pushing the machine once more, when another sound reached his ears. His heart leapt into his mouth, as he heard the car roar into life as the driver noisily revved the engine before driving off.

He jumped on the trail bike, turned on the ignition, and thrust his foot down hard on the kick-start pedal. The engine turned easily, but did not start, as it should have done, the engine still being warm. He thrust his leg down a second time then a third, then frantically another four of five times, still with no response. He could hear the noise of the high revving Toyota engine steadily rising as the car approached, accompanied by, the banging of the suspension on the stops, as the car thundered along over the rough road, coming rapidly towards him. As the noise rose, he could hear the pitch of the engine changing with Doppler Effect as it got closer. Still the motorcycle steadfastly refused to start.

'Damn!' he cursed as he realised the carburettor must have flooded when the bike was leaned over in the bushes. There is only one thing to do now, he thought, apart from pray. That's to try and bump start the bike.

He engaged second gear with the toe of his left shoe. He jumped off the machine, pulled in the clutch lever and started to push the bike as quickly as he could. Once the speed had built up, he let the clutch out, the engine fired briefly and a small puff of blue smoke floated from the exhaust. Then the wheel locked and the bike skidded along the track momentarily, till he pulled the clutch lever once more. The noise from the car was now deafening, he could only be just out of sight around the last bend. Ellis steeled himself for one last push, before the car caught him. Summoning every ounce of his depleted strength, he pushed the bucking machine as hard as he could over the ruts and bumps. Just when he was about to keel over with exhaustion, he let the clutch out. The engine fired and spluttered. Still he kept pushing, drawing on the last vestiges of strength in his body.

Then the car burst into sight fifty metres behind him, the powerful beam of the headlights pointing a huge accusatory finger of light at the frantic Ellis. The two fifty single cylinder engine eventually fired. Ellis revved the engine briefly, then jumped on board and let the clutch out fully. The front wheel rose dramatically off the ground, as the powerful engine transmitted its energy to the rear tyre. Ellis changed into third gear and the front wheel momentarily touched the ground before hitting a rut. The machine wobbled dramatically, which Ellis was just able to control. A quick look in his mirror made him feel relieved. He seemed to be maintaining the distance from the car, which weaved crazily from side to side behind him.

Kaduna was furious when he saw the motorcyclist up ahead on the trail. Someone was snooping. Someone had information and goodness knows what else about him. He accelerated frantically, hoping to crush the motorcyclist like a helpless fly, before he could escape. But the unknown person had just managed to get his machine going and was now starting to get away. The car was bouncing and leaping about and he struggled to avoid crashing into the unforgiving hard wood trees that fringed the edge of the jungle. He could not go any faster. Every machine had its limits, in each situation and this car was already over the limit for this confined space. He had reluctantly agreed to give one of the other pirates a ride back to the main road. The scruffy individual sat shaking, terrified in the passenger seat, eyes wide with fear, expecting the car to career into the menacing trees at any moment.

'Oti. Take the gun from the glove compartment and shoot that bastard.'

The other pirate did not respond. Kaduna punched him in the

ribs and screamed at him over the din of the engine.

'Take that damn gun and kill the bastard, or you will be dead meat. You hear?'

'Okay Boss. Okay, I do it.' The pirate reached forward to the glove compartment, rubbing his side and wincing with the effort. After a few seconds of searching the darkness, with the car lurching from side to side, he eventually located the gun. He took off the safety and pulled the barrel back, loading the first shell into the chamber. He pointed the gun out of the window, in the direction of the fleeing motorcyclist and started firing wildly at first. But subsequent shots got closer to the target, as he started to find the range of the bobbing and weaving machine up ahead.

Ellis was frantic as the bullets fizzed past, each one getting closer as the seconds ticked by; with his motorcycle lights now on full beam, all pretence of concealment gone, survival the only consideration. It took all his vast expertise of a lifetime on two wheels, to control the screaming, two stroke machine that leaped like a bucking bronco, as it careered along the rutted track, flat out in third gear. His heart must have been hitting somewhere between one hundred and thirty and one hundred and forty beats per minute, as the adrenalin surge flooded into his bloodstream. Then without warning, momentarily, he was consumed by a strange sensation, he no longer felt afraid. The whole scene, with its certain life or death conclusion, had actually become incredibly exhilarating. As he fought to control the wild animal of a machine, hotly pursued by heinous adversaries, he felt like he was on some kind of white-knuckle ride, at a theme park. If a .35mm slug or whatever was being fired, hit him squarely between the shoulders, for those few brief moments, he would not have cared. Then reality announced its arrival, as one of the bullets hit the seat inches from his leg. The feeling of exuberance quickly evaporated, replaced once again by abject terror, as he concentrated on evading a more and more, certain death.

He could see from the briefest of glances in his rear-view mirror, that thankfully, he was putting some useful distance between himself and the car. The bullets no longer came close, as the distance increased. It was starting to look like he might make it to the main road and the relative safety that it afforded.

But life is never that simple.

When he rounded the next turn in the jungle trail, he was stunned to see eighty metres ahead, some kind of truck lumbering slowly along, occupying every inch of the track. It's canvassed sides pushed the undergrowth along as it progressed. He realised immediately. It was Attandah's second truck, which had broken down on the motorway a few hours previously.

'Oh... shit!' he screamed. 'That's all I bloody need.'

There was no place to go. He was well and truly trapped. Behind him he had the crazy car driver, with the equally crazy gunman. While up ahead some half-asleep truck driver blocking his way. But in an instant, his years of study and specialist Interpol training came to the fore, with lightening rapidity.

There was only one thing to do, just the one chance. He quickly changed down to second gear then first, gently applying the brakes as he did so. Then when the bike was about ten metres from the truck, he yanked the handlebars to the right, skidded, and laid the bike down on the ground. He kicked away the machine towards the truck, as he slid along the ground. The stunned truck driver suddenly became alert and slammed on his brakes. As the Yamaha trail bike bounced and bounded along the track, the fuel cap flew off; spewing two stoke mix out over the red-hot engine. Eventually it hit the stationary truck, in that tantalising gap between the front bumper and the ground, bursting into flames as it contacted.

Ellis had lost count of the number of times he had fallen off bikes in his life, most at much faster speeds than he had been doing and on unforgiving tar or concrete roads. Much harder than the jungle track, which he was pleased to feel on impact, had considerable give as he slid along behind the machine. As the motorcycle bounced along the track towards the station-ary truck, he quickly staggered to his feet, a few yards behind the machine. Virtually as the bike hit the truck and burst into flames, he bounded past the opposite side of the vehicle, sweep-ing the hanging branches and leaves aside with his arms as he went. Miraculously, he was almost completely uninjured save for a few scratches on his right arm and some bruises on his right leg, which did not impede his progress.

Henry Kaduna could not believe his eyes when he saw what happened. As the bike hit the ground, it seemed to slide in slow motion, before bursting into flames beneath the truck. At first, he thought the goon next to him had somehow managed a lucky shot. But when the rider got up easily and sprinted off, he realised he was dealing with a professional.

He was not going to let this mystery man get away.

A few seconds after the bike crashed so spectacularly into the truck, he braked hard and his car skidded dramatically to a halt, less than two metres from the burning machine. He grabbed the gun from Oti and leapt out in pursuit of the rider, who had just disappeared round the side of the truck. He would not miss as his henchman had. Just one clear shot would be all that was required.

As Ellis ran towards the distant, though dim lights of the main road, he felt resurgent, almost victorious. There was no way the car could follow him, as the truck had unwittingly, though very effectively, blocked the track. New strength flowed into his tired legs. He had won this first, all-important round of the contest, between himself and his adversary. It now seemed increasingly like he had escaped almost certain death. The adrenalin kick flow-ing though his veins, made him feel like he had won a gold medal in the Olympics and the FA cup, all in one day. He ran steadily, the light on the trail improved by the half moon, which had now risen behind him.

He could see a pall of smoke in the distance, caused by numerous open wood cooking fires, typical anywhere in Africa, at this time of night. It was still over a mile to the road and he started to tire, as the effect of the adrenalin wore off, eyes never the less focused steely on the lights up ahead. Even through the numbing ache of chronic tiredness, his brain refused to think of anything else but escape, never once contemplating that he may still have been pursued.

Henry Kaduna, like the supreme athlete he was, burst out of the foliage which surrounded the burning truck, like a sprinter out of the blocks. He was fresh; his only recent exertion had been the car drive. He was determined to pursue this adversary to a satisfactory conclusion. He did not like loose ends and was hell bent on tying up this particular one. Once his eyes adjusted to the light, he could see a shadowy figure about fifty or sixty metres up ahead, running steadily.

He quickly assessed that he had no realistic chance of catching the intruder, at the speed the man was presently running and the lead he had established. So he decided to run as fast as he could to reduce the distance, then loose off a couple of shots from the .35 mm automatic he held in his hand. After two minutes of flat out sprinting, he had closed to about thirty metres and knew that any closer would be impossible. As not even someone as fit as him could keep up such a pace indefinitely. The man up ahead was clearly illuminated, by the dull silvery light of the half moon. Kaduna stopped, holding the gun with both hands till it became steady. He looked down the barrel, lined the sights up on the centre of the fleeing man's back and then gently squeezed the trigger.

The gun let out a feeble click.

He pressed the trigger again and heard the same telltale sound.

'Shit! Out of damn bullets,' he cursed and threw the gun to the ground. The frustrating realism now struck him, that his inept accomplice in the car had wasted the whole magazine during the chase.

He started running, at a moderate pace, hoping the man would eventually tire and he might be able to catch him. After a few minutes, completely without warning, the fleeing man suddenly tripped and fell. This was it, he would soon be on top of him and gut him like a pig with the stiletto he had in his pocket. He licked his lips in anticipation of the deed, as he rapidly closed on the prostrate man; reaching down and gripping the knife as he ran. He took the knife out of his trousers, pressed the smooth, stainless steel button and heard the immensely satisfying solid click, as the seven-inch razor sharp blade sprang into place.

Ellis lay on the ground and massaged his twisted ankle. One of the potholes had eventually caught him out and sent him tumbling. As he painfully, unsuccessfully, tried to rise to his feet, the ankle gave way and he fell back on the ground. Then he heard the unmistakable patter of feet, coming up quickly behind him. He felt immensely forlorn and vulnerable, as his eyes focused on the large, rapidly approaching shape of what could only be Henry Kaduna. He had seriously underestimated his opponents' strength and determination. The onrushing figure was now a mere fifteen metres away and closing fast. Then the nightmare intensified ten fold as he could see, in the dull moonlight, that the man was carrying a long pointed knife.

Unarmed, struggling to stand, and faced with what was undoubtedly an accomplished assailant, his mind was in turmoil, trying to think of how to protect himself. His heart was pounding like a steam hammer in his ribcage. Almost in a state of extreme panic, where he would be unable to think, resigned to a fate he had never had to contemplate. He was exhausted and at the end of his rope, but still the hideous shape came menacingly ever closer.

Then, another sound started to dominate the night air.

A car was approaching from the direction of the main road. He looked round quickly and saw the rear lights of a car, reversing rapidly towards him, engine straining in what was obviously full revs in reverse gear. Now it was completely over he thought. Trapped like an animal in a cage, between a maniac and a car.

Kaduna also saw the car up ahead, so he stopped running, uncertain as to whom it might be. He wanted to continue his run. Quickly stab the man on the ground and retreat victorious. But he soon wiped this option from his mind, reasoning that it would be foolish to risk possible death to achieve his objective. He didn't know who was in the car, or what weapons they possessed. He always liked the law of averages to favour him. So rather deflated, he crept towards the tall marsh grass for cover. He had made it his business over the years not to take chances, so he was not going to start now. A stiletto after all, was no match for any kind of firearm that the occupants of the car might have.

Ellis crouched, gaze transfixed on the approaching vehicle, saw the passenger door burst open and voice shout from the driver's side.

'Come on chap, we haven't got all day.'

My goodness! Ellis thought as he limped towards the car. It's Wilson!

Gratefully he collapsed on the passenger seat next to his associate, slamming the door behind him as he did so. Wilson let out the clutch and the heavy Peugeot surged forward, wheels spinning, throwing up a cloud of loose mud, as it moved off. Ellis lay back on the seat and let out a huge sigh of relief.

'Hell that was too close for comfort. That apparition had a stiletto and he would have seen me off, if you had not turned up. Thanks mate. Thanks a million.' Ellis said with a great deal of conviction.

'It's a good job you called in on the radio when you did. I was stopped on the main road and heard shooting in the distance so decided to get closer in case you needed help. But tell me Martin, what did you find out?'

'Well that's the good part. I've found out who the ring leader is. Remember you introduced me to a girl called Lesley at the beach two weeks ago?'

'Yes she is a croupier at Echo Beach Casino. I've known her for a while now. What's it got to do with her?'

'Well the guy she had with her, Henry Kaduna, is the same guy that was going to kill me a few minutes ago. I saw him at the small beach in the creek, giving all the orders and negotiating the deal with a trader called Mohamed Attandah.'

'Truly amazing, I am completely astounded. You have taken a terrible risk tonight, but come away with a huge piece of tangible information. Well done Martin.' He slapped the other playfully on the thigh and concentrated on his driving.

Henry Kaduna walked slowly back along the trail towards the blazing truck, frustrated at not having neutralised this latest threat. Whoever the bike rider was, he was highly professional, and that worried him. The man must have had intensive police or army training, to be able to creep up on them as he had done. The way he rode the bike and eventually slid off, so as avoid injury and make good his escape was quite awesome. He could not be in the employ of the police chief, as his methods were always of the crudest kind, never subtle.

No he thought. Someone somewhere, a lot higher up than Azubikas, had brought in outside assistance. The ramifications of which, did not bear thinking about. He briefly had a notion of packing his bags, grabbing Lesley, and heading for the airport. But Ekpe had told him the previous day, he had a feeling something big was coming up in a couple of weeks.

If it worked out to be something very lucrative, he would not be able to turn down such an opportunity. Kaduna made up his mind at that moment, as he walked disconsolately back along the jungle trail, that there was going to be one last final raid. Then that would be it! He would be packed and ready to leave right after that final attack. Then he would disappear into thin air. The world was a huge place and he was confident when the plane took off from Lagos, he would be untraceable.

He would be. All he had to do was make the plane after the final raid.

Chapter Twenty-Three

As Henry Kaduna walked thoughtfully along a rutted jungle trail just outside Apapa in Nigeria, three thousand miles away, at the southern most point of Africa, a Russian cargo ship was rounding Cape Agulhas.

The officers and crew of the M.V. 'Kapitan Penkov,' had enjoyed a calm, idyllic crossing from Singapore to Durban. The sea was like glass for most of the fourteen-day passage across the Indian Ocean. All on board had enjoyed many spectacular sunsets, where crimson and ochre clouds danced along the western horizon, orchestrated by a huge orange and red ball of fire.

But these apparently indelible memories had faded fast. Since departing Durban, South Africa's largest port, the fifteen thousand ton deadweight general cargo ship had been rolling violently. The culprits of this motion were the infamous Cape Rollers, which had stayed virtually on the beam all the way down the coast, making life extremely uncomfortable for all on board. The cargo, mainly crates of machinery, creaked and moaned within the hatches. The sailors went out on deck twice daily, to tighten the wire lashings and bridge pieces of the containers stacked two high on the hatch tops and along the main deck. They staggered round like drunks in the twenty to thirty degree rolls, hanging on like leeches to safety lines, lest they be cast overboard by the angry movement of the vessel.

Sleep was difficult, as the motion of the vessel would slide a seaman off his bed and onto the floor, just as if being pushed by a huge hand. Most people eventually slept on the deck, using life-jackets and spare pillows to wedge their bodies. Even the simplest action, such as trying to shave, proved almost impossible. When shaving cabinets were opened, the contents would erupt out onto the floor. So everyone on board was pleased when the ship eventually altered course, ten miles south of Cape Agulhas. The rollers now on the port quarter and the movement of the vessel reduced to bearable levels.

Captain Victor Borisenko stood on the bridge wing, leaning on the gleaming perfectly varnished mahogany Taff- rail and looked out at the unmistakable sight of Cape Agulhas lighthouse. A tall white finger with two broad red bands, that last sentinel right at the bottom of Africa, was clearly visible, even though the vessel was ten miles from land. He had seen it many times during his time at sea. He had thirty years seagoing experience and knew all about the South African coast, as he did most of the other passages and coasts of the world.

Since departing Durban, he had resisted the temptation to place the vessel right on the one hundred fathom line and squeeze an extra knot or two from the Agulhas current. The wind had been blowing force six from the southwest, promoting conditions ripe for phenomenal waves that had overwhelmed numerous vessels over the years between Durban and East London. But now his ship had at last left that particular problem behind and rounded Cape Agulhas.

They were now headed in a north-westerly direction, towards different and, in the captain's mind, infinitely more difficult problems. West Africa, as far as he was concerned, was one big problem. Stifling heat, accompanied with the all-pervading stench that permanently hung in the air, thieves that would steal anything that was not locked up.

Hordes of corrupt officials, eager to extort out of the vessel as much whisky and cigarettes as masters or chief stewards would allow. Last but not least in his mind, was the fact that there were more pirates than he ever wished to encounter. He was not looking forward with any degree of relish to the next few weeks.

The trip from Singapore to Durban, as expected at this time of year, had been very pleasant, though he had not enjoyed the passage like the rest of the ship's crew. They would congregate each night on deck, with cases of chilled beer and bottles of vodka to watch the sunset, or just use that beautiful event as an excuse to get drunk, as usual. This was fairly much the norm amongst Russian seamen, who used the vodka bottle as a crutch to forget their poor shipboard conditions and uncertain payment of wages. Captain Borisenko was from the old school of Soviet mariners and he had resisted the temptation to let his hair down and have a good time with the crew, keeping his distance and remaining aloof at all times. He retired to his cabin nightly with a book and a bottle of Jonnie Walker Red Label, his own particular crutch.

Now that the ship was headed inexorably towards West Africa, he thought there would be little peace for anyone till clear of the damn place. The recent report he had received, regarding the pirate attack on the 'Ville de Lyon,' had made chilling reading, so bad in fact that an aircraft carrier of the U.S. Navy had been called in the end, to help sort out the problem. He had taken the trouble to post this communication in the mess room, so that all on board would be fully aware what was waiting for them in West Africa. As he left the mess room, a number of the crew had crowded round the notice board, to see what all the fuss was about. Walking back to his cabin along the alleyway, he was perturbed to hear some of the crew laughing, as thought it was a matter for levity.

He had to admit to himself, that other matters on the ship also troubled him. Like the container down number two hatch tweendeck for instance, loaded under armed guard in Durban, with metal bars welded on its doors. It was very strange indeed, highly suspicious in fact. The agent had been evasive and non-committal when questioned. Anyway, it was below decks and pretty much out of harm's way he reasoned. He just hoped it wasn't something particularly nasty. Such as explosives, class 'A' chemicals, or even nuclear waste. That was the trouble with containers, he mused. Shippers could declare what ever they liked on manifests and put something entirely different in the container, a dreadful trade in he thought. In his opinion, it was much better ten or fifteen years ago, when everything was in open stow. Then the cargo on the manifest invariably matched up with what was on the ship. Now you could never be sure.

Another different, though equally worrying matter, was the watches he knew to be concealed in the engine room. A person of his experience missed very little on ships. The commissar had his ring of confidants, but so did he. Also he was an expert at using casual conversation, to manipulate people and unearth information. One such innocuous talk with the first trip deck boy Sergie Dimitri, had after some soothing assurances, then heavy threats, brought forth this particular gem. It made him glow warmly inside, like the comforting heat of log fire in a dacha, in the middle of a Russian winter. A pleasant thought, that the smug little commissar might yet be caught smuggling and wind up behind bars in the undoubted hell of a West African prison. Places he had on good authority would make the Gulag Archipelago look like a holiday camp on the edge of the Black Sea.

Undoubtedly, the man would try and squirm free of any accusation, by saying the captain was responsible. He had a way with words, which after all was his job. But Captain Victor Borisenko was ahead of his game, with a sworn statement from the deck boy of exactly who and what he had seen that particular night in Singapore. With that gratifying thought flowing through his mind, a thin mischievous smile flickered momentarily across his full Slavic lips as he turned and walked smartly toward the wheelhouse.

One deck below the bridge in the cabin of Commissar Kaminsky, the two ringleaders of the smuggling operation were having a quiet drink together. Laughing and joking convivially, as the level in the whisky bottle fell steadily. Relaxed and feeling even more confident than usual, the commissar looked thoughtfully over the rim of a cut glass whiskey glass, at the Estonian chief engineer. He had a similar glass; half filled with the golden brown liquid, which he sucked at slowly, savouring the taste, as if the liquid were too rare and precious to rush.

'Well not long now Chief, till we are rid of the watches, pockets stuffed full of dollars and naira. I tell you what, I'll even take you ashore in Lagos this time and buy you the best steak in town, how about that?' He placed his glass on the coffee table in front of him, with flourish.

'Steady on, Comrade. I don't want to risk death from hepatitis or something worse. I think I'll just be staying on the ship while we are in Lagos and for the rest of the West African coast for that matter,' the chief engineer said in an even tone. Ever cautious as usual, this consequently made him for the most part, an exceedingly dull person.

Kaminsky smiled benignly at the engineer.

'Oh come now Chief. Life is for living. I intend to spend some of my good fortune on a decent night out. Besides I've had all the injections and inoculations.'

'Me too but I won't be risking it.' After a few moments, brow deeply furrowed as he looked blankly at the whisky in his glass, the Estonian spoke again.

'Comrade Commissar. Do you still think this operation is tight as a drum? I mean there is no way the Old Man could have found out, is there?'

The commissar laughed loudly. Then spoke in hushed tones, one hand against his mouth. 'That old fool, I very much doubt it. Don't worry my friend everything will be just fine.'

Litbarski smiled thinly, nodded in assent and took another satisfying suck of his drink. He let his mind wander, as he looked at the mesmerising effect of the porthole chain, rippling back and forth with the motion of the vessel. His eyes fixed on the lumpy green swell that stretched to a cold grey horizon; he began to dream of his ambition in life. Escape from Russia by immigrating to Israel. He was actually Jewish, but kept this fact a secret from his shipmates, as over the years he had encountered bad reactions from some of these because of his religion. With the money from the watch smuggling, he would be able to buy a modest apartment for himself and his wife Nina with plenty left over, to set up a nice little car repair business. West Africa had been good to him over the years and was confidant, it would continue this time as well.

Martin Ellis paced slowly up and down the compound in front of Wilson's house. He walked at a sedentary pace and his feet inside his sandals were becoming quite wet, the long coarse tropical grass, still damp with dew from the previous night. This troubled him not, but in a strange kind of way he found the slight discomfort refreshing. It was just after nine-thirty in the morning. He had been too tired, after the exertions of the previous night, to get up with his associate at six-thirty, shower, and breakfast and drive in to the office and make pretence at being a P and I inspector.

Every muscle in his body ached from pushing the motorcycle along the jungle trail. His left ankle was painful and he was grateful that Ronnie had applied a huge towel full of ice to this, soon after returning last night. The morning air was still pleasant, warning up slowly to the undoubted cauldron of the West African noon. The sun's warm rays caressed his naked torso and nearby he could hear the chirping of grasshoppers and in the distance, the dull drone of the traffic rumbling along the motorway. As he walked, he rolled his head from side to side and stretched his arms and legs occasionally, to release the stiffness from within. He was enjoying the solace afforded by the compound, which enabled him to take stock of the events of the previous night and slowly analyse these. The phone calls he had made just after rising at nine a.m. had also provided good news.

Ellis was actually feeling in quite a jubilant mood, as within the space of hours he had acquired his second big lead. A few minutes earlier he had talked to both Ndofu and Johnson, to enquire if they had obtained any more information. Ndofu said that the stalls of Apapa and Lagos were already doing a brisk trade in six dollar Citizen Watches. So Attandah had wasted no time in starting to recoup his investment.

However the news Johnson divulged was much more important to the case. Apparently the previous day, he had seen Ekpe in earnest conversation with a well-dressed Nigerian who was tall and had a goatee beard. Once the conversation had ended, he had seen that person drive off at a pace through the crowded streets in a yellow coloured Toyota.

There was no doubt in Ellis's mind, who that the stranger could be.

That was the connection, Ellis was sure. That was how the pirate knew which containers to open when he attacked ships. The trusted head clerk of Bowman's was feeding him the numbers and probably where the containers were located. He had felt, during the interview with Ekpe many weeks earlier, that the man was hiding something. This information had confirmed his suspicions.

His second phone call that morning had been to the Interior Minister. Ellis had been able to tell him, the precise location where the pirates were landing and storing their contraband, prior to the goods being sold. He also informed him that he was hot on the heels of the pirate leader and would soon have a name and an address for him. The Minister congratulated Ellis warmly on his progress. He assured him, that specially trained elite forces were standing by, ready to act the next time the pirates struck. Ellis was greatly reassured by the man's enthusiasm and felt more confident now than he had for weeks.

The next thing on the agenda was to find out where Kaduna lived, which he thought would not be too difficult, as he knew where his girlfriend worked. To help with this part of the enquiry, Wilson had said he would make discreet enquiries amongst the ex – pat community, as to where the blonde croupier resided.

Chapter Twenty-Four

The events of the previous night, coupled with everything that had happened recently, had made up Kaduna's mind for him. Forget about that one last raid and get the hell out of Nigeria, before hell almost certainly caught up with him. He was halfway through packing his suitcases, when he heard a faint knock at the door of his apartment. Fearful of another visit from the police chief, he did not open the door, but pressed his powerful body against the door and spoke gruffly.

'Yeah. Who is it?'

A soft timid reply came almost immediately.

'Message for you boss, from Mr Ekpe.'

Kaduna relaxed slightly, it sounded like the youth Ekpe usually sent. But every wary and untrusting, he opened the door just enough for any message to be passed through, ensuring that the heavy security chain was properly engaged first.

'Okay sonny, throw the paper through.'

Almost immediately, a grubby crumpled envelope fell through the gap and landed on the floor a few inches from his feet, a shuffling sound was then heard as the messenger departed and made hurriedly for the stairs. Kaduna ripped open the envelope with disdain, slightly angry at the distraction and read the few scrawled words on the note within.

'I was right; something really big has come up. A lot of money.

We have to talk, meet me at the usual place at eight tonight.'

Kaduna crumpled the note up and threw it hard onto the floor, then resumed his packing. As far as he was concerned, there was only one place he would be that night. Thirty -five thousand feet above Nigeria, headed for what he hoped would be a life of luxury from the considerable profits garnered from his heinous trade.

He strode purposely back and forth between the various wardrobes and chests of drawers, choosing only the best, of his impressive collection of designer clothes and other possessions to take with him. But he could feel his demeanour changing rapidly.

Two powerful currents of thought coursed through his mind, as he tried to concentrate on packing. One part of him was screaming, to get out of Nigeria while there was still time. But unfortunately for Henry Kaduna, his Achilles' heel, greed, was winning the battle of his mind and willpower. The more he tried to erase it from his thoughts, the more prevalent the feeling became. The contents of the letter had said; something really big, a lot of money. He could not dispel these words from his mind, because Ekpe had never used them before. It must be something very special he concluded. Eventually, overcome by both curiosity and greed, which had generated a feeling of frustration and anger, he abruptly stopped packing and pushed the case angrily onto the floor of the apartment. Then he cursed under his breath, 'It had better be good, or I will kill that little bastard Ekpe.'

Ellis had never been much of a person for any type of gambling. Reasoning that whichever form it took, the majority of punters must always lose. Otherwise, the various casinos and gambling companies would never make a profit and would close down. None ever did, as far as he could see, the only gamblers who ever won were the ones that were extremely lucky. He was even more convinced of his theory, now that he had more than a week of gambling experience. Since the night of the incident in the jungle, he had decided to hang around the casino, where

Kaduna's girl friend worked, certain that the pirate would walk in one evening. Discreet enquiries had revealed the man to be a regular visitor and loser at this casino, which partly explained some of his need for large sums of cash.

He had been careful to keep his distance from the croupier, though she had recognised him and smiled pleasantly at him on one occasion. He always played on tables where she was not working, of which there were usually ten or twelve. But mainly he spent most of his time at the bar, slowly sipping a gin and tonic, or the local beer when he felt particularly thirsty. Perched on one of the high bar stools, with his back to the floor of the casino, he could keep an eye on the various comings and goings by virtue of the huge highly polished mirror on the opposite side of the bar.

Not an altogether unpleasant way of passing an evening in Lagos, he would think. In fact on occasion, engrossed in conversation with a particularly interesting person, he would almost forget the reason he was at the casino. To conclude the business that brought him to Nigeria in the first place and find out where the pirate lived. He was sure the villain would turn up eventually.

'Ready for another, sah?' Jonathan the friendly barman said rather expansively, knowing full well the answer.

'Yeah go on then, you've managed to twist my arm yet again,' Ellis said warmly to the man he had spent many an hour talking to over the last week. He was a virtual encyclopaedia of who was who in Nigeria and how often they visited 'his casino.' The barman always seemed to have some incredibly funny story to tell about the various clientele, whether they were just plain businessmen or government ministers. But his favourite topic of conversation by far, was his Lebanese boss and like most of the other staff, he hated working for him. Ellis was listening with amusement, to the barman's latest animated tirade against his boss and almost failed to notice the newcomer at the end of the bar.

'Hey barman, gimme a beer,' the new arrival said in a deep tone, devoid of any warmth or feeling. Jonathan stopped in mid sentence and without looking round, replied automatically.

'Yes sah. I'll be right there.'

Ellis lifted his eyebrow ever so slightly, and saw clearly reflected in the mirror behind the bar, a handsome well-dressed Nigerian with a goatee beard, two or three meters from where he was sat. The tall powerfully built man was standing, leaning with one arm on the padded edge of the bar counter. Ellis was stunned. It was him. The bird had at last come home to roost. He tried to act nonchalantly and not look again at Kaduna. But he found this a very difficult discipline, with the history of the man and the facts of the case buzzing round in his mind, like angry bees. But he knew he had to avoid staring at all costs, or risk drawing attention to himself.

Martin Ellis felt his insides turning to jelly, caused by a mixture of two great emotions, elation and fear. He felt a great sense of achievement, getting close to his adversary at last. But then on the other hand, the memories of that night just over a week ago, when he had come within a whisker of death, were all too fresh in his mind. Fortunately for Ellis, Kaduna took a quick sip of his beer and proceeded to the floor of the casino. Not noticing him, or remembering the encounter at the beach many weeks previously. The last thing Ellis wanted was a convivial conversation with the man.

As he walked across the floor of the casino, making for the blackjack table, Henry Kaduna was in a buoyant mood, pleased that he had decided to stay for one final job. The conversation last week, with shipping clerk Ekpe, had been truly amazing. His instinct, that something immense was about to happen, had proved correct. A Russian ship would be arriving in Lagos in a few days time. It had a considerable amount of valuable cargo on board. Radios, stereos, VCR's, and cameras all loaded in the Far East. But that was not what interested him. He was out to catch a much bigger fish. Ekpe had given him the number and the location on board, of a container that contained around twelve and a half million dollars. Kaduna had lambasted the little clerk, not believing what he had been told.

'Don't be stupid,' he had said a harsh edge to his voice. 'No one is going to send that kind of money on a ship. They would send it by plane under guard.'

'Yes that would normally be the case. But there is no trading agreement between Nigeria and South Africa. Planes don't fly from Johannesburg to Lagos. Even flying via a neutral country is extremely difficult to arrange, for one reason or another.'

Kaduna had been quite incredulous and had found the facts hard to believe, but on further prompting the reason became clearer.

'So if there is no trade agreement, what the hell is the money for?'

'The money is for oil.'

Of course, he thought. That was the only natural resource the South Africans' did not possess and had to obtain, from whichever source that would supply them. Still unsure, he had continued with his interrogation of the little clerk.

'I don't get it, Ekpe,' he said rather seriously, and then continued. 'The government would always want the quickest and most secure route for that kind of money. Surely they wouldn't take a chance sending it on a ship?'

Ekpe regarded him quietly for a couple of seconds, before replying. His demeanour had become more confident, with the prolonged involvement with Kaduna. He was feeling a certain sense of power, with the information he was able to obtain.

'Well perhaps it's nothing to do with the government. Perhaps someone else has sold the oil. Strange things can happen in Nigeria when money is involved.'

They certainly could Kaduna thought, smiling to himself as he walked towards his favourite blackjack table. Furthermore he mused, he was particularly adept at making other strange things happen. Usually in the dead of night, when bio-rhythms barely murmured, and security was at its most vulnerable. He would make sure the person waiting for that particular windfall, would be extremely disappointed. In this case, the potential gain heavily outweighed the risk involved. He had given a grateful Ekpe a large bundle of grubby and well worn naira notes, as well as three hundred dollars.

He felt thoroughly content and relaxed as he sat down, on the vacant chair near the end of the table. The fears that had almost made him leave Nigeria the ten days ago, now washed away, at least temporarily, by the good food and wine he had enjoyed that evening. He would have a few hours gambling, and then round off the night in fine style by ravishing the lovely Lesley. She looked particularly delicious that evening, as she dealt the cards to the eager punters sat round the table, wearing a tight fitting black dress, showing off her considerable assets. Kaduna was pleased that only one person at the table, would be experiencing those delights that night. He had noticed a familiar glint of anticipation in her eyes, when she saw him approaching the table. Yes he thought, he certainly had this lady exactly where he wanted her.

Kaduna caught Lesley's eye and threw four hundred naira rather disdainfully onto the middle of gaming table.

'Gimme twenty naira chips honey.' He looked directly at the croupier, the faintest of smiles flickering momentarily across his lips.

'Yes sir, twenty chips coming up.' She smiled warmly back at him, perfect white teeth showing between her luscious pink lips.

He started off with one square, placing a bet of twenty naira on this. The croupier dealt the cards. His luck was in, as he achieved an immediate blackjack. Kaduna felt pleased with his first hand, winning thirty naira in a couple of minutes, which boded well for the evening ahead. He would not have thought that however, had he seen Martin Ellis walking casually behind him, in the direction of the door. Ellis had watched his arrogant behaviour, since he had arrived at the casino. He was looking forward immensely to the time, in the not too distant future, when he planned to spoil his party in no uncertain terms.

While he had watched Kaduna from his position at the bar, a fleeting silly notion came into his mind, as he fingered the Interpol ID badge in his pocket. Walk straight up to him, flash the badge and arrest him on the spot. This of course was totally absurd, as he had no real evidence and no back up. The notion left his mind as quickly as it had arrived. He then paid his bill, bade the genial barman good night and made his way out of the casino.

Ellis walked out of the front doors, passed the perpetually smiling, bowing doorman. He skipped jauntily down the wide flight of steps and across the car park to where he had left Wilson's car. The night air was still and heavy with humidity. In fact it felt like a wall of heat, after the air conditioning in the casino. By the time he reached the car, he had already started to perspire freely and wiped some of this from his brow, with the back of his hand.

He got into the car, closed the door, and then promptly opened both windows. He looked at his watch, it was almost one a.m. There was little noise at that time of night, just the thump of the distant rollers on the beach. Croaking toads and chirping of grasshoppers could also be heard, and in the distance faint strains of music, from a radio or cassette player. He could still see the doorman and after around ten minutes, the man went inside for some reason. Ellis started up the car and drove slowly across the car park, till he had a much clearer view of the hotel entrance. He could also see the dusty rutted side road outside the car park, leading to the main road, which ran along the beach. It was a good vantage point. The only thing to do now was settle down and wait for the pirate to make a move.

Chapter Twenty-Five

A few hours earlier that day the M.V. 'Kapitan Penkov' had been discharging her cargo in Tema, the principal port of Ghana. Four gangs of stevedores were working the ship, steadily discharging containers and general cargo. On the jetty, customs men waited to inspect the seals of the containers before they were taken away to the stacking area, to await receivers arriving to claim their cargo.

Virtually all the ships trading to West Africa with this type of cargo, call at a number of ports in the various small countries in the Bight of Benin. They start at Abidjan in the Ivory Coast, before moving on to Tema in Ghana, then Lome in Togo. The vessels discharge a few hundred tons of general cargo, such as steel or machinery in each port, plus forty or fifty containers. Then before departure they load empty containers from the previous ship. After having called at the various small ports, the vessel then calls at Lagos, where the vast majority of the cargo on board is discharged.

The facilities in all of these ports are invariably in a state of disrepair. Shore cranes haven't worked in years, so ship's gear has to be used in each port, relying on poorly trained winch drivers, who may be the worse for wear, after over-indulging in ganja. The forklift trucks that carry the cargo to storage areas frequently break down, due to poor repair facilities and lack of spare parts. This all serves to prolong the time a vessel tends to stay in these ports.

Security of the cargo, ship's equipment and the crew's personal possessions is of paramount importance. As apart from the problems with piracy in all the ports on this coast, there is the additional problem of rampant pilfering and thievery. On board vessels visiting the area, everything of even the smallest value must be locked away and the final day before arriving on the coast is spent, securing the whole ship from top to bottom.

All stores have to be fitted with locks that can only be opened with a special spanner; the paint store may even be welded up. Hatches not being used are locked. The doors to the accommodation are locked, with the exception of one used for general entry and a crewman usually guards this twenty-four hours a day. The measures taken by ships are such that an observer would think the ship was entering a war zone. It is, but a different kind of war, a war of attrition between ship's personnel and virtually every stevedore on the coast, who try to remove ship's stores to sell ashore for a few dollars to supplement their meagre pay.

Looking down from the port side boat deck of the M.V. 'Kapitan Penkov' to the dusty dock, Captain Victor Borisenko was watching one such incident dramatically unfold. His afternoon walk up and down on the boat deck had been disturbed, by the sound of a commotion from the direction of the jetty. He had moved quickly to the ship's rail, to find out what was happening. He saw a bundle thrown from the bow of the small cargo ship on the berth directly behind his ship; this was caught by a skinny youth in dark, stained and ragged clothing. He could see that youth, like most of his counterparts, had no shoes on his feet as he sprinted below him along the dock, clutching the bundle under his arms. Suddenly a voice shouted out a warning.

'Stop or I will shoot!'

An army soldier in a green uniform with a black beret, drafted into the docks to help improve security, levelled his ancient rusted rifle at the fleeing youth. He issued the same warning once more, but in a louder voice with more urgency.

'Stop I tell you, or I will shoot.' But still the youth continued running. The soldier fired two shots in quick succession.

The captain expected to see the youth crumple to the ground, as he would not have missed from that range, or considerably more for that matter. Two puffs of dust erupted from the ground, a metre behind the youth. He looked quickly back as he ran, terror clearly evident in his wild eyes, before he turned sharply to the left and disappeared between two cargo sheds. The soldier shouldered his rifle and proceeded to give chase. The captain smiled to himself, thinking how lucky the youth had been. The whole episode was just another illustration of how desperate the people in this part of the world were; that a person would risk his life, for a few dollars worth of stores. Deep down, if he were totally honest with himself, he did feel a degree of pity for these people. Just as long as it was not his ship they were trying to steal from.

The incident now over, he resumed walking back and forth on the boat deck and reflected briefly on the coast so far. He was pleased that in the first two ports, Abidjan and Tema, thieving had been negligible. He had briefed his crew thoroughly before arrival and was seeing the benefit of this. There had been no sign of any pirates so far, though he had taken the precaution of drifting thirty miles out at sea, whilst waiting for a berth at both places. Vessels, who anchored off these ports, were invariably attacked. He had been around to long to fall into that trap. After another ten minutes or so of walking, he decided to return to his cabin and attend to some paperwork before dinner.

From the deck below where the captain had been standing, Victor Kaminsky, the ship's commissar, also witnessed the shooting incident. As he squinted up from under the rim of his peaked cap, he had seen the heavy-jowled features of the Old Man leaning on the rail, watching impassively the drama on the dock. He also was pleased with the way the coast had gone so far. He was cleverly mixing his daytime job, as an upstanding communist in charge of the vessel's morale, with a far more lucrative profession of smuggling.

He had negotiated favourable terms and substantial profits with persons from the port authorities of Abidjan and Tema for the watches. All the transactions, between the network of contacts he had built up over the years, had gone very smoothly. There had only been one slight murmur of discontent in the entire coast so far. A one ring customs official here in Tema wanted to buy a box of watches for his uncles' business in Accra. Kaminsky had refused, as he only had enough supply on board for the two and three ring officials. He promised to bring the man two boxes next trip, which seemed to placate him.

With the cash already in his hands, he had organised with the chief engineer for the boxes packed with the cheap watches to come up onto deck the previous night, and then be lowered into a waiting canoe. There was no harbour patrol in any of these ports at night time and canoes could travel back and forth unhindered. It never ceased to amaze him how quickly boxes of watches, could be brought from their place of concealment in the engine room and dispatched effortlessly, unnoticed, into a waiting canoe. Ten minutes on average was all it took.

It was good business and after all he reasoned it harmed no one. Everyone on the ship received an envelope with fifty or one hundred dollars. Even if they were in no way involved with the business. The crew thought it was wonderful to receive such a handsome and unexpected bonus and would spend the cash on wild drunken nights ashore, in the company of the local whores.

All crewmembers got an envelope, except the captain. Kaminsky knew he would be too suspicious, not want to be implicated and probably throw the money right back in his face. Who cared what he thought anyway, Kaminsky reasoned. He was just the captain. The real power in the ship lay with him. So he thought, at any rate.

His main concern at that moment was that he did not run out of watches before Lagos, because the authorities there would be seriously displeased if there were no watches available for them this trip. He would just let another five boxes go in Lome and that would leave about ten for his friends in Lagos. At this stage in the trip he felt quite content that everything was going according to plan and he was in full control.

Ships usually run like well oiled machines, with the various departments all pulling together collectively to achieve the end result. This is getting the ship and her cargo safely from one port to the next. No delays, no embarrassing episodes, which will ultimately cost the company money. That afternoon in Tema, as he sat behind the desk in his office reviewing the monthly wage account, Captain Borisenko was relatively content that his ship was meeting those standards. Of course, he probably had higher standards than some masters, but how they chose to run their ships was none of his business.

He checked the various figures in each row. Basic wage, leave pay, allotment, bond account, etc, adding them all up on his pocket calculator, to make sure the chief steward who prepared the account had not made a mistake. Either paying one of the crew too much, where the company would be out of pocket, or too little, which would provoke a great outburst from the aggrieved person, was not to be contemplated. The wage account had to be correct. It was just as important as the many other daily matters, to which he was required to give his attention.

The chief steward, a short rotund balding man from Vilnius in Latvia, was an old hand at the job and rarely made mistakes. But the captain still liked to check, as he had to sign at the bottom of the statement that it was correct. Like everything else on the ship, he was responsible. In this case to make sure the crew were paid the correct wages. That was the onerous part about his job; he was in command and was responsible for everything that happened on board. Any problem, that any person or department had, no matter how big or small, was his problem. Chief engineers in particular, faced with a major breakdown, would always think they alone had a mountain of worries till the problem was resolved. The master shouldered as much, if not more of that worry in such situations, as his vessel was going nowhere till the engine problem was cured.

As he progressed through the figures, finding nothing wrong, he could hear the rumbling sound of the winches running on deck, as the cargo was discharged from the ship. The lights in his cabin would dim slightly, if more than one crane was lifting at the same time and the ship would heel one or two degrees, as the cargo swung out over the ship's side. The steady beat of two eight cylinder marine diesel generators, far below in the engine room, were a constant noise whether in port or at sea. His walkie-talkie radio, hanging in its usual place, from a porthole dog behind him, would crackle into life every so often, as the chief mate conversed with the duty officer on deck. All of these sounds were normal ship sounds and he rarely noticed any of it.

But now a different type of sound, coming from the direction of the alleyway, made him stop work and look up, a puzzled expression on his wide Slavic face. A babble of shouting excited voices could be heard in the distance; a commotion, getting rapidly closer and louder by the second. As it reached its crescendo, four figures burst into his office. They were Ghanaian customs officers. A different crowd than had boarded on arrival. Three of these men had two bands on their epaulettes and one, far more senior who was obviously in charge, had four. 'This did not look good;' he thought and took a deep breath.

'Yes gentlemen. How can I help you?' He said in an official well-practised tone.

The tall impeccably dressed officer, in the green uniform of the Ghanaian customs service, four rings shining like beacons from his epaulettes, was the first to speak. The babble of voices subsided as he began to talk.

'You have a big problem, captain. I have reliable information indicating that your ship is involved in smuggling.'

'Not possible. This is a ship of the Soviet Union my friend, such a thing would not happen on this ship,' the captain said indignantly, raising his voice to add authority to his statement.

'Firstly, don't call me friend. Secondly, I don't care where the hell your ship is from. If this accusation is proved, you as master will be prosecuted,' the official quickly shot back at him a deadly serious look in his narrow dark eyes. The captain was momentarily taken aback by the ferocity and gravity of the customs man's reply, but he soon regained his composure and continued in an even tone.

'Very well, on what facts do you base this accusation?' He said rather resignedly, realising that this was a man who probably had considerable power and should not be taken lightly. The official reached into his pocket and thrust several cheap watches onto the desk in front of the captain.

'About ten boxes of watches like this were confiscated from a truck in Accra this afternoon. The driver was told he would face life in prison for being involved in smuggling, if he did not help us with our enquiries. He then told us the name of the person he was delivering the watches to. We traced that person, who with gentle persuasion soon told us the name of your ship as the source where the watches came from. What do you have to say now, Captain?' The customs officer's voice was rising, an unmistakeable note of triumph evident in his tone. The other three customs officers, heads nodding, grinned in appreciation of their boss's impressive oration.

'It's pretty thin evidence if you ask me. Still only on the basis of one man's say, his word against mine if you like. As far as I can gather from what you have told me, no one actually saw anything to implicate this ship.'

'The problem for you, Captain, is the receiver of these watches on shore, gave me the name of the person that he paid money to here on this ship.'

'Really, what was the name?'

'A person called Kaminsky.'

The captain tried to act shocked and surprised, but he had half expected something like this to happen for a while now.

'No, that's not possible. The man is the commissar on board this vessel. He would never be involved in something like this.' His protestations sounded noticeably feeble and weak.

'I'm afraid it is very possible that this man is indeed the culprit. How else could a Ghanaian citizen possibly know the name of this person on your ship?'

That was a fact the captain could not deny and did not argue any further.

The customs officer continued in an even tone. 'The hard facts are Captain, that this ship is going to be arrested until a fine of fifty thousand dollars has been paid by your owners.'

It was no use. Victor Borisenko had to admit to himself, he was beaten this time. He had to think of a way out of this situation, so this scandal would not get back to the owners in Russia. The only good thing in his favour was that this was Africa and these things could be negotiable, if handled correctly. In other countries, where authorities were well paid and had pensions to retire on, a situation like this would have been irrevocable. The room was silent with all eyes fixed on him. Suddenly the head customs man spoke again.

'Furthermore, I believe there are more of these accursed watches on board and I intend to search the ship from top to bottom, till I find them.'

So that was it, the captain thought. 'The watches were what the bastard was really after! There may be a way out of this yet.' He reached over and picked up the heavy metal telephone from its cradle on the bulkhead, at the side of his desk. He dialled 33, the commissar's number. After four rings the phone was picked up and a gruff voice was heard at the end.

'Kaminsky speaking.'

The captain then spoke quickly in an agitated tone in Russian, to the commissar.

'Something very serious has come up; I'm coming down to your cabin.'

'Excuse me gentlemen, please take a seat, I will be back in a few moments.' He gestured to the seats round the small conference table, in the corner of his office next to the door, as he squeezed past the four customs officers.

A few seconds later after bounding down one fight of stairs, he was in the commissars' cabin. He found Kaminsky standing in the centre of his cabin. He struck a somewhat arrogant pose, stood there legs slightly apart, hands out of sight behind his back. He even had his peaked commissar's hat on, just to emphasis exactly who he was. The captain recognised all the signs. Kaminsky had stood up as he realised a confrontation was imminent and had not wanted to be seated and give away the physiological advantage of height. Kaminsky spoke first.

'Yes, so what is this huge problem you have, that has made you disturb me?' he said in a clearly recognisable, derisory tone to the captain. Head tilted to one side one eye half shut. The captain would have liked to tear the man apart, as he so easily could have, but had to exercise maximum power on the self-restraint button.

'Well Commissar Kaminsky. I think you know what the problem is.'

Yes he knew exactly what the problem was. He had feared the worst when he saw the customs officers charging up the stairs to the captain's cabin.

'No Captain. I am not sure I follow what you mean.'

'Come on Kaminsky. Let's not beat about the bush. I have known about your little watch smuggling operation for some time now. Well the whole thing has just blown up in your face.'

'No,' he stated emphatically, before continuing in a confident mood, hands from behind his back, gesticulating grandly as he spoke. 'Whatever has been going on aboard this ship, you cannot pin any of it on me.'

The captain took two strides forward and thrust his face to within a couple of inches of the commissar's.

'Really, well it may surprise you to know, I have the sworn statements of three members of this crew that you are the organiser and ringleader of this watch smuggling business.'

Kaminsky was shocked to the core by the revelation, but ever the actor, did not let this show on his face. He took a step back from the menacing presence of the captain and used that brief moment to compose himself.

'Yes but if that is the case, these so called statements will be your own downfall, admitting you knew smuggling was taking place on your ship and took no action to stop it.' He laughed a shallow laugh, leering at the captain. 'All you have done in actual fact is to totally incriminate yourself,' Kaminsky said with conviction, a thin smile etched on his lips.

'I don't think so. You see the statements have no dates on them. I can fill the time and dates for today, then just send the customs officers ashore. Tell them I will conduct an investigation. Call them back in an hour and hand over the sworn statements, as damning evidence against you. The ship will be fined; you may even be jailed here in Ghana. One thing is for sure; you would be finished in the communist party.'

Kaminsky was totally stunned. He took his hat off, tossed it onto his table and slumped down on one of the chairs next to his desk, body bent over, head in hands. He realised now what had happened. He had just seen a different set of customs officers to the ones he had dealt with, proceeding up the stairs to the captain's cabin. It would no doubt have been the one ringer that he refused to supply with watches who had caused this problem. The little swine must have had friends in high places. The captain was right, he was finished. His standing in the party and his glittering career, mapped out all the way to the top, gone in the blink of an eyelid. Fighting back the tears, he kept his head bowed, partly in shame, though mostly in frustration.

Captain Borisenko stood back in silence, looking at the broken commissar, savouring the moment for a few seconds before speaking. The man had been a thorn in his side all trip, constantly interfering in the running of the ship and affecting his esteem amongst the crew. But the party man had seriously underestimated him, as he was tough as steel. That steel tempered under the jackboot, during the German occupation of his country in the Second World War. But Kaminsky had now been put firmly in his place. He started talking in a slow firm tone.

'Now listen here Kaminsky. There is but one way out of this, where all reputations can be salvaged.'

Kaminsky's head turned slowly upwards and he looked up at the captain, through watery eyes for a few seconds, before speaking in a barely audible whisper.

'Okay anything; just tell me what you want.'

Chapter Twenty-Six

'Why is you out on dis street so late at night?' the checkpoint guard said in a heavy African accent to Ellis, who peered blearily up at the scruffy soldier next to his driver's window. It was almost four in the morning and the streets of Lagos were deserted.

'Well actually I have been to the casino. It has only just closed,' Ellis replied.

The soldier, who had faded sergeant's stripes on the arm of his uniform, looked like he was high on Ganja, his speech was slurred, and he was unsteady on his feet. The boredom of sitting at the checkpoint for endless hours needed alleviating. The local pot obviously had been the answer. Ellis could tell he was going to be difficult.

'Don't you know dere is a curfew in dis town?' the soldier said rather indignantly.

'No I was not aware of any such thing.'

'You are a driver. You has to know the laws of the country before you drive your car so late at night.' Ellis knew there was no curfew, but the man had a gun and was obviously volatile, by virtue of the drugs he had taken. So remembering what worked best in this country, for these poor underpaid police or soldiers, he paid a few naira and he was soon on his way.

His mood brightened considerably as he took the slip road up to the freeway flyover, that the links the city of Lagos with Apapa, where Wilson's house was located. After all, he had achieved his objective of the last week. At last he had found where the pirate lived.

It had been almost two a.m. before Kaduna left the casino with his girlfriend. Despite the heat, Ellis had been dozing as he sat in the Peugeot. It had been the distinctive sound of a woman's high-heeled shoes, clattering down the wide marble steps at the front of Echo Beach Casino that stirred him. He had peered across the car park, to see Kaduna and his croupier girlfriend get into the same battered yellow Toyota, which had chased him in the jungle earlier in the week.

Kaduna had revved the car noisily and screeched out of the car park and up the track towards the beach road, throwing up a cloud of dust as he went. Ellis followed at a distance and eventually saw the Toyota stop and park outside, a relatively modern and smart looking three storey beachfront apartment block.

Fifty metres before the apartment block, Ellis pulled off the road and ran the car onto hard packed pebbles and sand between the beach and the road. He stopped the car and turned off the lights, regarding the apartments from inside the darkened car. Most of the residences were in darkness. Either unoccupied or the owners had already gone to sleep, as it was now almost three-thirty in the morning. Nigerians as a rule go to bed early and also rise early in the morning. He could see there were just three apartments showing any lights. He reached over to the glove compartment and withdrew a chunky pair of Minolta 35x80 binoculars and looked though them, tuning the focus wheel slightly as he did so.

In two of the apartments that were illuminated, he could see the tell tale flicker of a TV within, intermingled with the dull glow that emanated from them. As he turned his attention to the third apartment, his face lit up with a broad smile. The binoculars revealing quite clearly the two figures standing on the balcony, engaged in a heavy necking and petting session. The man was much taller than the woman, who clearly was white and had long blonde hair. At last he had found where the pirate lived.

Ellis noted the apartment was on the top floor at the end, furthest from the side road. He thought that it shouldn't be too hard to find when the time came. He sat and watched the two shadowy figures on the balcony, then after ten minutes or so, they disappeared inside. He then started his engine and drove slowly off the beach, onto the main road. Ellis took the precaution of only switching his lights on dipped, when he was actually driving down the road and out of sight of the apartment block.

Now as he turned off the freeway towards River Road, Apapa, he was content with his night's endeavours. The only hiccup had been the drugged up soldiers, but the memory of that incident was fast fading, as he was almost home and had achieved his objective for that night. The location of the pirate's apartment.

Ellis at last felt satisfied that all the parts of the jigsaw were falling nicely into place. He had photos, though somewhat hazy due to the poor light at the creek, of Kaduna arranging the deal for the sale of the contraband to Attandah. He also had the source of the information, as the clerk Ekpe in Bowman's office, had been seen a number of times talking to Kaduna. Also in his possession, were the numbers of stolen contraband from the ships' manifests, matched up with items he had purchased from the street stalls of Lagos and Apapa. He had photos of the contraband being unloaded from Attandah's truck to these stalls. Ellis even knew the location of the beach, where the pirates came ashore after attacking ships. All he needed now was to catch the pirates coming back after a raid. Then, with the assistance of the Nigerian Special Forces, he could arrest Kaduna and his henchmen as they came ashore.

After that, it would be the first available flight back to civilisation. A nice thought, as he pulled up to the gate in front of Ronnie's apartment block. The old watchman as usual was fast asleep in his hut, but the noise of the car approaching had woken him. Ellis still had to wait a few minutes before a face appeared at the gap in the gates, which eventually creaked slowly open. He waved at the night watchman as he passed, who acknowledged him by raising his head slightly. He quickly parked the car and made his way up to the apartment. Regrettably, he had to wake Ronnie, as the flat was locked from the inside with a heavy metal bar. A bleary eyed Wilson came to the door after a few minutes and let him in.

'So old chap, any progress tonight?' Wilson said evenly, no hint of irritation in his voice, after being woken in the middle of the night.

'Yes Ronnie, considerable progress. I now know where the bastard lives.'

'Excellent! Well done Martin. Sounds like there will soon, be an end to the matter.'

Kaduna stood peering through a crack in the heavy curtains of his apartment and watched in silence, as the car drove off the beach. Lesley came out of the shower and he heard her creep up behind him. This did not trouble him, even though he was thinking about the car and its occupant.

'Now what's so interesting out there?' Lesley spoke in a soft seductive voice. He could smell the intoxicating mixture of soap and perfume, as she stood close to him. He could feel himself becoming quickly aroused. It never took much.

'Oh nothing really, I just like to keep an eye on things. You never know who can be out there at night time, prowling round.'

Later as she slept deeply, Kaduna lay on the bed thinking about the car he had seen follow them back from the casino. He didn't miss much, which was why he had survived so long in his precarious position. It was probably the same person, who had been snooping round the jungle, a couple of weeks ago.

So now the stranger knew where he lived. Oddly enough, that did not perturb him very much. He would make arrangements, so that in the event of an emergency, he would not need to come back to his apartment.

Anyway, as an added precaution, and in life he had learned you could never take too many. He decided to pack the majority of his belongings, into a couple of suitcases and leave them with Lesley. She had a small apartment, which was attached to the Echo Beach hotel complex. When he obtained information from Ekpe regarding the ship, he would get her to book airline tickets. She could use her contact at the airport, to make some daily morning and evening reservations, around the date when the ship was supposed to arrive at the port. She had an arrangement with her friend at BCal, that as long as the booking was cancelled two hours before departure, he would arrange a refund. By this method, Kaduna would establish a secure escape route.

He smiled to himself. It was a good plan.

What that clever bastard in the car had actually achieved, was a negative result for all his efforts. His action had forced Kaduna to devise a virtually fool-proof escape plan.

Chapter Twenty-Seven

While the M.V. 'Kapitan Penkov' passed between the narrow, jagged breakwaters of Lome, the principal port of Togo, Gregor Kaminsky sat brooding in his cabin, an angry and unhappy man. His mouth was thick with fur and his head thumped as though it had been hit with a hammer. His bloodshot eyes were fixed on the last inch of whisky, which sloshed around in the bottom of the bottle. In Tema, the previous port, to placate the customs, the captain had made him surrender, all the boxes of watches remaining in the engine room. At the time, he would gladly have grasped at any proffered straw, no matter how thin, to avoid the stigma and disgrace of banishment from the party. Which would have been the case, had the ship been detained and fined because of the watch smuggling operation.

But now, two days later, when the dust had finally settled, he found the whole matter totally exasperating. As some how or other, the captain even knew where the contraband was concealed. To make sure all the boxes went off the ship, he personally supervised their transfer up onto deck and into a waiting customs truck on the shore. This was a disturbing factor in itself, as the old bastard must have known all along, what had been happening on the ship. It also meant someone in the smuggling chain had talked. Or perhaps, it was that little shit of a deck boy, who had seen the watches coming on board in Singapore. He vowed to give him a liberal dose of something particularly nasty, at an opportune moment later in the trip.

At the time, the chief engineer had been a positive embarrassment, with customs flooding into the engine room and it was blatantly apparent that the game was well and truly up. He had started blabbering uncontrollably, that his chance of immigration to Israel had been lost forever. Kaminsky had to shake him violently behind the control room, when no one was looking and assure him that his so-called dream would not be affected. Now though, with time to contemplate the lost revenue, he was extremely bitter towards the captain. He had not lost money on the deal, but his profits were substantially reduced. More worrying, there was the problem of the port authorities in Lagos. They would be expecting a fair sized shipment of watches. These were not people who took disappointment graciously.

Gregor Kaminsky was a dangerous man, who never forgot a bad turn in his life. People who had bullied him at school, found out years later, as he progressed upwards in the Communist party; he was able to weave a web of revenge around those unfortunates. A thin smile crossed his lips, as he thought of what he had planned, for the big fat slob of a captain. He would find out soon enough, what happened to those who crossed Gregor Kaminsky. With that satisfying thought, lifting his sombre mood slightly, he reached across and poured the remainder of the whisky into his glass.

Ellis looked up; from the worn dog-eared manila file he was scanning, with the overly attentive manager of Bowman's ship agency, trying to identify what ship might be the next target.

'So let's see, Mr Kafu. Looking at this list, it seems quite a few ships will be calling at Lagos in the next few weeks.'

'Yes that's right, for some reason the port is unusually busy at the moment,' the well-groomed Nigerian replied, in a rather flat matter-of- fact tone.

'It would appear you have two vessels arriving in the next two days, the first from Argentina, M.V. 'Cassiopeia' with a cargo of bulk wheat. The second is from the Far East with general cargo and containers.'

'Yes that's the M.V. 'Kapitan Penkov.' We are the main agents in Nigeria for Merca Flot, the Russian national line. There is usually one ship a month from that company.'

'Do you think I could view the cargo manifest to see what she has on board?'

'Of course, but please forgive me if I take a little time. Unfortunately my head clerk, Mr Ekpe is having his day off. So the manifests may take a few minutes to find.'

Kafu shuffled out of the room unhurriedly, a trait of all West Africans. Ellis noted and smiled warmly to himself at the African attitude. Why rush, it never achieved anything. That invariably was true. The rest of the world was in too much of a hurry to grasp such a valid point, Ellis mused.

During the few minutes that he was alone in the air-conditioned office, he savoured and appreciated the coolness the place offered, on another sweltering day in Lagos. Ellis sat back in the comfortable leather settee, at the rear of Mr Kafu's office. The only sounds to be heard were the whirr of the air conditioner and the tick, tack, of the various ancient typewriters in the main office. He closed his eyes and reflected on the state of play at that moment in time.

As far as he was concerned, the scene was set for a finale on the grandest terms. All the component parts of the case had eventually come rapidly together. Now sitting in the office where the vital information was originally leaked from, he wondered where the little criminal, Ekpe, was at that moment. Ellis thought wryly that he in particular would be viewing life from a different aspect, when the conclusion was eventually reached. As for the main perpetrator, the arrogant brute, Henry Kaduna, he now knew where he lived and thanks to Wilson, he also had the address of his girlfriend. The noose was certainly tightening round that person's neck in no uncertain terms.

The door creaked open and Mr Kafu walked ponderously towards Ellis with some files in his hand.

'Here you are. These are all the manifests of the vessel in which you were interested.'

'Thank you Mr Kafu,' Ellis said pleasantly, as he began to leaf though the papers.

The first dozen or so sheets were of little interest to him, or any pirate for that matter, as these pertained to the steel cargo the ship had loaded in Japan. When he reached the cargo loaded in Taiwan, his pulse started to quicken slightly. This was containers, half of which was machinery and spare parts. The other part was electronic goods, radios, stereos, cassette players and other high value electronic cargo.

There were fewer manifests for the final two ports, Hong Kong and Singapore. However mixed in with containers of toys and plastic flowers, was a considerable amount of high value electronic goods. All told, the ship was like an Aladdin's cave if you knew where to look, this ability his adversary had acquired long ago.

Yes there was no doubt, Ellis concluded, this ship would be too much temptation for Henry Kaduna and his henchmen. Ellis put all the papers neatly back into the folder and passed these to Mr Kafu, who was busy signing some forms behind his desk.

'Well that would seem to be every thing for the moment. What is the vessels' ETA?'

'I received a telex from the master an hour ago, stating that he has just left Lome in Togo. So he will be arriving at the fairway buoy tomorrow afternoon at 1600 hours.'

'I see,' Ellis said thoughtfully. 'Do you know if they will be berthing on arrival?'

'Well that is the problem. As I said before, the port is quite busy at the moment so they may not berth immediately. They may have to anchor or drift off for one or two days.'

If the master did decide to anchor, Ellis was sure that the pirate would find the temptation too great and would pay him a visit in the dead of night, as he had so many others in the past. But this time there would be quite a surprise waiting for him, when he eventually came back to the shore. Ellis looked forward with relish to that final encounter, which would see the heinous pirate and his comrades arrested and thrown in jail. Never to trouble innocent merchant ships again.

Ellis thanked Mr Kafu for his help and made his way out of the office, into the scorching afternoon heat. He was due to meet Ronnie and some of his expat friends for sundowners at the Apapa Club. A nice thought, the sound of ice chinking in a frosted glass of gin and tonic. But as it was still early, he decided to go back to the apartment, shower and change into fresh clothes before joining the others.

As he drove unhurriedly along Creek Road towards Ronnie's apartment, he was in an extremely relaxed and content mood .The traffic on the road was light, with the just occasional car containing one or two expats, or wealthy Nigerians in marked contrast to the rest of the traffic. This consisted of dilapidated cars, or yellow buses of the Lagos Apapa Bus Co. They would lumber away from the pavement, packed to the seams with sweating workers returning home after a day's work.

'That was Africa for you,' Ellis thought, the ultimate land of the haves and have-nots. Unfortunately for Africa, more so than other continents, there was a vastly disproportionate number of the latter. This in itself helped to explain why life was so cheap on this continent. It also helped to explain, the mentality of someone like Henry Kaduna; a ruthless cold-blooded murderer, who would stop at nothing to achieve his goals. Ellis had first hand experience of this, from his encounter with the man two weeks previously, a man not to be taken lightly at any time, a formidable adversary. Ellis nodded his head thoughtfully, as he drove along. He would treat this person with the utmost respect; until the mission had reached what he hoped would be, a rapid and successful conclusion.

Chapter Twenty-Eight

The sea was like glass, flat calm without the slightest zephyr of wind. The ship was rolling very gently on the low ocean swell as it proceeded from Lome to Lagos, a short voyage of around 23 hours. Thomas Kolskis, the second mate of the M.V. 'Kapitan Penkov', who was on the twelve to four watch that afternoon, felt very content with his life. People on the ship, and in particular the Old Man, had talked incessantly about the so-called hell of West Africa. But he, for one, was far from convinced that the place was as bad as it was purported to be. Especially when he reflected on some of the places he had visited during his time at sea. Places like Japan for instance, a virtual sea of ships, most of which were not complying with the collision regulations and the weather, either blowing a gale, or dense fog, a nightmare of a place. Or the English Channel, with its countless crossing ferries, plus many coasters and fishing boats. The Wandelaar pilot boarding ground, near Flushing in Holland, was another bad place in his experience, especially in dense fog, when ships embarking, or disembarking pilots in a confined space, tended to be erratic and unpredictable in their movements. West Africa, in direct comparison to those locations, was almost idyllic with crystal clear visibility and not a single ship in sight. What a pleasure.

There had been a few minor instances of pilferage since arriving in Abidjan a week previously, but this was not a major problem. As for pirates the captain's pet subject, which he was virtually paranoid about, although they undoubtedly existed, he felt the whole thing was blown out of all proportion. Only the most naive and unprepared ships would be affected by that particular problem. Russian ships were always prepared. Prepared for the Third World War if necessary, he thought wryly.

He stood in the centre of the wheelhouse looking towards the bow, watching the ships' Velle cranes describe shallow arcs on the distant horizon. The din and vibration of the ship's engine and generators blotted out most of the sound outside the ship's wheelhouse. So when the twin-engine plane passed close by at the same height as the bridge wing, he was shaken out of his daydream in no uncertain terms.

'What the hell was that?' he shouted loudly.

Sernoski the duty A.B. who was equally taken aback, but relaxed and un-stressed at all times, said in an even tone.

'Oh, just some hot shot pilot from an oil company or something, really nothing to worry about Sec.'

'We'll see Sernoski. I bet the Old Man is up here in a few seconds.'

The A.B. knew the captain better than the second mate. In his cabin just below the bridge, Victor Borisenko had paid the plane scant heed, barely looking up from his pile of paperwork, recognising immediately the source of the noisy intrusion on his concentration. It would soon be time to go to the bridge, in preparation for arrival at Lagos.

The Nigerian pilot of the plane, Koffe Enazas, was having a great time that afternoon. The businessman, who had chartered his twin-engine light aircraft for a flight to Lome, was interested in shipping. He had encouraged Koffe to dive down from their cruising height of three thousand feet, to have a closer look at the various ships in the area.

'Yeah that's a Ruskie,' the businessman's voice crackled over the intercom.

'I bet we sure woke them up sir, I don't think they saw us coming,' Koffe replied, laughing after he had spoken. The businessman also laughed. They would be at Lome international airport in another half an hour.

Koffe had been chartered for the return trip and would have to hang around the airport for the rest of that afternoon, till the man had concluded his business in Lome and was ready to return to Lagos.

Koffe was a great bear of a man, with a large round jovial face, that topped his broad heavily muscled shoulders. He had learned to fly with Air Nigeria and after a number years had saved sufficient, to purchase a second hand Piper Comanche PA 30 light aircraft. He preferred the life as a charter pilot as opposed to working for a big airline. The planes were a joy to fly, and there was plenty of variation in the trips he made, either along the West African coastline or further inland to some jungle airstrip. He was making a comfortable profit on his small operation. As he looked down at the silvery ocean, he could see another ship a few miles up ahead. A tanker this time, low in the water, its wake spreading out for miles behind on the calm sea.

'Do you want to take a look at that one, sir?'

'Naw, we'll leave this one in peace I think.'

'Okay, whatever you wants, you is paying.' Koffe banked the aircraft and headed in towards Lome airport.

On the M.V. 'Kapitan Penkov' at that time, the captain had just walked out, from the chartroom to the wheelhouse. The pulses of both the duty A.B. and the second mate quickened slightly, with the appearance of the ship's master. He as they expected, proceeded to bark out various orders and commands in almost military style.

'So Second Mate, have you been in contact with those sons of bastards at East Mole Signal Station?'

'Yes sir, I've tried a few times, but no reply as yet,' the second mate said, a slight tremor of nerves perceptible in his voice.

'Okay keep trying channel 16. Channel 14 is worth a try sometimes also. What revs are the engine on at the moment?'

'We're down to eighty-five now sir.'

'How far from the accursed pilot station?'

'Just eight miles sir.'

'Very well. Put the engine on stand by and come down to full ahead manoeuvring.'

'Aye aye sir.' The second mate pushed the yellow button beside the telegraph, which rang irritatingly loudly, until one of the engineers pushed his button in the engine room, to confirm the command from the bridge had been accepted. The second mate then pulled the handle of the telegraph upwards, to slow the engine down to full ahead manoeuvring.

The captain could see the outline of the two moles outside Lagos, which protected the channel into the port, quite clearly on the radar screen. The variable range ring gave the distance from those moles as 7.2 miles.

'Right, Second Mate, let's bring her down to half ahead. There's no point getting in too close if we do not have confirmation that the pilot is on his way out to us.'

'Okay sir half ahead.' The second mate pulled the handle of the telegraph up another notch to the half ahead position. The engineers answered this command almost immediately and a few seconds later the engine revolutions reduced by twenty, the ship vibrated slightly as the engine passed through its critical range.

After five minutes with a distance on the radar to the closest mole of six miles, the captain reduced speed to dead slow ahead. Still there was no answer from the signal station, as the ship crept ever closer to the breakwaters. Eventually, after half an hour of calling the signal station, word came through that the pilot was on his way. The vessel was instructed to wait one and a half miles from the breakwater, with the pilot ladder rigged on the starboard side, at one metre above the water.

The captain was relieved to hear that he would be berthing that afternoon, instead of having to drift out at sea all night. He approached the breakwaters cautiously, steaming at dead slow, barely maintaining steerageway. The master constantly scanned the channel behind the breakwater with his powerful Russian binoculars, for any sign of a pilot boat approaching. He stopped the engine and had almost reached the one and a half mile position when the VHF radio suddenly burst into life.

'Kapitan Penkov dis East Mole Signal Station,' a thickly accented Nigerian voice announced, in an arrogant tone. The second mate was going to answer the call, but the captain snatched the VHF handset from him.

'Give that to me,' he said tersely.

'Yes East Mole, this is the 'Kapitan Penkov'. We are waiting for the pilot one and a half miles from the west breakwater,' an anxious tone, noticeable by those on the bridge, in the captain's voice.

'You has to anchor captain, the pilot boat, she broken down. Maybe you get your pilot tomorrow morning if dey has fix the boat.'

Captain Victor Borisenko felt like exploding and screaming down the VHF at the hapless person on the other end. But he had learned at a very early age in command, that kind of demonstration served no purpose and once again his deep self-resolve, kicked into gear. He took a deep breath before replying.

'Okay East Mole Signal Station. We will be steaming back out to sea to drift for the night and await your orders.' He placed the handset back on the VHF set and turned towards the second mate.

'Very well Second Mate, nothing for it but to steam out to sea and drift around all night. Let's go half ahead on the engine. Helmsman, hard starboard wheel.'

'Yes sir half ahead.' The second mate took two strides forward to the engine telegraph and pushed it down three notches from stop to the half ahead position. It rang noisily for a few seconds, till the engineers answered the movement. The second mate smirked to himself. As there had not been a movement for five minutes, the engineers were probably dreaming again. The vibration through the wheelhouse, told the captain that the engine had sprung into life. Its deep rumble could be heard quite clearly, as it permeated its way from the engine room up to the bridge. The funnel behind the bridge, made the characteristic fut, fut, sound as the exhaust gas and smoke made its way out of the narrow tubes and into the atmosphere. All very reassuring sounds. He leaned on the bridge window ledge, directly in front of the helmsman, watching the ship's head come steadily round and point out to the distant horizon.

The gyro repeater clicked steadily with the passing degrees of the compass card, while the ship rolled gently as it came beam on to the low swell. The master steadied the ship up on a southerly course and was just about to order full ahead on the engine, when all sounds from the engine room and the funnel suddenly ceased.

The engine had stopped.

The telegraph needle shot back up to stop and the second mate brought the handle up to stop position in response.

'Shit,' the captain shouted. 'What the bloody hell is up now? Tell the chief officer to get ready to drop the port anchor.' Suddenly the bridge phone rang. The captain strode purposefully across the bridge and picked it up.

'Bridge, captain speaking.'

'This is the chief engineer,' said an agitated voice on the other end of the phone.

'Yes Chief what's the problem?'

'Difficult to tell Captain but it seems to be a problem with the fuel.'

'How long will it take to rectify Chief?'

'Once again difficult to say. If the fuel valves are blocked, we will have to change all of these. I'll get all my men on this, but we must wait for the engine to cool first, so I guess we are looking at about two hours minimum.'

'Very well Chief, do the best you can and keep me posted on

any developments.'

The captain replaced the phone and looked round at the second mate.

'How far to the breakwaters?'

The second mate quickly looked in the radar.

'Just a shade over two miles sir.'

'Okay tell the chief mate and the bosun to stand by the anchor up forward, just in case we need them.'

The captain knew it was a serious situation, to be in such close proximity to the shore with a dead engine. But he was not about to anchor the ship, in what he knew was an area of high pirate activity. There was a still a good chance that the east flowing Guinea current, would carry them along the coast, away from Lagos and perhaps slightly further out to sea. He decided to wait half an hour or so, before committing himself to dropping the anchor.

Suddenly, quite dramatically, the heavy curtain that separated the chartroom from the bridge, slid noisily back. He looked round, to see Kaminsky the commissar standing there in all his finery, peaked cap and all. Just about the last person he would have wished to talk to, at that grave moment in time.

'Why has the ship stopped Captain? We seem to be very close to the shore.'

'A problem with the engine.' The captain replied curtly.

'Shouldn't we drop the anchor?'

'I will decide when we do or do not drop the anchor, if you don't mind, Comrade Kaminsky. I'm in command round here,' the captain replied in a sarcastic tone.

'Yes, yes, of course you are in command comrade, I was merely thinking out loud.'

Kaminsky walked slowly past the captain and onto the bridge wing. An imperious air about him as if he owned the ship, an evil smirk etched onto his thin lips. He knew exactly why the engine had stopped. Fuel oil and salt water don't tend to mix too well. It had been a relatively simple task to perform. The deck fire line was usually kept pressurised on this coast, as fire hoses could be used as a first line of defence to help repel boarders. Or at least fill up their boats with water and sink them. That was the rather crude theory at any rate.

The previous night he had simply taken a fire hose, which was tied to the ships rail. He put the nozzle into the air vent of the service oil fuel tank and opened the hydrant valve. The tank had not been hard to find, a nice shiny brass label on the end of the air pipe, announced to the whole world the location of the tank, so critical to the running of the vessel. It was from this tank, that the fuel pumps sucked the oil that went directly to the main engine. The whole operation had taken less than five minutes. Ironically, after half a bottle of whisky one night, it was his accomplice in the watch smuggling operation, the chief engineer, who had mentioned his fears of the vulnerability of that particular tank.

He had no idea when his actions would make the ship stop and couldn't believe his luck, where it had happened. It was the only thing he could think of to get back at the captain, for the humiliation he had suffered in Tema. Now he had placed the captain in the middle of his worst nightmare. As the prospect of having to anchor overnight off Lagos, the pirate capital of the world loomed large. Kaminsky however, would be tucked up in his bunk, as all hell broke loose round about him. If the ship got attacked it would be nothing to do with him. After all, as he had just been reminded, he was not in command.

Inside the wheelhouse, Captain Borisenko was starting to feel the first signs of tension creeping insidiously into the muscles of his shoulders. Of course his countenance would never reveal to an observer how he was feeling. It would not be correct for the boss to look anything less than 100 per cent in command at all times. But nevertheless, he was starting to get a very bad feeling about the whole situation.

Half an hour later, the captain was disappointed to see, the ship had not drifted along the coast as he had hoped, but had in fact drifted closer to the land. They were also closer to the deadly jagged breakwaters, which would tear the bottom out of any ship unfortunate enough to run aground on them. The afternoon on shore breeze, had proved to be stronger than the east flowing current and the vessel had drifted northward, half a mile over the last thirty minutes. At that rate of drift, they would be aground in one and a half hours. A decision would have to be taken before it was too late. He had just phoned the engine room, but the news was not good. The chief engineer informed him that one of the fuel valves had seized in its socket and would take at least two hours to release. 'Nothing for it,' he thought resignedly, he would have to anchor to stop the ship grounding. The threat of piracy paled in comparison to the very real threat of losing the ship.

The rusty black anchor of the distant cargo ship hit the water with a dramatic splash. A cloud of mud and rust, thrown off the gypsy on the windlass as the anchor chain rattled out, partly shrouded the foc'sle and the three ship's crew letting go the anchor. Henry Kaduna adjusted the focus ring of his powerful binoculars, eyes straining slightly, to read the rust-streaked name on the bow. After a few seconds he smiled and said the name quietly. 'M.V. 'Kapitan Penkov."

That was it! The ship he had been waiting for. He could not believe his luck. He had been quite prepared to risk another attack in the port against that particular vessel; such was his desire to get the treasure trove of cash, he knew to be on board. But now the vessel had anchored off the breakwater, it was in the perfect location. Just like an apple ripe for picking he thought brightly. The scene was now set, tonight would be the last attack. He decided to get into his car and go round to Asamwa's shack and tell him to find the rest of the pirates and instruct them to be at the clearing in the jungle by two in the morning.

His mind now concentrated on his plan of action. Whilst bedlam ensued on the ship as it always did. The scum running riot amongst radios, plastic toys, children's clothes and other low value merchandise on deck, he would head straight for number two hatch and the special container in the tween deck. He planned to break off any locks on the access hatch to the hold, with a pair of high tensile steel cutters, then go down into the hatch and break open the container. He'd fill a small rucksack with as much cash as possible, then get straight in a canoe and make his way back to shore. It was a simple plan. Those were the best in his experience. The least amount of things to go wrong, the more chance of success the plan would eventually have.

Martin Ellis had been listening to the VHF radio in Wilson's office and had heard the conversation between the signal station and the Russian cargo ship. So he knew it would not be berthing that day. What he was not prepared for, was what he could see through binoculars, from Wilson's office on the second storey of the building. The ship seemed to be anchored just off the breakwater, the worst possible place.

He was surprised to find his emotions decidedly confused. He should have been elated that the bait was there; to at last bring the case to a conclusion, to catch the evil Kaduna and put an end to piracy off Lagos. But no, he was actually worried about the fate of those seamen, at anchor so close to the land. A deep sense of responsibility ached inside him.

He had to at least warn them. Warn them of the dangers, so that they would not be taken completely unawares. He picked up the VHF handset and called the ship. This quickly responded to his call. He asked to speak to the captain. After a few minutes, a deep heavily accented Russian voice boomed out of the VHF loud speaker.

'Yes, station calling the M.V. 'Kapitan Penkov,' please identify yourself.'

Ellis took a deep breath then replied. 'This is Mr. Ellis from the Britannia P and I Club.'

'Yes okay, but we have our own P and I Club. You are nothing to do with us.'

'I am fully aware of that Captain. But I see your ship is anchored very close to the shore. I was just calling to warn you that this is a very bad area for piracy. In the last two months, four ships have been boarded and robbed. These pirates are armed and they recently shot some of the crew on a ship. It really would be safer if you heaved up your anchor and steamed out to sea.'

Ellis was unprepared, for the response that came booming out of the VHF set.

'Who the bloody hell are you to tell me about pirates, mister? You can't honestly believe I would anchor here if I had any choice in the matter. I have an engine problem and cannot move till it's repaired. So thank you for your advice, over and out.'

With a sigh of resignation, Ellis put the handset back in its cradle. There was nothing else he could do. Their fate was undoubtedly sealed. He walked slowly over to the land phone and dialled the Interior Minister's number. After a few seconds, he was connected to Chief Endofu. He told him that he was certain a pirate attack, would happen that night and to prepare his forces. Ellis was a little surprised, though pleased, when the chief asked him to visit his house around 7:00 p.m. to meet with the major in charge of the Special Forces, so that they could discuss the best way to apprehend the pirates.

Before the meeting, he had a light dinner with Ronnie in his apartment and told him what had transpired earlier in the day. Wilson had been pleased that at last, it would appear, the final chapter was about to be written in this business. Wilson, ever cautious and careful, insisted Ellis take one of the Motorola radios with him. Lagos was a dangerous place at night time and drivers were often stopped and attacked at traffic lights by armed robbers. He already had the Minister's phone number, which Ellis had given him at an earlier date.

After the meal, Ellis borrowed Wilson's car and drove the ten miles or so to the Minister's opulent residence, on the northern outskirts of Lagos. There was a moderate amount of traffic on the various roads he had to negotiate. The only minor source of frustration was the two army checkpoints that he had to pass through. At these places, scruffy half stoned soldiers peered in through the driver's window at him, before waving him past. Apart from that, the short trip went off without incident and he arrived at the house, just before 7:00 p.m.

He was shown into a large, luxuriously appointed living room, with several comfortable deep armchairs and a long settee that could have accommodated four or five people. The floor was of polished grey marble, adorned with a number of brightly coloured native rugs. There were several pots dotted around the room, with Yucca trees and other tropical plants growing in them. The curtains were drawn and air conditioning unit whirred rather noisily. The Minister met him half-way across the room and greeted him expansively, almost if he were an old friend. He was a slim man of medium height, aged around forty-five, Ellis guessed. He was dressed in traditional garb, white flowing shirt and baggy trousers, both inlaid with intricate blue patterns and a matching plant pot hat.

'Inspector Ellis, please come in. I am so pleased you were able to come here tonight for this little meeting and I was able to meet you at last,' the Minister said, smiling warmly as he shook Ellis's hand.

'Thank you Minister, I will just be happy when we eventually bring this awful business to a satisfactory conclusion.'

'Yes yes, me too. Please come over here and meet Major Owaragee of the Special Forces Unit.' The Minister led Ellis over to one of the deep armchairs at the far side of the room, where Major Owaragee was sitting. He was a small slim weasel of a man, with a thin moustache and cold narrow eyes that appraised Ellis critically as he approached. He was wearing a black beret and green camouflage uniform, with a highly polished brown leather belt and matching holster. His black boots were so shiny you could have seen your face in them.

He sat back relaxed in the chair, with one hand slowly stroking his chin as he regarded the approaching pair. The Minister introduced Ellis to the major, who surprised him by remaining seated and shaking his offered hand, without the courtesy of getting up to do this. A gesture of supreme arrogance, which irritated Ellis and from his point of view the meeting got off to a bad start.

The Minister indicated for Ellis to sit down next to him on the large settee, which was located close to the majors' armchair. There was a large mahogany table, with huge legs carved in the shape of baying elephants, in front of him. A selection of cold drinks, ample glasses and a few wooden bowls full of nuts and other snacks had been placed on the table. The major was drinking a tall glass of beer, between small handfuls of nuts, the crumbs of which, could be seen on his immaculate uniform.

'Please, Inspector Ellis, help yourself to a drink and some appetisers.'

'Thank you sir, but I've just had dinner and I am fine for the moment.'

'Well we may as well proceed with the meeting. Inspector Ellis, if you would like to start with the information you have, that leads you to believe the perpetrator of this pirate activity will strike tonight.'

'Yes I must say I am fairly certain he will organise an attack tonight. You see there is a large cargo container ship anchored very close to the breakwater at the moment. He cannot move out to sea, as he has a problem with his engine. I have seen the manifests in the local agent's office, for that particular ship. There is a considerable amount, of high value cargo on board and I feel that it would be too tempting for our villain to pass up.'

The major regarded Ellis through his cool impassive eyes, his face devoid of expression. There was a brief moment's silence before the major spoke, a slightly sarcastic note apparent in his voice.

'How do you know that the pirate is aware of the high value contents of the ship? For all he knows it may be containers full of machinery.'

'Well during my investigations over the past few months, I have found the source of the pirates' information. A clerk in one of the shipping offices is tipping our friend off, with the container numbers and their positions on the ships.'

'That man should be shot for betraying his trusted position,' the major proclaimed indignantly, raising his voice as he did so, hitting the top of the armchair with his clenched fist.

'I don't know about shooting him, but a lengthy term in prison is certainly warranted for the clerk I would say,' Ellis interjected in a level tone. He was faintly amused at the major's outburst.

'Let us not digress, gentlemen. What is your plan for when the pirates come ashore, Major?' the Minister said evenly.

'Quite simple, we will give them the option to lay down their weapons and surrender. Then transport them, in a number of trucks I have arranged for the purpose, to Kala Kiri prison for interrogation. Of course, if they are obstinate, we will use whatever force required, to apprehend these criminals.'

'What time will you advance to the jungle clearing, Major?' the Minister enquired.

'That depends on what time they decide to attack. I have dispatched a jeep and three men with binoculars to the end of the East Mole. As soon as they see any sign of an attack, they will radio my main unit, stationed out of sight behind the Community Nine. We will then move down the jungle trail and be in position when the raiders return.'

'You are certain of the location then, Major?' the Minister prompted

'Oh yes. I am one hundred per cent certain of that. I personally went with the map that Inspector Ellis made and checked the location. We even found a number of empty cartons there. It is definitely the correct place,' the major replied confidently

'What time are you going to pick up Inspector Ellis?'

'Ha!' The major let out a short sharp laugh, a sly glint in his eye. 'He won't be needed any longer on this case. I think Nigeria can take care of its own problems from now on, Inspector.' The major, who was looking directly at Ellis, made a dismissive gesture with his hand. Ellis was shocked and sickened to the pit of his stomach, by this casual dismissal by the major. But before he could say anything, the Minister rounded on the major, his voice rising considerably as he spoke.

'I beg your pardon, Major Owaragee. This has been an Interpol operation, conducted by Inspector Ellis right from the beginning. I must insist that he is there tonight. Besides, he is the only one who can recognise the pirate leader. We must confirm this Kaduna fellow is taken tonight, or in a few weeks we will be right back to square one.'

The major's outburst had clearly taken the Minister by surprise and he was noticeably angry with the man for putting him in such an awkward position.

The major raised his hand in a gesture of submission.

'Very well, Minister, if you insist. I will send a car at 2300 hours to the residence of Inspector Ellis. Excuse me if I had underestimated his importance to this mission.'

Ellis was seething and glared menacingly at the major. He felt like throttling him right there in the Minister's living room. If the mission of tracking the pirate leader had been given to someone like him, the man would have never been caught. After a few seconds Ellis started to regain his composure. He was determined to stay focused and see the mission through to a conclusion, at virtually any cost.

The Minister spoke next, sensing the tension between the two men.

'Now now gentlemen, let's all pull together on this operation and ensure a successful result is reached. So there is just one thing before you leave, Inspector Ellis.'

The Minister reached under the heavy mahogany table and brought out a handgun in a tan shoulder holster. He placed it on the table and slid it slowly towards Ellis. He then took an envelope from the centre of the table and placed it next to the gun. 'Your boss in London instructed me to issue you with this weapon. There is a letter in the envelope, which entitles you to carry a firearm in Nigeria. It also states that you are on Interpol business and are to be given entry to any area you require.'

Ellis was surprised to be presented with a firearm in this manner, but he was also very relieved to know that he would be armed. As it was impossible to say how the mission would work out and what danger he would find himself in, before the night was over. He picked up the holster and slid the gun out, to see which model he had been given. It was a Browning 9 mm automatic. He was familiar with this type of weapon and deftly clicked the lock catch on the magazine. It popped out and dropped down into his outstretched palm. There was a full magazine in the gun, thirteen bullets in total. There was no spare clip, so he would have to be judicious, if he ever had to use the weapon.

He thanked the Minister for the gun. Then after a few minutes had elapsed he said good-bye to him and the sullen major and made his way outside to Wilson's car. He carefully folded the letter and placed this in his back pocket. Next he reached under the seat and wedged the holster into the framework. Then, before he started the car, he checked under the seat to make sure he could find the gun easily. Past experience had taught him, that such details could be the difference between life and death in an emergency.

It was just a few minutes before 8:00 p.m. as he turned the Peugeot onto the main road. The radio Ronnie had given him was still sitting where he had left it on the passenger's seat. So he picked it up and called Ronnie, who answered after a few seconds.

'Hello old chap, where are you now?' the familiar voice crackled out of the walkie-talkie.

'Just left the Minister's house. I should be back at your place by half past.'

'Ten four Martin I'll put a brew on.'

'That would be just the ticket thanks. See you soon, over and out.'

'Yes,' he thought rather mordantly, as he drove though the dimly lit streets of Lagos. He needed a cup of tea, or something stronger even, to take away the bad taste left in his mouth from the encounter with the major. Not the type of person you would want standing behind you in a tight situation. Anyway he reasoned the plan for the mission was relatively straightforward. There would be in all likelihood, a much stronger and better-armed force of soldiers than pirates. They would also have the element of surprise on their side.

The trip back to Ronnie's house went much the same as the outward journey. He was stopped at the same two checkpoints, where once again he was waved past. A few minutes later than he anticipated, he turned into Harbour Road. His mind was very active as he picked his way slowly round the potholes, methodically going over how he thought the mission would unfold. The street was very dark; the only light provided by the dim looms emanating from the residences, either side of the road. He could see the light a hundred metres away, outside the gate of Ronnie's house.

Then suddenly, from nowhere, a car pulled out in front of him and stopped. Dark uniformed figures rushed towards him and one pulled open the car door.

'You is under arrest. Get out of the car and com with us.'

'What? You must be mistaken. I'm a police inspector with Interpol,' he replied in an incredulous tone.

'That cannot help you here. Dis Nigeria, we have nothin' to do with any Interpol. Now get out the car before I shoot you.' The tall thin policeman, dressed in a black uniform and beret, unbuckled the flap of his holster and took out his gun. Fear gripped Ellis' heart, as he slowly, resignedly got out of the car. 'I'll bet that damn major is responsible for this mess,' he said to himself, as he was bundled unceremoniously into the back of the police car.

But he was wrong. It was nothing to do with the major. Henry Kaduna was responsible for his arrest. After the encounter in the jungle and then being followed home by Ellis, he had put the word out on the streets of Lagos for some information. It had not taken long for this to materialise. In fact ironically, he had tracked down Ellis considerably quicker than the converse. He then phoned Police Chief Azubikas, telling him that an undesirable element was at large in Lagos. Kaduna cleverly waited till the night of his final mission, before having Ellis arrested, so that he would be free to act at will when he attacked the ship.

Martin Ellis knew none of this, as he sat wedged between two burly policemen, as the car bumped its way along the road to Kala Kiri prison. Every emotion possible was flooding back and forth in his mind, like a vicious rip tide. Gnawing frustration at missing out on the conclusion of months of work, despondency and depression, at the apparently hopeless situation, but most of all fear of the unknown, and what awaited him at their destination. He had heard grim tales of African prisons. A frisson of dread vibrated through his body, as the car approached the huge dark foreboding walls, of what he knew could only be, Kala Kiri prison.

Less than four miles away from where Ellis was arrested, Litbarski, the chief engineer of the Russian cargo ship, cursed as yet another attempt to free the jammed fuel valve failed. His men were exhausted. They had worked virtually non-stop since the engine had broken down and had even skipped dinner at five-thirty, in an attempt to get the engine repaired. But now all his men were on their last legs. Breakdowns never happened at eight in the morning he thought, always the end of the working day, or in the middle of the night. But now there was an even bigger problem, most probably related to the bad fuel which had caused the initial trouble. The indications pointed to a seized crosshead bearing. A major repair, it would take at least ten hours. A depressing thought. He went to the control room with a heavy heart and phoned the captain's cabin with the bad news.

Victor Borisenko took the chief engineer's grim news surprisingly well. In fact he was resigned to spending the night in this exposed position. He was just thankful that the anchor had held firm on the sandy seabed and they had not drifted onto the breakwaters.

The deck department had been divided up in to watches of four men, working six hours on, six hours off, patrolling the decks with batons and powerful flashlights. He had resisted the temptation to give the crew firearms, from the substantial armaments at his disposal, for the time being. Cargo and stores was one thing, but if any pirate tried to enter the accommodation that was entirely different.

Up on the bridge, the third mate had the radar on six-mile range, with the gain turned up slightly to give a better warning, of the approach of any small craft. The ship was lit up like a huge Christmas tree, with all the deck lights switched on. As the ship rolled easily from side to side on the low swell, cargo clusters swayed back and forth on ropes at intervals along the ships rails, illuminating the waterline. The seaman on watch with the third mate went from one bridge wing to the other, training the searchlights back and forth into the inky night, like a guard in a prison somewhere, searching for signs of a breakout. The ship was in a state of high alert, much more than those previously attacked in this area.

Junior seaman Sergie Dimitri lay in his cabin trying to sleep. He had been designated to patrol with the twelve to six watch. Everyone knew that was the worst time, when pirates were most likely to strike. Of all the duties on board, he loathed having to get up at midnight. He could never sleep before that watch, as there was always too much noise in the accommodation. Radios were blaring, doors banging and crew talking loudly. People ashore, would never believe what it was like, to do the twelve to six watch. You were always exhausted when you started at midnight and felt worse as the watch progressed. Tonight he was certain would be the most horrible yet.

Earlier that evening, as they had eaten their evening meal of greasy pork and green coloured potatoes, the crew were unanimous that this ship was a prime target for a pirate attack. If that was not enough to scare the hell out of any first trip seaman, he had the additional worry of the commissar. He had been told in no uncertain terms, that retribution would be slow and painful, for his part in the downfall of the smuggling ring on board. He felt wretched, as he thrust his face into the smelly sweat soaked pillow and tried yet again, to get some sleep.

Chapter Twenty-Nine

It was almost midnight, when Henry Kaduna parked his yellow Toyota, at the back of the Echo Beach Holiday Inn. He enlisted the assistance of a night porter, to help him up to Lesley's apartment, with his two smart grey matching Revlon suitcases and a heavy black grip. She was sitting pensively on the bed, smoking a cigarette as he dumped the cases down by the wall at the entrance of the bedroom. He crossed the room and sat down on the bed next to her. A deep frown etched on his brow.

'Hey what's up with you? Tomorrow we get the hell out of this place. Going to great places like I promised and you're sat there looking like that.'

'Well I'm sorry. I can only look the way I feel. I just get a real bad feeling about tonight.'

'Listen, the job will be no problem. I'll be back here before you know it. Look, here are the flight tickets I picked up this afternoon, first-class all the way to Gatwick England. Hey, I tell you, tomorrow night we will be living it up in London.'

Eventually she smiled and ground out the cigarette. She took his head in her hands and gave him a long passionate kiss. He could feel himself becoming aroused and after a few seconds, he gently pushed her away from him, not wishing to take the edge off his mental preparation, by going the whole way with her. Though it would have been easy to make love with her and he was sorely tempted, but sense prevailed for once. He would need all his wits about him later. It would have been foolish to indulge.

He lay back on the bed, caressing her long silky smooth blonde hair for a few seconds. He felt relaxed, but was at the same time looking ahead with relish, to the action he would instigate later that night. Everything was set, for one final big raid. The ship was a sitting duck and so close to the shore, that he would be on and off, in the blink of an eyelid. The two tickets he had given Lesley were for the 10 a.m. BCal flight, direct to London Gatwick. This time tomorrow, he would be in a four star hotel in London, with enough money to keep him and Lesley for years.

There was nothing to stop him, now the smart Interpol agent Ellis, was 'banged up' in Kala Kiri prison. He smiled to himself, as he remembered just how easy it had been, to find that bastard. There were not many white men in Nigeria, considerably less that fitted his description. Eventually, he had remembered meeting him at the beach. All arrogant and self possessed, trying to chat up his girlfriend. Kaduna had failed to realise initially, that it was the encounter on the beach three months previously, which made Ellis the only person capable of recognising him.

He looked at his watch. The luminous dials showed ten past midnight, it was time to make a move. He got off the bed and walked toward the door, picking up the grip as he went.

As he went out the door he looked round and said in a flat even tone.

'Don't worry, everything will be fine. I'll be back in a few hours, be ready to leave when I get back.'

'Okay. You take care though.' Lesley replied, a note of concern in her voice.

Down in the car park, a dark brown Renault was waiting. A youth of about seventeen sat eagerly behind the driver's wheel. He was one of the newer members of the pirate gang and had been on the previous attack. Kaduna got into the passenger's side, slinging the grip on the back seat.

'Hey boss you okay?'

'Yeah. Let's get a move on, we are wasting time.'

The car pulled out of the car park and made its way along the beach road towards Apapa. Any roadblocks they met on the way paid them scant heed and most just waved them through without having to stop. Eventually, they arrived at the jungle clearing just before one in the morning.

Kaduna got out of the car and was greeted by Asamwa, who seemed as stoned as ever. Like most of the crew the man never learned. Kaduna quickly changed into the combat uniform and boots that were in the grip. He thrust a pistol down in his belt and picked up the Uzi machine pistol, which he slung in front of him. At the bottom of the grip there was a small rucksack, which contained the heavy wire cutters and a large flashlight he would need on the ship.

He picked up the rucksack and put this on his back, adjusting the straps so the fit was comfortable and then walked to where the canoes were beached. When he reached the edge of the creek, he was amazed to find not just three canoes with his gang, but closer to six or seven. He turned and faced Asamwa, angrily gripping the collar of his grubby, virtually threadbare shirt and thrust his face to within a few inches of his cowering accomplice.

'Who the hell are all these people?'

'Hey boss stay cool. They must have heard what was going down and decided to com along. They is all pretty poor with starvin' families and needs to try to get ahead.'

He did not like surprises such as this. Three canoes full of men were plenty for this job. But he quickly reasoned, this was the last time and he was after something entirely different to the others, so it was immaterial how many took part. In fact, the extra numbers might well help his cause, creating more bedlam and confusion than normal.

'Okay, but tell them we paddle the last half mile to the ship and everyone must be very quiet. I will kill anyone who makes a sound.'

'No problem boss. I already told them what to do.'

'Right, let's get a move on.' Kaduna waded out knee deep into the dark warm water of the creek and clambered into the canoe he normally used, glaring at the pirate who was leaning on the powerful one hundred horsepower Evinrude outboard, at the stern.

'I hope you checked this bloody motor over today and that there is plenty of fuel?'

'Oh yes boss. Don't worry. The motor, she running real fine and I has a full can of gas down here.' He kicked a plastic petrol can on the bottom of the boat, to draw it to the attention of Kaduna. He merely grunted, as he made his way past the other pirates to the front of the boat. In the dim light, he recognised a few of them who mumbled words of greeting to him as he passed. Most were armed with long bush knives, though a few of the more seasoned pirates had pistols.

A few seconds after he sat down on a hard wooden thwart right up in the bow, the powerful outboard burst into life and the canoe broke free from the shallows. The deep-sided dug out canoe headed out into the middle of the creek, blunt bow rising slightly, at the prompting of the hundred-horse power engine.

There was no moon and the night was inky black. Kaduna could hear the high pitched roar of the other canoes, as one by one they set off from the shore and followed his canoe out to sea. His eyes soon became accustomed to the dim light and he could easily make out the dark shapes of the palm trees, which lined the bank of the creek. Soon the gap in the low headland was visible and as his canoe approached this, the bow stared to rise and fall easily, as it felt the remains of the ocean swell that found its way naturally into the creek.

Eventually, the canoe powered its way past the headland and out to sea. The swell became more pronounced now, and the canoe rose up and down the rows of smooth waves that processed towards them, throwing the stern high into the air as the canoe moved forward. The man driving had to hold on tightly to the outboard, or risk being cast into the angry black ocean by the motion of the canoe. The other occupants gripped the rough wooden seats or thwarts, to avoid being thrown to the bottom of the canoe.

The ship was not hard to see, even though it was still over three miles away. In fact, a huge glow lit up the eastern sky, near the breakwaters. It looked as though every available light had been turned on.

Kaduna smiled wryly to himself. The ship seemed almost to be advertising its presence. As if inviting all and sundry to board for a giant party. A thin finger of light from a small low powered searchlight, traversed up and down from the bridge wing, as a rather pathetic discouragement to potential boarders. A couple of shots from a pistol would soon put that out, he thought confidently. The rest of the lights would be extinguished in a similar manner.

Once the canoes got to within half a mile of the anchored ship, the engines were switched off. The dozen or so occupants of each canoe eagerly grabbed the long brightly painted paddles and began paddling rhythmically in virtual silence, towards the unsuspecting vessel. The thunder of the surf crashing down on the beach would probably have drowned out the sound of the canoe engines, but Kaduna always believed in having every possible advantage at all times.

It did not take long till the canoes were less than one hundred metres from the ship. Approaching from the direction of the bow, where they would be hidden from observers on the bridge. Even the radar would fail to pick up the canoes, due to the shadow sector created by the bow and the ship's masts and cranes.

Kaduna knew there would be seamen waiting on deck, hoping to discourage or repel potential boarders. He had seen figures walking up and down, wearing white overalls and yellow hard hats, with powerful torches flickering off the sides of the containers as they patrolled along the deck. He could even see a head with a hard hat, looking over the bow in the direction of the oncoming canoes. Somebody was in for a hell of a shock very soon, Kaduna mused to himself, a thin ever confident sneer etched across his lips.

Sergie Dimitri was that sailor on the bow and he felt very discontented with his lot in life at that instant, almost wishing he were back in Odessa, working twelve hours a day on the collective farm. Having had no sleep at all before midnight, now, two hours later, he could hardly keep his eyes open. The coiled ropes near the windlass were a temptation dangled in front of his eyes, as an inviting place for half an hour's sleep.

Initially, he had been petrified at the thought of patrolling up and down on the deck on pirate watch, dressed in his white boiler suit, a perfect target for someone with a gun, hidden in the darkness beyond the glow of the ship's lights. The bosun who was in charge of the twelve to six deck patrol, had to threaten him with a dose or severe violence, to get him to walk along the deck at midnight. But now, he was just hot, sweaty, tired and depressed. Exhaustion had taken over as the dominant sense in his body. So, as he leaned on the bulwark at the forward end of the bow, with ever such a slight breeze cooling his sweaty face, he dozed off briefly.

When he woke up a few seconds later, he did not believe at first what his eyes were telling him. There, not twenty metres from the bow, coming straight towards him, were a number of canoes.

He watched transfixed for a few seconds, as the long ugly black dugouts skimmed silently out of the darkness over the pitch-black surface of the sea. A number of shadowy figures could be seen on each craft. For a split second, he thought it was some kind of nightmare or trick his imagination was playing on him. But no, this was really happening to him.

Fear hit him instantly like a hard punch in the stomach. Adrenalin surged into his blood stream. But instead of heightening his senses and making him think clearly, all it did was induce blind panic, into the eighteen-year-old seaman.

He could think of nothing but getting back into the accommodation, behind the security of the heavy steel watertight doors. He turned and ran to the steps that lead down from the foc'sle to the main deck. He bounded down them two at a time, hands sliding along the rails as he went. Had he slipped on the way down those steep, greasy stairs, he would have undoubtedly broken a leg. But he was lucky and ended up on the main deck, still in one piece.

He ducked under the chain lashings of the containers, on the deck next to number one hatch. Then with his head bowed a few inches, he hurried as fast as he could beneath the containers from number two hatch to aft. His heart was pounding and he was panting heavily for breath, as he made his way aft and to safety.

In his wild panic, he had forgotten to do one simple thing. The reason he was posted on the bow in the first place. Inform the rest of the ship that a pirate attack was imminent. There was a speaker close to where he had been standing. An Amplidan talk back system. All he had to do was depress the lever and utter two simple words. 'Pirates forward.'

Then the rest of the ship would be aware that they were being attacked. He only remembered this, as he passed the end of number three hatch. It was too late to go back. A phone call from the deck office would have to suffice, he thought.

Suddenly from nowhere, a huge shape leapt out of the shadows and two huge gnarled hands grabbed him by the collar of his overalls.

'Where the hell do you think you are going in such a hurry, my little first trip shit,' the bosun bellowed into his ear.

'P…P.P.P. Pirates… forward… lots. We have to get back in the accommodation Bosun, there are too many.'

'Too many, we will see about that lad. You are coming back with me, to see what the hell is happening. A few years ago, people who deserted their post in this Navy, wound up getting shot. So you had better back me up or else.' The bosun's words had dramatic effect on the terrified seaman, suddenly realising that the bosun posed a much greater threat than the pirates. He had no choice, he would have to comply. The bosun felt the seaman stop struggling and he relaxed his iron grip slightly.

'Okay Bosun. No sweat. It's just I was on my own. I kind of panicked. It won't happen again.'

'That's more like it lad. Now did you inform the bridge when you saw the pirates?'

'No, sorry, I was in too much of a hurry to get aft.'

'Okay never mind son.' The bosun gripped the walkie-talkie that was suspended from voluminous chest and pressed the talk button. 'Bosun to bridge. Come in bridge.' A few seconds later, the anxious voice of the second mate crackled back from the walkie-talkie.

'Yes Bosun what's the problem?'

'Report of pirates forward, I'm taking the junior seaman to go and have a look.'

'Oh shit! There was no sign of any thing on the radar. Okay I'll tell the Old Man. You both be careful, the slightest sign of trouble, come straight back aft.'

'Yeah, Okay Sec. See if you can contact the other two guys, they don't have radios but you may be able to shout down to them from the bridge wing. They were hanging round the poop deck last I saw them. Tell them to come forward.'

'I'll see what I can do.'

The two seamen began to creep cautiously forward, stopping every so often and listening for anything untoward. The bosun led and Sergie was comforted ever so slightly to have his huge mass in front. But he was still immensely terrified and could feel his hands shaking.

His resolve was being fast eroded and the temptation to flee becoming stronger by the minute. As they approached the port side of number two hatch, the bosun turned round and whispered in his ear.

'There's a boat alongside here.'

'H… h… h… how do you know?'

'Listen, you can hear hushed voices below.'

Sergie listened for a few seconds and sure enough, the barely perceptible sound of the odd word he did not understand, came drifting up from the side of the ship. They both stood motionless for a few seconds listening.

Then a different sound. Chink chink. Metal on metal. Looking along the ship's rail, Sergie could see a hook with a line attached. Then more chinking sounds. Just a metre from where he was standing, he saw a hook clatter against the top rail before falling and finally fastening to the rail below. Another hook and line missed and fell back towards the sea. The Bosun moved up towards the position where the first hook was attached, four or five metres away. Sergie followed close behind. Heavy breathing sounds could be clearly heard, someone was obviously struggling up the ship's side.

'Why don't we just cut the lines, Bosun?'

'Because I have a better solution lad.'

A few seconds later, bony black hands appeared then scrawny arms, which pulled a dark body up to deck level. A distinctive African head was visible, complete with short black curly hair. The bosun's right arm came sharply backwards and delivered a sickening blow to the African's head, with his short thick wooden club.

The man, who should have been killed instantly, let go of the rail and fell screaming to the boat. He hit his head on the heavy hardwood gunwale of the canoe, seven metres below and split his already battered head open like a ripe melon.

Suddenly there was much shouting and other noise from the canoe. More hooks and lines were being attached to the ship's rails, though further forward at number one hatch. Another figure appeared at the rail. This time the bosun's club smashed the man's fingers and he too fell screaming to the water. The bosun thrust his face close to Sergie's. He could see his eyes were bright with triumph. The bosun always liked a good fight, it was in his nature.

He would often be involved in fights shore side. Sergie could never remember him being beaten.

'You see kid, nothing to it. As they try to come on board, just smash them with your club. The others will be along soon; we won't let these bastards even set foot on our ship.'

Sergie was feeling more confident and less nervous now, he gripped his club and was about to strike the next head to appear, when something caught his eye above the bosun.

It was a pirate.

He must have come on board on the starboard side. In a flash, the dark figure dropped down like a panther off a tree, right behind the bosun. Sergie shouted at the top of his voice.

'Watch out Bosun, behind you.'

But it was too late. Henry Kaduna slid the seven-inch long, two-inch wide Jim Bowie hunting knife, into the bosun's back, between the fourth and fifth ribs, burying it right up to the hilt. The bosun let out a spine chilling, blood-curdling scream as the huge knife went straight through his heart. He fell silent and slumped lifelessly like a sack of potatoes to the rust encrusted deck.

Sergie threw down his club and ran aft as fast as he could; banging his arms and head a number of times as he went. But he felt no pain in his desperate bid for survival. Kaduna saw the youth running, took out his pistol, aimed carefully and fired one shot. It hit Sergie between the shoulders and he tumbled to the ground mortally wounded.

The luminous dials, on his Rolex sports watch, showed one twenty in the morning. He was surprised, that this had not been taken off him on entry to the jail. By this time, Martin Ellis had languished in a stinking cell at Kala Kiri prison, for almost five hours. Alone in a very small place of incarceration, that had barely enough room to walk up and down. The cell was the same length, as the single bed that occupied most of the area and only two or three feet wider. The only light available, was that which spilled in under and above the steel door. A filthy bucket caked with excrement lay near the door and the stench from this, was all pervading in the tiny cell.

Grim sounds of wanton misery filled his ears from all corners of the prison. Men were moaning, crying and pleading for water. As no air moved in the prison, it was like the inside of a furnace. In the distance, the unmistakable sound of the lash could be heard above the general din in the prison, as a heavy leather whip landed with considerable force on bare skin. An agonising scream would pierce the air after each stroke.

He had sat alone undisturbed since his arrival, the sounds from hell his only companions. His training told him that this was all part of the softening up process, that they would come for him soon enough. Ellis was determined whatever they did to him; he would not let the side down by screaming like the wretch in the distance.

Very despondent, he sat on the edge of a filthy mattress, which was covered in dark stains. The worst thing as far as he was concerned, was that not a soul knew of his predicament. He could be days or weeks here, before help arrived. All thoughts of a spectacular end to his mission were effectively dispelled from his mind, as he contemplated his immediate future and how to deal with the worst-case scenario, torture, which seemed with each passing minute to be on his future agenda.

Ellis was so absorbed with his thoughts, that he almost didn't hear the heavy key turn in the ancient lock. He looked up despondently as the door creaked slowly open, muscles in his stomach suddenly tight as a drum, his pulse rocketing into overdrive. A tall thin guard, with a gaunt face, motioned with his free hand for him to get up and move out of the cell, uttering a single word.

'Com.'

Ellis got off the bed and walked towards the apparition at the door, legs feeling like jelly as he put one foot in front of the other. The guard motioned for him to turn right and spoke in a deep, though detached tone.

'Op the stairs.'

In the dim light he could see a second guard, slouched nonchalantly on the stairs. When the metal cell door clanged shut behind him, this guard led the way up, his heavy army type boots scuffing the worn concrete steps as he moved. Even though the sounds of misery receded as they walked, Ellis was feeling very apprehensive as they progressed up five or six flights of stairs.

Eventually to his surprise, they arrived at some kind of outer office. A single light bulb illuminated this area, which had a grey metal desk and a wooden chair. Other wooden chairs were dotted around the room, on top of some threadbare brown carpet. At the end of the room was a highly polished mahogany door, with a large brass doorknob. As Ellis approached, he could see engraved in the door what appeared to be ornate carvings of the African bush. The guard knocked on the door and a voice boomed from the other side.

'Come in.'

The guard opened the door for Ellis and he could not quite believe his eyes. He was entering an extremely plush office, quite incongruous to its grim surroundings. Classic paintings adorned the walls, thick red carpet over the floor, linen drapes at the windows. At the far end of this room, sat behind a huge executive style desk, was an extremely fat balding African, his face framed by heavy-jowled cheeks. Small, bright though compassionless eyes peeked out from between folds of flesh. His appearance sent a chill of apprehension through Ellis. The man looked evil and capable of anything.

'This must be Azubikas the police chief,' he thought, that Head Office had warned him about. There was a comfortable armchair right in front of the desk. But the police chief did not offer it to him, but started talking almost immediately Ellis entered the room.

'Ah, so you are Inspector Ellis from Interpol. Yes?' The man said leaning over slightly as he spoke. Ellis has to swallow before he could talk, as he was dehydrated and his mouth was bone dry.

'Yes that's correct.'

'There has been a mistake. It seems my men arrested the wrong man last night. They were sent to your street to arrest an East German; he also has fair hair like you. Please accept my apologies for this error.' A thin smile was etched across the corpulent police chief's thick lips.

There had been no mistake. Azubikas had meant to arrest Ellis to help Kaduna's latest mission to be successful. He knew exactly who Ellis was, but wasn't about to get involved in torture, or anything like that with him. After all, there was a whole jail full of prisoners with which he could amuse himself.

He had intended to keep Ellis under lock and key till the next morning at least, but he had just received a phone call from the Interior Minister, who had threatened the direst of consequences, if this man were not released immediately. So having no choice, he would have to release him. Besides, the pirate had probably finished his business by this time.

Ellis was extremely relieved at his unexpected release, though slightly perplexed that he had been subjected to this unnecessary ordeal. His confidence almost fully returned he was determined to let this common jailer know his feelings. He looked straight into the man's beady snake like eyes, took a deep breath and spoke in a slow measured tone.

'Well I am not amused to be held in this prison, with no reason, for five hours. I was involved in an extremely important mission tonight, with the Nigerian Special Forces, which may well be compromised because I have failed to be there. I told your arresting officer I was with Interpol, but he would not listen.'

The police chief was not accustomed to people answering him back and took great exception to Ellis doing so. His face instantly contorted with anger, as he raised his voice, almost shouting at Ellis.

'How dare you talk to me in such a tone? You has to know, Lagos is a dangerous place. People will say anything to avoid arrest; my men were merely following orders. It was a simple case of mistaken identity. My sergeant will escort you from the prison and one of my cars will take you back to your house. That is the end of the matter. Now get out of my sight, before I throw you back in the cells.' Azubikas thumped the heavy desk with one of his meaty paws, to emphasise the point.

Without saying another word, Ellis turned quickly and made for the door. Half an hour later he was back at Wilson's apartment, head spinning at the various changes in fortune, over the previous five hours. He hoped desperately, there would be still be a chance to become involved, with the conclusion of his mission. It was still only two-thirty. Anything was still possible, depending on whether the pirates had taken the bait. He was certain they would have. It was just too tempting a target to miss.

He found Wilson, pacing up and down nervously in the living room of the apartment. A flood of relief washed over his face, when he saw Ellis enter the room.

'Oh thank God you have been released. I didn't know if they would let you out tonight or not.'

Ellis was amazed that Wilson had even known he was incarcerated.

'How did you know I had been arrested?'

'Well the last time you called on the walkie-talkie, when you put it down the button must have jammed or been resting against a part of the car, because I got nothing but engine sounds, you singing and then a hell of a commotion when you were dragged out of the car. There was also a lot of shouting in the street at the time, so I went out to investigate and found the car. I talked to one of the neighbours, who was leaning over his balcony at the time and he told me what had happened. I then phoned your pal, the Interior Minister, which seems to have done the trick and got you released, thankfully.'

'That's incredible Ronnie, I hadn't realised that and once again, I am in your debt.'

'Oh think nothing of it chap, we've got to get you pronto to where the action is tonight.'

'How do you mean?'

'Well Martin, at the moment Kaduna and his cronies are ransacking the Russian cargo ship as you so correctly predicted. The VHF has been alive for the last hour with calls from the ship, trying to raise help from shore. Typically there has been no response from this end.'

'I had better get a move on then. It's best really, if I go on my own Ronnie. It may get rather hot when they come ashore. I'll take the radio, so that at least we can maintain contact through the night.'

'Okay Martin, it's your show. Here's the car key.' He reached down to the marble topped coffee table and tossed the key to Ellis, who caught it easily.

Once back in the car, he reached under the seat, to check if the gun was still there. He was relieved to find it was. So he took off his damp perspiration-soaked shirt and manoeuvred his left shoulder into the holster. Then he put his shirt back on and started up the car.

The drive to the jungle clearing at Badagry Creek, took just under forty minutes. There were a number of army jeeps parked on the edge of the jungle, inhibiting his progress. Eventually he decided to park up, and walk the final hundred metres.

He had only been walking a few seconds, when he was challenged by a soldier dressed in camouflage gear and slumped against the side of one of the parked jeeps. Ellis quickly reached into his back pocket and produced the document given to him earlier by the Minister. The soldier, who had a small flashlight, checked the document and then indicated to Ellis that he could proceed, he met another soldier as he approached the clearing, this time the man was an officer. A first or second lieutenant, he wasn't sure as he could not see clearly in the dim light, if he had one or two pips on his shoulder.

At his request, the officer showed him to where the major was positioned. This was at the edge of the clearing, behind some low bushes, with a clear view of the silvery creek, which snaked away towards the sea. Ellis was unsure of the welcome he would receive, still convinced that the major was the person behind his arrest.

The night air was very still and the only sounds audible emanated from the jungle, provided by a plethora of toads, crickets and tropical birds. The major heard the approaching footfalls and looked round, expecting to see one of his officers. He was quite amazed to see the Interpol Inspector. He was still puzzled, not knowing why he had not returned with the driver at 23.00 hours.

'So you have decided to join us at last, Inspector Ellis. I'm surprised that you so are late for your own party, as you say.' The sneering intonation of the major's speech prompted Ellis to challenge him head on.

'Well, if you had not had me arrested, I would have been here on time.'

The major looked him quite incredulously and said, with a deal of conviction.

'I haven't the faintest idea, what you are talking about. The car was sent for you at the arranged time, but for some reason you was not there.'

'That's because I was banged up in Kala Kiri prison.'

'Well if you were, I can assure you it was nothing to do with me. I have enough to occupy my mind tonight, without getting involved in arresting Interpol agents.' There was a note of finality in the way the major had spoken that made Ellis realise that his arrest might well have been nothing to do with him. He decided on a more tactful approach, to get back on better terms with the man.

'Okay, okay, Major. Listen, I'm sorry if I jumped the gun somewhat. But I have had a rather fraught few hours. And we didn't exactly part best of friends after the meeting, so you must forgive me for jumping to conclusions.'

There was a few seconds of silence, before the major nodded his head slowly then spoke, 'All right Inspector Ellis, I accept your apology. Let us now concentrate of what is happening here tonight.'

Ellis let out a subdued sigh of relief.

'So what's the situation at the moment, Major?'

'Well, quite a number of these pirates have been attacking the ship for almost an hour. My men on the breakwater counted no less than seven canoes, but as of yet they show no sign of leaving the ship and coming back to shore. When they do arrive here, I have forty armed men positioned around this clearing, so there will be no escape for any of these criminals.'

'So I suppose the only thing for us to do is sit quietly and wait.'

'Yes that's all we can do Inspector Ellis.'

Chapter Thirty

On board the ship, the pirates were having a thin time. Most of the containers they had opened were full of machinery, with the occasional one full of clothing. Kaduna had another interest on this vessel, so selfishly he had not bothered to pinpoint the location of any other high value cargo. As the ship gently rolled, the doors of the opened containers banged back and forward. Occasionally, a pirate stumbling round in the darkness, would cry out when an arm or leg was trapped by one of these loose doors.

Using old turnbuckles they had found scattered around the deck, the ragged band of pirates continued to break door seals and anti- pilferage devices. Eventually a group of them came upon some cargo of real worth. A whole container stacked from top to bottom with Panasonic cassette radios. The pirates who uncovered this treasure trove let out great whoops of glee, attracting the attention of others who were searching different areas in vain.

Soon boxes of cassette radios were being thrown onto the deck. The pirates, now fuelled with hyper enthusiasm, having seen the potential for previously unheard of riches, started to throw the boxes down into the canoes, many metres below. Some of the boxes smashed open as they landed in the canoes, wrecking the contents. Others missed completely and landed in the sea.

Eventually, one of the pirates had enough sense to start lowering the boxes three at a time, with the ropes used for boarding.

The others quickly caught on to this idea and the container was soon emptied. When they had finished, three of the canoes were packed to the seams with the buff coloured cartons and wallowed slowly back and forth, next to the black rust-streaked hull of the vessel. With four canoes still to fill, they went in search of more booty, like a hideous army of vagrants advancing steadily along the deck, breaking open containers as they went.

Meanwhile up on the bridge, Captain Victor Borisenko was seething with anger at the wanton pilferage happening on his ship. The noise which had a first been hard to hear now sounded like some kind of giant birthday party, at his expense. The shouts of triumph and laughter flowed up from the deck, not far from the accommodation, assaulting his ears. He was sorely tempted to order the sailors to open fire with the Kalashnikovs from the armaments locker. But he knew he would not be able to justify that action at any later enquiry. But he swore vehemently, if anyone tried to enter the accommodation, he would issue the order.

At this time, down in port side of number two tween deck, Henry Kaduna could clearly hear the sounds of bedlam on the deck above him. He had just located the precise container he sought. A few minutes earlier, he had gained entry to the hold, which had been relatively easy. The mild steel bolt, with a welded nut at the end securing the entrance hatch, had taken the minimum of effort to shear off with his heavy-duty cutters.

He had congratulated himself on quickly negotiating that first obstacle. But now he stood in the oven like tween deck, the air dank and heavy with the smell of stevedore's urine, his earlier elation had evaporated with what he had discovered. Instead of two seals and an anti pilferage device to cut through, he found the door of the container had actually been welded shut, with iron bars that passed round the door locking bars. He cursed loudly and kicked the container a few times in his rage.

'Bloody stinking lousy bastards. What kind of shit trick is this to play on me?' He said quietly, voice laden with rage.

He shone his large torch all over the door, checking to see if there was any way he could use his titanium bladed cutters to break the welds, but it was useless. This was one container that he would not be able to enter. He admitted to himself reluctantly, that he had been a fool to believe, no special precautions would have been taken, with such a valuable cargo inside. He was just about to go up on deck and perhaps try for the captain's safe, to at least salvage something from the night's endeavours. But he could not pull himself away from the dull red container. After a few moments, having calmed down slightly, he became more objective.

'There has to be a bloody way. There always is,' he said aloud as he shone the torch down one side of the container, then down the next. But all he saw was the impenetrable corrugated sides as the torch beam scanned the side of the container, looking for what he did not know.

He almost missed it in the dim light, as his torch scanned impatiently up and down the container's sides.

But something had caught his eye and he now traced the beam much slower, until he found out exactly what it was. At first he could barely make it out in the dull light. But as his eyes slowly became adjusted he saw it more clearly. Located one metre along the side of the container, around 30 centimetres up from the deck was a small jagged tear in the metal, perhaps only five centimetres long. Probably caused by a careless forklift driver in a port somewhere, it happened all the time to containers.

The strength of a container was in the base, to support up to twenty-five tons of cargo weight. Also the frame at each end and the lifting holes at each corner, were immensely strong. The sides however did not need to be so strong and were only made of very thin mild steel, corrugated for vertical strength.

An idea began to form in his mind. He took the cutters and put the tip into the tear and pressed down on the handles. Amazingly the tear was now twice the length. The special cutters, with a bit of effort were able to cut through the thin metal side of the container.

He tied the torch to the bar on the door of a container close by and began cutting methodically.

Twenty minutes later, absolutely soaked in sweat, he had managed to cut a long gash in the container, almost one metre long by fifty centimetres wide at the top and bottom. He laid the cutters on the deck and carefully pushed the metal apart, using one of his feet. The flap bent back surprisingly easily, until he had a hole he could just squeeze through.

Cautiously he climbed into the pitch-black interior of the container, ever careful of the jagged edges of the newly formed aperture. He shone the torch round the container, which was virtually empty of cargo, save for the large pile of mail sacks at the far end.

Somewhere amongst those was the special sack he was looking for.

He picked up the various sacks carefully, feeling the contents within. The first was definitely mail. As was the second and the third. He threw these sacks to the other end of the container near the door, well clear of the original pile. Next were a few sacks containing what were obviously packages of some kind. Possibly the medicines Ekpe had mentioned? Nothing so far that felt remotely like bundles of money.

He had almost searched the whole pile of sixty-three sacks and was growing increasingly despondent, as he approached the last few, thinking the whole exercise had been a huge waste of effort.

Then, the next sack he picked up felt altogether different to the others. Yes, he could feel the outlines of the neat blocks of bills within. He was jubilant, having found what he had come to the ship to steal.

He reached down and unsheathed the Jim Bowie knife, its huge blade stained with the dried blood of the bosun. He slit open the thin cord tie with the lead seal attached at the top of the mail sack and dumped the contents on the floor. When he saw the multiple bundles of dull green hundred-dollar notes spill out of the sack, he almost jumped for joy. It was a fortune and it was all his. He scooped up the bundles and quickly pushed them into the small rucksack he had brought for the purpose, which was crammed full once he had finished.

Then he carefully made his way out of the container, through the tween deck, up the metal ladder and onto deck. Once out of the hold, he closed the access hatch behind him. He was thankful to be up in the cool night air, after the furnace of the hatch. His whole body was buzzing with the thought of what he had been able to accomplish in the previous half hour.

This money, combined with the money already salted away in his various bank accounts, would mean he would never have to work again. He was a rich man; something he could never have dreamed would happen to him, when he left the Sahel region in Northern Nigeria as a youth, almost twelve years ago. His only thought then was survival.

All that remained now was the relatively simple task of getting off the ship and ashore as quickly as possible.

As he walked forward to where he had left his canoe, he had to wade through and climb over many ripped cardboard boxes and piles of cargo the pirates had thrown haphazardly down from the hatch top containers. The whole foredeck area looked like the aftermath of a huge children's party. This was to a certain extent true, he thought wryly to himself.

The hubbub made by the pirates as they opened even more containers was akin to that made by a mob, on the verge of losing control. It was none of his concern. He felt no loyalty to any of them. They could do whatever the hell they wanted as far as he was concerned. As he looked over the ships rail, the lights of the shore could be seen quite clearly glowing, just a couple of miles away. That's where he would be in a few minutes, he thought confidently to himself.

The canoe was where he had left it just aft of the bow, level with number one hatch, bobbing up and down on the shiny black swell that rolled past the ship. He quickly slid commando style down the rope that had been attached to the rail when he arrived at the ship, legs apart at the end of the descent, landing solidly on one of the heavy thwarts, of the bouncing hull of the canoe. The bottom of the dug out was strewn with a considerable number of cartons thrown down by the pirates on deck. At the aft end was the same pirate who had driven the canoe out to the ship. He was leaning casually back on the aft gunwale, hands behind his head.

'Okay. Get this canoe started and back to shore as quickly as possible,' Kaduna shouted; a note of authority in his voice.

'But what of the rest of the boy's boss? An the canoe she no full.'

'Bugger them. They can ride in one of the other canoes. Start the motor up now or you can swim back to the shore, you little shit.'

'Okay boss, okay. No sweat.' The pirate knew Kaduna to be a man of his word and not to be crossed at any time. He scrambled quickly over to the outboard and pulled the starter cord a few times, till eventually the engine spluttered then fired. Kaduna cast off the rope that held the canoe to the ship and the canoe pulled quickly away, from the dull black ship's side, turning to starboard in the direction of the shore.

On the deck of the ship Asamwa had seen Kaduna leave. With Kaduna gone, he was now the leader of the attack. This was his big chance to finally get ahead. Over the years, Kaduna had always taken the lion's share, of anything they had looted from ships. Asamwa had always resented this, though was in too much awe of the man's reputation as a cold-blooded killer, to have said anything. Being essentially a very simple minded person, he had frittered away his ill-gotten gains over the years, on booze, whores, gambling and Ganja. But now a great chance to make some real money had presented itself.

'Hey you two leave that kinds of shit alone. We got more important tings to do.'

Two rookie pirates close by, who were bent over ripping open yet another carton of cargo, stopped what they were doing and turned towards Asamwa.

'What you talkin' about man,' the taller of the two said.

'We's gonna to attack the accommodation. The captain he have plenty money in his safe and the crew too. An there may be women in the accommodation, that we can have fon with.'

A huge grin spread across the features of the taller pirate, who let out a whoop of childish glee then gave the other rookie pirate, a high five-hand shake.

'Okay brother lets do it.'

The three of them crept furtively along the deck and were joined by the remaining four pirates on the ship. There was now just one canoe tied up alongside, the rest of the canoes, heavily laden with booty and pirates were wallowing slowly in the ocean swell, heading towards shore.

When the group reached the first steel door, at the forward end of the accommodation on the port side, they released all the securing dogs and tried to pull the door open. But it would not budge, obviously secured by a bolt, or some other arrangement from within. It was the same with the next three doors they tried. Some of the pirates became discouraged, saying that they too wanted to head back to shore. But Asamwa soon quelled their discontent, saying he had an idea that was sure to work. It was something he had seen Kaduna do on a previous raid.

Right at the aft end of the accommodation, they found another watertight door. Strangely, this opened easily. This was the carpenter's store, which one of the ships crew must have forgotten to lock. Inside the store it was pitch black, so Asamwa struck a match. As it fizzed into life, casting the dullest glow round the room, Asamwa's eyes flicked from one corner of the space to the next. At last he found what he was looking for. There, quite close to the door, was a ten-pound sledgehammer.

The pirates then proceeded up a ladder and along the boat deck, a look of wild excitement visible on Asamwa's face. Now he had the means to get into the accommodation. They were all armed with pistols and knives and he was certain the crew would quickly surrender. Then the fun could start in earnest.

The band of pirates soon arrived at the windows of the crew's mess. Doors on the main deck and boat deck of ocean going ships were always substantial, watertight and made of steel. The portholes on the main deck always had metal plates behind, as protection in heavy weather. But windows on the boat deck were only made of toughened glass, the threat of waves decreased on this higher deck.

Asamwa smashed the ten-pound sledgehammer against the glass window, but it made little impression at first. Eventually, after five of six strikes, the window began to crack and eventually the glass shattered. One of the pirates screamed as a flying shard hit his forehead and blood trickled freely down his face. Asamwa paid the man no attention, intent on smashing the rest of the glass and gaining entry.

Finally, when the remaining jagged edges had been smashed away, Asamwa started to climb carefully through the window.

That would be his last act on earth.

The Russian sailor hidden in the darkness of the mess room, not three metres away from the pirate, depressed the trigger of his Kalashnikov AK 47 assault rifle. Asamwa's body was caught in a deadly hail of bullets and was tossed about like a rag doll, eventually falling blood-splattered and riddled with holes to the floor of the mess room.

Outside, three other pirates who were close behind Asamwa were also caught in the deadly fire. One took hits to the face and died instantly, the other two suffered wounds to the arms and chest and fell screaming in agony to the deck, blood pouring from their wounds onto the shiny green steel deck.

The Russian moved quickly to the window, keeping his body close to the bulkhead so that the gun only pointed out to the boat deck. Out of the corner of his eye, he could see the two men screaming and writhing on the deck. He fired a short burst into them and the awful sounds were silenced. Hands as steady as a rock, he coolly depressed the button of his of the walkie-talkie mike, which was attached to the lapel of his overall.

'Come in Captain this is A.B. Serkov.'

'Yeah, go ahead Serkov.'

'I nailed four of them Captain. But three escaped along the deck. Do you want me to take them out as well?'

'No leave them. They can tell their friends what happens when you try to rob innocent merchant ships.'

The sailor smiled wryly. He had not enjoyed himself so much since he was a sergeant in the Russian Army, mowing down the locals in Afghanistan.

On the foredeck of the ship, the remaining three pirates ran in absolute panic, tripping and falling as they went, on the debris from the containers that they had strewn there previously. When they reached the canoe, two of the men slithered quickly down the ropes, while the third, eyes wide with terror, just dived straight into the inky black water. Coming up to the surface a few seconds later, arms thrashing wildly as he bobbed up and down on the swell, trying desperately to reach the canoe. Eventually he found the strength to cover the few metres of water and the other two men helped him on board. The fourth man at the stern, who had been left with the canoe, pulled frantically at the cord of the outboard, which eventually spluttered and sprang into life.

The last canoe moved away from the ship quicker than the others had, only being half full of booty and with just the four men on board. After about ten minutes, they had drawn level with the little convoy of canoes, sluggishly making its way to the not so distant shore. An anxious nervous voice called across the short expanse of water.

'What the hell happened back there man? We heard the shootin'.'

'Whole load of bad shit man. Four of the boys and Asamwa just shot to death.'

'My God!' came the reply 'I think am gonna to leave this kind of thing alone in future.'

'Yeah me too. Its jost too dangerous.'

'What of Kaduna?'

'He left real early. I guess he must be nearly on the shore now.'

'I wish I was on shore, at my place right now. I get a real bad feelin' about the whole thing.' Another voice replied in a weary tone of voice.

The small convoy of dugout canoes wallowed its way over the rollers towards the entrance to Badagry creek. The occupants of the canoes were shocked and traumatised by the horrific conclusion to the attack on the ship. By now, every one of them was praying earnestly for a safe return to their homes on the on the shore.

This was not going to happen.

Chapter Thirty-One

Martin Ellis crouched behind the thick green bushes that surrounded the small sandy beach. He had been there almost an hour by this time and it felt like every inch of his sweat-soaked skin was alive, with every insect, in this part of the jungle.

He constantly scratched and mopped away the sweat, which trickled from his forehead and into his eyes.

The major regarded his extreme discomfort with a look of sly derision, which Ellis was not slow to notice but he decided to say nothing. He could see the luminous hands of his watch inch slowly towards five- thirty. The sky in the east showed the first tentative signs of the new dawn, as shafts of dim light illuminated the small powder puff cumulus clouds above Lagos.

The sounds of the jungle behind him seemed to fill his ears. Though he told himself, it was probably his discomfort that had subconsciously amplified these sounds, croaking of toads, buzzing of insects, clicking of crickets and the occasional shrill of a parakeet. In the distance, the surf could be heard crashing dully onto the steep beach either side of the inlet.

But now another sound, barely perceptible at first, began to accompany those he had become accustomed to. It was the high-pitched drone of an outboard motor. The pirates were on their way back at last, he thought to himself. Soon, very soon, the whole affair would hopefully be brought to a successful conclusion. His pulse quickened slightly, anticipating the imminent confrontation with the adversary he had chased for so long.

His eyes strained in the darkness, to pick out the first sign of the returning canoes. A few minutes later, he began to make out the large bow wave, of the first heavily laden canoe. Then, close behind, another could be seen, then another. The light was improving fast now, as it does in the tropics. It seemed to Ellis like a whole fleet of large canoes, wallowing from side to side with the weight of cargo they carried, was heading straight towards him.

The trap was perfectly set. He hoped all the soldiers positioned round the beach would remain silent and resist the temptation to open fire, till all the men from the canoes were on the beach, so that none would have a chance to escape. But he need not have worried, that was exactly what the major had told his men to do.

The first canoe ground softly ashore, on the gently shelving beach. The driver killed the outboard and the men on board scrambled eagerly into the warm shallow water of the creek and began throwing cartons onto the beach. Within a matter of minutes, the other canoes had pulled alongside the first one, their occupants chattering excitedly as they roughly tossed the contents of the canoes onto the beach. Soon large piles of dented cartons began to form next to each canoe. Ellis looked towards the major and spoke in a whisper,

'Now's the time Major, what's the plan?'

The major laughed softly.

'You really don't know, do you Inspector Ellis?'

'I'm afraid I don't, please tell me.'

'The plan Inspector is to kill all these scum.'

'What! I thought they were to be arrested,' Ellis said, a nervous edge to his voice.

'They are killers, they deserve no mercy.'

Before Ellis could protest further, the major stood up and shouted at the top of his voice, 'Open fire men.'

The noise was deafening, as rifles and automatic weapons

opened fire on the unsuspecting pirates less than fifty metres away. Behind Ellis, a great cacophony of screeching flapping birds rose, panic stricken from the jungle to the safety of the sky above. As the wall of hot lead ripped into the pirates, most fell instantly, screaming and writhing to the ground.

Others tried to get back in the canoes, but were mown mercilessly down, before they had gone a couple of metres. One or two hid behind the mounds of boxes and fired a few defiant rounds back from their rusty, ancient firearms. But the withering fire from the soldiers, scythed mercilessly through the cardboard cartons and into the last few remaining pirates cowering behind.

In less than a minute it was all over. It was a massacre! The only sounds coming from the direction of the canoes were the anguished moans of a few mortally wounded pirates. Soldiers quickly moved from cover, checked the bodies and pumped a few more rounds into any wounded that they found.

Ellis was in a state of shock. In all his time in the police and Interpol, he had not witnessed such carnage. It took him a good few seconds, before he could summon the strength to stand up and follow the major to the killing ground. Even then, his hands were trembling and his legs far from steady.

Nothing could have prepared him for the sickening sight he encountered, when he arrived at the scene of the slaughter. There were around forty pirates lying motionless. Some had the tops of their heads blown clean off, others with hideous gaping wounds in their faces. All the corpses had multiple gunshot wounds. The pathetic rags they wore, now heavily blood-stained. Some of the dead were no more than children, fifteen or sixteen years old, perhaps on their first raid, sucked up by fervour and the temptation of easy pickings. They had paid a heavy price for becoming involved. Ellis felt deflated and more than a little saddened by the tragic scene in front of him.

Eventually, he was able to detach his mind from the trauma of the grisly scene. He methodically checked each body closely, to make sure that at least Kaduna had perished in the slaughter, to bring partial justification, to the hideous act just perpetrated.

But there was no one amongst the dead, who remotely resembled Kaduna in size or appearance. It was not possible that he could have escaped from such intense gunfire. No human on the planet could have survived that deadly storm. Finally, he turned to the major and tried to speak, though the words would not come and he had to swallow a couple of times, before he could talk.

'Kaduna is not amongst the dead.'

'Impossible. He could not have survived that fire.'

'Well he is not here. Did your people at the breakwater say how many canoes were involved in the attack?'

'Well it was very dark at the time, they said six possibly seven canoes'

'That's it Major. There must be another canoe still out there. No doubt he will have heard all the gunfire, so for sure he will try and come ashore in another location.'

Kaduna had indeed heard the gunfire and saw the jungle a few miles to the west of his canoe, illuminated dramatically by the multiple flashes of the guns, like a huge macabre fireworks display. 'So they had been waiting for him,' he thought darkly. It was fortunate he had decided this time, to land closer to his apartment on the other side of the breakwater from the entrance to Badagry Creek.

But even though he had narrowly escaped certain death, his problems were far from over. The outboard engine that had been troublesome to start, had backfired and spluttered many times on the way to the beach, till eventually it gave up the ghost completely. He was furious with the other pirate in the boat and felt like smashing his head to a pulp with the butt of his pistol. Though sense told him that action, no matter how gratifying it would have felt, would have exacerbated the present situation even more.

It would be a miracle, if two men paddling could beach the

canoe through the heavy surf, without it turning over. With only one person it would definitely have been impossible. He had ordered the protesting pirate to help him dump the cargo from the boat, which was weighing it down deeper in the water. Eventually, all but a few boxes of radio cassettes had been hefted over the side and were floating behind them. The outboard had also been dumped, to further lighten the boat.

The Guinea current was making the canoe drift slowly eastwards and towards the angry surf crashing noisily on the shore, barely one hundred metres away. They paddled steadily, just maintaining steerage-way, as the smooth tops of the surf rolled past them.

Kaduna was immensely strong and fit, but the other man was like so many of his countrymen, scrawny, thin and undernourished. Kaduna could see he was flagging fast and he had to paddle on both sides of the canoe, to make up for the other man's shortfall.

The beach inched closer and the sound of the surf became thunderous, as it erupted in front of them. Every muscle in Kaduna's body ached, he was gasping desperately out of his tortured lungs for breath; as he frantically dug the pointed paddle into the sea either side of the canoe. The huge surf that towered behind them, was no longer rolling under the canoe, but the tops were now breaking and starting to swamp the canoe.

'Keep going you bastard or I'll kill you,' he screamed at the terrified pirate in the bow of the canoe. It was not far now, less than twenty metres. Kaduna continued to paddle furiously.

The next wave, even larger than the last, caught the aft side of the canoe, turning it beam on to the swell. The heavy dugout canoe was rolled over like an empty barrel by the immense force of the wave, spilling the two men into the angry boiling frothing sea.

Kaduna could feel himself sinking. The rucksack on his back was now saturated.

The money inside, soaking up the water like a dry sponge, making him heavier by the second, dragging him down inexorably to the bottom of the ocean. As the next wave crashed overhead he tried to pull towards the surface, but it was no good. It felt like a giant pair of hands was pulling him down deeper to a certain death.

It was a simple choice. He would have to release the rucksack, or die. So he pushed the straps over his shoulder and felt himself rise slowly to the surface.

Eventually after what seemed an eternity, his head broke the surface and his bursting lungs gratefully gulped down the warm salty air. His arms felt like lead, as he tried to swim towards the shore, his army combat uniform and heavy boots full of water. He couldn't kick the boots off because of the way they were laced up. He felt what little strength he had waning fast and a watery grave clearly beckoning him. Trapped between the shore and the powerful undertow, he felt resigned to a fate he thought he certainly did not deserve.

But help was to arrive from a totally unexpected source. The next wave caught him and dumped him violently on the beach. He was dazed but had enough sense to scramble a few metres up the beach, using the last vestiges of his strength before collapsing exhausted on the dry sand.

After a few seconds he vomited violently, a result of exhaustion and the warm seawater he had swallowed. He laid here for fully ten minutes, just staring at the small white clouds, drifting across the light blue morning sky, marvelling at the fact that he had somehow made it to shore alive. Eventually, as he was supremely fit, his strength slowly flowed back into his aching muscles and he was able to sit up, albeit in a slightly dazed condition and take in the scene around him.

He could just make out the heavy dug-out canoe about fifty metres away, rolling back and forth, as each successive breaker hit the beach. Some of the boxes they had dumped had also washed ashore, the cardboard packaging, remarkably still intact. Between him and the dugout, was the motionless body of the other pirate.

Like the canoe, rolling back and forth as the waves attacked and retreated from the beach, like so many lines of soldiers.

Kaduna's head ached badly; it felt as though it had been hit with a machete. He rubbed his eyes and slowly began to see more clearly. Eventually after another five minutes, he felt strong enough to stand up and his vision had returned virtually to normal.

He could hear the excited babble, of distant voices. As he looked along the beach, he could see the local villagers, running along the waters edge, their baggy pants and shirts flapping in the breeze, as they ran towards the cartons, which were strewn along the beach.

It was time for him to get as far away from this place as possible. He was just about to turn and leave, when something in the wash of the surf, near the dead pirate caught his eye.

It was the rucksack.

Amazingly, the sea had thrown that onto the beach, just as it had the rest of the contents of the canoe. Grinning, he waded out cautiously a few metres into the surf, reached down and easily retrieved the heavy rucksack.

He couldn't believe his luck. He was thankful to have survived the canoe turning over and narrowly escaped drowning. The money had seemed less important, when faced with the real possibility of death, but now he had survived and still had the money. He had an excellent feeling about how the rest of the day would now work out, as he turned and slowly staggered off the beach.

Martin Ellis sat tensely next to the major in the back of the army jeep, as it bumped, bucked and weaved along the jungle trail. A few minutes earlier, the soldiers on the breakwater had reported a canoe coming ashore, about a mile east of their position. Ellis and the major, in the company of another other jeep full of soldiers, were proceeding as rapidly as the jeeps' suspensions would allow, along the narrow jungle trail.

Ellis thought morosely that it would take at least forty minutes to reach that position, by which time Kaduna would be well clear. Bad luck with the men stationed on the breakwater as well. Because their jeep had broken down, they would only be able to give chase on foot. But he still had a number of trump cards yet to play. He knew where Kaduna lived and also the address of his girlfriend. He would surely go to one of those locations. If he were not at either of those places there would only be one place remaining. The airport.

As the jeep tore along the track at an alarming speed, Ellis held on to one of the sides, to stop himself being thrown around. The noise of the engine, revving high in third gear and the suspension pounding up and down made conversation impossible. But Ellis was glad in a way, as he was able to focus all his thoughts on his quarry. He was sure Kaduna would try to flee the country immediately, with the massive furore that his latest pirate attack was bound to create. News had filtered through about the murder of the two Russian seamen and the machine-gunning of the pirates on the ship.

Ellis slowly went over in his mind the various options available to Kaduna. His thoughts drifted towards the croupier. Perhaps he would take her with him as cover? A couple travelling together were less conspicuous somehow than a person alone. All he would achieve travelling with the croupier would be to draw attention to him, as Ellis knew her identity as well as his.

Lesley sat nervously in her little apartment, behind the Holiday Inn casino. She didn't normally smoke very much, but the tension was getting to her, as she ground out her tenth half smoked cigarette in only a few hours. If smoking was supposed to calm the nerves, she thought dryly, it wasn't doing a very good job on hers, that morning in Lagos. He had told her to be dressed and ready to leave by seven o'clock. It was an hour from the Holiday Inn to the airport and he had wanted to be at least two hours early, to make sure there was no foul up with the tickets. It was almost seven o'clock and she had expected to see him long before now.

A brief sketchy bulletin, she heard on the early morning news, turned the tension screw in her body a few notches further. The newscaster had mentioned, that local residents on the outskirts of Apapa, reported machine gun fire had been heard, from the direction of the creek. Sources said it was a Government clean up campaign against pirate gangs. How awful, she had thought, as hideous images of Henry Kaduna face down in the swamp, riddled with bullet holes, were thrown up in graphic detail by her imagination.

She was about to reach for yet another cigarette, when she heard a key rattle impatiently in the lock then suddenly the door burst open. Kaduna quickly entered the room, slamming the door behind him. She was shocked at his extremely dishevelled appearance. He looked like he had been fighting a war. All his clothes were crumpled, torn in a number of places and covered in dark patches.

'You ready to leave?' he said in a monotone, as he went towards the bathroom with a rucksack, which dripped water on the marble floor as he moved across the room.

'Yeah I'm ready. Where have you been? I've was worried something had happened to you.'

'Oh something happened to me all right. But I came through it Okay just like I do most things. Do me a favour, honey. Bring my briefcase into the bathroom, will you?'

She found the expensive black leather briefcase near the dressing table and took it to him in the bathroom. What she saw in there took her breath away. Kaduna had emptied the contents of the rucksack onto the floor of the bathroom. A great sodden pile of U.S. dollars lay there. It was a fortune. Where the hell had he been, to get so much money, she thought nervously. Kaduna was frantically squeezing water out of these bundles, down the drain of the shower.

'Right honey, get all the towels you can find and start trying to get some of the water out of this cash. Dry it then stack it in the briefcase, while I get changed.' He strode past her into the living room.

Without asking any questions, she did as instructed. Hands shaking visibly, with a combination of nerves and excitement, she picked up the various bundles, wrapped them in a towel and padded them down, to absorb some of the water. Then she lined the briefcase with a face towel, before stacking the bundles of damp green notes neatly inside. The briefcase was soon crammed to capacity and she could barely close the lid. There was still around twenty of the bundles lying on the floor, that she was unable to fit in the brief case.

During the hours that Lesley had sat alone waiting for Kaduna, she had agonised over her decision to leave Nigeria with him. After all, it was not as if she was in love with the man. Lust perhaps, but love no. She knew he was rich, even before this latest revelation and that was always important to a girl of her aspirations. She wanted the best that money could buy. Besides, she had a distinct feeling, if she suddenly disappeared, he would have sought her out, with heaven knows what consequences. She knew full well that he had a violent temper and a short fuse.

Now however, after having seen the fruits of his latest crooked adventure, she really did wish she had run earlier that night, when the temptation had been gnawing at her insides. But now it was too late, she was in too deep. If she tried to back out now, he would probably kill her. 'What a mess I've got myself into this time' she thought, rising from the bathroom floor.

On returning to the bedroom, she found Kaduna had divested himself of his hideous army uniform and was now the picture of elegance. Dressed in a light grey suit, crisp white shirt and neatly knotted blue tie, highly polished black Italian leather shoes completed the remarkable transformation. He had even cut off his goatee beard and was just finishing trimming it with an electric razor. She found herself staring at him. He was quick to notice.

'What's up? You look like you've seen a ghost.'

'I'm sorry if I stared. It's just the change in you is rather amazing.'

'Well, surely you didn't expect me to travel in that shit, did you?' He pointed to the green army uniform in a crumpled pile of on the floor, a look of mock disdain on his face.

'Of course not,' she replied rather tamely.

'That was the old Henry Kaduna and he stays right here with those clothes.'

'Well that certainly is good to hear. Anyway I definitely I prefer the new Henry Kaduna,' she replied. A smile flashed momentarily across her pink lips.

'Good.'

He turned his wrist to reveal a wafer thin Cartier dress watch and exclaimed, 'Hell, look at the time, almost quarter past seven. We will have to get moving or we will miss the flight.'

She suddenly remembered the pile of money that remained in the bathroom.

'Oh! I couldn't fit all of the money in the briefcase; there is still some on the floor through there.'

'Well, all my cases are locked. Could you fit the rest of the cash in your hand luggage?'

'Yeah, no problem.' She retrieved the damp bundles from the bathroom and placed them at the bottom of her travel bag.

They quickly made their way out of the apartment, each carrying their own cases, then down the stairs and into Kaduna's ancient Toyota, which was parked close to the entrance. They were soon on their way to the airport, driving along the back road that led to the freeway. Lesley felt better now. Somehow more assured that everything would work out all right in the end and blissfully unaware of the manhunt that was in progress in Lagos at that precise instant, for the person sitting right there next to her.

'So what's next Inspector?' The major enquired rather flatly.

They had just broken into Kaduna's beachfront apartment and found no sign of the occupant.

'It's a short ride to the Holiday Inn to see if he has gone to his girlfriend's apartment.'

'Okay let's get moving,' the major said, gesturing to his men to start back down the stairs again. He called the sergeant in charge of the other jeep on the walkie-talkie and told him to proceed to the Holiday Inn and stop all cars leaving the car park.

Less than ten minutes later, they entered the croupier's apartment. The door had been unlocked. Ellis was dismayed to find they had only just missed the pirate and his girlfriend. At least this was the location the pirate had come to after the raid. His sodden boots and army garb were still lying on the floor where he had left them. They could only have left a few minutes earlier, as a cigarette, pink lipstick on the stub, was still smouldering in the ashtray.

'Right Inspector, that's two blanks in a row. What do you suggest now?' The tone of the major's voice indicated he was becoming impatient. Ellis frowned. The finer points of police work would always be lost on a man like him.

'Two blanks, that's true, but it's been worth checking both locations. Look here, major.' He pointed to a small metal trash bin, beneath the dresser.

'It looks like our man decided to shave his beard off, before moving on.'

'Really, I never even knew he had a beard.'

'Exactly,' Ellis thought to himself. But had the presence of mind not to say what he was thinking. 'Furthermore, by the look of that cigarette, we are now right on their tails. Only one place they can be now. The airport.' Ellis said confidently.

While Martin Ellis and the Nigerian Special forces pursued Henry Kaduna to the airport, two miles away, just off Lagos breakwater, the officers and crew of the MV. 'Kapitan Penkov' was in a state of shock, still trying to come to terms with the events of the previous night.

Just before sunrise, after the last canoe had departed, Captain Borisenko ventured along the deck with two heavily armed sailors, and found a scene of wanton destruction. As if a giant had gone crazy, opening containers and tossing the contents around like confetti. Cartons, boxes, crates, electrical goods, toys, everything imaginable strewn round the deck of the ship.

They had found the young seaman near the forward end of number four hatch. A single bullet wound between the shoulder blades. He was alive when they found him, but died before he reached the ship's hospital. The body of the bosun located beside number two hatch was quite cool to touch .The captain deduced he must have died instantly a few hours ago. Both bodies had been transferred in body bags to the meat room in the ship's fridge space. This was standard procedure, till an autopsy could be done ashore on the bodies to establish the cause of death.

'Do you want me to bag up the four pirates as well Captain?' Andropov the slim fair-haired ships doctor had asked.

'No, leave the one in the mess room where he fell. I don't want any doubt as to what happened here, when we get to shore. The other three on the boat deck, I have something else in mind for them.'

After a brief tour of the deck, he had seen all he needed so he returned to the bridge. He was only there a few minutes, when the chief engineer called to say the engine was now repaired and the ship could move off any time. The captain graciously thanked the chief for his endeavours, over the previous twelve hours. He and his men must have been at the point of collapsing with exhaustion by that time.

As he looked out from the wheelhouse, towards the shore, he pondered morosely the events of the last few hours, saddened by the loss of his two loyal crewmen. He had seen the trees just be-hind the shore lit up by multiple flashes that he knew could only be gunfire. The dull muted sound of automatic weapons could be clearly heard, as it drifted across the short expanse of water, towards his ship. 'It sounded like someone had prepared a reception committee for the thieving bastards,' he thought. It made him feel slightly better, but unfortunately it had been too late for his dead crewmen. A voice beside him brought his attention back.

'Excuse me sir.'

He turned round to see the chief officer standing next to him.

'Yes what is it?'

'While you were on deck, the pilot station called us up on the VHF. We are getting a pilot at 0800.'

'Okay, the sooner we get into this place the sooner we will be able to get the hell out of it. We better test the bridge gear and give that beat up engine a few movements back and forward. I don't want to risk going between those breakwaters, unless it is one hundred per cent working. I'm going down to see the bosun's mate. Give me a call on the radio when the engine's tested and we are ready to heave the anchor.'

'Aye aye Captain,' the chief officer replied as the captain disappeared through the door that led down from the bridge.

Chapter Thirty-Two

Lesley was relieved to at last reach the BCal check-in desk. The sight of the Nigerian check in clerk in her smart tartan BCal uniform was quite incongruous, but a strangely comforting factor in her confused life at that moment. She was thankful that the trip to the airport had gone without incident. The traffic on the freeway was very light, so the trip only took a little over forty-five minutes.

They checked in two cases each and obtained their tickets for the first class section of the aircraft. Then they made their way through security and passport control to the embarkation area. Kaduna went to a small kiosk and purchased two coffees and three packets of toasted bread. He gave her a coffee and one packet of the toasted bread, but she was not hungry and pushed it to one side of the plate. He wolfed down his two packets and then ate her packet as well, making an attempt at levity, by remarking that he had been out at work all night. She laughed nervously at the comment, puffing on her cigarette. She would be unable to relax till the flight was actually airborne and heading back to civilisation.

Glancing at the gold Cartier watch he had bought her, soon after they met, the time read 09.30. They would be boarding the flight soon. As she looked over towards the departure gate, she could see the same smart clerk that had checked them in initially, tapping the microphone on her desk. After a few seconds she spoke.

'British Caledonian Airways would like to announce the departure of their flight to London Gatwick. Would all First and Business Class passengers come forward now for immediate boarding, thank you.'

'Okay girl, you ready to move?' Kaduna stretched and then reached down for his brief case.

'I most certainly am,' she replied.

They both got up, like any normal couple travelling from one destination to the next, with passports and boarding cards in one hand, hand luggage in the other. There were four or five other people in the short queue in front of them, who were being checked through quite slowly, considering the smallness of the numbers involved. Lesley looked up at Kaduna and smiled nervously at him. He nodded reassurance at her. Things were going to be all right from now on.

They were just about to hand over their boarding cards and passports for checking, when a man appeared from nowhere and stepped in front of them.

'Right, that's far enough.'

Lesley had to use all her willpower to suppress a huge scream. A heavy-set white man, with short fair hair, was pointing a gun right at the chest of her boyfriend. She recognised him immediately. It was Wilson's friend, Ellis, who she had first met at the beach party and seen at the casino a few times since.

'Okay Henry Kaduna. Your game is now up. I'm arresting you for numerous acts of piracy and murder. Put your hands in the air.'

An Army major stood near the end of the short queue and two other armed soldiers blocked the entrance back to the terminal.

Kaduna, cool as a jungle cat, looked Ellis right in the eye. 'Oh no, no, no.' He shook his head in disbelief. 'I'm afraid you have the wrong man. My name is Milton Obokwe. I've never heard of this person, Henry Kaduna.'

He smiled benignly at Ellis, who was taken aback for a split second by his adversary's calmness. That was all Kaduna ever needed in situations such as this, a split second of indecision. His wrist moved with lightning speed and his brief case knocked the weapon out of Ellis's hand.

The gun flew into the air and landed behind a row of red plastic chairs, ten metres away. It narrowly missed an elderly couple, who stood transfixed as the lethal weapon arched towards them, then clattered noisily on the marble floor of the departure lounge.

Kaduna then used all his considerable strength, to push Ellis backwards into the crowd of passengers waiting in the queue. Ellis knocked over a child and a young woman as he stumbled then fell, finally ending up sprawled on the floor. As he looked up, he saw Kaduna disappear rapidly out of the twin doors leading down to the stairs to the boarding area for the buses, which took passengers to the various planes.

Ellis quickly scrambled to his feet and pushed roughly past the startled passengers, who had been waiting in the queue. He reached the door and yanked on one of the handles. But the door only opened slightly. Kaduna had jammed something between the handle of the free door and the standing door. Ellis tried it a few times then gave up, looking round for the next boarding gate. It was only a few metres to his left.

The major and one of the soldiers were already running in that direction. Ellis was quick to catch them up and they burst through the doors and down the wide steps two at a time. They eventually arrived panting at the ground floor and rushed through another door, out onto the edge of the runway. Ellis looked frantically round, shading his eyes with one hand, as the bright sun glared down from a clear blue sky.

Kaduna was nowhere to be seen.

'Damn!' he cursed clenching his fists.

Suddenly the major's walkie-talkie crackled into life.

'Com in Major,' an excited voice said.

'Yes sergeant, go ahead.'

'There is a man with a brief case, runnin' towards the hanger area at the side of the main terminal.'

'Come on Major, over there!' Ellis shouted over the din, as a newly landed plane gave maximum reverse thrust on its jet engines.

The three of them ran as fast as they could towards the hangar area. The humidity was very high and the air temperature already around thirty degrees centigrade. The heat from the sun, absorbed by the white concrete apron areas, radiated back upwards. It felt like they were running though an oven with the heat turned on full. Within a few seconds Ellis was drenched in perspiration and constantly wiped his eyes to keep the hangar, one hundred metres away, in clear view.

Kaduna was a desperate man as he approached the hangar. His trick of jamming an umbrella, ripped from under the arms of an elderly passenger in the queue, in the door handles, had gained him valuable seconds. But now he could see three distant figures running in his direction. The pack was closing in fast. He knew unless a miracle happened his number was well and truly up. He had not come this far in life, to be defeated at the final hurdle.

Suddenly at the side of the hangar only twenty metres away, the engine of a light aircraft burst into life.

Koffe Enazas had just finished the pre- flight checks on his air-craft. He was booked for a flight to Port Harcourt, with an oil executive who sat in the back seat, engrossed in some papers. The executive had been delayed by twenty minutes, but this did not perturb Enazas, as these people always ran on tight schedules, and were invariably a few minutes late. The only problem now was, he has missed his take-off slot at nine forty and the airport was quite busy at this time with arrivals and departures. He was just about to call the tower and ask for permission to take off, when his whole world was turned upside down.

In a flash Kaduna leapt onto the wing of the light aircraft and pulled open the door to the passenger's seat. He jumped in and closed the door behind him. Then he pulled out his automatic pistol and pointed it straight between the eyes of the petrified pilot.

'Right, get this plane moving or you are a dead man.'

It had all happened with such incredible swiftness, that it was a couple of seconds before Enazas could fully grasp what had happened and blurt out a few terrified words.

'C... c... c... can't. Need permission for take off.'

Kaduna looked briefly over his shoulder and could see three figures closing rapidly on the plane. He cocked the trigger and pressed the muzzle of the gun hard against the pilot's forehead and screamed.

'This gun is your permission to take off. I won't tell you again. Move this God-damned plane or you are dead.'

'Okay... Okay' the pilot screamed back terrified, then added, 'Take the gun out of my face. I have to see where I'm going.'

Kaduna turned away from the pilot and opened the window of his door. The pilot adjusted the pitch of the propellers and the aircraft moved forward, slowly picking up speed. The three figures were still closing rapidly on the plane. The nearest soldier seemed about to fire his rifle. Kaduna took careful aim and fired two shots. The second shot hit the soldier in the thigh and he fell screaming in pain to the ground. The other two stopped running and the plane eventually pulled away from them.

The executive in the back sat perfectly still as if glued in place, too terrified to say anything. He was probably wishing he had not been late for his charter flight, but resigned to whatever fate had in store for him now. Visions of his wife and seven children flashed before his terrified eyes. He was starting to get a very bad feeling, that he would never see any of them ever again.

The pilot had regained some of his composure, now that he was not staring down the barrel of Kaduna's gun. He spoke loudly, to be heard above the din of the twin Lycoming 160 HP four-cylinder piston engines.

'We need permission from the tower. It is too dangerous. A plane may be about to land for all we know. We might all get killed.'

'Never mind. That's a chance I'm prepared to take. Get this plane airborne as quickly as possible.'

'All right, you're the boss.'

The windsock at the side of the runway indicated a slight southerly breeze, so the pilot turned the Piper Comanche PA 30 to starboard and headed to the north end of the main runway, as yet unnoticed by the tower. As the small plane rose and fell easily on the uneven surface of the taxi runway, its occupants were unaware of the events unfolding outside the aircraft.

Now that the plane was moving quite quickly to its take off point, Kaduna had forgotten about the men who had been chasing him. He was lulled into a false sense of security, cocooned in the cosy cockpit of the plane. So when the aircraft turned onto the main runway, ready for take off, Kaduna was horrified to see two men standing less than one hundred metres away. Martin Ellis and Major Owaragee had seen the direction the plane was moving and had cut across the grass verge between the runway and the taxi way.

The air traffic controller, who had been dozing in his chair in the tower, had now woken to the fact that an aircraft was about to try and take off without having been cleared by him. He was in charge of this airport and nothing happened without his permission. His authority was being severely questioned by the impudent pilot of light aircraft. The controller went virtually berserk, screaming down the microphone in the control tower. Enazas could not make out what the man was saying in his headset. He leaned towards Kaduna and spoke urgently.

'Control is trying to call us. I can't make out what they are saying. Sounds important.'

'To hell with them pilot, let's get this plane in the air,' Kaduna screamed wild-eyed at him.

Then he reached over using the butt of his gun and smashed the face of the small compact radio on the dashboard, rendering it inoperative. The pilot regarded him briefly, a look of astonishment fixed on his face. He sighed and shook his head in resignation. Then he put the brakes on briefly and changed the pitch setting on the propellers to maximum. The small aircraft started to shake and vibrate quite violently. Enazas released the brakes and the plane lurched forward, rapidly gaining speed.

Ellis saw the small plane taxi round to the end of the runway and begin its take off. He spoke urgently to the major, who was holding an FN semi-automatic rifle that he had taken from the wounded soldier.

'Right Major, aim for the tyres.'

The major crouched, one knee on the ground and took careful aim. Ellis had his pistol, ready to fire a few shots when the plane got closer.

Kaduna could see the figures at the side of the runway were aiming guns at the plane. He quickly stuck his automatic pistol out of the side window and began firing wildly at the two men.

The hiss of bullets whizzed passed the major and Ellis as the plane approached. One thudded into the side of the runway, sending splinters of tar into the air. The major did not panic but held his ground. The left side tyre of the rapidly approaching plane was looming large in the sight of his rifle. Thirty metres away now, he couldn't miss. He pressed the trigger. Click. The gun had jammed. He tried again but the same thing happened. Click. Click. He threw the gun down on the ground in disgust and frantically tried to un- holster his pistol.

Ellis started firing his gun at the tyres of the plane. But it was travelling too fast by this stage and all his shots were well wide of the mark. The plane flashed passed in an instant, at over one hundred miles per hour. He caught a brief glance at Henry Kaduna's face, a sly grin of triumph on his lips. Immensely content, no doubt that he had won the final confrontation, Ellis thought rather despondently.

Another hundred metres further down the runway, at not even the halfway point; the light aircraft began to rise steadily from the ground. Settling back in the passenger's seat, Kaduna looked nervously out of the front window. When the nose of the aircraft rose above the trees in the distance, at the end of the runway and eventually blue sky filled his view, Kaduna let out a great sigh of relief. He was enormously pleased be on his way out of Lagos after such a close call with the law.

But his troubles were not over.

'Oh my God! Look behind us,' the businessman in the rear seat said urgently.

The pilot glanced nervously in his rear-view mirror. Henry Kaduna irritably turned his head round to see what the fuss was about. His eyes soon focused on the tiny window behind the rear passenger and filled with horror. A huge Jumbo jet was heading directly for them. Koffe Enazas the pilot was frozen in shock at the control column of his aircraft. He gripped the handles so tightly that the knuckles of his hands turned white with the effort. The awful ache of mortal dread flooded through his body. His chest suddenly felt like it was held in a vice, he was barely able to breathe.

The pilot of KLM 004 from Amsterdam to Lagos did not at first notice the light aircraft by the side of the runway. He was at the end of a long flight and as a result of fatigue his reactions were predictably slower. So he could not believe his eyes, when the tiny light aircraft just taxied onto the runway and began to take off.

He was on final approach, fully committed to landing. Frantically and with the assistance of the co-pilot, he pushed the engine power levers forward back up to full power. Then he pulled back on the control column, in attempt to gain height and avoid the light aircraft.

For a few agonising seconds, it looked like there was going to be a mid air collision as his plane stayed at the same height and the light aircraft continued to rise to that level. But miraculously, the Jumbos nose began to rise slowly as the four hundred ton plane clawed its way skywards again. Eventually he passed over the light aircraft by no more than thirty metres and let out a huge sigh of relief, extremely relieved to have avoided an almost certain disaster.

The cockpit of the Comanche turned dark, as if the sun had suddenly set, as the huge Jumbo roared overhead. Kaduna shouted to the pilot.

'Hell that was close!'

'We is still finished,' the pilot calmly replied.

'What!' Kaduna said, a look of sheer incredulity on his face.

Just then, the small plane was hit by the massive wash of turbulence caused by the four huge jet engines of the Jumbo, forcing it to lose control and somersault through the air like a piece of waste paper, fluttering in the wind. The screaming occupants were thrown back and forth in their seats, heads and arms banging on the side of the cockpit.

They were probably all unconscious when, as a result of the massive forces inflicted on the tiny aircraft, the port wing snapped clean off. The light aircraft quickly spiralled downwards, crashing into the jungle beneath, smashing through branches and erupting in flames when it finally hit the ground.

Martin Ellis stood on the edge of the runway, dumbstruck by the shock of the previous few seconds. He had been certain he was going to witness a major catastrophe, as the Jumbo seemed certain to collide with the light aircraft. The noise was deafening, from the engines of huge plane passing close overhead, as it suddenly came up to full power. Both he and the major were almost swept over by the force of the jet wash. Then miraculously, somehow, the Jumbo managed to avoid the small plane. He then watched awestruck, as the light aircraft went out of control and crashed into the jungle.

As he made his way slowly back to the airport terminal building with the Nigerian major, Ellis' thoughts were in turmoil. He should have been elated. The pirate was now undoubtedly dead. No one could have survived such a terrible plane crash. But what had really shocked him were the lengths that the pirate had gone to in a bid to try and escape capture. Almost causing an air disaster, where many hundreds of innocent people would have been killed.

The major was the first to speak, as they crossed the concrete apron to the airport terminal building.

'Well Inspector Ellis. That's quite a morning's work we have had. Perhaps not the conclusion we would have both wanted. But nevertheless, I suppose we can say the case is well and truly closed.'

'Yes Major. That's the end of this particular pirate and his gang. What about the plane wreck and the bodies?'

'Don't worry about that. I will organise some people to retrieve the bodies, if there is anything left of them and notify the family of the poor pilot.'

'Good. I'd appreciate it if you could drop me off at my associate's house, in River Road, Apapa.'

'Sure no problem the jeeps are still out the front.'

The major's voice was drowned out, by the sound of the KLM Jumbo landing safely on the runway behind them.

At 11.15 that day, the M.V. 'Kapitan Penkov' approached the berth at Tin Can Island. The trip from the anchorage to the berth had been a tense affair. The pilot boat had refused to come out past the breakwater, complaining that his engine was still not good. The master then had the harrowing task of bringing the vessel through the breakwaters. This was made even more difficult by the high swell that was running, reducing the manoeuvrability of the vessel noticeably. The jagged edges of the breakwaters were waiting as always to punish severely the slightest mistake.

A large crowd of stevedores, port officials and general riff-raff, watched the ship approach the berth. There was even a reporter and a photographer from the local newspaper. Captain Borisenko stood on the starboard bridge wing, with the Nigerian pilot and could hear a distinctive buzz of excited conversation, emanating from the crowd on the dock.

On the dock itself, one of the stevedores, awestruck at what he saw, said to his friend.

'My God! It is a terrible thing.'

His friend, mouth hanging loosely open, nodded silently in agreement.

The sight made some of the men feel like vomiting. One or two could even be heard retching at the front of the crowd. Others could look no more and turned their backs to the ship. Because hanging from the fore mast of the vessel, were three bullet ridden corpses covered in flies. Birds were pecking away at what remained of the eyes. One body had only the sockets of its eyes remaining. It truly was a gruesome sight. No one in the crowd had ever seen anything quite as bad. Hanging from the neck of each corpse was a white placard, with crudely painted letters in black that read, 'PIRATE.'

The bosun's mate had pleaded with the captain, before the ship left the anchorage, not to go ahead with this idea. But the captain was adamant, he was sick of innocent ships being the target of pirates and he wanted to make a statement that the whole world could see. Exactly what people risked if they turned to piracy as a route to easy money. To let all would-be pirates know that they risked a horrible death, similar to the three gruesome corpses hanging so dramatically from the mast.

He certainly achieved his objective. Pictures of the dead men hanging from the mast were on the front page in every paper in Nigeria the next day. Some papers in Europe and USA even ran short stories on inside pages, with the same hideous images. His message struck home with the various bands of pirates that operated in Nigeria. For many months after Captain Borisenko and the M.V. 'Kapitan Penkov' sailed from Lagos, pirate activity ceased completely. The Nigerian government even ran nightly anti-piracy patrols for a short while with the boats provided by the UN.

Then with the passage of time, as the hideous images faded, and the hunger-pains became unbearable; cries from their starving children ringing in their ears, the temptation to earn easy money from unarmed merchant ships became too hard to resist. Slowly the pirate activity crept back. Now regular attacks can be expected off the coast of West Africa and all merchant ships have to be on full alert when waiting at anchor or drifting off this coast.

Lesley Granby eventually left Lagos, later that day. The original flight was delayed, as one passenger had not handed in his boarding card. They all had to reclaim their luggage and check in again. It took many nerve-racking hours before the aircraft was finally airborne and she was on her way back to England. The events at the airport involving Henry Kaduna, had left her numb. She felt sure that the smug British cop would arrest her. But to her immense relief this did not transpire.

Later, sitting there in the sumptuous comfort of her first class seat, she was slowly beginning to unwind. She had smoked almost continually all day and now the packet was empty. She reached down into her hand luggage, looking for another that she had purchased at the airport, but had difficulty trying to locate the slim shiny packet. She thought it must have slipped down the side of her airline bag, as she hurried to board the plane. She groped round in the depths of the bag and then her hand touched something damp. Her hand recoiled in horror and then suddenly remembered.

It was the money.

She had forgotten all about that. A thin smile crossed her lips. Perhaps things would work out just fine after all...

Authors Note

This book is fiction, as are all the characters within; any resemblance to any actual person is purely co-incidental. However, piracy is not fiction and this has occurred in West Africa and many other parts of the world, for many years now, both before and after the period that this book has been written about.

The level of piracy these days in West Africa is still a great concern. But it is not as serious as in other regions of the world, such as the South China Sea, the Straits of Malacca, Indonesia and the coast of Somalia. There were over three hundred attacks in these areas last year. Most of these attacks came from highly organised gangs with modern weapons, boarding ships from powerful launches while the vessels were under way. Ships and their cargoes have even been hijacked and the crews set adrift in lifeboats at the mercy of the sea. These pirates continue to murder a number of ship's crew each year.

Some of the worst places are now patrolled, but very few pirates are actually caught. This is due to the huge areas where pirates operate and the lack of resources available. It would take hundreds of patrol boats to have a noticeable effect.

Meanwhile, pirates continue to thrive and can still attack unarmed merchant ships with complete impunity and will continue to do so for the foreseeable future.

26

The number of acts of piracy in Nigeria in the first ten months of 2007.

ISBN 142512182-9